I0550666

Faith or Fate

By John Ruggiero

CMD Media, LLC

Elizabeth, New Jersey

Copyright © 2013 by John Ruggiero

Published by CMD Media, LLC

All rights reserved. This book or any portion thereof may not be reproduced or used in any manner whatsoever without the express written permission of the publisher except for the use of brief quotations in a book review.

This is a work of fiction. Names, characters, businesses, places, events and incidents are either the products of the author's imagination or used in a fictitious manner. Any resemblance to actual persons, living or dead, or actual events is purely coincidental.

Edited by Paul Hadsall, Jr.

Additional editing by Dr. Alice Farmer

Printed in the United States of America

First printing May 2013

Second printing June 2013

ISBN 978-0615812984

CMD Media, LLC

1139 East Jersey Street, Suite 503

Elizabeth NJ 07201

http://cmdmedia.net/

Acknowledgements

For two years I worked on this book, rewriting it several times over. I would like to thank the following people for assisting me in reaching a goal that I did not think was possible.

For taking on the enormous task of both proofreading and editing, my sincere thanks go to Paul Hadsall for his tireless patience. I could not have asked for a better editor. His opinions, ideas and critique were instrumental to me throughout the process of completing the book.

For believing in me and my story enough to finance the publishing of the book, I have to thank James Devine. I will be forever grateful to James for providing me with a great editor and for all of his support on so many levels during this entire process.

To all of my family and friends who have been there for me through the good times and the bad I would like to sincerely thank each and every one of you. Without your support, none of this would have been possible. Life is filled with peaks and valleys. It's the time you spend in the valleys that make you realize who the people are that are there for you and whom matter most.

Dedication

This book is dedicated to my mother Marie Ruggiero. As a single mother of four she was both mother and father to me. She taught me more about how to be a man than any male role model could ever do. She taught me how to be responsible and that having children means that you make whatever sacrifices you have to in order to do right by them. She is by far the strongest person I have ever met and I admire her more than any other person on this planet.

I may not say it enough, but I love you mom and thank you for everything you've done for me.

Faith or Fate

Chapter 1

The sound of fighting woke seven-year-old Thomas Greggs from a sound sleep.

"Keep pushing my buttons bitch, just keep pushing me," his father yelled.

His mother screamed back, "Where the hell have you been, Dan? Every night for the last month you've come home late and drunk! I'm sick of it!"

Thomas pulled the covers over his head and closed his eyes tight. He tried as hard as he could not hear what was happening. Thomas started to breathe heavily and he felt the tears starting down his cheeks as he heard his father getting louder and louder.

There was a loud crash and then Thomas' mother screamed. Thomas tossed the covers off of him, snuck towards the door and peeked outside his bedroom door. He saw his mother getting up off of the floor, her eyes red from tears.

"Keep your friggin' hands off of me, you bastard!"

"You brought this on yourself, Marie! You never know when to keep your mouth shut!"

"I hate you! You're nothing but a lousy drunk," Marie shouted. "I wish you wouldn't come home at all, you son of a bitch!"

This sent Dan over the edge and he ran towards his wife. Marie knew what was coming so she crouched to brace herself for the attack. When Dan grabbed her, Marie tried to slap him in the face but Dan blocked her easily.

"Oh, you want to hit?" he asked sarcastically.

Thomas watched in horror as his father held his mother against the wall with one hand and punched her in the face with the other. Marie screamed out in pain then held her face before sliding down to the floor.

Thomas couldn't watch any more. He pulled open his bedroom door and yelled, "Stop it, stop it, please!"

Dan turned to look at his son. "Get the hell back in your room and go to bed," he yelled. "This doesn't concern you!"

"Leave her alone, please," Thomas begged. Through his own tear-filled eyes, Thomas saw his mother sitting on the floor crying and holding her face.

Thomas' enraged father yelled, "I told you to stay in your fucking room!"

As Dan started walking towards his son's room with his hand raised, Thomas quickly slammed the door then locked it. Dan grabbed the handle and pounded on the door with his fist.

"What the f…," Dan yelled when he tried a second time to open it. "Thomas, open this Goddamn door right now! Do you hear me boy? Open this door right now or you're gonna get it, so help me God!"

Thomas leaned against the door with his eyes closed and used all of his might to hold it shut. He was terrified that his father would break the lock. "Leave him the hell alone," Thomas heard his mother shout. She started crying really loud again. "Leave us both the hell alone," she pleaded.

Dan turned to face her again and shook his head in disgust. "You're fucking pathetic," he said. "I'm going back out; take one of your fucking crazy pills so you're normal when I get back."

Dan sat in his car for a moment, shaking his head while muttering to himself. He was tired of being told what to do, he was tired of all of his responsibilities and he wanted to be able to come and go as he pleased without this constant nagging. Seeing Thomas standing there crying made him think that his son was just as crazy and weak as his wife. Dan considered going back into the house to tell him so, but he knew it wouldn't do him any good. So, instead, he started his car and drove back to the bar.

Back inside the house, Thomas heard the front door slam, but he still waited to make sure his father was gone. He heard his mother weeping quietly, and he opened his bedroom door slowly. Thomas looked around the living room. Then he ran towards his mother and hugged her. She held him tight in her arms and they both cried.

Thomas looked up at his mother's face. Her eye was swollen and red. Her top lip was bloodied and discolored on the right side. Thomas also noticed the blood on the back of her hand as she took his hand and walked him back to his room. He could see that this was from a large bloody scratch that ran down most of her arm. "Please sleep with me Mommy, I'm scared," Thomas asked.

"I will Thomas." Marie replied, "Just let me wash my face and brush my teeth and then I'll be right in." Thomas nodded and forced a smile before going back to his room.

Marie reluctantly went to the bathroom fearing what she might see in the mirror. With the light on she could see her lip was bruised and swollen, her neck was red and there was a surface cut that ran the length of her right forearm. She cleaned up the best she could and went into the room with Thomas. She could see he was still shaken by what had occurred so she tried to bring back some sense of normalcy for him.

She read him a story, the same as she did every other night. She then turned on his Spiderman nightlight and kissed him goodnight before climbing into bed beside him.

Thomas lay still and remained quiet until he was certain his mother had fallen asleep. He then reached both his hands up, closed his eyes and touched his mother's arm gently so not to startle or wake her. He kept his hands in place until he felt his chest tighten, which always made him choke back his breath. He waited a second or two until the pain in his chest subsided and then he exhaled softly and slowly. Thomas whispered, "I love you Mommy."

This was the only way Thomas ever used the gift that he was born with, a gift that he kept secret from everyone.

Thomas was now exhausted, but in order to sleep, he had to follow the same ritual he did every night. As his eyes grew heavy, he looked to the left to make sure his closet door was closed.

Thomas was like every other seven year boy; he had a very healthy fear of the monster that lives in the closet and the monster that lives under the bed.

Once he saw that the closet door was closed, he let out a big yawn. He took one last look at the digital alarm clock on his dresser that sat right next to his Spiderman lamp before turning onto his side and falling asleep.

The next morning Marie was surprised to find that there weren't any of the usual aches or pains that she normally woke up with after a fight with Dan. She was alone in the room so that meant Thomas was already up and about. Marie sat for a moment at the edge of the bed before getting up then her mind began to wander. "How did it come to this?" she thought. "What kind of life is this for poor Thomas?" She felt herself begin to sink into the darkness so she quickly caught herself and got to her feet. Marie made the bed, straightened out the room then headed for the bathroom. But before turning on the light she braced herself for what she was about to see. Surely the swelling had worsened and everything was discolored or bruised by now.

When she flipped the switch, she was amazed to find that there wasn't a mark or blemish to be found. Even the scratch on her arm was gone. How was this possible? Was she in a haze from hitting her head on the wall after being pushed last night? Maybe she imagined the bruises because it had happened before so many times? All at once Marie felt both anxious and depressed because she couldn't remember. She was almost in a panic as she opened the medicine cabinet and reached for her bottle of Trimipramine. As she swallowed it down with a handful of water, she closed her eyes while repeating the words in her head, "Just calm down, just calm down."

When she looked in the mirror again, Marie immediately focused on the bags under her eyes and the lines on her face from years of abuse and worrying. Although others had told that she still looked great for her age, she just couldn't see it. She was the same weight she was when she met Dan in high school, 120 lbs. Also, she had the same long straight jet black hair and the same crystal clear sky blue eyes. Yet all she could see was the split ends and the darkness under her eyes. She was only 28, but she felt like she was 48.

She took one longer stare in the mirror and she told herself that she wouldn't allow herself to wallow any longer. Thomas had seen enough last night and she would not allow him to see her fall apart in front of him. So she took a deep breath, washed her face, brushed her teeth and left the bathroom to see what her son was up to.

Thomas was in the living room sitting where he always sat, in the dark blue recliner chair that was older than Thomas. It sunk down when anyone other than Thomas sat in it and it made a horrible squeaking sound when you reclined it back.

All of the furniture in their house was old. It was one of the many things that added to Marie's depression. It had all been purchased before Thomas was born and most of it came from garage sales or flea markets. Marie had always been a very neat and organized person and the house was always well maintained. However, she was always embarrassed when they had company over because the sofa and loveseat didn't match. One was blue like the recliner and the other was brown. Also, like the recliner, the cushions were worn and they would sink to a very noticeable level.

The coffee table that sat in the center of the room was faded and nicked, the carpet was worn and the 20" color television would change to just a green tint sometimes. When this happened, you would he to give it a tap on its side to adjust the color again. The rest of the house wasn't much different. Every room needed a paint job and had something that needed to be fixed or repaired. There never seemed to be enough time or money.

The garage, which was Dan's space, was always kept immaculate. Every tool had a place or a holder, the work bench was always clean of clutter and even Dan's music collection was neatly kept. Each cassette was in its case, stacked in alphabetic order.

Thomas was staring at the TV like a zombie as he ate a bowl of Cap'n Crunch while watching PBS. As Marie watched him she couldn't help but smile as he lifted the spoon up to his mouth without looking at it even for a second. Of course this meant that half of the cereal and some of the milk wound up either in the cushions of the chair or on his Spider-Man pajamas.

Marie was taken back for a second by how much he resembled her. He had the same pale skin tone, the same jet-black hair and the same sky blue eyes. Marie knew it had always been a thorn in Dan's side that his son had none of his features. On many a drunken night, Dan questioned her as to whether Thomas was even his son at all.

But truth be told, Thomas was definitely his mother's son. He was a very smart student, advanced in every subject. He wanted no part of sports or children oriented television. Thomas would rather watch a program about something related to science or nature than Scooby–Doo or a baseball game. Like his mother, Thomas was very much an introvert. Marie remembered having all of these same qualities when she was younger. She remembered being teased and picked on just like Thomas was for being strange or different. She felt terrible for Thomas because he didn't have any friends.

Marie was again lost in her thoughts until Thomas rushed past her towards the kitchen.

"Gotta get dressed for school," he shouted. "I don't want to make the bus driver wait again; he doesn't like that at all!"

Marie snapped out of her fog and laughed out loud.

"Ok honey, you get washed up, brush your teeth and comb your hair while I iron your clothes."

Fifteen minutes later they stood on the porch as the bus stopped in front of the house. Marie handed Thomas his lunch box then zipped his coat. She gave him a nod of approval and smiled as she said, "Have a good day honey."

Thomas yelled, "See ya later, mom!" as he raced down the stairs.

As Marie watched the bus pull away, she felt the depression set in again. She felt ashamed because it was getting to the point where she couldn't even hold it together in front of her son anymore. She had pleaded with Dan over and over to find her a doctor that had more experience with her condition. However, Dan would either just ignore her or he would tell her that all of the other doctors were too expensive.

Marie was able to hold her tears in until she was back in the house with the door closed behind her. She looked at the picture on the mantel of her and Dan during happier times and asked out loud, "How did it come to this?"

She took the picture off of the mantel and stared at it. As her tears dripped onto the photograph, Marie remembered happier times with Dan. She could remember almost every day they spent together. It wasn't always like this, she told herself. He was different, they both were different.

The Marie that Dan first met was a bookworm like Thomas; she was very smart and very shy. She just missed being valedictorian and had no social life. Her parents were very strict and didn't allow her to date; not that it mattered much because boys didn't seem to be interested in her.

Dan, on the other hand was a blonde, brown-eyed god with a perfect smile. He participated in all sports but baseball was his passion. He was the star pitcher on the high school team. After he went undefeated during his freshman and sophomore years, minor league scouts began to attend his games on a regular basis during his junior year.

Dan's love of baseball was passed down to him from his father. George Greggs was a hardworking man who demanded a lot from his son, but Dan knew that his father was proud of him and loved him very much. George was a huge Yankees fan who had a brief stint in the minor leagues himself. He would spend hours in the yard with Dan after work teaching him how to pitch, hit and field.

George's other passion was cars. When his baseball career didn't work out, he took a job as a mechanic and eventually opened his own shop. When they weren't playing baseball or when it got too cold to play outside, George would spend hours teaching Dan how to fix and rebuild cars. George would always tell Dan, "It's important for a man to know how to fix a car." But deep down George didn't want Dan working with his hands his whole life like he had to.

George saw that his son had a God-given talent and pushed him to get better and better. His manner of teaching was demanding, but it was always positive. George never belittled his son and he always tried to pick him up when he was down.

George kept a scrapbook of his son's entire baseball career. There were trophies lined three deep on the mantel in the living room. He would brag to anyone who would listen that his son was going to make it to the 'biggies'. He said, "It was just a matter of time."

Three months before Dan's senior year, George had a massive heart attack and died. Dan was devastated because he had lost a huge part of himself and looked to alcohol for relief. He started to attend every party he would hear about and drink until he passed out. Soon every weekend wasn't enough and he was drinking alone in his room during the week as well. When friends began to distance themselves from him, Dan leaned on the only person he thought he could trust, his baseball coach.

Coach Miller thought Dan was his ticket to his dream of coaching in the minors. He would tell anyone who listened that he and Dan were very close. Furthermore, he was instrumental in Dan learning to pitch the way he did. The other coaches ate it up and after Dan's first year with the team, the local media and some prestigious state colleges were paying serious attention to Coach Miller.

Coach Miller knew Dan's father death was going to have an effect him, but he had no idea that it would be as bad as it was. The coach was amazed when he first met Dan because he was a ready-made ballplayer. He had seen kids come to him with talent before, but none were on the level of Dan Greggs. The coach worried about what was at risk for both of them if he let Dan free-fall after his father's death. Their long-term goals were in sight. Coach Miller wasn't going to let anything screw it up, not even Dan.

When the rumors reached him regarding Dan's drinking, the coach immediately took action. Coach Miller knew Dan wasn't the sharpest tool in the shed so he had to make sure Dan had help meeting his academic needs so he could continue to pitch. He knew his young star also needed a shoulder to cry on so it would have to be a girl who would be willing to put up with that sort of thing.

When Coach Miller entered the library to meet all of the potential tutors, he knew the second he laid eyes on her that Marie Donaldson was the one. She was nerdy and she wouldn't even make eye contact, but she was still kind of cute. She was the type of girl that the coach had seen drool over Dan from afar. She was perfect.

Marie was encouraged to tutor other students by her guidance counselor. She was told that colleges needed to see something more than just good grades on her transcript. After reviewing several afterschool clubs and going over the list of volunteer work available, Marie was at a loss. So when her counselor mentioned tutoring it seemed like a good fit so she agreed to do it.

When the counselor mentioned that she would be tutoring Dan Greggs exclusively, Marie lit up like a Christmas tree. She thought Dan was the hottest guy on the planet, but he didn't even know that she existed. She was also nervous about it. Dan was used to being around the pretty and popular girls at school. Marie didn't think she was anywhere close to being in a league with them.

On the day of their first session, Dan entered the library with the head cheerleader, Maggie Layson, at his side. Marie could easily see what made her so popular with boys, but looks were all she had. Maggie was in three of her classes. From what Marie had seen, she knew Maggie had better use those looks and that body to marry a rich man.

Dan knew from the minute he said good bye to Maggie and sat down with Marie that she had a crush on him. Her face was flush and she couldn't stop smiling. Dan, of course, played the gentleman's role and offered his hand while introducing himself. Marie shook his hand and replied nervously, "I know who you are, my name is Marie."

Dan initially thought Marie was cute in a nerdy way and very smart. There was definitely something about her that was unlike any of the girls he knew and he was drawn to it in a weird way.

With Marie's help, Dan was able to get back on track academically and regain his focus for baseball. It was just as Coach Miller planned. Marie was so enamored that she did all of Dan's homework for him and she became a much-needed shoulder to cry on. Dan's drinking tapered off and he was having the season of a lifetime.

Dan almost seemed possessed out on the mound. He pitched every game and threw every pitch with his father in mind. He just wanted to make his father proud because he knew for certain that George was watching from the heavens. Dan was on top of the list in every major high school baseball category. There were now calls coming in to his coach every day with offers of college scholarships and talk of being drafted by big league teams. He pretty much had his pick of anything he wanted.

Dan's baseball dreams came to an end on a night he was pitching the best game of his life. He was working on a no-hitter in the bottom of the 7th, but Dan was tired and he didn't have much left in the tank. In his illustrious career he had never pitched a no-hitter, but that would change tonight, Dan thought.

The count was three balls, two strikes and Dan felt tightness in his shoulder as the batter fouled one ball off after another to stay alive. Dan's team had a 1 – 0 lead, but one mistake could change that – the opponent's best home run hitter was the plate.

Dan ignored the tightness and reared back to throw two more fastballs, but both were fouled off. He became angry and he remembered what his father would yell out to him from the stands when he saw Dan was tiring: "Heat it up kid, put some more on it."

So Dan reached back then threw a fastball high and inside. Swing and a miss, strike three!

But Dan never saw the swing. As soon as the ball left his hand, he heard a pop and his shoulder burned like it was on fire. The crowd first cheered the strikeout, but came to a hush as Dan dropped to his knees and yelled out in pain.

Two surgeries later to repair a torn rotator cuff and several torn tendons in his elbow, Dan's baseball career was over. It wasn't long after that he began his downward spiral.

He started drinking more again and all of his baseball friends abandoned him. Coach Miller suddenly had no time for Dan anymore. He always had a meeting to go to or someplace he had to be.

Marie was well aware of what was going on. Although he was home schooled for a while because of the surgeries, she still heard the rumors all throughout the school about Dan's drinking and about how he had changed.

On the day he returned to school Marie was called into her guidance counselor's office and told that she would no longer be tutoring Dan. She was now being assigned to tutor Ryan Olson, the football team's star quarterback. Marie quit the program on the spot and told the counselor it wasn't right what they were doing. She finally became aware that this program was designed to keep the jocks academically eligible for sports. She cursed herself for not seeing that before.

When she finally located Dan, he was sitting in the dugout at the baseball field. He looked so lost and alone all of the sudden. He was no longer the high school god he had been before and he didn't know how to deal with that. When Marie sat beside him, he looked over at her and smiled. High school god or not, she still melted every time he smiled.

"I heard the news about you not tutoring me anymore," he said. "Did you come to say goodbye?" Marie took his hand and smiled back. "I'm not like the others, Dan. You should know that by now." Dan smiled again, leaned into her and kissed her. They spent the next hour just sitting and talking in the dugout.

Marie made it her mission to get Dan to graduation with the best grades he ever had. She called him at night to make sure he was home and going to bed at a decent hour. She called him in the morning to get him up for school. When she arrived to pick him up in the morning, she always had a bagel and a coffee for him. At night he would eat dinner over at her house after they studied.

The world had abandoned Dan, but Marie was there for him in every aspect as his lover, his tutor and his friend. Although everyone else referred to him as damaged goods, she still saw him as the high school god. Whether he meant to or not, Dan took full advantage of the situation. But in Marie's eyes he was still as amazing as he was before he got hurt, if not more. She was able to actually get to know the real person now, not the arrogant jock who had all of the ladies drooling over him.

It was true and she knew it firsthand. After he injured his arm Dan had really changed. He was more sensitive and vulnerable now. He was also very romantic. Marie felt as if she had won the lottery because she had the perfect man. She didn't care what anyone else thought, she had the hottest guy in school and he was all hers.

After graduation Marie got a full-time job and paid for Dan's tuition for a technical school specializing in automotive repair. They agreed that Dan would finish technical school, get a job and then he would help pay Marie's tuition through college; but, of course, that didn't happen. Dan graduated, found a job and kept promising her that the next year she could go to school. Then when time came around, he would promise again. All the next years never came. Time went on, Dan started drinking again and Marie got pregnant.

They were married at the town hall three months before Thomas was born. Marie wanted a real wedding but Dan said they couldn't afford it. He promised her that they would have a real wedding the following year, but that next year never happened either.

As she sat at the edge of the bed thinking, Marie knew that her issues started much earlier in her life. It wasn't just Dan that made her this way; there were other things that changed her as well.

Marie was adopted when she was 21 months old and she never knew her real parents. She would have never known that she was even adopted if it wasn't for Uncle Rob. She could still remember the exact moment she found out like it was yesterday.

Marie's parents had thrown her a sweet sixteen party in their backyard. It was a big cookout with many family members in attendance and a few girls that Marie had known from the neighborhood. They weren't really friends of hers; they were the daughters of her mother's friends. It wasn't that Marie didn't like them. She just didn't associate with them, not even today.

Good old Uncle Rob was drunk as usual and hitting on Marie and the other girls. He had staggered over to Marie while she was talking with them and he grabbed her from behind to hug her, only this was no regular hug. When he reached his arms around her to squeeze her he crossed his arms in front of her with both his hands. His hands wound up on her breasts.

Horrified, Marie shouted, "Get off me, you old pervert! For God sakes, I'm your niece, sicko!"

This caused Uncle Rob to let go and he stumbled backwards.

"What's the big deal?" he said, "It's not like we're blood relatives."

"Uh, yeah we are, you drunk old fool," Marie replied. "I'm your sister's daughter; I believe that makes us blood relatives!"

"You ain't no one's daughter," Rob said, slurring his words and laughing. "You was adopted. Everyone knows my sister Ruth couldn't have no kids, something to do with her ovaries, so they got you instead."

Marie's Aunt Sue overheard the yelling and rushed in to push Rob away, but it was too late; the damage was done. Marie stood in shock as she watched Aunt Sue push Rob away while cursing at him. "You stupid drunk son of a bitch," she yelled. "What in God's name have you done?"

Marie turned to look at the other girls who were now standing silently with their mouths hanging open. Out of the corner of her eye, she watched as Aunt Sue left Rob and quickly made her way to Marie's parents who were standing by the grill talking to another couple. She watched as Aunt Sue tapped her mother on the shoulder to get her and her father's attention. There was an eerie quiet as they both leaned in to hear what Sue was saying. Suddenly almost in unison, they both lifted their heads as if stunned. You could then see them scanning the party to see where Marie was until their eyes met hers. Once their daughter was in sight, her father took her mother's hand and they rushed to where Marie was standing.

Marie remembered how they had explained everything to her about how she became a member of the family. They also explained the reason they had never told her she was adopted. They had both agreed that if they were going to adopt a child, that the child would be their child.

They explained to her that they had seen too many talk shows in which couples had adopted a child and when the child was old enough they told tell him or her that they were adopted. They said in almost every case, the child felt different about their adopted parents and wanted to seek out their biological parents. Her father assured her that this always led to all kinds of issues for the child and the adoptive parents. So that's why they both agreed that they did not want this to happen with their child.

Marie's mother told her that all of the family members knew about their struggles to have a baby. They told every one of their plans to adopt and explained that they did not want the child to ever know that they were not her biological parents. The only way the truth would come out is if there was an issue in which the medical history of the parents was needed.

Marie remembered the shock and the hurt she felt that day and how she hated Uncle Rob from then on for opening his stupid mouth. The truth did help make sense of a few things to though. Marie and her father had never been close. She was never Daddy's little girl.

Her father was a drinker, like his brother Rob, who would verbally and physically abuse Marie and her mother on occasion. Marie had never felt a connection to him and now she knew why. He must have never really accepted her as his own.

Years later, after her father passed, Marie's mother would explain that her father was the one who was responsible for them not being able to have children because his sperm count was too low. Of course her father being a proud man, he had told everyone it was his wife's ovaries that were the problem because he was afraid it would make him look like less of a man.

After the secret came out, Marie's mother and father started fighting a lot more often. Soon her father became more distant than ever. It had reached the point where Marie had heard the word divorce thrown around more and more.

On the outside, Marie was the same as always. Her grades didn't suffer and she kept up with all of her tutoring responsibilities. But on the inside she was quickly crumbling. She found herself sitting alone in her room a lot. There was no TV or radio on, she would just sit and stare while her mind drifted. She would start crying or feel like she was going to cry for no reason at all. There seemed like there was no truth or no hope in the world. She was the invisible girl with no friends and no real family.

A car horn beeped outside and brought Marie back to the present. She looked at the clock and noticed she had been sitting lost in thought for a half hour. There was still a lot to do around the house and she had to get motivated. She let out a long sigh, wiped her eyes then went on about her business of cleaning the house and doing the laundry.

Chapter 2

The Greggs lived in West Orange, which is one of many suburban towns in New Jersey. It was built on a mountainous terrain. The 'upper level' of the town or the top of the mountain consists of very large homes and mansions. From about half way down the mountain to the edge of the lower level is the middle class area. Down at the bottom of the mountain towards the town's border is the poor area. The Greggs lived right on the boarder of the middle class section, a few blocks away from the low income section.

Dan, Marie and their only child, Thomas Greggs, lived in a small two-story home that resembled the other houses on their street. The houses were all only about 25 feet apart and were designed with the same floor plan. The front room was always the living room, and off of that was the dining room. At the opposite end of the dining room there was a doorway that led into the kitchen where the only touch-tone phone in the house could be found hanging on the wall. To the left of the dining room was a small hallway that led to a small bathroom, followed by a small bedroom which in the Greggs' house belonged to Thomas. On the second floor there was a large master bedroom, a large bathroom and a spare bedroom. Attached to the house on the left was a small one-car garage. In the rear they had a fenced-in yard that was bigger than you would normally find in a residential neighborhood.

The only major difference between their house and the rest of the houses on their side of the street was the color of the house and the roof. The Greggs' house was painted beige and it had a brown roof. The paint was cracked and peeling in several places. Dan had said on many occasions that he was going to have aluminum siding put on, but it never happened.

The house to the right belonged to their neighbors the Morgans, Kate and her father Kyle. Their house was blue with a grey-shingled roof.

Kate was an only child like Thomas. She was two years older than Thomas and never really spoke to him or anyone in his family.

Kyle, on the other hand, took a liking to Thomas right away. Once he got past Thomas' shy side, Kyle found him to be really smart and very polite for a boy his age.

Kate's mom divorced her dad and moved to Florida with another man when Kate was three, leaving Kyle to raise his daughter on his own.

Kyle was 34, tall and athletically built, with short brown hair and brown eyes. He worked as an insurance agent, and he was always dressed in khakis and a button-down shirt during the week. On the weekends, he either wore a pair of jeans and a t-shirt or sweatpants and a t-shirt. He was a very outgoing man. He would always wave hello and talk to everyone in the neighborhood. In the winter when it would snow, more times than not, Kyle would shovel the Greggs' walkway because Dan was either at work or passed out on the couch.

Kyle was a big Yankees fan and so was Kate; they went to many games together. She was tall and thin, with long dirty-blonde hair and brown eyes like her father. Kate was very much the tomboy from the time she was little. She always wore blue jeans and a t-shirt with a black pair of converse sneakers.

Kate was also very good at baseball for her age, so good that Dan had once drunkenly commented, "Kyle, somebody made a mistake. I ended up with your girl and you ended up with my son." Kyle just nodded and smiled politely. However, he was thinking what an asshole Dan was and how he felt bad for Thomas.

At the age of nine, Kate was the best player on her little league softball team. She could hit and field better than any girl in the league, even the older ones.

It was about more than baseball to Kyle though. It was about spending time with his daughter. While playing catch or fielding fly balls Kate would talk and talk. She would talk about school, her friends, her favorite TV shows and even about her mother on rare occasions. Kyle would use this time to learn about what was going on in her life outside of home. Of course it would be years before Kate would understand this.

Kyle would sometimes invite Thomas to come over in the yard to play catch with them or to the park to watch Kate practice hitting and fielding. Kate, of course, hated it. She didn't want to share her time with her father; she wanted her Dad all to herself. "Why couldn't Thomas play with his own dad?" she would think as her Dad talked to Thomas.

The first time Kyle invited Thomas over to play catch, he was surprised how adamant Thomas was about not joining in. When Kyle tossed the third mitt Thomas's way and said, "C'mon kiddo, put it on, you're playing," Thomas just stared and shook his head. "C'mon, kiddo, don't worry about it, I'll show you how to catch. Don't be afraid or embarrassed."

When Kyle noticed the sad look in Thomas' eyes, he said, "Hey, it's ok kiddo, no big deal, you can just watch us." Thomas nodded before walking a few feet away and taking a seat in the grass.

"See, I told you he was a weirdo," Kate said sarcastically.

"Hey, you knock that off right now," Kyle said to her sternly as he looked her right in the eyes. Kate felt embarrassed and muttered an apology to Thomas. He smiled and said, "It's okay," then watched for a half hour as they continued playing.

After they finished, Kyle waited until Kate went inside before running to catch up with Thomas. "Hey, kiddo, wait up a second. I'm sorry about what Kate said. Sometimes she doesn't think before she speaks," Kyle said. "If you don't want to join us in playing catch that's fine, you can still hang out whenever you feel like though, okay?"

Thomas smiled again without making eye contact and nodded. To Kyle, it seemed like Thomas wanted to say something but he was holding back. "Hey, you know, if there's every anything you want to talk about or if you ever need someone to talk to when your mom's not around, you can talk to me if you want," Kyle said. "Ask Kate, I'm a pretty good listener and I have been known to give good advice a time or two."

With that Thomas laughed, and Kyle laughed as well.

Kyle put his hand on Thomas's shoulder and said, "See ya later kiddo," as he turned to leave. He was very surprised when Thomas called out, "Mr. Morgan, wait!"

Kyle walked back towards him and said, "What's up kiddo?"

Thomas looked at the ground and bit his lip for a second before speaking. "My father tried to teach me how to catch a baseball a few times in back yard. I tried really hard at first but the glove seemed way too big for my hand. Dad kept throwing it and I kept missing it and he got really mad," Thomas said. "'C'mon, Thomas, you're not even trying,' he'd shout. I would tell him again and again, 'I am Dad, really,' He said, 'Well try harder, you can do it.'

"But he just kept yelling at me, and I gave up. He kept yelling until I started crying and my mother yelled at him to stop." Thomas then paused as a tear rolled down his left cheek. "He said, 'Why do I even bother with you, go back inside and watch TV or whatever the hell it is you like to do. I give up.'"

Kyle felt sad, angry and helpless, then he thought to himself that it's probably the way Thomas feels everyday dealing with Dan.

Kyle put his hand on Thomas's shoulder again and said, "It's ok, kiddo, I understand. Sometimes people don't think before they speak and say things they don't mean, even adults. I've talked to your mom and from what I hear you are really smart. And as you get older, you're going to find that you are good at so many things that you never thought you would be. Just keep your head up and don't let others tell you who you are. You just be you and everything else will work itself out, okay?"

This time, Thomas looked Kyle right in the eyes and smiled as he nodded.

"Ok then, kiddo, I gotta go, Kate's waiting for her PB&J sandwich, I'll see you later."

"Ok, bye Mr. Morgan," Thomas said before running back towards his house.

"Call me Kyle," he shouted back before heading home.

Chapter 3

Four months later is when Thomas decided to use his gift for someone other than his mother.

It was a warmer than usual mid-March day. Kate came home from school and asked her Aunt Janet if she could ride her bike in front of the house. Janet allowed her but reminded her put her helmet and knee and elbow pads on.

Kate nodded, grabbed her helmet and headed out. Janet was watching Kate ride but her mind was on a million different things. She didn't notice that Kate wasn't wearing her knee or elbow pads. Kate was riding on the sidewalk, passing by a house a few doors down when she was startled by a large dog that charged the fence that it was behind. She lost control of the bike and crashed onto the ground and screamed as she fell on her right elbow.

Janet heard the scream and came out of her daze. She ran toward Kate, who was now crying hysterically and holding her arm. It was already swelling and it was discolored from the elbow to the forearm.

Marie was inside cooking when she heard the scream. She ran to the front door and saw Janet leaning over the injured girl. Thomas heard it too and ran to join his mother.

Marie opened the door and shouted, "Janet is she okay? Is there anything I can do?"

"Marie, I think Kate broke her arm," Janet yelled back. "Please call an ambulance." Marie hurried inside to call then she and Thomas went outside to stay with them until the ambulance arrived.

Thomas felt terrible as he watched Kate squint her eyes and cry from the pain. "I want my dad," she begged. Thomas couldn't help but think that his dad would be the *last* person he wanted if this had happened to him.

When the EMTs arrived, they loaded Kate into the ambulance. As Janet was getting into the back with her she asked Marie to let Kyle know what happened. "I will," Marie said. She looked into the ambulance to where Kate was sitting and said, "You'll be fine, Kate."

The EMT closed the door and the ambulance sped away.

The following day, Thomas was kicking a soccer ball back and forth across his backyard. It rolled to the fence that separates his yard from Kate's. When he got to the fence and looked down at the ball, something else caught his attention.

Kate was walking around in a circle and talking to herself in her backyard. She was wearing her team's baseball cap and she had a baseball glove on her hand. Thomas noticed that it was on the wrong hand. Kate's other arm was covered by a cast that went from her shoulder to her wrist.

"Hi Kate," Thomas shouted. Kate stopped walking and looked over at Thomas. She had a really sad look on her face and it made Thomas sad too. "Are you okay?" Thomas asked.

Kate stared at him and shook her head. "Do I look okay, stupid?" she shouted at him. "Do I, Thomas?"

"I'm sorry Kate," Thomas said softly as he looked at the ground.

"I'm gonna miss the entire season!" she said. She felt like crying but she didn't want Thomas to see.

Thomas didn't say anything; he just looked at her sadly.

"You don't understand," she said and she began to walk away.

"I can help you," Thomas shouted.

Kate stopped and slowly turned to face him again.

"What did you just say?" Kate asked.

"I can help you," Thomas said again.

Kate laughed bitterly, "Are you nuts? How can you help me?"

"Wait there," Thomas said.

He then walked around the house and joined her in her backyard.

"Well?" Kate said sarcastically.

"First you have to promise not to ever tell anyone about this," Thomas said.

"What the heck are you talking about?" Kate asked.

"Promise!" Thomas insisted, "Promise you will never tell anyone about what I do."

"Sure," Kate said, "Whatever, I promise, ok?"

Thomas nodded then reached for her cast.

"That hurts!" Kate shouted. "What the heck do you think you're doing, stupid?"

"Sorry," Thomas said softly. "I have to touch it."

Kate looked at him, confused. Thomas again reached for her arm with both hands and this time he lifted it a little. Kate watched as Thomas inhaled deeply and closed his eyes. He looked as if he was in pain and she was just about to tell him to knock it off when it happened; the pain was gone!

Thomas exhaled and opened his eyes. Kate grabbed her arm with her good hand and pushed down. There was no pain at all!

"What just happened?" she asked.

Thomas didn't answer. "Remember, Kate, you promised," he said and then he ran back to his house.

Kate walked back inside the house, rolling her arm in big circles. Kyle had just finished the dishes when he saw her. Kate had a big smile on her face and she was moving her arm up and down, side to side and rolling it all the way around. Up to an hour ago, she couldn't even look at the cast without saying her arm throbbing.

Kyle dried his hands and then caught up to Kate as she was approaching the stairs. "Umm, how's the arm feeling honey?" he asked.

"It feels really good dad, I think maybe the doctor was wrong," she said. Kate wasn't even finished with the sentence before she had the arm going in all directions again faster and faster. Kyle rushed over and grabbed her arm to stop her.

"Hey," he said, "Easy there! You might do even more damage to it."

Kate pulled away and said, "It's fine, dad, really."

"Listen honey," he said, "It might feel better right now for whatever reason, but that doesn't mean it's okay. You saw the x-rays the doctor showed us. Let's just take it easy and not move it so much until I can take you back to the doctor tomorrow?"

Kate smiled and nodded. She *knew* Thomas had done something incredible for her. She couldn't even begin to imagine how, but he did it.

After that day, Kate started hanging out with Thomas all of the time. She even started to look after him at school, taking on the role of a big sister to protect him from bullies and others who would make fun of him. Kyle couldn't figure out what caused the change in Kate's attitude towards Thomas, but he was very pleased that it happened. He assumed it had something to do with what she had gone through with her arm, but he just couldn't make the connection.

Thomas had never been happier because he had finally had a friend. Before long, his normal routine would be to come home from school, spend time with his mother talking about his day, complete his homework and then go over to the Morgan's house leaving just before his father arrived home from work. At first Marie was concerned about how much time he was spending over there. But when she noticed that Thomas was happier and more confident, she came to think of it as a good thing.

Thomas saw the Morgans as the perfect family. Kyle was a great dad who listened to his daughter and took an interest in everything she cared about. Kate loved her dad too and the fact that she didn't have a mom didn't seem to bother her at all. This made Thomas think often of how good his life would be without his father around. He found himself wishing his father was gone on those many nights when he heard Dan yelling in the other room.

Thomas's relationship with the Morgans made that situation a lot easier to bear. Kyle was always there to listen to him vent about what was going on at home. Although Kate didn't quite understand what he was going through, she would always try to cheer him up.

Throughout their preteen years Thomas and Kate were inseparable. When they weren't in the house hanging out or watching movies, they were either taking turns riding her bike or going to the arcade. During the summers they would spend their days at the town pool during the week with Aunt Janet and on the weekends they would go to the beach with Kyle.

Kyle would try to invite Marie and Dan along, but they would always refuse. Kyle knew Marie loved the beach, because Thomas had told him so, but for some reason she wouldn't go with them. Kyle always assumed it was because Dan wouldn't let her.

When Kate reached the age of 13, things started to change. She started to make more friends in middle school and she was becoming very popular. Thomas, on the other hand, maintained his status as a shy, introverted outcast.

Kate's friends didn't like the idea of her dragging Thomas along everywhere. Therefore, she tried to accommodate everyone as best she could by dividing her week up into days where she hung out with Thomas and her other friends.

Thomas didn't take this well, in fact he was very depressed when this started happening. He still didn't have any other friends. He found himself alone in the yard again, staring at the same old ball he used to kick around.

One afternoon Kyle noticed him out there and invited him over. They had dinner together and Kyle told him that he could still come by any time he wanted to whether Kate was home or not.

"Thanks, but I can't," Thomas said.

Kyle smiled at him and replied, "Hey, now that she's gone hanging out with her friends, I have no one to talk to either. You'd be doing me a favor saving me from being in this house all by myself talking to the walls."

Thomas agreed and that's the way things stayed until Kate got a boyfriend at the age of 14.

Once Kate fell head over heels for Andy Wolkowski, she forgot that everyone existed, including Thomas. She even gave up baseball. Andy was a junior in high school while Kate was still a freshman. Although Kyle was dead set against it, Kate still agreed to be his girlfriend. Kate cut off all contact with Thomas because Andy was jealous of the relationship they had. He didn't want her hanging out with any other guys. When Kate tried to explain this to Thomas, he was hurt deeply and he wouldn't leave his room for weeks except to go to school.

Thomas heard a rumor about Andy. People said that he dated a lot of freshmen. He used them and then got rid of them. Of course when he tried to warn Kate about him she wouldn't listen to a word he said.

For three months Kate ate, breathed and drank Andy Wolkowski. But true to his reputation, Andy dumped Kate when she refused to let him get by second base. To make matters worse on the day he broke up with her, he went around telling everyone that he got a lot further with her under the bleachers at school.

Kate was devastated because this was her first boyfriend as well as her first love. As soon as Thomas heard about the breakup so he went to Kate's house to see how she was doing. He wound up staying up the whole night with her talking in her living room. He tried to take her mind off of it and make her laugh as she cried from time to time.

Of course, Thomas had no point of reference when it came to this sort of thing. All of the girls he liked wouldn't spit on him if he was on fire. He just tried to do the best he could by just being there for her.

Kyle would try to join them from time to time and Kate would cut him off by saying, "Dad, we're talking okay?" in her sad, sniffly voice. Kyle would look to Thomas for some kind of reaction and Thomas mouthed the words, "It's okay." Kyle smiled at him then disappeared into the hallway where he kept listening.

Three days later on his way home from school, Thomas saw Andy walking with another girl. He saw red as he watched Andy slide his hand from around the girl's waist to her butt. Although Thomas wasn't sure, this girl was probably Kate's age and more than likely another freshman.

Thomas was not a violent person by any means. All of the rage that he carried towards different people and things he kept bottled up inside. He was just about to turn to head down a different street to get home when he stepped on a branch that cracked so loud it caused Andy to turn around and look back.

Thomas stood frozen for a moment with the anger building inside him as he stared at Andy with this other girl. Andy looked at him with a smug look on his face and laughed. "What, is she sending her crazy stalker gay friend to follow me now?"

It was the first time in his life that Thomas had reacted without thinking. It was as if his rational mind had left him and all that was left was rage.

Andy was surprised as a much smaller and lighter Thomas charged at him and pushed him down. Thomas was able to get one and only one punch in while he could hear the girl shouting, "Get off of him, you freak!"

Andy managed to force Thomas off of him and onto his back. Thomas tried to get a hold of Andy's arms as Andy punched him again and again in the face. The fight was stopped when an adult who was passing by intervened. As Thomas lay there with his eyes closed, his mouth full of blood and his head aching, he heard Andy yell, "You and your girlfriend better stay away from me or it will be worse next time!"

The stranger walked with Thomas all the way home to make sure he was okay. Once they were in front of his house, Thomas thanked the man and told him he had to go in through the back door. The man asked one more time if he was sure he was all right before going on his way. Thomas hid just out of sight until the man disappeared around the corner. He touched his face and yelled "Owww," out loud because it hurt so much. He had never allowed himself to be in pain this long, so this was a first for him.

As he closed his eyes and placed his hands on his chest he heard a familiar voice from behind him. "Oh my God, what the hell happened to you?" Kate asked.

Thomas let out a sigh and turned to face her. "Jeez, who did this you?" Kate asked as she approached him.

Thomas held up a hand to stop her. "Please just give me a second," he said. "This really hurts a lot."

Thomas then started the process again of closing his eyes and healing himself. When he was done, Kate just stood there with her mouth open. "Amazing," was the only thing she could think of to say.

Thomas stared at her as she studied him and let out a long sigh. There was no way she was going to let this go and he knew it. "I ran into Andy on the way home from school," Thomas said. "He was with another girl. He said some really mean things to me and I just lost it. I'd like to say I got the better of him, but at least one punch in and I think I bruised his left eye. I'm very proud," he joked. They both laughed and Kate hugged Thomas tightly.

"You did that for me?" she asked. "Why would you put yourself through that after the way I treated you when I was with him?"

When she let go Thomas could see she had a tear in her eye. He smiled and gave her a light shove on her shoulder. "I did it 'cause you're my best friend and I am your brother from another mother," Thomas said, hoping for another smile. They both burst out into laughter and Kate replied, "You sure are."

They talked and laughed in the yard together for another hour or so before Kyle opened the back door to let them both know dinner was ready if anyone was hungry.

That night everything in Thomas's world was good again. He was back with the family he wished he was part of. As far as he was concerned, the beating he took was well worth it.

Chapter 4

December 27th, 1991 was a date that would stand out in Thomas's life. He made a choice that would affect everything else for years to come.

It was on this cold, gray winter day that a now fourteen and a half year old Thomas was stuck home alone with his father. Kate, Kyle and Janet had gone to upstate New York to spend Christmas with a cousin. They were coming home that day, so every so often Thomas would look out the window to see if they were back. His mother was at the ShopRite picking up groceries.

As usual Dan was drunk in the garage working on a 1967 Camaro that he had swindled away from a widow less than a year ago. The woman's husband had died and she had absolutely no knowledge of cars at all. Dan got lucky, because he was the first to answer the ad she had placed in the paper. He lied and charmed the elderly woman in believing the car needed more work than it was worth. He offered to take the car off her hands for $500. The elderly woman had no one to advise her so she trusted what this nice man was telling her and she sold him the car. Dan came back later, with Marie, put his license plates on the Camaro and drove it away with a grin that stretched from ear to ear. He knew that car was worth at least $5,000 and possibly double that.

Thomas was in the living room trying to avoid him by watching television. His went from channel to channel until he got to MTV. R.E.M's video "Losing My Religion" was on. Thomas put his head back and closed his eyes as his mind started to wander while he listened to the lyrics. Michael Stipe sang, "That's me in the corner, that's me in the spotlight losing my religion, trying to keep up with you and I don't know if I can do it. Oh no, I've said too much. I haven't said enough."

The thought of religion had always been such a mystery to Thomas. There were so many questions and no one could seem to explain religion in a way that made sense to him. His mother had told him there was God and that there was the Devil. She explained that when you died you would be judged on what kind of person you were in life. The good ones went to heaven and the bad ones went to hell. It sounded simple at first, but from what he had heard and read, everything was a sin. It all just confused him so he tried not to think about it very much.

His eyes were getting heavy and he was just starting to drift off when he heard a loud crash come from the garage. Thomas quickly sat up, reached for the remote and lowered the volume of the television so he could listen.

He knew better than to just go into the garage and ask if everything was okay. His father had been drinking pretty much the entire day and this usually made him one mean cuss to deal with. Thomas didn't want any part of that. He had learned that lesson the hard way over the years. So the routine now was when his father would come inside for a minute, Thomas would go into his room. As soon as Thomas would hear the door to the garage slam again, he would then go back into the living room. This was something that was done on a daily basis. Thomas wanted no part of his father and it seemed like the feeling was mutual to him because Dan didn't even attempt to talk to him anymore.

Thomas had reached the point long ago where he didn't like being home at all. It was on days like this when he was left alone with his father that Thomas had a constant knot in his stomach. It was almost as if he was holding his breath the whole time until his mother got home.

Suddenly, there was a second loud crash. This time it was followed by his father shouting out in pain loudly enough that Thomas could hear him in the living room. Thomas got to his feet and ran to the garage. He opened the door and his father was nowhere in sight. There were no other sounds but the radio blasting out some song from the 70s and the sound of his breath.

"Dad, are you in here?" Thomas shouted. "I heard a noise and you sounded like you hurt yourself, are you okay?"

When there was no response, Thomas walked over to the radio and turned it off. Standing there with only the sound of his breathing in the room, Thomas began to look around. Out of the corner of his eye he saw his father lying face down on the floor.

Two portable workstations that had been filled with tools had fallen down on top of Dan when he fell or fainted, accounting for the loud crashes Thomas had heard moments ago.

"Dad, are you okay?" Thomas shouted as he rushed over to his father's side. When Thomas lifted the carts off him, Dan's body jerked suddenly.

He turned over onto his back while clutching his chest before crying out in agony. "It's my heart, Thomas; call an ambulance for Christ sakes!"

Thomas jumped to his feet and was about to run to the phone, but instead he stopped. He stood for only a few seconds in that spot thinking, but it seemed like hours had passed. He had decided that he would have to tell his father about his gift and heal him. For just a moment he thought that maybe this would be the thing that brings them closer together and that things would get better between them.

"What the hell are you doing, stupid?" Dan yelled before crying out in pain again. "Are you trying to kill me? Call the damn ambulance!"

Dan took a few deep long breaths and attempted to get to his feet before collapsing again. Thomas started to rush towards him. "Neither you nor your mother can survive without me, you hear me?" Dan shouted. "I am the only thing that keeps this worthless family together! You are worthless... you always have been. You were never my son... I'm ashamed that you even have my last name. You can get the hell out and go live with your friends next door for all I care! He already has one daughter over there, I'm sure he won't mind another one."

Thomas stopped dead in his tracks and stared at his father. Those words hurt more than the million hits or punches he been subjected to over the years. As he watched his father get into the fetal position and cry out in pain, Thomas suddenly felt nothing. He was numb. It was as if everything was moving in slow motion as he walked out of the garage and into the kitchen. Thomas' mind was a blur until he heard the operator's voice on the other line. "911, what's your emergency?" Thomas gave her the details as well as the address, but couldn't remember the conversation immediately afterward.

Thomas calmly hung up the phone, walked to the living room and stood there waiting for the ambulance to arrive. As he listened to his father cry out and cuss him there was only one thought that went through his head: "Let God decide."

If it was meant to be, then his father would make it. It was no longer in Thomas's hands. This seemed fair to Thomas. After several minutes had passed, his father became silent. Just as Thomas stood contemplating whether he would check on him, he heard the sounds of the sirens on his street.

Thomas walked over to the window, opened the blinds and watched as two EMTs exited the vehicle then went to the back for the gurney. He closed the blinds and waited for the bell to ring before opening the door to let them inside. When one of the EMTs asked where his father was, Thomas pointed towards the kitchen and calmly said, "Through the kitchen there's a door to the right that leads to the garage, he's in there." Without saying another word they rushed past him through the house and into the garage.

Thomas continued to wait in the living room while listening to the EMTs frantically tried to resuscitate his father. He could hear one of them say over and over, "Let's try it again. Clear!" followed by the sound of a thump.

Thomas looked out the window again and saw a crowd was gathering. His neighbors were all standing next to the ambulance while talking to each other and pointing towards the house. It all somehow seemed surreal to him, like it wasn't real and he was dreaming.

The front door swung open and Kyle Morgan was standing in the hallway breathing heavy while covered in sweat. He rushed into the living room and stopped suddenly when he noticed Thomas standing in the corner looking out the window.

"We just pulled in when we saw the ambulance outside! Are you alright Thomas?" he asked while sounding winded. "What's going on?"

Thomas didn't answer him. He wanted to, but the words wouldn't come out. Instead he lowered his head and closed his eyes tight before the tears came streaming down his face. Kyle was just about to go over to him and comfort him when he heard voices coming from the kitchen.

As he hurried towards the voices, he saw two EMTs come out of the garage with a gurney. Kyle immediately noticed that they weren't moving quickly and that there was a blanket covering the head of whomever they were pushing. Kyle also noticed that the hand sticking out of the side of the blanket was covered in grease. Kyle suddenly felt sick because he knew it was Dan, and he knew he must be dead.

The men stopped for a moment when they noticed Kyle and asked if he was family. When he said he wasn't, they were about to continue on passed him. Although Kyle knew the answer he felt he had to ask to be certain. So as they passed him by he asked the EMT closest to him if Dan was alive.

The man didn't say a word, but his facial expression along with the quick shake of his head said it all. Kyle stood stunned for a moment at what he had seen before the realization had occurred to him that Thomas must have seen the whole thing and that he was alone dealing with it in the other room.

When Kyle got back into the living room he saw Thomas standing in the doorway watching the EMTs make their way through the crowd and into the ambulance. He stood behind and noticed that they didn't put their siren on when they pulled away. He knew exactly what that meant.

Thomas just stood there with tears streaming down his face as the people in the crowd pointed at him while they talked amongst themselves and shook their heads with looks of sympathy on their faces.

"If they only knew," Thomas thought to himself. "If they knew what a monster my father was, they would feel no sympathy at all." At that moment, he felt no shame at all as he imagined how much better his and his mother's life would be without his father's constant abuse.

"If this is true, why I am crying?" he wondered. In a sudden moment of pure guilt and clarity, two thoughts entered his head, "Am I the reason he is dead? Could I have saved him?"

The thoughts lingered until Kyle put his arm around him and walked him through the crowd, over towards his house. Kyle waved people off and stared them down as they shouted, "Is he all right?" and "He's not dead, is he?"

Once they got inside Kyle's house, Kate rushed over to Thomas and hugged him tight.

"What happened?" she asked, "Are you okay?"

Kyle looked her in the eyes and shook his head sadly. "Kate, Thomas said his mother is at the ShopRite, please sit with him while I try to get the number."

Kate nodded and as Thomas started to cry, she guided him over to the couch. He sat with his head in his hands while she rubbed his back and tried to comfort him. Meanwhile in the kitchen, Kyle called 411 to get the number of the local ShopRite. But by the time he got the number and had her paged, no one responded.

When Kyle came back into the living room, he stood near Thomas, watching Kate rub his back. He didn't know what to say to comfort him. He didn't want to tell Thomas that his father was dead. He thought it was best if he and his mother consoled each other. But still his heart broke for Thomas.

Kyle left Kate and Thomas alone while he waited on the porch for any sign of Marie. It was only another 20 minutes, but it seemed like an eternity before he saw her car appear on their street and pull into the driveway.

Kyle really hoped beyond hope that she would be there for her son and together they would console each other to try to get through this. But he had a feeling in the pit of his stomach that things were going to get even worse, if that was possible. He knew Marie sometimes had a hard time dealing with things and he worried this would send her over the edge. Kyle's fears were realized soon after she got out of her car.

Chapter 5

Kyle ran through the words that he was about to say to Marie in his mind, but he never got a chance. As Marie approached her house, she found it strange that a group of her neighbors were gathered in front. When they all looked at her car simultaneously and pointed to her, she had a bad feeling that something was wrong.

Nancy, the neighborhood busybody who lived across the street, came running over to Marie as soon as she closed her car door. Nancy was a widower in her late 60s and everyone knew that her life revolved around the daytime soaps and neighborhood gossip.

"Marie honey, I have something to tell you," she shouted as she approached. The rest of the crowd -- two other couples from across the street and a bunch of kids from the neighborhood – trailed right behind her.

Kyle heard Marie yell so loud that the whole street probably heard her. "Oh my God! Is he ok? Please tell me he's ok!"

Kyle ran outside as fast as he could. He could hear Marie talking, but she wasn't making sense at all until she made eye contact with him. Thomas heard his mother too and he quickly ran to the window.

"Kyle, where is Thomas?" Marie yelled.

"He's fine Marie," Kyle responded, "he's inside with Kate."

"Does he know about what happened to his father?" she asked.

"Oh my God! I can't believe this," Marie cried as she dropped to her knees on the ground. "Dan's father died of a heart attack and so did his grandfather. Is he dead Kyle? Please tell me he's not dead."

Thomas wanted to go to her so badly but he couldn't face her. He couldn't look her in the eye and explain to her what had happened. He feared she would never forgive him.

Kyle put his hand on Marie's shoulder and tried to console her. "Come inside and let's call the hospital, or I can take there if you want me to drive you."

It was at the moment that everything spun out of control and Kyle was helpless to stop it.

Nancy was rubbing Marie's back the whole time she was talking to Kyle. When he asked her to come inside the woman blurted out, "I don't know, it didn't look good honey, they had the sheet over his head when they drove him out of here."

Kyle stood in shock as the words hung in the air for only a second before Marie screamed, "No!" She then quickly got to her feet and ran to her car while crying hysterically.

Kyle ran behind her, pleading with her to let him drive her but Marie didn't listen.

By the time Thomas made it through the door and down the porch steps, his mother already had the car speeding away in reverse. Thomas chased after her begging, "Please mom stop the car, you can't drive like this," but Marie never heard him. Instead she dropped the gearshift into drive and sped away up the street.

She didn't get far though. As she tried to make the right hand turn at the end of the street, she sideswiped a parked car and crashed into a telephone pole.

Half of the neighborhood was now out of their houses watching this drama unfold. Several neighbors made it to the car before Kyle and Thomas could. They could hear Marie screaming on the top of her lungs for everyone to get away from her. Someone had opened the car door to try to help, but she started kicking and scratching at the neighbor who reached for her hand.

Thomas forced his way through the crowd and finally got close to his mother. At first she didn't recognize him, so she tried to push him away. Thomas grabbed her hand and said, "Mom, it's me."

Marie became calm, but only for a moment. Just long enough to hug Thomas and say, "How could this have happened? I can't live without him." Thomas hugged her tight and whispered, "I'm so sorry, Mom." Marie squeezed him tighter and tighter as she began to cry hysterically again.

Thomas heard the sirens and he could see the red lights approaching behind the crowd of people. He held his mother until one of the officers approached and asked him to step back. When he tried to let go his mother grabbed him tighter and wouldn't let him. He kept repeating to his mother over and over, "It's gonna be ok Mom, they just want to see if you're all right," but Marie wouldn't let go.

Finally one of the officers grabbed Thomas from behind and forcefully pulled him away. Marie didn't follow him out of the car; instead she buried her face between the driver's seat and the door, crying uncontrollably again.

For several minutes, the officer tried to talk her out but Marie didn't respond. It then took two officers and two EMTs to remove Marie from the car. She kicked and screamed the whole time as everyone from the neighborhood watched in shock.

All Kyle could think about was Thomas. How traumatic must it have been to see his father die right in front of him, followed by a complete breakdown by his mother?

Kyle could relate to this in some way. When he was 21, he lost his father to Hodgkin's disease. It wasn't a sudden death like what Thomas had witnessed. But it did happen rather quickly. He was diagnosed in the month of June, by October it had spread to his lymph nodes and he passed in late November. Kyle watched his father go from being a 6ft 2" man in great shape to a frail, bald man who couldn't get out of bed or even feed himself within a span of six months.

All Kyle could do for Thomas now was to be there for him as a friend and offer his support as someone who had been through this.

It was about 9:30 p.m. when the phone rang at the Morgan house. Kyle had finally gotten Thomas calm enough where he could give him something to eat. So Kyle let it ring the first time. When whoever it was immediately called back, Kyle got up to answer it.

It was Dr. Lessner from West Orange General Hospital. He apologized for calling so late and said he had gotten the number from Marie Greggs. The doctor told Kyle that Marie would be staying at the hospital for an undermined amount of time in the psychiatric ward.

"Mr. Morgan, it was determined that Marie Greggs was at risk to herself. She needs to be evaluated and treated before being released. Mrs. Greggs asked me to apologize to you and to ask if you would look after her son Thomas while she was away. She also asked that you tell Thomas that she loves him and that she will see him soon," the doctor said.

Dan's wake was three days later. The only people who attended the one day of viewing were Kyle, Kate and Thomas. As strange as it seemed, Thomas was actually surprised by the turnout. He assumed that because his father was a good bullshitter, someone would have taken a liking to him along the way enough to want to come by to pay their final respects. That wasn't the case, though. Instead, Thomas sat in a quiet room with Kate and Kyle for two hours with his father's body not ten feet from him. Kyle tried to encourage Thomas to go up to the altar to pay his respects, but Thomas refused. The image he had in his head of his father saying those terrible things to him was still fresh. He couldn't bring himself to go up to face him now and fake sadness.

He thought about what Kyle and Kate must think of him, but at this point it really didn't matter. He just wanted to get through the wake and the funeral tomorrow. After that he and his mother would work on making things better for each other. He was certain that the worst part of their lives were behind them. They would finally have the chance to be as close as Kyle and Kate were.

Chapter 6

Marie arrived home on January 18th and at first Thomas was scared that things wouldn't get any better. His mother was medicated to the point where she was like a walking zombie. For the first few weeks after she got home, she slept most of the time.

Thomas called the doctor at least once a day and he would always take the time to explain the boy that this was to be expected with the new medication Marie was taking. Her body had to adjust to it.

The doctor was right; after almost a month, Marie was up and about. She started cleaning the house again, cooking dinners and driving to the store. She would even visit with Kyle and some of the other neighbors.

One day, she asked Thomas to come with her to the cemetery with her. Marie told her son that she felt terrible that she couldn't attend the funeral and she wanted to see where Dan was buried.

Thomas didn't want any part of it. In his mind, his father was gone and he didn't want to relive any of it. But his mother kept asking, pleading with him because she didn't want to go alone, so Thomas reluctantly agreed.

The ride to the cemetery was long and quiet. His mother didn't say a word and she didn't put the radio on. He could see that she was gripping the steering wheel tightly and biting her lip from time to time. He stared over at her, waiting for a response, but she was completely focused on the road. Thomas stared out the window, hoping this would be over soon.

Thomas started to feel sick as soon as he opened the car door at the cemetery. He felt lightheaded and he began to sweat as he relived the day his father died in his head. When he leaned over to dry heave, Marie rushed quickly to his side.

Much to his surprise, his mother seemed to completely understand what he was going through at that moment. She put her hand on his shoulder then gently pulled her son towards her to hug him.

"I understand, honey," she said calmly. "This must be very overwhelming after what you saw. If you're not ready, just stay in the car and I'll come back when I'm done, ok?"

Thomas felt ashamed because he wanted to be there for his mother, but he just couldn't do it. He couldn't handle staring at that headstone knowing his father was in the ground below it. He didn't look at him in the coffin for the same reason.

Marie gave him a kiss on the cheek before turning around. "I'll be back soon," she said. Thomas stood outside the car and waited until she was out of sight before he got back inside.

He sat there with his mind racing for over an hour. As the time went on, he worried more and more if his mother had suffered another breakdown after seeing the headstone. He eventually got out of the car and sat on the hood until he saw her approaching.

When she got back in the car, Thomas was surprised again to see that she wasn't an emotional wreck. The new medication seemed to be working now, but he feared that if it stopped for any reason, she would try to hurt herself. Thomas was terrified of losing the person who meant the most to him. To lose his mother would mean that he had lost himself.

When they returned home, things seemed to be fine too. Marie made dinner and they sat and watched TV together until it was time for bed.

As Thomas was lying in his bed just about to drift off to sleep, he heard his mother crying. At first it was low and intermittent, but it quickly became a louder, heaving, sobbing type of crying.

Thomas got out of his bed and ran for his mother's room. He gently knocked and there was no response, so he opened the door. His mother was pacing back and forth with a picture frame in her hands.

When she stopped for a moment near the window the street lamp outside lit up the picture enough for Thomas to see the past. It was his mother's favorite photo of their family. She loved it so much that she had it made into a 9 by 12, which she then had framed. She was so thrilled with the way it turned out that she displayed it in the center of the mantel in the living room.

This picture always stood out to Thomas because it was the only one he had seen that showed his parents happy together after he was born. After that, the pictures were mostly of Thomas and his mother. Any picture with Dan in it was either taken in the garage or at some kind of family function where he would be standing talking to someone else.

Marie had told her son about her favorite picture many times through the years. No matter how many times she told the story, it always made her smile and she couldn't get through it without laughing out loud at certain parts.

"You were just a baby in this picture, only a few months old," she told Thomas. "Your father and I were invited to a Christmas Eve party at his Uncle Raymond's house and of course your father was dead set against going.

"He was being a real Scrooge that year and he wanted nothing to do with the whole holiday experience. Anyway, I forced him to go and we all get dressed up. Of course your father complained about that because his idea of getting dressed up is tucking his t-shirt into his jeans. As you can see, I wore my favorite green dress with my red heels and a red Santa Claus hat. For your father, I picked out the one pair of dress pants he owns, and a green shirt.

"The funny thing was, right before we left I gave him a Christmas Eve present. He was all excited about it until he opened the box and saw that it contained a red tie with a Christmas tree on it along with a black and white Santa hat that had the word HUMBUG written on it.

"I dressed you in this adorable pair of red jammies that had little green reindeer all over them. I also got you a little Santa hat too, but you cried when I put it on so I had to take it off.

"Anyway, when we arrived at the party you and, of course, your father, were miserable. But after spending time with the family and seeing how everyone was enjoying themselves, he really loosened up. They all loved the hat and the tie, and we had the best time. This picture was taken right before we sat down for dinner with the family. We were in his uncle's living room in front of his Christmas tree. Raymond had a magnificent 8 foot tree that was lit with various colors."

In the picture, his father had his one arm his mother, who was holding Thomas while she smiled from ear to ear. Dan's other arm was extended in a toast like fashion as he extended the drink he was holding outward. He was also smiling in the picture like Thomas had never seen before or since.

Every time he saw that picture it made Thomas wonder if they were both happier before he was born and there was no proof that he had seen in the last fifteen years to make him doubt that thought.

When Marie noticed Thomas standing there, she looked ashamed. "Are you ok mom?" Thomas asked as he took a step towards his mother.

"I'm fine Thomas," she replied. "Today was just a little tougher on me than I thought it would be. Just give me a little time to myself to work through it and I'll be fine."

Thomas nodded and turned back to the door.

"I'm sorry you have to see my like this, Thomas," Marie said as she wiped her nose. "I'm doing the best I can to be a good mother, but it's hard right now."

Thomas looked at the picture again for a moment, and then he looked into his mother's eyes.

"How could she have loved him that much?" he thought to himself. "He was horrible to her, to the both of us."

"You are and have always been a great mother," Thomas said while trying not to cry. "I would be lost without you."

Marie tossed the picture on the bed and rushed over to embrace Thomas. She cried for a while as she hugged him tightly before looking him in the eye. "I'm sorry I scared you Thomas," she said.

"It was just his one time and there was nothing you could do," he said to reassure her.

Marie then hugged him again and whispered in his ear. "I don't want you blaming yourself for what happened to your father, Thomas. The doctor said that even though you were with him, there was nothing you could do. There wasn't anything anyone could have done to save him."

Thomas let go of her then took a step away from her while looking her in the eye. The words she said echoed in his head over and over while he watched her wipe her tears.

"I'm going back to bed now, Thomas. Don't worry, I'm ok now."

With that Marie walked back over to Thomas and kissed him on the cheek. Thomas returned to his room and lay in his bed staring at the ceiling. He listened to hear if his mother was crying again.

When the house became quiet, Thomas felt his eyes getting heavy and he started to drift off. When the words his mother had said popped into his head, "There was nothing you could do," Thomas' eyes opened again and he didn't sleep the rest of the night. He kept thinking the same thing, "what have I done?"

As the months went on Marie's medication was changed several times to correspond with her peaks and valleys. After that initial visit to the cemetery, she changed her scheduled visits to the therapist from once a week to three times a week. The increased therapy along with the proper mixture of medications finally resulted in a calmer, more logical Marie.

Thomas had gone through a change as well. Since his father's death, he spent almost no time at all with the Morgans. He didn't want to be away from his mother. He did the best he could in school, but his grades were slipping. None of that seemed to matter to him anymore; his mother was his only concern and the rest of the world didn't matter at all.

Thomas intercepted all of the progress reports from the school because he knew it would only make his mother worry more. Truthfully, it was impossible to concentrate on anything when his mind was always on what his mother was doing or if she was ok. He didn't need her blaming herself for that when none of it was her fault. It was his decision that changed things.

Both Kyle and Kate made it a point to pop in from time to time just to check on him. They didn't want intrude on whatever healing process that Thomas and Marie were going through, so they were very short visits.

Thomas missed talking to both of them a lot, but he was having a hard time dealing with everything that had happened. He didn't want to leave his mother's side, it was true, but he was also afraid to look Kate in the eye. He didn't know how he could answer her unvoiced question: "Why didn't you heal your father?"

As a true friend and sister, Kate kept his secret as she promised she would. During their visits, Thomas could see her eyes studying him every time Kyle tried to talk to him about his father or console him. How could he ever explain to her that he let his father die because he hated him and he wanted him out of their lives?

Although Thomas considered them both family, he could never explain why. He was afraid he would immediately be compared to the uncaring monster that raised him. For Thomas, that would be a sentence worse than death.

Thomas was still worried about his mother's fragile mental health and when she mentioned that they were now having money issues. Thomas couldn't sleep soundly at night.

Marie had explained to Thomas that his father had a life insurance policy worth $25,000. She said the money was just about gone because she had used it for the funereal costs and living expenses. She had mentioned getting a full-time job, but she was concerned that no one would hire her because she had no prior work history.

Thomas mentioned this to Kyle during a visit and Kyle immediately called his sister. Two days later, they both came by Marie's house to discuss a job opening for a receptionist/file clerk at the law firm where Janet worked. Janet explained to Marie that she had already spoken to her boss and the job was hers if she wanted it.

Marie was ecstatic and cried because she was so happy. Over the next eight months she earned the position of office manager and was offered tuition reimbursement to go to college at night.

This was definitely a time of peaks. Thomas began to think that maybe he was right. God did decide after all and maybe He decided that they were better off without his father.

With Marie back at work full time, Thomas began spending a lot more time over the Morgan house again and everything seemed right in the world. He should have known it couldn't last.

Chapter 7

July 16th, 1993 was another day that Thomas would remember always. He made a choice that would affect his life forever, one that killed Thomas Greggs and gave birth to The Healer. Thomas would relive this day over and over in his mind for many years, tormenting himself with thoughts of what if. He often thought if he had it to do all over again, Kyle Morgan would be dead.

Thomas was now 16 and a junior in high school. Kate was attending a state college that was less than four miles from home. She had received several softball scholarships to other schools, but she didn't want to go far from home. She didn't want her father be alone.

Although she didn't know what he was dealing with, she could tell something was wrong. Kyle had lost some weight and there were days when he arrived home from work only to go straight to bed. When she would question him about it, he would just say, "I'm getting older honey, not as spry as I used to be."

That day, Kyle had gotten out of bed with the worst headache and he felt nauseous. He knew he should just blow off work and spend the day in bed, but he had a meeting scheduled for 10:00 a.m. that he couldn't miss. So he sat on the edge of the bed for ten more minutes giving himself an internal pep talk to get going. When he finally got to his feet, he suddenly felt woozy and the room began to turn slowly.

Kyle staggered to the bathroom and held onto the sink to keep himself upright as he took long, deep breaths and closed his eyes. The sickness passed, so he opened his eyes and washed his face with cold water before having some toast for breakfast.

This all seemed to come out of nowhere. In the beginning, Kyle felt fatigued all of the time, like he could never get enough sleep. Then this cough started that would come and go for no reason on what seemed like a daily basis. None of these things sent off any alarms though. Kyle attributed it to stress at work and maybe some allergies that were developing as he got older.

It was the lump on his neck that he noticed when he was shaving that scared him. Kyle knew better than anyone what the symptoms of leukemia were and he prayed he would never have any of them. His greatest fear was that he would die young like his father did and leave Kate alone without any parents at all. He waited two weeks and when the lump didn't go down, he went to see his regular MD. When the results from the blood work came back, he was immediately referred to an oncologist named Dr. Strausberg.

Kyle's initial impression of the doctor was that he looked much younger than 40 years old. He was a tall and thin man with blonde hair that was cut in an almost military style. He was in great shape and he had a tan that made him appear as if he had just come back from a trip from some island.

What impressed Kyle the most about his doctor was that he spoke to him as a person. Dr. Strausberg took his time explaining everything and answering every question. Kyle never felt rushed even though he was certain that he was running over into someone else's appointment time.

During his initial visit, Dr. Strausberg actually appeared to be getting emotional himself when he was explained to Kyle that he had leukemia and that it was in an advanced state, stage four. When he said that the prognosis wasn't good, he reached over and placed his hand on Kyle's shoulder to comfort him.

That was pretty much all that Kyle could recall from that visit. Everything became "cloudy" after that and he entered what could only be categorized as a numbing haze. It was as if his mind had shut down to save him from dealing with the pain from what he had heard.

Either way, the truth was clear: he was dying and nothing could save him. After further tests, Dr. Strausberg told Kyle that he had less than six months to live depending on how aggressively the disease continued to spread. As was the case with his father, it had already spread into the lymph nodes.

When Kyle returned home that day, he immediately called his sister and told her the news. As Janet broke down on the phone, Kyle made her promise repeatedly that she would always be there for Kate and that she would take care of her like she was her own. Janet replied, "of course I will." He struggled with the "how and the when" to tell Kate. He kept putting it off and eventually a month had passed in a blink.

Kyle sat alone in the kitchen eating his toast and drinking his orange juice alone while listening to an all-sports radio station. He picked up his plate and his glass then carried them over to the sink and washed them before heading back to his bedroom.

He was just about the open his closet door when the same feeling overtook him. He tried to make it back to the bed so he could sit but the room began spinning faster and faster. He reached for the dresser to balance himself, but Kyle missed and instead landed with a solid thud on the floor. His breathing became shallow and he started to lose consciousness. His thoughts drifted to Kate and how he would probably never live to see her get married.

Kyle tried to lift his head up, but it felt like it weighed 200 pounds. "Please God, not now," he whispered. Two minutes later he was unconscious.

Next door, the day was like every other day for Thomas during summer vacation. He woke up late again because he always seemed to have a hard time falling asleep at night. It started right after his father died and his mother came home from the hospital.

At first, Thomas stayed awake so he could check on his mother from time to time because her depression worried him. But when things got better for her, Thomas found that for some reason his sleeping habits didn't. Even when she was sleeping peacefully and Thomas would close his eyes, sleep would not come.

Instead the demons would.

That's how Thomas would describe what would occur when he would close his eyes and a million bad and depressing thoughts would come rushing in one after the other, nonstop.

It always started with thoughts of his father.

He would relive every moment and every detail of the day he died. Then he would think about his mother and the guilt he felt for hurting her by not saving his father. He would give anything in the world for her just to be happy, including putting up with his father again.

Then thoughts of school would enter his head, "Why I am so different?" he thought. "Why are there no girls interested in me, what's so wrong with me?" It always ended with staring at the ceiling while feeling angry and sad. To break the cycle, Thomas would sit up in his bed and turn on the TV or read. He would eventually fall asleep with the TV on or a book on his chest.

He looked at the clock, which told him it was 9:50 a.m. It was Monday, so his mom was already at work. That meant he had to take care of a few chores around house and make dinner for her later.

About the same time next door, Kate was waking up late herself. Only it wasn't for the same reason as Thomas. Kate was out with three of her friends and didn't get home till after 1:00 a.m. Her dad was asleep then, but she was sure there would be a lecture when he got home from work.

Kate got out of bed and was headed to the bathroom when she happened to glance over to the window and noticed that her father's car was still in the driveway. She walked into the kitchen to see if he was there, but he wasn't. She looked up at the clock on the wall and it was 9:37 a.m. Her first thought was that he had stayed home to "straighten her out," as he put it. He hadn't done this in a while, but she had been staying out late a lot with her friends recently and she knew he didn't approve of it.

Kate listened for a second to see if she could hear him anywhere in the house, but there was nothing but silence. Then she thought that maybe he had car trouble and Aunt Janet drove him to work. He did complain from time to time about how he wanted a new car because the one he had needed a lot of work and had a lot of miles on it. Still, there was something that made Kate feel uneasy.

She went to the fridge and poured herself a glass of orange juice. She stood for a minute drinking it and listened again. She then walked back to the window and looked at the car again. After a minute of staring and thinking, she decided to go to her father's room. His door was closed, but that wasn't unusual either; he always closed the door to his room when he left for the day.

When Kate opened the door and said, "Hey Dad," the first thing she saw was the bottom of her father's legs on the floor sticking out from behind the bed. She ran to him and immediately noticed that his face had a blue tint to it and he was barely breathing.

"Oh my god, Dad, wake up!" Kate screamed. "Please wake up!" She looked up at the heavens and begged, "Please God, don't take him from me, help me, please someone help me."

At that moment she heard a loud bang outside that made her look in that direction instinctively. Through her tear-filled eyes, she saw Thomas dragging the aluminum garbage cans from the side of the house towards the curb.

"Thomas, oh my God, Thomas," Kate shouted as she ran for the door.

Thomas had just turned back towards the house when he saw the Morgans' door fly open and Kate come running towards him. She was still in her pajamas and she was screaming something at him but he couldn't make sense of it at first.

"Oh please, Thomas, you have to help my father! He's dying!"

"He's what?" Thomas asked as Kate grabbed his arm and pulled him towards her house.

"Come on," she yelled and they both started running.

Kate ran so fast that Thomas fell behind her and couldn't keep up. He ran up the steps then through the open door and stopped while breathing heavy.

"Where are you?" Thomas shouted.

"Back here in my father's room," Kate answered. "Please get in here!"

At that moment, Thomas felt such a terrible feeling of déjà vu come over him. It was the nightmare scenario that he had lived over and over in his head since his father died. He entered the room to see Kate standing over Kyle's lifeless body and said to himself, "oh no, please, not again."

"Thomas please help him!" Kate begged.

Thomas had never saved a person before. He had only healed bruises, cuts and broken bones. He was scared he couldn't do it and of how much it would hurt Kate if he failed.

Kate interrupted Thomas's daze by shouting again.

He looked at her for moment. She met his gaze and said softly, "Please." as the tears streamed down her face.

Thomas knelt beside Kyle then gently put his hands on Kyle's chest before letting out a sigh. "Kyle is a good man." Thomas thought to himself, "Good men don't deserve this." Thomas looked up at the heavens for just a second before repeating the word Kate had said, "Please." He then concentrated and closed his eyes.

The pain in his chest was immediate and more severe that it had ever been before. He held his breath until he couldn't stand it anymore before letting go of Kyle and turning away. After taking a few deep breaths, he turned around to see Kyle staring back at him looking absolutely confused. Thomas smiled at him before a tear ran down his face.

"What's going here?" Kyle asked. "What happened?"

Kate reached over and hugged him tightly as she cried out loud for several minutes. Afterwards they both helped Kyle back up onto his feet and into the kitchen. Although the memories of what happened were still so fresh in his mind, Kyle couldn't get over how great he felt all of the sudden. He was no longer feeling fatigued or sore. In fact he felt as if he could get up and run around the block if he wanted to.

Kate went to the refrigerator, got him a bottled water and placed it in front of him before asking him "Are you sure you are okay?" three times in a row. When he replied that he was fine, she ran over to Thomas, who was standing in the corner, and hugged him tightly while crying.

She kissed his cheek and whispered, "Thank God for you, Thomas, thank you so much."

There were many truths shared that day in the Morgans' kitchen. Kyle had told them both about his diagnosis and the prognosis. He tried to explain to Kate why he couldn't tell her even though he knew it would be hard for her to understand. He told her that Janet would in her life after he was gone in whatever capacity she needed her to be and that she would never be alone.

He said that he was happy to know that she would always have someone like Thomas in her life and that he would always be family. Thomas listened and smiled because deep down he knew he had healed Kyle. It was just a feeling he had that he would get after healing himself or his mother. He even felt it after healing Kate. It was something that he couldn't describe; he just knew that it worked.

He got so caught up in the moment and the closeness between them all that Thomas decided to reveal something of his own. He told Kyle about the ability his was born with and how he used it to heal his mother. He told him about Kate's arm and everything that had happened that day.

Kyle sat with his mouth opened while he listened, looking over at Kate from time to time as she nodded in agreement. "Could this be possible?" Kyle thought to himself. But then there never was any logical reason to explain Kate's broken arm not being broken anymore, was there?

"That's what happened to you," Thomas said. "Kate came to get me when she found you passed out and barely breathing on the floor. I think you might be ok now."

Kyle shook his head back and forth in stunned disbelief. "Wait, this isn't real is it?" he asked.

Thomas smiled again then said, "Go get checked out tomorrow and let me know what they say." Thomas stayed the rest of the day until his mother got home from work.

Kyle found it hard to believe, but still he continued to feel great the entire day. As he went to bed that night he prayed for the first time in a long time. "Please let this be real." he said. "I can't feel this good only to have it come crashing down on me tomorrow." It took a while, but Kyle eventually fell asleep. When he woke up the next morning, the first thing he did was make a call to the office to let them know he wasn't coming in. The next call he made was to Dr. Strousberg's office to schedule an urgent appointment.

Chapter 8

Kyle and Kate sat in the waiting room of Dr. Strausberg's office for 15 minutes before Kyle was escorted into an examining room. Kyle bit his fingernails the whole time while Kate tried to talk to him about various things to distract him from thinking so much.

The assistant called his name and escorted him to an examining room where Kyle sat alone for another 10 minutes and continued to bite his nails. He went over in his head again and again what he was going to say to the doctor. He reworded it each time, but every time it sounded like a crazy story made up by a desperate man.

When Dr. Strausberg entered with Kyle's file in hand, he was immediately surprised by what he saw. When he had met with Kyle last week, his patient looked very fatigued and pale. He warned Kyle to take it easy and advised him to stop working.

Today, Kyle seemed alert and the color was back in his face. In fact when he saw the doctor walk in he smiled and said, "What's up doc?"

Dr. Strausberg returned his smile and replied, "You tell me, Kyle. Why are you here?"

As Kyle explained to him what had occurred yesterday, the doctor just nodded from time to time as he reviewed his file. When Kyle finished Dr. Strausberg let out a deep sigh before placing his file on the countertop.

"Kyle, I know this must be really hard on you and believe me, my heart breaks for you. But to come in here and tell me that you believe some teenage boy 'healed' you of advanced leukemia? C'mon, Kyle, you know better than that."

Kyle laughed and stood up to face the doctor.

"I know this sounds crazy, believe me I do, but I think it's real. Thomas healed my daughter's broken arm when she was 9; I just found this out yesterday. I don't know how he can do it, but I feel better than I've felt in a long time. Please just run the tests again even if you think it's a waste of time. Please just do it for me."

Dr. Strausberg gave Kyle a look of pity as he placed his hand on his shoulder. "Why would you want to put yourself through this, Kyle?" he asked.

Kyle looked him in the eye and said, "Because I believe he really can do it. I feel it in my heart, I think he healed me."

Even though he believed that it was a complete waste of time that would lead to yet another heartbreaking discussion, Dr. Strausberg agreed to run the tests. He told Kyle to go to the hospital and that he would call ahead to set things up.

After Kyle thanked him profusely and left, the doctor reviewed the file again while shaking his head from side to side. He asked one of his assistants to set up the tests. As she wrote them down, she paused for a moment then asked, "Didn't we just do these tests on him not too long ago?"

"Yeah we did," Dr. Strausberg replied. "The poor guy thinks he was miraculously healed by some kid who lives next door to him. He is just looking for any kind of hope at this point, no matter how unrealistic it is. I just couldn't say no to him."

Alice looked at the doctor like he had two heads. "He thinks a kid healed him?" she asked.

"Just make the calls and make sure the tests get done, ok?" the doctor said. "Also tell them it's a rush and to let me know as soon as the results are in."

The next day, the hospital called with the test results. Alice put it on hold and notified the doctor.

"I'll take it in my office," Dr. Strausberg replied.

Alice sat watching the light blink with nagging curiosity inside her. Although it sounded like such a crazy notion, she was a devout Catholic and deep down she did believe in miracles. She was certain that if she waited it would be just a matter of moments before the doctor would come out to tell her to call Kyle and have him come in to break the news to him that nothing had changed. But she had to know, so she listened in. What she heard next almost made her drop the phone.

All of Kyle's tests came back negative; there was not a trace of leukemia in his system.

She continued to listen as the doctor argued with the person on the phone repeating time and time again, "This was not possible." He became so agitated and frustrated by this person insisting that the test results were accurate that he slammed down the phone.

He shouted "stupid idiot" so loud that the two people who were in the waiting room looked up from their magazines and laughed.

Alice quickly hung up the phone and grabbed some paperwork to appear occupied before he made his way to the front desk.

The door swung open and Dr. Strausberg said, "Call Kyle Morgan back and have him go to West Orange General Hospital tomorrow. Tell him we're going to run the same tests."

"Is there a problem, doctor?" she asked while trying to act confused.

"Just take care of that for me please, Alice," he said sternly.

She did as she was told. Even though she had heard it with her own ears, she was 98% sure that the next set of tests would yield a different result.

After work Alice met up with a four friends at a local bar. She was about three drinks in when she blurted out, "I may have witnessed an actual miracle at work today."

It didn't take much prying for her to tell the whole story. She didn't mention his last name, but she said the name Kyle several times along with the name of the hospital he went to for the tests. She even said that they wouldn't know for sure until West Orange General re-tested him.

The story was repeated four more times at various water coolers the next day and eventually a call was made to the Channel 5 news department. It wasn't long after that an unidentified source at the hospital confirmed the results. An hour after that another source at West Orange General was on standby, if the new results were the same it would be the lead story on Channel 5.

The following day, Dr. Strauberg got the call from West Orange General. The test results were the same. The doctor was dumbfounded and beside himself. He had them check it three times and the results were the same every time.

"How was this possible?" he thought to himself. Dr. Strausberg called several of his colleagues and none of them could offer an explanation for what had occurred. The only advice they could offer was "test him again."

When he asked Alice to call Kyle and have him come in, she could tell by the look on his face something wasn't right.

"So, was it a made up story?" she asked.

He paused for a moment as if he was searching for the right words before responding.

"Nothing has been determined yet. Just call him and tell him I need to see him as soon as possible."

As soon as Kyle entered the office he could tell something was off. The doctor's assistant gave him the strangest look before saying hello and asking how he was doing. He waited only five minutes before he was told to go straight down the hall into the doctor's office. The door was open and Dr. Strausberg was sitting inside with Kyle's file in front of him.

"Have a seat, Kyle," he said.

Kyle sat leaning forward with his elbows on the desk with a knot in his stomach waiting to hear the results.

"How are you feeling Kyle?"

"I feel great, Doc," Kyle replied. "Please don't make me wait. I've waited long enough and I haven't slept in two days, please just tell me either way."

Dr. Strausberg knew there was no explanation that he could offer that would make any sense at all so he placed the file down, walked to the other side of the desk and sat on the desk in front of Kyle.

"As you know we tested you several times using different facilities with different labs," Dr. Strausberg said.

Kyle took a deep breath in and let it out slowly to prepare himself for whatever he would hear next.

"The results were checked again and again by several experts and the results were the same. There is no sign at all of the disease present."

Kyle leapt to his feet and screamed out loud, "Oh my God, oh my God!"

He jumped up and down around the room before falling to his knees.

"Is this real? Please tell me this is real."

"I can't explain it," Dr. Strausberg said as he placed his hand on Kyle's shoulder. "I would like to do more tests, but you seem to be cured, or um 'healed' as you called it. I'm a man of science Kyle and this isn't possible in my world; there has got to be a reason for it."

Kyle got to his feet and hugged the doctor. A thought occurred to him and he started to laugh. The last time he had seen a doctor this confused was when Kate broke her arm. That's when it really hit him -Thomas really *could* heal people.

Chapter 9

The results of Kyle Morgan's second set of tests spread through the Channel 5 newsroom like wild fire. When they reached the desk of a young ambitious field reporter named Robert Van Putten, he knew he had to do something. He had sneaked into the producer's office and read the whole file. This teenager named Thomas Greggs had healed his neighbor and family friend of leukemia. As if that wasn't a big enough story, was he home alone with his father when he died of a heart attack? This kid and this story was his ticket to the big time and he knew it.

Robert immediately ran to find the producer to beg for the assignment so he could be the first on scene when the story broke. Although there were several other seasoned reporters in house, Martin Shulman liked what he saw in Robert. There was a hunger in his eyes that Martin himself had when he was Robert's age, only when Martin was 25 there wasn't a producer who could see his inner drive or someone who knew how to use it to the station's advantage. Now at the ripe old age of 33, Martin was content with his life. He had worked his way up through the ranks at the station, he made a decent salary and the money he inherited from his parents allowed him to live very comfortably. With no wife or kids, he didn't answer to anyone. He could come and go as he pleased and that's the way he preferred it.

He had long since given up on taking chances and bucking the system, but that all started to change after Robert started working for the station.

Robert was initially hired to do all of the human interest or wacky stories, but when Martin met him he saw that his new reporter didn't fit the part at all. Robert looked like he just got out of the military. His wore his short brown hair in a buzz cut and ended every response with 'sir'. Robert looked very intense all the time as his green eyes studied you when you spoke. He was the same height as Martin, 5-foot-11, but Robert was in much better shape, appearing as if he worked out almost every day.

They hit off from their very first meeting and Martin found out quickly that Robert had something that he had never had. Robert had blind ambition. A day didn't go by that he wasn't pitching a story or picking the seasoned reporters brains for information. It wasn't long before Martin started to mentor Robert and hang out with him after work.

Although Martin tried to pace Robert and bring him along slowly, it wasn't long before Robert was out in the field working on lead stories. But that wasn't enough for Robert and Martin knew it. Robert wanted to be the center of attention, he wanted all eyes on him and nothing was going to stop him from reaching that goal.

So as Robert begged and pleaded in his office to go to West Orange, Martin thought long and hard before giving in. "Ok, grab a cameraman and go," Martin said. "But be careful with this one, ok? You'll get the exposure you're looking for either way, but stay away from the Greggs' house because the boy is a minor and his name hasn't been made public yet, you hear me?"

Robert smiled from ear to ear and then crossed his heart with his finger.

Martin smiled as he watched Robert run out of the room without saying thank you or even good-bye.

Thomas was with the Morgans, having a celebratory dinner after an afternoon filled with many thanks, hugs and tears. As they ate, Kyle had a nagging thought in his head, "Would Dr. Strausberg tell anyone about Thomas?" Kate said that Thomas made her promise not to tell anyone before healing her.

She also wondered why Thomas couldn't save his father, but she knew it was obviously something Thomas was not ready to talk about. As they sat in the kitchen eating their meal, they all seemed to pause at the same time when they heard the name Thomas Greggs coming from the television in the other room.

Thomas looked like a deer in the headlights as he stared over at Kyle and dropped his fork. He ran into the next room, with Kate and Kyle right behind him. They all watched in shock as the reporter mentioned "The young man who was now being referred to as 'The Healer.'"

"Again, we have confirmed reports from two anonymous sources at both Livingston Grace Hospital and West Orange General Hospital. Kyle Morgan has been cured of stage four, critical leukemia. He now has and I quote, 'no signs at all of the disease in his body.' The official word from both hospitals has been 'no comment at this time.'"

Kate kept her hand cupped over her mouth the whole time, not believing what she had heard. Thomas just stood there with his head down and his eyes closed as he pushed both of his fists down into the couch. Kyle frantically searched for the words to say, but he was interrupted before he could find them.

There were three loud bangs on the front door. Everyone froze and looked at each other. The knocking continued until Kyle approached the door and shouted, "Who's there?"

Robert knew better than to announce who he was so he mumbled something loudly and started to bang again.

Thomas and Kate were now standing behind Kyle as he slowly opened the door to peek outside. Once Robert heard the sound of the handle, he motioned to the cameraman before forcing the door all the way open.

"Mr. Kyle Morgan," he said loudly, you are in fact the man who was miraculously healed by the boy who lives right next door to you, isn't that true?"

Kyle stood frozen with his mouth open, unable to speak as the light from the camera shined in his face.

"Isn't true that you were suffering from stage four leukemia? With only months to live, you told your doctor that someone had healed you. You must be thrilled to be alive. Sir, can you please comment?"

From behind her father Kate shouted, "Get the hell out of here!"

Kyle pushed the reporter back and asked him to leave. "I have nothing to say, you have it all wrong."

The reporter stood his ground, shifting his weight towards Kyle as he continued on. "You should be grateful sir; it seems you have been blessed by a true miracle, what do you have to say about that?"

Thomas had reached his limit. He lunged forward with all of his might and pushed the reporter as hard as he could while shouting, "Get the fuck out of here!"

Robert fell backward into the cameraman before landing on the ground. The cameraman caught the whole thing. He knew he had gold, so he shouted to Robert, "I think that's the kid!"

Without missing a beat Robert was back in action. "Is that not in fact the boy who healed you Mr. Morgan? Is your name Thomas Greggs?"

Thomas stared into the camera as he heard his name shouted out to the world, wishing he was anyone else or anywhere else in the world at the moment. The anger welled up inside him again, but before he could get to the reporter, Kyle shoved the cameraman back then slammed and locked the door.

Kyle turned to hold Thomas back as he screamed, "Goddamn you, you said my name, God damn you!"

Robert didn't stop though. Kyle could still hear him reporting through the door on his porch as he forcefully pushed Thomas back into the living room.

"Kate, call the police! Tell them to get this piece of garbage off of my porch!"

The damage had already been done. By the time the police arrived, half of the neighborhood had seen the report and they were gathering in front of the house or on the street. As time went on more news crews arrived along with more police. Within two hours, the street was cordoned off for local traffic only and it was filled with people.

Marie had no idea about the chaos that surrounded her home as she made her way home from work. She was tired from working ten straight hours, the last two of which were spent alone in her cubical with only the maintenance people in the building with her.

By the time she got to her car, her head was throbbing and she just wanted to get home to soak in a hot bath. When she turned the ignition, the radio came on and it seemed so loud that it made her head pound, so she quickly turned it off. She drove home in silence except for the sounds of her occasional yawns.

She was on Main Street and only a block from turning left onto her street when she noticed that everything had suddenly stopped. She rolled down her window and tried to see what was causing the traffic jam but all she could see were people and cars. She assumed something really bad had happened like a big car accident. Those were the only occasions when people would all stop to gather and stare, she thought.

As she got a little closer, she noticed that a policeman was standing in the road diverting everyone from her street. When she drove up to him she said, "I live on that street, officer. Is there something wrong?"

"Sorry ma'am, but I just got here," the officer said. "They told me the street was already filled to capacity with onlookers and the media. I was told to divert all traffic and tell those who live here like yourself that you would have to find a parking spot on another street for the time being."

"Park somewhere else?" she repeated. Her head was throbbing and the last thing she wanted to do was walk several blocks back to her house. "So you have no idea at all what caused this?" she asked. "Was there an accident or fire, was someone hurt?"

"I'm really not sure, ma'am," the officer responded. "I heard something crazy, but I think someone was pulling my leg." Before he could expand upon that several cars honked together in unison. "Please move on so we can get things moving again," he said to Marie as he waved her on.

She wound up parking four blocks away. She grabbed her purse, locked the car door and walked as fast as she could so she could see what was going on. When she reached the corner, she could see most of the attention was focused in the area around her house. This scared her so she began to push her way through to get a closer look. When she got close enough, Marie could see that all of the attention seemed to be focused on her house and the Kyle's house next door. Policemen were standing guard in front of both houses and reporters were lined up filming in front of the crowds.

Marie's heart dropped as her mind raced through all of the things that could have happened. She frantically pushed her way to the front of the crowd and through the reporters. The closest policemen stopped her, "Excuse me Missus, but you can't go in there."

"The hell I can't," Marie said. "That's my house and I need to know what is going on. Where's my son?"

Inside Kyle's house, Thomas was pacing like a caged animal as he periodically looked outside at the growing crowd.

Kyle had tried to speak to him several times but Thomas couldn't even turn around to acknowledge him. Kate told her father to give him his space and that's what he did.

Time dragged on as Thomas watched for his mother's car. He went through a hundred different things he would say to his mother to explain this situation, but not one of them offered any kind of reason for why he couldn't save his father.

Kyle and Kate were in front of the television watching the madness that was taking place outside their door when they noticed a woman talking to one of the policemen in front of Thomas's house. Within seconds she was surrounded by all of the reporters shoving microphones at her. Kyle didn't know what to do when he saw the lone policeman trying to keep them all back as he radioed for assistance.

"Oh my God, that's Marie," Kyle said without realizing he had spoken aloud.

Thomas bolted through the doors and down the stairs. Someone from the crowd shouted, "Look, there he is!" but the reporters couldn't respond fast enough.

Thomas rushed into the crowd and pushed, punched and pulled his way to his mother's side. When he reached her he could immediately see that she was frazzled and very confused. Marie reached out to hug her son but he took her hand and pulled her though the crowd.

Both Thomas and Marie were struck in the face by cameras or microphones several times. Overzealous reporters grabbed and pulled at them while trying to get them to stop long enough to comment on camera, and both Thomas and Marie had torn clothes by the time they got away. Thomas just put his head down and kept repeating to his mother, "Don't Stop!" until they were safely back inside Kyle's house.

They stood in the hallway hugging and crying together. They were both just relieved, more than anything, that the other was okay. Thomas knew there was no way around it, so he took his mother's hand to lead her into the living room where he would attempt to explain everything.

She sat on the couch and Thomas was just about to begin when the news began to rebroadcast the clip from earlier when the story first broke.

Marie sat quietly staring at the television as the reporter talked about Kyle being healed and how the test results had twice come back negative. She never looked at Thomas though they referred to him as 'The Healer' several times. She just stared at the television until the clip was through and they returned to the live feed in front of the house.

Thomas, who was standing the whole time, walked over to his mother and placed his hand on her shoulder. He was surprised when she jerked away from him and stared into his eyes.

"I'm sorry Mom," Thomas said softly. "I never knew how to tell you. I didn't want anyone to know. I feel like a freak."

When the tears started to stream down his cheeks, Marie stood up and hugged her son tightly. "It's ok, Thomas," she said.

She released him and looked him in the eyes. "You saved Kyle's life, that's amazing," she said before hugging him again. When she let go this time she had a more serious look on her face as if she were trying to work something out in her head.

"You can really do this?" she asked.

Thomas didn't say anything; he just looked at her and nodded.

Marie looked at the floor and remained silent for a moment still appearing as if she were lost in thought.

"Who else did you help, Thomas?" she asked. "How long have you been able to do this?"

Before Thomas could manage a reply she asked another question, but this time he could hear the strain in her voice. "Why didn't you ever tell me about this?"

Thomas had seen that look many times and he had heard that strain in her voice many times as well. In every instance it was the first few rocks in the avalanche that was about to come down.

"Mom, let me go over and get your pills first, then I'll tell you everything, ok?"

Thomas headed for the back door when his mother yelled, "Answer me, Thomas!"

Thomas stopped cold where he was standing and took a deep breath before turning around. "I've been able to do this for a while now," he said calmly. "I've healed myself many times for as long as I can remember just cuts and bruises, stuff like that.

"I healed Kate's arm because I saw how upset she was. I knew how important softball was to her and I knew that the time she spent with her father playing catch must have been great.

"And um, I have healed you a lot of times after Dad umm...," Thomas said softly.

Marie put her hand over her mouth because it was all so clear to her now. There were so many nights and so many fights where she could swear there were bruises or blood on her body only to wake up the next morning to find that she was fine.

"Was this possible?" she thought to herself.

As she pondered the extent of what Thomas could do, a thought came into her head.

"What about you father?" she asked, "Why couldn't you heal him?"

Thomas looked away and searched his mind for an answer but there wasn't one.

All he could think of to say was, "I um... I couldn't mom".

He was surprised when his mother didn't accept that answer and pressured him for another.

"You said you had this ability as long as you can remember," she said sternly. "You healed yourself, you healed me, you healed Kate and you even saved Kyle from what might have been certain death.

"Your father died right in front of you, with you in the house, why couldn't heal him?" Marie demanded.

Thomas fumbled for words trying to explain, "I don't know what happened Mom, I uh, I don't know," he said.

"Did you try Thomas? Did you even try to save him?" Marie asked with her voice cracking.

Thomas started to turn away, but Marie grabbed his face with both hands.

"Look me in the eye, Thomas, and tell me you tried to save him."

Thomas closed his eyes and tried not to cry. He took another deep breath before responding to his mother with anger in his voice. "I went in the garage that day and I was going to heal him. But he yelled at me and said horrible things to me. That's the kind of man he was *all the time*, Mom!

"He hated me and he beat you! I let God decide that day and we're better off without him!"

Marie let go of Thomas and stepped away from him. He would never forget the look on her face for as long as he lived.

She reached into her pocket and pulled out her car keys. Thomas ran towards her and pleaded, "Mom, where are you going? You can't go out there!"

She didn't stop, though. As she walked past Kyle, he also tried to stop her.

"Marie wait, just hold on for a second!"

Thomas followed his mother to the door and grabbed her arm.

"They won't leave you alone; we need to stay here for a while."

Marie stared into Thomas's eyes with a look of rage.

"I need to be away from you," she said coldly.

Thomas couldn't think of anything to say to make this any better. He wished he could take back what he said. He wished even more that he didn't say it at all, but he did.

As she reached for the door Thomas began to cry again, "Mom, please, I'm sorry," he said.

"What have you done Thomas? How could you have done this to me?" Marie opened the door and disappeared into the crowd.

Chapter 10

Thomas sat alone in the Morgans' living room for hours waiting for his mother to return. After she had left, Kyle tried to speak to him but Thomas blew up, telling him it was his entire fault.

Thomas asked if he could be left alone until his mother came back and Kyle left. Kate heard the conversation from the other room and when her father walked past her with his head down, she put her hand on his shoulder.

"He doesn't mean it Dad," she said. "He's just really hurt and really confused. Just give him his space for a while."

Thomas sat on floor in the hallway, staring at the wall. He stayed there like that for two hours until he fell asleep. When he woke up the next morning on the couch he didn't even recall Kate waking him so Kyle could help him to the couch. He immediately thought of his mother and hoped she had come back.

Thomas got to his feet and quickly walked around the house. Kyle and Kate were asleep in their rooms, but his mother was nowhere to be found. He ran to the window and checked the driveway near his house, but his mother's car wasn't there. Most of the crowd has dispersed, but there were still several TV news crews outside and he also noticed a small group of people standing together holding candles talking amongst themselves.

"I thought I heard someone walking around out here," Kyle said from behind him.

Thomas lowered his head because he was ashamed by what he had said to Kyle last night, but he was also still angry so he didn't respond.

"If you're hungry, I can fix you something," Kyle said. "When was the last time you ate something?"

"She's still not back," Thomas said softly, without turning around.

"I know she's not," Kyle said sympathetically. "I called the police late last night and they're looking for her. They'll find her Thomas, she'll be all right, you'll see."

When Thomas didn't respond, Kyle walked closer to him.

"I am so sorry this turned out this way, Thomas," he said. "I only told the doctor because I thought I could trust him. He must have said something to somebody and this all happened. I would never hurt you or your mother in a million years, Thomas. You gave me back my life and my family; I could never thank you enough or repay you for that."

When Thomas turned around Kyle hugged him and they cried together.

The next three days were agonizing. Bigger crowds of people were gathering every day. But now the crowd was mixed between your average nosy bodies who were hoping to catch a glimpse of something news worthy and what the media referred to as 'The Faithful'.

The faithful consisted of the holy rollers and those who traveled from within the state with the hopes of being healed by Thomas.

During that time, Thomas hardly talked, slept or ate. The media had gotten wind of Marie's disappearance and now the biggest story in years had just gotten bigger. It was in every newspaper and featured on every network's nightly news broadcast.

Kyle would try to stay positive and continually reassure Thomas but he knew something was wrong. He had a really bad feeling as the days passed.

On the morning of the third day Marie was missing, Kyle was sitting in the living room drinking coffee alone. It was 6:30 a.m., Kate was asleep and Thomas was in the shower. Kyle was beyond fed up with the news so he was watching a rerun of Gilligan's Island.

Suddenly the news broke in and the world turned upside down.

"This is Ron Guildright and we interrupt your program for breaking news," the television said.

"The car that is believed to have belonged to Marie Greggs, the mother of Thomas Greggs, also known as 'The Healer', has been found in a lake off of Washington Road. Marie has not been seen since Tuesday when she was reported missing."

We now take you live to the scene where field reporter Robert Van Putten is on site."

"Thank you Ron," Robert said.

"According to my local law enforcement source, a contractor named Jack Nanson stopped to change a flat tire along this stretch of Washington Road this morning and made a gruesome discovery.

"Nanson noticed tire marks and several broken trees going down this embankment. He followed those tire tracks to the lake, where he saw the back of a 1982 black Pontiac Sunbird submerged underwater.

"Nanson rushed back to his truck and drove down the road to a store, where he called police.

"The car has since been pulled from the lake and we are awaiting further details."

"We have not been able to confirm an initial report that one person was inside the car when it was excavated, but this appears to be a tragic end to this story we've all been following. We will interrupt your local programming as more details come in."

Kyle dropped his coffee on the floor and yelled in pain when it splashed onto his foot. He ran over to shut off the television before anyone came into the room.

Kyle's mind raced. "Oh my God, this can't be happening," he said out loud. Kyle didn't realize it, but his daughter had come into the room. He almost jumped out of his skin when he heard Kate say, "You can't believe what's happening, Dad?" At that moment, Kyle couldn't think of a gentle way to share the news. "They found Mrs. Greggs' car in a lake," he said quietly.

"Oh my God!" Kate yelled. "Was she inside?"

"I don't know. Thomas doesn't know yet so keep it down."

As if on cue, Thomas walked into the room, still drying his hair with a towel.

"Thomas doesn't know what?" he asked.

There wasn't even time for an answer before the knock on the front door. Kyle looked at Thomas and was about to speak when there was a second, louder knocking. A deep voice said, "Mr. Morgan, this is the police, please open the door, we need to speak with you, it's urgent."

As Kyle passed them, Thomas looked at Kate and noticed she couldn't look him in the eye for some reason. He could tell she wanted to cry but she was holding it in. He stared at her wanting to ask what was wrong, but he wasn't sure he wanted to know.

Instead he went to join Kyle at the door. Kyle was talking to two policemen and nodding his head a lot. When he closed the door, Thomas could tell that he was very upset.

"Is it my mother?"

Kyle let out a deep breath and turned towards Thomas. With tears in his eyes he said softly, "I'm sorry Thomas, they found her car in a lake. Your mother...she was inside, she's gone Thomas."

Thomas felt as if someone had dropped a building on him and his legs gave out as he hit the floor. It seemed as if every excruciating pain-related emotion he had was turned up all at the same time and it was consuming him. He screamed out, "No!" as he punched the floor with his fists until they bled. "I did this!" he screamed over and over.

Kyle rushed over to him first, then Kate came running in from the other room.

Thomas cried and screamed until he couldn't anymore. Then he just went silent, staring straight ahead like a zombie as he rocked himself back and forth.

After a few hours of talking to Thomas and trying to console him, Kyle had to call his sister Janet. He explained to her what had happened even though there was no need; she had seen it all unfolding on the news. He asked if she could come over for a while because the police needed someone to identify the body and there was no way he was going to subject Thomas to that. Janet arrived 15 minutes later and was shocked by the chaos that she saw taking place on her brother's street. She, too, had to fight her way through the crowd and show identification to get into the house.

Kyle went to the morgue and saw that it was indeed Marie who was lying on the table. He immediately became overcome with guilt and sadness. He felt ashamed that the first thought that entered his head was how close he had come to being the one who was lying there and how the fate that would have been his daughter's belongs now to the boy who saved his life.

Kyle kissed Marie on the cheek then whispered, "Rest in peace Marie, I'll look after Thomas, I promise."

The whole drive home, the guilt was eating Kyle up inside. If he had never mentioned to the doctor what Thomas had done, Marie would still be alive.

"What had he done?"

No one was available to make the funeral arrangements, so Kyle took it upon himself. He learned that Marie had a will and in it she stated that if she were to pass, then Kyle Morgan would be Thomas's legal guardian until he reached the age of 18. An attorney from his sister's law firm told him that Marie had the will made up about six months after she started working there.

Chapter 11

The media circus of Marie Greggs' wake and funeral rivaled that of a very well-known politician or celebrity. The police set up a barricade around the entire building and Thomas, Kyle and Kate had to sneak in through the back door after riding in an unmarked police car with tinted windows.

Kyle escorted Thomas to the first row of chairs with Kate following behind them. Just as they were all about to sit down, Thomas asked if he could have the front row to himself. Kyle wasn't sure what to say or do, so he looked to Kate. Although she seemed very concerned, she nodded her head in agreement and motioned to her father to follow her to the next row.

Thomas sat staring at the coffin as person after person came to give their condolences. He couldn't help but compare it in his head to his father's wake where no one came to pay their respects.

When the last of them passed him by, Thomas got up from his chair and approached his mother. This was the first time he had seen her since that fateful night. The first thing he noticed was how peaceful she looked. The last image he had in his head of her was of her filled with rage and confusion. This was the way he wanted to remember her. She appeared as if her troubles were all gone and she was finally resting.

He reached out and touched her hand, than held it for a moment. He placed his other hand on her arm and closed his eyes. He held his breath waiting for the pain his chest to start, but he felt nothing. She really was gone forever.

Thomas opened his eyes again and looked at his mother's face one last time with tears rolling down his cheeks. He knew this was the last time he would see her.

He then lifted her hand and held it up against his face. "I love you mom, I'm so sorry for what I've done," he said softly. "I will miss you more than you will ever know, please forgive me someday."

Thomas gently lowered her hand then turned around. He noticed there were some more people waiting to approach him to offer their condolences, but he walked away from them and went back to his seat where he sat staring at one of the floral arrangements.

When he looked back at the coffin, he remembered a conversation he had with his mother about death. It was just after his Nana Theresa died. Nana had passed and she was in a 'better place' his mother told him. Like all other kids his age wanted to know all about that better place.

So she explained, "Heaven was a wonderful place where you meet up again with the people you cared about. In heaven, no one is sick or in pain. No one is sad and everything is beautiful."

Thomas remembered thinking, "Sounds like a great place, good for Nana, she must be happy." He also remembered asking, "Why do we have to wait until we die to get to this beautiful place?"

His mother thought for a moment and then replied, "Because, Thomas, life is a journey. At the end of it you will be judged by God. If you were a good person who didn't hurt anyone or commit crimes, you will be allowed to spend eternity in this beautiful place." Thomas remembered being frightened by this story and it must have shown because his mother stroked his hair and said, "You have nothing to worry about, Thomas, you will always be a good person."

Thomas closed his eyes and the words echoed in his head, "Where no one is sad and everything is beautiful." He wondered if his mother was happy in this beautiful place. If anyone deserved to be there, it was her. But if this place did exist, was she reunited with her parents and was his father there?

"How could my father be there?" Thomas thought. "He wasn't a good person at all." This made his ponder his fate, "How will I get to that place after what I have done?"

He had so many thoughts and questions, and no one to answer them. Thomas put his head in his hands and began to cry when he felt someone sit down in the chair beside him.

He saw bright white pants, socks and shoes. When Thomas moved his hands, he saw a black man wearing a white blazer and a yellow tie looking at him with concern.

"It's ok, son," the man said sympathetically. "There's no shame in letting it out."

Thomas had no idea who this stranger was, so he quickly turned to see if Kyle was behind him, but both he and Kate were in the back talking to Kyle's sister Janet. The strange man lifted his hand seemed as if he was going to put it on Thomas's shoulder; this made Thomas angry. Without saying a word he got up and moved several seats over to get away from the man.

"I don't know you," Thomas said.

"No, you sure don't," the man replied.

The man got up out of his chair and fixed his suit, before walking back over to Thomas.

He then leaned over, offered his hand then said, "I'm William Johnson, also known as Reverend Billy Johnson."

Billy was 40 years old, tall and slightly overweight, but he carried it well. He was bald and his goatee was tinged with gray hairs. He always wore expensive white suits. His redeeming quality was his charisma. He was so charming and easy to talk to that he made people feel like they'd known him forever.

When Thomas didn't accept his handshake, Billy said, "Ok son, that's fine. I understand."

Thomas looked away, and Billy tried to get a read on him. This was another one of Billy's talents. He could always figure out what made people tick and it didn't take long. Billy rubbed his goatee for a minute and said, "You know, I lost my mama when I was about your age."

When he saw that Thomas didn't turn back towards him he continued, "I was raised by my Aunt Betty. My brothers and I had no one else to turn to." Thomas turned his head slightly, not quite facing Billy, but enough that he could see the reverend out of the corner of his eye.

Billy continued on, "My aunt was a good woman and I loved her, but she wasn't my mama, that's for sure." When Billy looked down and let out a sigh Thomas glanced over at him.

"Where was your father?" Thomas asked softly.

"My daddy was an abusive drunk who was never around and when he was he wouldn't show me any attention. He treated me and my brothers like we were invisible. Well, he got in a fight one night at a bar and almost killed a man. He was sentenced to 12 years in jail.

"My mama moved us soon after and didn't tell anyone where we was going. I never heard nothing about him after that. Didn't care to either to tell you the truth. I know it's not right to say this, Thomas, but I never cared for the man and certainly not the way I cared for my mama, not even close to it."

Billy could tell he was starting to get through to Thomas. He had done his research prior to this meeting. He knew all about Thomas' parents and he knew he could use it all to befriend him.

Thomas imagined that Billy was reliving those old memories in his mind like he had done many times himself.

Billy waited a few seconds before making eye contact again and forced a smile.

"My aunt passed too when I was 16," the reverend said. "She was a woman of strong faith and she instilled that in me. After she passed, my brothers and I were practically raised by members of the church. It seemed like each member took turns letting us stay with them. They would feed us, clothe us and made sure we stayed in school. It really enforced my faith in people and in God. I made sure I did all that I could to repay them for their kindness. I worked around the church, did odd jobs at their houses, anything to return the kindness they had shown to me and my brothers."

Thomas looked at the empty chair next to him for a moment, and then motioned for Billy to sit.

"Thank you, Thomas. You would think with me being on my feet most days preaching that I would be in better shape, but the years have a way of wearing you down."

Thomas almost smiled, but when Billy moved, the boy's eyes focused on his mother's coffin again. Billy knew to take Thomas' mind off of it and to make a connection, he had to keep talking.

"So I received a scholarship to Louisiana College where I studied the Bible among other things and earned my degree. From there I returned to my hometown and became a Reverend at the church I had belonged to for all those years. It's my way of giving back to the community and the folks at the church who gave me so much."

Thomas just nodded his head and stared at the coffin. Billy knew he was losing Thomas' attention and he would not allow that to happen.

"You see Thomas, we all have a purpose," Billy said. "There is a path for all of us and sometimes we can't see it--especially in times of struggle or tragedy when we are at our lowest. I know sometimes it seems like we were only put on this earth to suffer and things will not get any better. I can tell you, I know this; I lived it too, just like you. But then something happens; one day it all makes sense and you find that path that leads to your purpose.

"I lost the most important people in the world to me and I was in unimaginable pain because of it. I was spiraling out of control and I was lost, just like you. But I had something Thomas, something I don't think you have ever had. I had faith, Thomas.

"Faith that all the suffering wasn't for nothing, faith that there is a higher purpose and a reason for everything that happens, faith that I will be able to make a difference and that I will be welcomed into heaven with open arms to be reunited with my mama and aunt when my time has come.

"Even at my lowest, I had faith," he said softly. "We were not made to suffer, Thomas that is not our purpose in this world. We are tested from time to time, this is true, and some are tested more than others. My purpose was shown to me by the kindness of others and through that kindness I found my path.

"I was given a gift, Thomas, through my faith and the kindness of others. I made it my life's 'mission' to help others find their path, to find their faith."

Billy pointed a finger at Thomas and said, "You have been given a gift, too."

Thomas turned away again, with all of his pain and anger visible on his face. Billy put his hand on Thomas' shoulder and this time the grieving boy didn't move away. "You have been given an extraordinary gift," Billy said softly. "A gift the no one else in the world has received, Thomas. Yes, you have lived a hard life for someone so young. But I can see that you have a good soul in spite of what you might think of yourself."

Billy then looked at Marie's casket and said, "That woman loved you, Thomas, and I know that you loved her more than anything. It's written all over you."

Thomas began to cry and he put his face in his hands. "I couldn't save her," he said softly. "It was my entire fault. This is no gift, this is a curse!"

"Thomas, it was not your fault," Billy insisted. "Hey," he said and patted Thomas on the back. "Look at me."

Thomas looked up slowly.

"Your mother had a mental illness. She couldn't handle the magnitude of this gift you have. It overwhelmed her, just as it is overwhelming for you. She was a good woman who loved you very much and nothing can change that."

Thomas lowered his head and started to cry again.

Billy rubbed his shoulder and said, "Thomas, I was given a gift, shown a path by extraordinary people and their kindness. I am here to do the same for you when you are ready."

Billy leaned down and whispered, "I will help you find that path. I will show you that same kindness then you will find your purpose and your faith.

"Just give me that chance when you are ready, I'll show you how special you are and why you were chosen for this gift."

Kyle finally noticed that a stranger was sitting next to Thomas, talking to him. Something about the man set off an alarm in his head. When Kyle started to make his way over to them, Billy noticed and knew it was time to leave. The reverend took a card out of his wallet and placed in on Thomas's leg.

"Take this card and put it in your pocket, he said. "You can reach me at this number day or night if you need anything. Even if you just need someone to talk to, I will be there for you."

Billy stood up and again looked at the concerned man who was fast approaching them. "Use it when you're ready, but only you will know when you are ready to find your path. Take care and God bless, my friend." With that Billy fixed his blazer and walked away.

Kyle shot a quick puzzled look at Billy and sat down next to Thomas, who hugged him and broke down crying. Kyle asked Thomas about the stranger, but the boy didn't want to talk about it. Kyle decided to wait a few days before approaching Thomas again about it.

Billy motioned to two men who were standing off to the side in the back of the hall and the three of them left the funeral home together. Along the way, Billy stopped to hand the police officer who let him into the parking lot another hundred dollar bill. He had already given the man two hundred dollars on the way in.

After they got inside Billy's black Cadillac, his brother Jerry asked, "So how did it go, man?"

Billy smiled and said, "It went well."

"'It went well?'" Jerry asked, confused. "Well did you get him or not?"

Billy shook his head, and then playfully slapped his younger brother on the cheek.

"Take it easy my brother. It may take some time but he'll come around, you'll see."

"I hope you're right," said the driver, Billy's older brother Bernie. "We ain't making shit off of our congregation right now. We need this kid to go national and start making some serious money, that's the plan, right?"

"Like I said," Billy replied, "give it time and he'll come around. I planted the seed today. That's all I wanted to do."

"Did you give him the old, 'my mom's dead and I was raised by my aunt' speech? How you found your calling and shit?" Jerry asked.

Billy laughed "Of course. It works every time, especially with the women. Only this time I told him my daddy was an abusive drunk who was in jail, too!"

They all laughed when they heard that because their daddy really was in jail--only it was for stealing money from the church, not a bar fight.

The three men spent the entire drive back to Virginia talking about what they were all going to do with all of that money when "The Mission" was up and running at full speed.

Chapter 12

After his mother's service Thomas went to live with the Morgans. It was not an easy transition for him at all. He had fallen into a deep depression which caused him to isolate himself from Kyle and Kate as much as he could. Kate kept telling her father to give Thomas his space and that he would come around, but Kyle secretly worried that the grieving boy would try to do harm to himself at some point.

After a few weeks, the media exhausted every angle of the story and most of the camera crews went away. Because they had no access at all to Thomas, Kyle or Kate, the story started to turn into more of a tale then an actual event. Medical experts were now appearing on every network offering possible reasons for Kyle's miraculous recovery.

The Believers, however, did not dissipate. Their numbers increased every day. They would stand on the sidewalk during the day and some of them would camp in the park that was a few blocks away at night. The police did the best they could to keep them away but it was becoming too much for them. The town was dedicating a lot of men and a lot of man-hours to keeping people away from the house and the government was getting fed up. When Kyle received the first letter requesting that he provide his own security, he called the municipal building and raised hell. It didn't do him much good; the latest letter had an end date for the family's police protection. After that, officers would no longer be stationed outside of the house.

Kyle was right to worry about Thomas because he was having thoughts of suicide all of time. He was a prisoner now inside this house, considered a freak by some and The Healer by others. He could see the toll it was taking on both Kyle and Kate. Thomas' own feelings were mixed about this because on one hand he did feel bad that they were suffering through this with him, but on the other hand, if Kyle hadn't blurted out his secret none of this would have happened and Thomas' mother would still be alive. He wasn't sure if his relationship with Kyle could ever be the same. Kate, on other hand, didn't give up on trying reaching Thomas. She came and talked to him every night whether he would respond or not.

Every so often, Thomas would look out the front blinds at the people who came to the house. Kate had told him that they were different religious groups and people who were hoping that Thomas could heal them. He would stare at them with their candles. Some were in wheel chairs, some were in crutches, some had oxygen tanks and some were just old.

A few times, someone would run through the police barricade and rush towards the house screaming Thomas' name. "Thomas, please help me!" or "Help my son!" or my daughter, mother, father or wife. There was a small part of Thomas that wanted to go out there and help them all. But there was a bigger part that wanted this to be over, that cursed what he was and cursed what he had done.

As the days turned into weeks, Thomas eventually started to open up to Kate more and more. Because he was unable to sleep, Kate would stay up with him until he drifted off. He wanted to tell her about Reverend Billy and what he had said, but something made him hold back. He wasn't quite sure why at the time, but he had started thinking about a way to disappear from New Jersey and reinvent himself someplace else where no one knew anything about him.

Thomas knew that was just a foolish dream because Kate and Kyle were the only family he had left. Even after all that had happened, he knew deep down that these were the only two people in the world who cared about him.

After six weeks, Kyle had to go back to work or he'd lose his job. He hoped it would return some sense of normalcy to his life, but all everyone could talk about was the incident involving Thomas. All day every day for the first week, one person after another sat at his desk asking him to retell the same story.

As much as Kyle tried to change the details of the story by telling them his cancer was exaggerated and that he was taking an experimental drug, they still asked about Thomas and his mother. Kyle started to withdraw from the people he worked with because they were acting no different from the people who met him on street. It wasn't enough to explain it once; they all seemed to be digging for something that they hadn't heard on the news so they could tell everyone they knew. He wasn't sure why, but he started to feel like he didn't fit in anymore.

Things had gotten a lot tougher for Kate too. Thomas was now being homeschooled because he could not leave the house without being approached. Now all of her friends -- and some that she didn't even consider friends -- were asking if they could come over her house to meet Thomas.

A few Kate had considered close friends stopped speaking to her when she kept telling them no. It angered her how they all talked about him and what he went through like it was an episode from some drama series on TV. She got into many arguments with people she didn't even know when she overheard them talking about Thomas' father's death and how he watched him die. It got so out of hand that Kate was even offered an 'A' for the whole year by a teacher who wanted to bring her sick mother to see Thomas.

Kate became isolated as well, spending most of her time at home because the real world didn't seem so real anymore. She realized everyone seemed fake and everyone wanted something from her.

Thomas could see clearly what was going on around him and he wanted a change. Not just for him, but for the Morgans as well. He had been staring at the card Reverend Billy had given him every night for the last two weeks thinking about what he said about his purpose. Surely his purpose wasn't to be locked up in a house for the rest of his life while hurting the people who were left that cared about him.

Thomas told himself that he would wait for a sign and that he would know when the time was right for what he needed to do. Three weeks later, Thomas got his sign.

It was 2 p.m. and Thomas was home alone. He had just finished watching something on TV when he wandered over to the front window to peak out of the blinds. As his eyes scanned the crowd, a couple who was standing off to the left by a policeman caught his eye. They had a little boy with them who was about 4 years old.

The father was talking to the policeman and pointing at the house, while the mother's attention was on two girls on the other side of the house who were arguing loudly. Thomas smiled as he noticed little boy. He looked as happy as he was bouncing up and down while holding onto his mommy's hand. Every so often he would look up and say something to her, but she was distracted, so he would just continue bouncing. Thomas stared at the boy and couldn't help but wonder if something was wrong with him.

Without thinking about it, he pulled the cord on the blinds so they went all the way up, giving Thomas a better view but exposing him to the crowd. The little boy looked right at him and smiled. Thomas laughed and smiled back before waving to him. The little boy waved back for all of two seconds before he was bouncing away again, lost in his own world.

As the crowd reacted, the boy's mother looked down to see what her son was doing and noticed he was waving at Thomas. "Oh my god, Frank!" she yelled to her husband, "It's him!" she said as she pointed towards the window.

Frank looked away from the policeman and towards the window. Standing there was the boy who may be the only hope for his dying son.

"Ok, get back," the policeman said. "I told you both, you can't be here."

Thomas had made his way to the front door and opened it just in time to hear the boy's mother beg, "Please officer, my child has a kidney disease and the one kidney he has left is showing signs of failing, we have to see him, please!"

Thomas walked onto the front porch and the whole world seemed to stop – everybody froze and stared at him. The eerie silence made Thomas feel uncomfortable. Across the street, a van door slid open and two men jumped out, one with a camera and one with a microphone in hand.

The two policemen who were left to conduct crowd control worried they wouldn't be able to stop this crowd if it charged towards the house. One of them immediately got on the radio and asked for all of the backup he could get ASAP.

"Please everyone, just stay back where you are," Thomas said, sensing that things could get out of hand really fast because of what he had done. When the crowd ignored him and started to move forward, Thomas went back inside and pulled the blinds down so no one could see him. He waited until he heard sirens, then he peeked out to see three more police cars parked in front of his house. He watched as the six police officers exited their vehicles and stood alongside the first two in a show of force.

When the crowd backed away, Thomas came out onto the porch again.

He didn't speak this time, instead he made eye contact with the family who had the four-year-old boy and motioned for them to come with him.

As they approached, one of the policemen reached out his hand to stop them because he didn't know what he was supposed to do.

"Please let us through," the mother pleaded, "he wants to help us!"

Before the policeman could react, the little boy let go of his mother's hand and ran towards the porch. Thomas walked to the bottom step to meet him and said, "Hello there, what's your name?"

"Henry."

"Why hello Henry, I'm Thomas."

He reached out to shake Henry's hand, but instead the younger boy gave him a high five, which made Thomas laugh.

Thomas made eye contact with the policeman. "It's ok," he said.

When the policeman hesitated, the boy's mother begged, "Please sir, he'll die if Thomas can't help him."

Officer Michael Rutt knew there was a very good chance he would be reprimanded, but being a father of two he let them through.

Thomas invited the family inside the house. He noticed that Henry's parents were nervous and seemed almost in awe of him. Thomas introduced himself again and extended his hand.

Henry's father took Thomas' hand and gave him a firm handshake. "The name's Frank Connelly," he said. The handshake was so firm that it made Thomas say, "Ow!" and shakes his hand to stop the sting.

"Darn it Frank, what are you thinking?" scolded Henry's mother, Lucy. "You could hurt his hands and then he won't be able to help Henry!"

"Oh Jeez, I'm sorry Thomas," Frank said nervously. "Are you ok?"

Thomas smiled and nodded as he led them into the living room. He had never seen adults act like this around him and it struck him as being kind of funny.

"Please, don't be nervous," he reassured them, "Believe or not, I am totally normal." The fact that he even had to say that made Thomas giggle a little.

They sat and talked for a while but Thomas could tell that they were anxious. He asked if they were ready and they all replied "Yes," Henry offering the loudest response.

Thomas asked them to have Henry lay down on the couch. He then asked Frank to hold Henry down gently by his shoulders and he asked Lucy to hold him down gently by his feet.

When they were ready, Thomas stood beside Henry thinking that this was the sign; this is what he was meant to do. He was just about to put his hands on Henry's chest when Henry cracked a big smile and looked up at his father.

"Dad, after this can we go to McDonalds?" Henry asked.

Everyone in the room laughed and eased the tension.

"Sure thing champ," Frank replied. "Anything you want buddy."

Thomas looked at Frank and nodded with a smile. He then looked up at the ceiling to focus and took a deep breath. He closed his eyes as he laid his hands down on Henry's chest and he immediately felt it. It was like a lightning bolt being shot into his chest. He felt it all the way down to his fingers. It lasted for only about 30 seconds and it was gone.

Thomas smiled before he opened his eyes because he was sure that it had worked.

He sat with the Connellys for another 15 minutes talking to them and explaining what his life had been like up to this point. By the time they left, Frank and Lucy could both see that he was just an ordinary kid, and their hearts went out to him for what he had been through. As Thomas walked them to the door they thanked him for the thousandth time.

"You are very welcome," he said, "I'm glad I could help." He could see that they were grateful, but he could tell that both still had some doubt if miracle healing was really possible. As if he were reading their minds, Thomas reassured them, "Go get him checked out, you'll see, everything is ok now."

With that, Lucy started crying and gave Thomas a big hug. "Bless you," she said. "Thank God for you, Thomas."

Thomas said nothing, he just nodded. Frank extended his hand, but Thomas just looked at it and said in mock horror, "Oh no, not again!" Everyone laughed, and Frank grabbed Thomas and gave him a big hug too.

When Thomas opened the door, everything was quiet outside. There were now three camera crews positioned right behind the police. Each one of them snapped to attention and started broadcasting as soon as the door opened. Before Thomas could even say goodbye, two policemen came rushing up the stairs to escort the Connellys away before another yelled to Thomas to get back inside.

As he stood alone in the living room, he contemplated what he had just done. "There was no turning back now," he thought to himself. Change was coming, that was for certain. Still, thinking about that boy and the look of gratitude in his parents' eyes...it all felt right to him. "Maybe I've found my purpose," Thomas thought.

Later that evening, the Reverend Billy Johnson was outside his Virginia home barbecuing when his brother Bernie came running out of the back door. "Man, you gotta come see this!" Bernie said.

"What's going on man?" Billy asked. "Can't you see I'm cooking here?"

"It's that kid you went to see," Bernie said. "He's on the news, practically every channel!"

Billy, Jerry and Bernie went back inside the house then sat and watched as the reporter recounted all the day's events. "It is total pandemonium here on this quiet street in West Orange, New Jersey. Earlier today, Thomas Greggs, who is being referred to now by the people gathering here as 'The Healer,' came out of his house, chose a couple from the street to invite inside and used his so-called healing abilities on their young son. We have yet to determine what the boy's condition was or if whatever Thomas has done to him have made a difference. There were several witnesses to the event and they are amazed."

The screen switched to a man and a woman who live across the street.

"We hadn't seen Thomas since his mother passed," the woman said. "We heard all the rumors and we've seen all the people gathering but we didn't know what to believe. But now this happens and wow! We're waiting like everyone else to see if this is real!"

"An anonymous source has just told NBC that the couple's names are Frank and Lucy Connelly. We were able to confirm from our source at West Orange General Hospital that they have a young son named Henry who has severe kidney issues. We were informed that the Connellys went straight to West Orange General to have Henry checked out. We will continue to have live updates as this story progresses."

Bernie looked over at Billy and noticed that he had that Cheshire cat smile on his face. "Man, could you believe that?" Bernie said.

"Oh yeah, I believe it," Billy said. "It won't be long now. No sir, it will not be long now," Billy shouted again as he pumped his fist in the air.

"What are you talking about now, man?" Bernie asked

"Listen, after it comes out that this Henry kid is healed and the world finds out that Thomas did it again, it will not be long before the pressure is way too much for that family he is staying with and he calls me. He's got no one else to turn to. "What'd they call him, 'The Healer'? I like that," Billy said and smiled again.

Billy could tell his brothers were still confused. "Look," Billy said, "there are already people and reporters bothering those people every day because Thomas saved that man Kyle Morgan. But, the people weren't 100% sure it was something Thomas did or some other kind of medical miracle. Even when it was mentioned that he had also healed the man's daughter too, people were still skeptical. Now the faithful," Billy said as he made the quote signs with his fingers, the faithful believe, that is for damn sure.

"But after this here," Billy said as he pointed at the TV, "everyone will believe, and they are going to flock to the house from all corners of the globe seeking out The Healer. That family will not be allowed to breathe. Who can live like that, hmm?"

Billy smiled again ear to ear as he pointed to the TV and said, "There's the winning lottery ticket, my brothers. Guess what, I don't even have to go to the store to buy it! Nope, that ticket is going to come right to me and when it does, it will be like we are printing our own money."

The next morning the report came out that Henry Connelly's kidneys were completed healed. Not only was the kidney that was failing healed, the other kidney was now functioning again as well. Mr. and Mrs. Connelly were on every news station praising Thomas and thanking God for him the next day.

Chapter 13

The days after were just as Billy predicted; it was pandemonium at the Morgan house. The media was everywhere. Some of them were stationed round the clock on the street while others followed Kate and Kyle everywhere they went.

It got so bad that Kyle's boss suggested that he should take his vacation early and get away from the office. When he went to speak to his manager, Kyle's boss said, "We're not *asking* you to do this Kyle; we're *telling* you to take some time."

The three of them were now secluded in the house together with the world watching. Kyle felt tremendous guilt for what Thomas had gone through, but he wasn't happy at all that Thomas had made a spectacle of himself after things were starting to return to normal. He was well aware that it sounded hypocritical, especially after Thomas saved his life, but this madness that surrounded them now was really getting to him. As the days turned into weeks without it letting up, Kyle started to reach his limit.

On the other hand, Kate stood by Thomas. She was proud of him for helping that boy and she told him so. She could tell he was confused by Kyle's reaction to what he had done, so she waited until he went back to his room to talk to him. When Kate told him she was proud of him, Thomas lost his look of depression and started to seem happy and confident.

Thomas confided to her that he hadn't felt that good in a long time. He told Kate that words could not convey the look in Henry's parents' eyes when he motioned for them to come inside. "They looked at me like I was an angel or something," he said. "I changed their lives and saved that little boy." He paused, lost in thought for a moment. "No, not just the boy, I saved that family."

Kate smiled because this was the first time she had seen Thomas beaming like this since he healed her arm years ago. "Your gift was meant to help people like Henry," she told Thomas. "And that's just what it is – a gift, not a curse."

Kate knew that whatever she said, and however happy Thomas seemed in the moment, his thoughts would always wander back to his mother. He'd been unable to really feel happiness since her death.

"Hey, I will always be here for you, Thomas," Kate said while looking in his eyes. "For the good and the bad, you know that, right? We are more than friends, we are family. Whenever you need someone to talk to, cry with or laugh with, I will always be here.

"Remember, you were *my* angel first, long before this Henry kid ever came along, so don't forget that."

Thomas laughed and smiled at her. "I could never forget that," Thomas said.

At the moment he wanted to tell Kate about what Billy had said about his purpose. He wanted to tell her that he was thinking about joining up with him to make a difference in other lives like he did for Henry. He wanted to share everything with her, but he was afraid. Instead he became very serious, "No matter what happens down the road Kate, you will always be my big sister and I will always be there for you too when you need me, I promise."

Looking back later on the conversation they had that night, Kate realized that they were saying goodbye to each other without even knowing it.

Thomas slept in the spare bedroom that was right off of the kitchen. At night the only light in the room was from a night-light that Kyle had plugged in one of the outlets near the stove. It was the early morning hours and Thomas was awake again staring at the ceiling. His mind wandered back to when his mother was alive and he could see her smile clear as day. A feeling of calm came over him and he was just about to fall asleep when he heard someone walk into the kitchen. He heard footsteps approaching the room and he didn't feel much like talking, Thomas closed his eyes and pretended to be asleep.

He could hear whoever it was enter the room, pause for a moment and then close the door to his bedroom. When whoever it was turned on the light in the kitchen, the light from under the door made it so Thomas could see the room around him.

Thomas' eyes scanned the room for a second and they stopped on a cross that Kyle had hung in the corner. For some reason it made Thomas think again of what Reverend Billy had said to him about finding his purpose. His thoughts were interrupted by the sound of the footsteps again followed by Kyle talking in a low tone. It was definitely Kyle, but he couldn't make out what he was saying.

When Thomas looked over at the clock and saw that it was 2:14 a.m., his curiosity got the better of him. He got of bed, went over to the door and opened it very slowly. He peeked out into the kitchen and Kyle wasn't there.

He heard Kyle's voice again in the living room, so he got as close as he could without being seen.

"I don't know Janet, I think maybe all of this is becoming too much for me to handle," Kyle said.

"I mean I love Thomas like he was my own son, but we're prisoners now. We can't even leave the house."

Kyle paused for a moment they continued, "There are still people approaching me and Kate everywhere we go.

"My boss pulled me into his office the other day and told me that all of this was becoming disruptive to the company. He said that it was costing the company money for the additional security that was required. My company had to get a court order to stop the reporters from coming within so many feet, but that doesn't stop the wackos. They wait for me in the parking lot begging me to take them to Thomas."

There was another long pause in which Kyle muttered, "Uh huh," several times. "Goddamn it, I can't take this anymore Janet," he said. "Some of the neighbors won't even talk to us anymore and those who do are telling me that they are putting their houses up for sale." There was another pause followed by a sigh, "I don't know how much longer I can take this before I crack, Janet. Something has got to give so we can get our lives back."

Thomas had heard enough so he went back to his room, closed the door slowly and sat on the bed. He thought about his mother and how she took her life. He knew Kyle was a lot stronger than his mother, but he couldn't take that chance.

Saving Henry was the sign he was waiting for. It was clear to him now more than ever. It was time to move on to find his purpose.

Thomas listened with is ear against the door as Kyle hung up the phone and walked out of the kitchen. He waited until he heard Kyle's bedroom door close before getting dressed.

Thomas went to the linen closet and grabbed several pillowcases so that he could pack all of his belongings in them. He went to the back door, checked to see if anyone was in the area and then ran out into the darkness.

He knew there would still be people out in front of his house, so went through several back yards so no one would see him. About six blocks away there was a 7-Eleven convenience store. He found a pay phone outside and pulled a wrinkled old card out of his wallet. The first attempt at a collect call went unanswered so he started to panic, not knowing what to do next.

Billy had just gotten home an hour or so ago. He had gone out with his brothers to a bar and left with a woman who recognized him from church. He had just finished a tough week and he wanted to let off some steam. He had been trying for almost a year to make a name for himself as a preacher with no luck. Although he was very popular in the community, the money just wasn't there. He wanted so much more for himself and it just wasn't happening.

Even the female perks weren't what they should be. Billy was sure that tomorrow, when he spoke to one of his brothers, they were going to razz him about how the woman he just left was fat or ugly or both. But "Hey," Billy thought to himself, "That's why God made alcohol."

The truth was that Billy was just like his father. What he told Thomas about his father going to jail when he was younger was true, but he didn't get locked up for beating someone. His father, Marshall Wilson, was a 64-year-old former minister who was arrested for embezzling money from the church that he worked at for 10 years.

It was their father who taught Billy and his brothers, 'the game', as he called it. It was his father's story about finding one's purpose that Billy had used in most of his cons as well. He had heard his father tell that story to so many of his lady friends through the years. He adopted it as his own when he and his brothers hit the road. Billy modified it a little as needed, but it worked as good for him as it did for the old man back in the day.

Billy and his brothers were preachers just like their father. They would follow their father from church to church watching him preach while growing up. When they were old enough, they each took their turn trying to branch out on their own. Billy was the only one who had any success because he seemed to have a knack when it came to connecting with people young and old. He father noticed this and started to limit his appearances on stage. When they got to Virginia, Billy was 17 and ready to preach on his own but his father wouldn't let him. This caused a rift between them which made Billy contemplate moving forward on his own someplace else after he graduated high school.

Marshall knew it wouldn't happen because his other sons, Bernie and Jerry, were loyal to him. He also knew that the three of them were inseparable and that Billy looked out for the other two. If Billy were to leave, he wouldn't do it without his brothers. This Marshall was sure of.

But that didn't stop Billy from learning every aspect of the preaching game in anticipation for when his time finally came. Bernie and Jerry were lazy and just along for the ride. They were content greeting people, leading them to their seats and collecting the donations. Neither had an ounce of ambition, but they were trustworthy and they were loyal.

Another thing Billy learned from his father at a young age was how to play the role of the preacher and still be a ladies' man. To the faithful at the church he appeared to be a loyal husband and a devoted father. But in reality, Marshall was a man with an oversized ego who would partake in many extramarital activities.

When it became too much for his wife to endure, she packed her bags and moved back in with her parents out of state. She asked the boys who they would rather live with and they chose their father.

Billy was the oldest, 11 at the time, and he idolized his father. He wanted more than anything to be just like him. His brothers just mimicked whatever Billy did and followed along. Billy was really impressed that wherever they went, everyone knew his dad. It didn't even matter to him that he never heard from his mother again. In his mind, he wasn't lying to Thomas about his mother being dead because, in a sense, she was dead to him and his brothers.

One of his father's biggest faults was that he liked to live a flashy lifestyle. He liked to wear expensive clothes and a lot of gold jewelry. He also lavished gifts on many of his lady friends.

As he got older, Billy realized his father was taking money from the church and he warned him that he wasn't being smart about the way he was doing it. Billy told him that it was way too obvious and that sooner or later someone was going to say something.

But because of that ego of his, because he thought, "Everyone was his friend." Billy's father just kept taking more and more until it caught up with him one day. When that day came, Billy and his brothers left town and didn't return for a year. Billy hated his father for what he did. He was happy in Virginia with his girlfriend, Neesy. They had plans together, she was going to go to a local college and he was going to start preaching on his own near whichever college she chose. Instead he had to leave in shame and not look back. This too was another lesson he had learned from his father, how to cut your losses and move on.

They wound up in North Carolina because they had a cousin who lived there. Bernie got a job at a gas station and Jerry worked at a movie theater. Billy worked in a warehouse during the week but it wasn't long before he started attending a local Baptist church. He used a different name at the church because he was concerned that people would know what his father had done.

Within two weeks he befriended the church staff as well as the entire congregation. He portrayed himself as a man with a dream of being a preacher someday. Because of his charm and his personality, everyone believed the tale he told about losing both of his parents at an early age.

"God gave me the strength and wisdom to grow up fast in order to look after my two brothers," he said. "Only my faith kept me going every day. It was only through prayer that I came to know my purpose and that was to spread His word to anyone who would honor me by listening."

In only a month after joining the church, Billy was preaching alone on the last Sunday of every month. Three months later, as his popularity grew, he was preaching *every* Sunday to a mostly packed church. By the end of the sixth month, Billy had quit his job at the factory and he was the only preacher at the church.

Even though he was doing well and preaching on his own, he still thought of Neesy every day. He wanted so bad to see her again, but he waited a year until he thought the memory of what his father had done had faded before he headed back to Virginia with his brothers to make amends. Even though he could remember it all vividly, like it happened yesterday, it still all seemed like it was a lifetime ago to him.

As he looked at his face in the rearview mirror while sitting in his driveway he saw a much older man and he wondered to himself if he would ever reach the heights he had dreamed of as a younger man. Thoughts of the past lingered in his mind as he closed the door to his car and staggered into his house.

Once inside he listened for Neesy to see if she was up waiting for him before heading to the shower. As he took of his clothes he smelled them before placing them in the hamper. It was as he suspected, they reeked of smoke and of perfume. Since this was routine to Billy, he knew exactly how to handle it. He grabbed up the rest of the clothes that were in the hamper, headed down to the basement and tossed them all in the washing machine. After putting in the detergent and starting the machine, he made his way back upstairs to bed where he slid in as gently as he could next to Neesy.

His head was just starting to throb and he had just started to drift off when he heard the first ring. By the time the phone rang a second time; his wife reached over and picked it up.

"Collect call from who?" she said.

Billy heard what she said and he immediately opened his eyes. "Now who the hell in your family is calling us collect in the middle of the night?" Billy said angrily.

"Thomas Greggs," she said. "Who the hell is Thomas Greggs?"

It took a second for the name to register to Billy, but then it clicked. "Give me that, Neesy," Billy said as he grabbed the phone away from her.

"What the hell is going on?" Neesy asked as she covered her eyes to shield them from the light Billy just turned on.

Her husband waved her off with his hand and said, "Yes, I'll accept the charges!"

Neesy watched as Billy spoke to this Thomas person for several minutes. He didn't say much at first except, "uh huh, I understand." Then Billy opened the nightstand drawer and pulled all of its contents out until he found a pen. He looked around for something to write on, settling for a paperback book that his wife was reading.

Neesy looked over and noticed he wrote, "The 7-Eleven, Main Street, West Orange, NJ."

She glanced over at Billy with puzzled expression, which made him look back at her and shake his head as if to say, "Don't ask." Billy kept assuring this Thomas person that he was here for him and that everything would be fine from now on. Then Billy the preacher kicked in with a speech about faith and God.

Billy explained to Thomas that this was in fact a sign for what God had in mind for him then he kept going on about his purpose. He finished the conversation by saying, "I'll be there in four hours, son."

Without saying a word to Neesy, Billy hung up the phone and immediately started dialing again.

"Four hours?" Neesy asked. "Are you going to tell me what's going on?"

Billy ignored her and hit the phone's disconnect button. "Damn it, pick up the damn phone you idiot!" He dialed again, but still got no answer. Frustrated, he slammed the phone down and got out of bed to get dressed.

"I gotta go to New Jersey right now, Babe," he told Neesy. "This is really important, something I need to take care of right now."

"Is Thomas really a woman, Billy?" Neesy asked with an edge to her voice.

"Nah, nothing like that," Billy said as he laughed. When he noticed Neesy still looked at him with disapproval, he said, "Thomas is that healer boy they keep talking about on the news."

"That's his name?" Neesy asked. "Well what does he have to do with you?"

Billy already had pants and a shirt on before she asked. He was now putting on his shoes and reaching for his keys while heading for the door.

"I can't get into that right now, Babe," he said. "I gotta go pick up that boy now and bring him here."

"Wait, what did you just say?" Neesy asked. "You're gonna bring him *here*?"

"No time to explain," Billy said as he put on his jacket and opened the bedroom door. "I will tell you this though, our lives are about to get a whole lot better," he said with a big smile on his face. "Go back to sleep hon, I'll see you in a few hours."

Billy didn't wait for a reply. He hurried down the stairs and into his car.

Chapter 14

Two years had passed since Thomas left the Morgans and disappeared off of the face of the Earth. Kyle reported him missing the following morning as soon as he noticed that Thomas wasn't in his room. For about three weeks after, it seemed like everyone in the world was looking for him.

Kyle wouldn't say it to Kate, but he feared that Thomas had taken his life somewhere and it was just a matter of time before someone found his body. It made him feel even worse for his daughter; because she would run to the phone every time it rang, hoping it was Thomas. His call never came and Kyle could tell that even she was starting to lose hope after a few weeks.

The crowds of the faithful and those who wanted to be healed had dispersed about two weeks after Thomas' disappearance, leaving only the reporters who wouldn't let up.

As bad as the attention was when Thomas was living with them, it got much worse when he went missing. The story brought around the clock coverage, constant phone calls and helicopters flying overhead one after the other.

Robert Van Putten, who had made a name for himself by being first on the scene when The Healer story broke, begged his producer to let him stick with this story and milk it for all that it was worth. Robert was quickly making a name for himself as someone who would do anything for a story and his producer Martin Shulman had no problem with it as long as the results were exclusives.

Robert rummaged through the Morgans' garbage, harassed Kyle's sister and even tried to bribe someone from the phone company to tap the Morgans' lines, just so he could be the first to uncover where Thomas had gone.

Alas after weeks of searching, rumors and speculation, there was no scoop. Thomas had just vanished in the middle of the night. No one knew for certain if he was dead or alive… no one except for Billy Johnson.

Eventually the media moved on to the next big story. Even Robert gave up once he got a tip from one of his sources that Mayor Harold Bertlin of Parsippany had been having an affair with his wife's sister who was now pregnant with his baby.

While a sense of normalcy finally returned to Kate and Kyle's lives, it had come at a cost. Kyle blamed himself for everything that happened even though Kate tried to convince him otherwise. He became withdrawn and started drinking. It got so bad that after six months, Janet and Kate had to perform an intervention.

Kate put on a strong face in front of her father, but she also blamed herself for what had happened to Thomas. But unlike her father, Kate didn't believe Thomas was dead.

Kate's belief was confirmed late one night when she picked up a late night phone call only to hear silence on the other end of line. It wasn't the first time this had happened since Thomas left, so Kate did as she always did - she waited a moment and then asked, "Thomas is that you?"

Kyle quickly got sick of these types of calls and dismissed them as being from some of the wackos who think Thomas still comes around. He told Kate to hang up right away, but she never listened to him.

On this particular night, Kate was just about to ask again if it was Thomas when the actual sound of his voice almost made her drop the phone

"Just listen Kate and don't say a word, ok?" Thomas said.

When Kate didn't reply he continued, "I just wanted to let you know that I am alive and well. I've been meaning to call for months, but I never knew what to say and whatever I said wouldn't make much sense to anyone but me at this point.

"I had to go, but I'm sorry for the way I left. I should have told you both so you didn't worry or at least left a note. This is for the best trust me. I had to put that place and everything about it behind me forever.

"Take care of yourself and I wish nothing best for you and your father; you two deserve nothing but happiness. Thank you for all that you've done for me and for being there for me when I needed you both."

Before Kate could say a word, she heard the phone click followed by a dial tone. When she hung up the phone, she had tears in her eyes. She remembered how Thomas often said he felt that he didn't belong anywhere since his mother died. When they would watch the news together and it was all about him, Thomas would say he wanted to disappear.

He often said he wanted to be a nobody again and that if he knew when he was little how good it was being a nobody, he would have never complained about being one.

Just knowing he was alive and well would have to be good enough. Even though Kyle was pleased to hear the news, a big part of him wished he could have talked to Thomas that night before he left. They had no other choice at this point than to accept his decision and hope that he would call again one day.

In Virginia, life was much simpler for Thomas. The property they were all living on had been in Billy's wife Neesy's family for generations.

There were three houses situated on three acres of land. It had all been left to Neesy when her mother had passed. To get to the property itself, you had to turn off of the main road and go down a gravel road. It took a minute or two of driving through a wooded area before you came to a clearing where the main house was visible on the top of a small incline.

With Neesy being an only child, Billy's family became her family after they were married. She let Bernie move into one house and Jerry move into the other and they lived there rent-free with their families. All that she would ask of them was to make sure they kept up with the landscaping and repairs of the homes. They lived in the two smaller one level ranch houses on the property. There were two more gravel roads on either side of the main house" If you followed the road to the right for a minute or two, you could see Bernie's house in the distance and if you followed the road on the opposite side, that's where Jerry lived.

Both houses consisted of two and a half bedrooms, a living room, kitchen and one bathroom.

The main house that Neesy and Billy lived in was the house Neesy was raised in. It was beautifully kept when her mother was alive and Neesy made sure it stayed that way. The two story house had a wrap-around porch and a triangle-shaped grey shingled roof. The house was sky blue with the edging around the windows and the porch painted white.

On the morning when Thomas first arrived at Billy's house, the first thing he noticed as he got out of the car was the perfectly trimmed bushes that were on both sides of the stairs in the front of the porch. As he got closer he noticed there were flowers in front of the bushes. They were all different sizes and colors, but he thought they were beautiful and he couldn't recall ever seeing anything quite like them.

As he waited for Billy, his eyes continued to scan the front of the house. He got the feeling like this was where he belonged, away from everyone and everything. No reporters, no crowds, just the sounds of the birds and a cool breeze on his face. It was very peaceful and that's exactly what he needed.

Once they went inside, Billy called out to Neesy and she called back, "In here, honey."

"Come on with me Thomas, I'll introduce you the missus," Billy said.

While he was standing in the front hallway, the first thing Thomas noticed was the stained hardwood floor he was standing on. It was as clean and shiny a something he had seen on TV during a basketball game.

Billy hung his jacket on the long coat rack, then took his shoes off and placed them in a section underneath the rack where Thomas could see a bunch of other shoes neatly lined up together side by side.

"She's real uptight about these floors of hers, Thomas," Billy said with a smile. "Rule number one, the shoes come off as soon as you enter this hallway."

Thomas smiled back and Billy said, "Ok, good, now follow me."

At the end of the hallway was a flight of stairs that went to the second floor and to the right of that was the entrance to the living room. Thomas' jaw dropped at the size of the living room alone - it was twice the size of his.

Thomas noticed that the coach, the loveseat and the two recliners all were covered in plastic. The fabric was all the same under the plastic, white with some kind of red flower type pattern to it. There was a fancy throw rug in the middle of the room and a large wooden coffee table that was polished just as good as the floor was. It looked more like a museum to Thomas then it did someone's living room.

"Hey, Billy, where's the TV?" Thomas asked.

Billy laughed and put his hand on Thomas's shoulder. "Oh, this isn't a living room, Thomas," he said with a smile. This here is what Neesy refers to as a sitting room. There's a TV in the kitchen and in the bedrooms upstairs as well. Don't worry, son, we're not Amish."

With that, they both laughed and walked into the dining room.

Thomas again stood with his mouth open as he saw the large table that was made of the same dark as the coffee table in the sitting room with eight matching chairs around it. Again he marveled at how he could see his reflection on the surface of the table. Hanging on the wall was a large painting of the Last Supper with a small light above it to illuminate it.

On either side of the room were matching wooden hutches. The one on the right was fancy dishes and silverware and the one on the left was filled with various porcelain dolls. There were at least eight on each of the three shelves and none of them resembled the others. Thomas thought they looked kind of creepy, but he would never say that to anyone in the house.

As Billy motioned him into the kitchen, he could see a woman leaning into a large white refrigerator. The kitchen itself was also larger than most kitchens Thomas had seen in his neighborhood.

The floor was tiled in an off white color and the cabinets were a light stained wood color with dark green counter tops. Off to the right was a kitchen table and chairs that matched the cabinets.

Thomas watched as Billy walked up and hugged his wife from behind. She laughed and he kissed her on the cheek several times before she kissed him back. Thomas felt uneasy and didn't know what to do with him, so he looked around the room. There was nothing out of place on the counter tops and they were all wiped clean. When he located the small TV in the corner, he stared at it until Neesy and Billy were done.

"Now this young man here is Thomas Greggs," Billy said as he and Neesy approached him.

"Thomas, this is my lovely wife Neesy Johnson."

Neesy noticed that Thomas looked scared and shy as he extended his hand. Her heart went out to him because she had watched the entire tragedy that had been his life unfold on the news like everyone else. Neesy couldn't help herself. She gave Thomas a motherly sympathetic look before forcing a smile and hugging him.

Billy laughed as he saw the look of surprise on Thomas's face as she squeezed him tighter. When she let him go, she held onto his face with both hands while looking him in the eye. "You must be hungry for being on the road so long, when was the last time you ate something?"

When Thomas shrugged his shoulders, she gave Billy a stern look before leading Thomas over to one of the kitchen chairs. "You sit right here and I'll fix you some breakfast. How do you like you eggs, honey?"

Thomas looked at Billy for guidance and Billy smiled again. "You better answer her, Thomas, or she'll cook every kind you can imagine," he said and laughed out loud.

"Umm scrambled I guess; if it's not too much trouble."

"Scrambled it is, they'll be ready in a minute," Neesy replied.

When Neesy's head disappeared back inside the refrigerator, Billy stood next to Thomas and put his hand on his shoulder. "I gotta go take care of a few things," he said. You hang out here for a while with Neesy and I'll be back in a bit."

He was scared of being alone in a strange place and he was just about to ask Billy if he could go with him when Neesy poked her head up above the refrigerator door. "He'll be fine with me; you go ahead and do what you need to do."

Thomas watched as Billy left the room and then he sat quietly staring at the table, not knowing what to say. When he looked over at Neesy, he could see that she already had the eggs cooking on the stove and she was putting four pieces of bread in the toaster. Thomas watched her go back and forth, only stopping from time to time to reach her hand around and place it on her lower back. He saw her wince and pauses for a moment before moving onto to something else.

From looking at Neesy, Thomas assumed she was much younger than Billy. She was tall and thin with a light brown complexion. She had medium length straight brown hair and brown eyes. She didn't have any wrinkles whatsoever and she had perfect teeth. Thomas thought she looked a lot like the mom from *The Cosby Show*. She even sorta dressed liked her, Thomas thought to himself. She was wearing a brown pair of slacks with a yellow blouse and a white pair of tennis sneakers. On her neck was a gold chain with a cross.

When she was finished cooking, Neesy placed the plate in front of Thomas and poured him a glass of orange juice. As Thomas ate, Neesy carried on a one-sided conversation about her family. Thomas nodded his head occasionally, trying not to seem rude, but his thoughts were on the Morgans and the decision he had made to leave.

When Thomas finished eating Neesy took his plate and dumped what was left in the trash. The bag was full so she grabbed the strings and attempted to pull it out of the container. She stopped suddenly and grabbed her back.

"You need me to get that for you?" Thomas asked.

"No, I'm alright, just getting old. You just relax and watch TV; I can take care of this."

Thomas forced a smile as he looked at her with concern. "I'll get it," Thomas said as he pulled the bag out of the container. He tied the strings as he watched Neesy walk towards the sink to wash the dishes. He saw her take a deep breath before turning on the faucet and he could see the strain on her face.

She didn't even hear him come up behind him and she was startled when she heard his voice, "Don't be scared, this won't hurt."

Before she could finish saying, "What are you doing?" Thomas already had his hands on her back.

It took about 30 seconds and as soon as he let go, Neesy realized her pain was gone. She looked at Thomas with her hand covering her mouth in disbelief. For years, she had tried different treatments and medications that did nothing to relieve her back pain.

"Did you just?" Neesy asked with a look of disbelief on her face.

Thomas smiled, "Go ahead and try reaching for something."

Neesy smiled back, and cautiously reached up to grab a can off a high shelf.

"My God," Neesy said, "you *are* real!"

From that moment on Thomas and Neesy had an instant connection. She became a good friend, a mother figure and she looked out for him.

After cleaning up, Neesy took him on a tour of the rest of the house. The upstairs consisted of three large bedrooms and two bathrooms. Every room was as neat, clean and orderly as the rooms downstairs. The only difference as that all of the rooms upstairs were carpeted, with the exception of the bathrooms. Neesy and Billy's room had a brown rug, a king size bed with a beige comforter and assorted throw pillows. There were two large black dressers, another dresser with a mirror attached to it and two matching night stands on either side of the bed. Above the bed was a large wooden cross with Christ on it.

There were also various other religious statues on all of the dressers as well along with pictures of Billy and Neesy that looked as though they were taken throughout their years together.

The other rooms were just basic guest rooms, with a full size bed, a single dresser, a TV and a nightstand.

It took Thomas quite a while to adjust to life outside his small world in New Jersey. He felt terrible about how he left Kyle and Kate without an explanation. He wished he'd told them how much they meant to him.

There were so many nights within those first few weeks of being kept inside constantly that Thomas just wanted to leave and head back to the Morgans. Having time to reflect, he could almost understand how Kyle revealed his secret. He knew when it came down to it; Kate and Kyle were the only two people he could trust. He was certain that they had been offered a lot of money to tell all about him after he had gone, but they hadn't said a word.

When he found himself missing them, he would always think back to the conversation he heard between Kyle and his sister. With the media coverage all but gone now he imagined that things are just as calm for the Morgans now as they were for him. All that he wanted for them was to have peace again in their lives. This was same peace that he was now able to find.

One of the rules that Billy put in place was that Thomas he could not leave the house at all for a month or two because his picture was on every news channel. Billy also convinced Thomas to grow his hair longer and bleach it blonde. He then bought Thomas brown colored contact lenses to hide those baby blue eyes of his.

Thomas's eyesight was perfect, so this took a lot of getting used to. But over time Billy introduced 'Jeffrey' (named after Billy's favorite uncle who passed) to everyone he knew and everyone in the church.

Billy told everyone that Jeffery was a troubled young man who recently lost both parents in an automobile accident. According to the story, Jeffrey was hitchhiking along the East Coast trying to get to Florida and that Billy discovered the boy sleeping inside the church one rainy Sunday morning "So he did what any God-loving man would do." He took Jeffrey home, fed him, and offered him a place to stay.

Chapter 15

As the months went on, Jeffery had become one of the family. He started attending Sunday church and listened to all Billy's sermons. The congregation itself was entirely African American, but it spanned all ages. From what Thomas could tell, it was mostly working class types of people and entire families. They had the same thing in common and it was very obvious, they all had a very strong belief in their faith.

Thomas watched from the side of the stage most times and was amazed by the way Billy held everyone's attention. He seemed so passionate about what he was preaching and it moved Thomas as well as everyone else in the audience. Billy seemed to mean every word he was saying and he spoke in a manner that made each person feel like he was connecting directly with them.

Billy's style of preaching, if you could call it that, was to talk about ordinary living and struggles. He would talk about everyday life and intertwine it with quotes from the Bible, and he made the connection between the two seamlessly.

The few preachers Thomas had seen on TV were always screaming or jumping up and down to get the crowd to react. Billy didn't need any of that. Simple sincerity was enough.

The whole ceremony was flawless. The choir always knew the perfect song to sing and they always were right on cue. For night services, Billy would adjust the lighting himself so that the audience was in a warm dimly-lit room that created a candlelight atmosphere. The stage, on the other hand, had a lighting change with every story Billy told and every song the choir sang. Somehow, Billy always got it right and it looked perfect.

For some reason Billy was never satisfied, no matter how well things went, and this confused Thomas. Everyone left happy and the senior pastor always had a smile on his face, yet Billy always appeared to be frustrated after a service when he would talked to his brothers. Thomas would see Billy handing both of his brothers' money while shaking his head in disgust.

The business part of the church was a mystery to Thomas and he wanted no part of it. From what Thomas had gathered from hearing bit and pieces of conversations between Billy, his brothers and the senior pastor, the church was doing very well, but Billy was not getting the appreciation he felt he deserved. When he got together with his brothers he would repeat the mantra, "It's just a matter of time before we don't need any pastor or any church, we'll make the rules."

Eventually, Thomas started to help out at the church by doing odd jobs and assisting with whatever functions they would have. This meant that

Thomas was spending a lot of time with the family as well. They seemed to take accept him as one of their own and they treated him that way.

What Thomas liked most was just being around normal people in a normal family. In Virginia, with this family, he was just plain old 'Jeffery' and not, 'Thomas the amazing healing boy!'

One of the things that Thomas had come to like the most about living there was the interaction between Billy and his wife. Sure, they would have their arguments, but it was nothing like he was used to at home. In fact when Neesy and Billy argued it was always Neesy who got the last word. They reminded him more of a sitcom then a married couple.

Neesy was definitely the boss. There was no doubt about that. But they were also very affectionate with each other. There seemed to be genuine love there. Billy would always kiss her goodbye when he left and hello when he came back. They were always hugging and he saw them slow dance a time or two in the kitchen.

Billy would always say to Thomas, "Boy that woman is a big pain in my ass, but I love her!"

The only issue he could see between them was that Billy would spend a lot of time out of the house. Neesy told Thomas that there was a lot of church-related work that required his attention. Thomas asked to go and help out several times, but Billy would tell him that it was related to the 'business part of the church' and that he wouldn't be of any help.

Thomas noticed that on those nights when Billy went out, Neesy always seemed depressed. She would spend the night with Thomas either playing cards, or a board game or just watching TV. Thomas didn't mind it at all because he loved spending time alone with Neesy. She was one of the easiest people to talk to that he ever met. He could confide in her and talk to her about everything. She had such a way of putting him at ease, just like his mother did.

During one of their card nights the discussion of death came up.

Neesy believed "When it was your time it was your time." She believed it in her heart and she told Thomas on more then on occasion that "God has a plan for everyone."

She then confided in Thomas that her mother had passed three years ago and that it devastated her. Neesy's father left her mother before she was born. For as long as she could remember, her mother worked nights. When Neesy was an infant and toddler, her mother would take care of her during the day, only sleeping when her daughter would go down for a nap too.

When Neesy was old enough to go to school, her mother would make her breakfast, put her on the bus and then sleep until she got home. When she got home it was homework, dinner and then bath time. Then every night at 9 p.m. her mother would her them off at Mrs. Keenston's down the hall.

Neesy's mother wanted her so bad to be a doctor and encouraged her to go to college. They became her goals as well until she met Billy during her senior in high school.

"My mother had told me that we were getting a new preacher at the church and that he had three sons that were around my age," Neesy told Thomas. "Next thing I know Bernie, Jerry and Billy are going to my high school.

"Now my mother was always a spiritual person, Thomas. She dressed me up and took me to church every Sunday without fail. My mother would always get so mad at me when I would fidget in my chair. She would tap me on the leg and give me 'the look,' which was always followed by her saying "Listen for once, you might learn something."

"I remember there being such a buzz around town before Reverend Marshall was even in town. People who had seen him during their travels referred to him as flashy and full of energy. When he finally made it town, he replaced the entire choir on the first day. He said it was time for a fresh new start and he wanted people who matched his energy. It was a really surprising move, but the town responded positively by packing the church for the first time in a long time."

"As I looked around during his first service, I could see that the old guard was sitting together on the right hand side of the church looking agitated and cynical. But everyone else was newcomers.

"I went to that same church every Sunday and there weren't more than 25 people at most on a good day. But on this day, it was standing room only.

"I remember I was talking to my girlfriend in the row behind me when suddenly the Reverend Marshall's voice came booming over the church speakers, but he was nowhere to be seen. 'Thank you all for coming ladies and gentlemen, today is a new day so give thanks to God', he said. The new choir came in and started singing before Reverend Marshall made his big flashy entrance. It was like nothing we had ever seen in our town.

"The reverend was dressed in a canary yellow suit with no tie. He was completely bald and he had a black goatee, and he was wearing three big gold chains around his neck. One was a chain that had just a plain gold cross on it, another was a chain with Jesus' head on it and the last was a big gold plate with the words, 'In Marshall We Trust' engraved on it.

"He asked everyone to be seated before picking up the Bible, kissing it; then putting it back down. He preached the whole night without looking at it once. The old guard hated it-- in fact my mother complained the whole time-- but the new folks came back again and again because it was unlike anything that had seen.

"Eventually, I met Billy and found out that he was already very involved in every aspect at the church. He helped script most of the sermons his father preached and nobody knew it. Besides the physical attraction, I was also attracted to the amount of ambition he already possessed.

"I had to try and try to get his attention. Billy had the same personality as his father and everyone liked him, especially the girls. When he finally introduced himself and we got to spend some time talking, we hit it off right away. People talk a lot about finding their soul mate, but I knew soon after meeting him, that he was mine.

"Now my mother wasn't found of the Reverend Marshall at all--she referred to him as a used car salesmen or a game show host. She didn't care much for his sons either. There was a rumor around town was that they were sleeping with every teenage girl that attended the church. So my mother forbade me from having anything to do with any of them.

"Of course, this made her me to get to know Billy even more, because there sure weren't any characters in town like the Wilson men. We had been dating about a month behind my mother's back before the news broke that Billy's father had been arrested for stealing from the church.

"The next day, Billy was gone and I didn't see him again for another two years.

"When he returned, he hooked back up with his brothers. I heard he had changed his name and that he begged the church to let him preach there. He explained to them again and again how he had no knowledge at all about his father's thefts.

"It took him almost a year of volunteering at the church and helping out at all of their events before he earned their trust back. Six months after that, he was not only back preaching at the church, he was the only preacher they had.

"He had to work to get me back too, but not that hard," Neesy said with a smile.

"I was in college living on campus and Billy would come up to spend every weekend with me. We had to date in secret because my mother would never approve. The truth finally came out when I had to tell my mother I was pregnant and Billy was the father. I told her I was leaving school for a year and then I would go back.

"Thomas, I thought my mother would have had a heart attack and disown me when I told her. Instead she told me that she knew all along that I was with Billy again, she had heard the rumor around town. She looked me in the eye and asked if I truly loved Billy and if he made me happy, and I said that he did.

"I was shocked when the next words of her of mouth were, 'When will you be married?' She gave me that look again and said that she could tolerate a lot of things, but her daughter having a baby out of wedlock wasn't one of them.

"We were married almost three months later to the day."

Thomas looked confused all of the sudden and Neesy knew what was coming next.

"We lost the baby during birth," Neesy said while sniffling. "He was two and half months premature and he was stillborn."

"I'm so sorry," Thomas said.

Neesy put her hand on Thomas's shoulder and said, "It took some time, but I've gotten over it.

I told you, God has a plan and a child was not part of mine." Neesy told Thomas that Billy took it really hard and that they tried several times but it just wasn't meant to be. Thomas nodded and forced a smile. He had come to respect and admire Neesy so much over such a short time and she had become very dear to him.

"Well, where was I?" Neesy said. "Oh yes, back to my mom, like I said, she passed three and a half years ago and it was tough for me. I won't lie Thomas; I was in a state that I thought I might not be able to come back from.

"I spoke to her on the phone one day and she was asking when we were coming for a visit. I was busy doing stuff around the house, so I blew her off and told her within the next few months I would visit her. She died three weeks later from a massive heart attack.

"I thought of that last conversation I had with her a million times. I tortured myself with thoughts of how I wished I would have told her that I loved her one more time; instead I was worried about getting dinner done before Billy got home.

"That was a tough time, Thomas, and you know what brought me back? Some people just got up and sang some of her favorite songs or cried. They also told stories and spoke of sweet memories of my mother. It really helped the healing process and I can't thank him enough for that."

Thomas could see that she really meant every word she was saying.

"So I know what you went through, Thomas, and what you're still going through. I want you to know that you are family now. We are here for you to talk to, to laugh with or to cry with. Whatever you need, Thomas, you aren't alone."

Thomas looked away as the tears started to build in his eyes, and Neesy came over to hug him.

Just then Billy walked into the room. "Is uh, everything ok?" he asked when he noticed Thomas and Neesy crying and hugging.

Thomas let go first and wiped his tears quickly with his sleeve. He didn't like to cry around men, because his father would always tell him to "toughen up" if he ever saw tears. Nessy could see that Thomas was embarrassed, so she looked over at Billy and said, "Everything's fine" as she stepped away from him.

She noticed that Billy was giving her the "what the hell is going on?" look, so she waited until Thomas went into the other room.

She then whispered to Billy, "It was nothing, we were talking about his mom and he got upset."

Billy nodded and checked if he could see Thomas around the corner. "Well is he all right?" Billy wanted to know. "Because I have to talk to him about appearing at the church on Sunday. I want to get this whole mission thing going."

"Give it a few hours, maybe after dinner," Neesy said. "Don't bother him with it right now, ok?"

Billy sighed then shook his head. "Ok, I'll wait," he said, "but this is important, Neesy. It's going to change all of our lives. We are going to preach the word and heal people all over the country, you watch."

Neesy knew that look too, it was Billy's excited, "I want the world to know me!" look. She grabbed his face and kissed him on the lips. "After dinner," she said.

Billy was pleased to see that the talk Thomas had with Neesy must have done him some good. When he came down for dinner, he was in a much better mood and he seemed really relaxed. Billy waited until Thomas excused himself and was heading into the living room before he approached him.

"Thomas, do remember when we first met and I spoke to you about a purpose?" Billy asked after they stepped out the back door and onto the screened porch.

Thomas laughed a little. "You with the 'purpose' and Neesy with the 'God's plan,'" he said while making the quotation signs.

Billy laughed and said, "Well, it all kinda ties together when you think about it. Thomas, there are signs in this world that we can't ignore and they are meant to show us the path we were meant to take. You were given a gift and we were meant to meet, this I am sure of.

"Now my path has shown me that I was meant to spread his word to the masses, and you? Well that gift of yours was given so that you could heal, Thomas. There lies your path."

Thomas didn't respond. He just stared straight ahead lost in thought. Billy wasn't sure which way it would go, so he decided that he was really going to have to sell it to Thomas. He knew Neesy wouldn't approve of his methods, so he took a quick look inside before continuing.

Billy got up, sat down next to Thomas and placed his hand on the boy's shoulder while looking him in the eyes. "Thomas, what happened to your mother and father was tragedy. I know you would give anything to go back in time and do it all differently."

When the blank stare vanished and his expression turned to anger, Billy could tell that hit a nerve.

"I can't go back, though," Thomas said angrily. "And I will never be forgiven for what I've done."

Thomas matched Billy's stare. "You know, I hear all of your sermons. I listened closely to each one when you talk about the grace of God. Why is there no grace for me then?" Thomas demanded. "God hates me and this is a curse, not a gift. Don't you see that?"

Billy could see that Thomas was coming unglued, so he switched gears and took a gentler approach.

"What about that boy Henry you saved, Thomas?" Billy asked. "That was a selfless act and you made a huge difference in that family's life with you ability. I could see it in your face as I watched on TV, you felt good about what you were able to do for that boy."

Thomas was just about to say something when Billy cut him off.

"Thomas, there are men, woman and children in this world who are sick or dying. Some of them are beyond medical assistance and some can't pay for the help they so desperately need. There are also people out there who have injured themselves and can no longer work to provide for their families, people who pray every day for a miracle. Maybe just maybe, God wants *you* to be that miracle, Thomas.

"Maybe you haven't used your gift as you should have, maybe you using that card I gave you and coming here was one of those signs I was telling you about? I thought I knew what my purpose was, Thomas, but then you came here and it was another sign for me that my purpose has changed."

Billy could see Thomas was taking it all in and he knew he had to seal the deal. "You know what Thomas? If we do this, there just might be forgiveness for us both in time."

"What do you need forgiveness for?" Thomas asked.

Billy lowered his head and let out a sigh. He then stared off into the distance for a moment before looking back at Thomas.

"We all have done things we are not proud of Thomas," he said. "I'd be lying if I said there wasn't a skeleton or two in my closet."

Thomas nodded as if he understood and forced a smile.

Billy nodded in agreement, and then stood up to go back into the house.

"If I do this," Thomas said, "everything will change for you and your family. They'll keep coming and they won't stop. That's why I had to leave the Morgans. They made their lives unbearable."

"What about you, Thomas, how did all that attention affect you?" Billy asked.

Thomas paused and thought about it for a minute because it was a question that he had never considered before now. "To tell you the truth, there was a part of me that actually liked it a little after I helped that boy," Thomas said sounding embarrassed. "The crowd was cheering afterwards and I really felt important.

"But there is another part of me who likes the quiet normal life with you and your family. I feel like if I start healing people, then I can never have the normal back and neither will you or Neesy."

Billy smiled, walked up close to Thomas and put his hand on his shoulder. "Look, I don't do anything without a plan, Thomas, Neesy will tell you that. I have one in place to take care of everything you mentioned. I already have things in place to protect you and the family; you can trust me on that.

"As far as you getting to live the normal life, well there can still be a Jeffrey. We can buy wigs and disguises so you can go out when you want to, just like the celebrities do."

"What does Neesy think about all of this?" Thomas asked.

Billy responded by laughing and saying, "Son, do you think I can even go to the bathroom without checking with that woman?"

They then both laughed together.

"I'll let you know tomorrow, ok?" Thomas said.

"Sounds good," Billy replied.

After staying up most of the night thinking about it, Thomas decided that what Billy had said made sense. It just might be the only path for him towards forgiveness and understanding why he was given this gift.

The next morning at breakfast, Thomas told Billy he would do it.

Billy's next move was to call the local newspaper and TV news station and tell them that Thomas Greggs, The Healer, had contacted him. He told them that any media personnel were invited to see firsthand the start of what he referred to as The Mission. He then explained that The Mission would consist of him preaching the word of God followed by a healing session for the faithful conducted by none other than Thomas Greggs.

An hour later the story was on every major network.

Chapter 16

During the years since Thomas' disappearance, neither Kate nor Kyle had forgotten him. But they moved on with their lives.

Kate changed the day her father almost died. She went from being a carefree teenager who loved to hang out with friends and party to a responsible young adult who sometimes took life way too seriously. After Thomas left, she realized that her father was all she had in the world and she would not risk losing him again. For a while, it was almost as if the roles were reversed and Kate had become the parent. Whenever she was out or late coming home from school, Kate would call and check on her father.

Kyle would reassure her time after time that he was cured and that he never felt better, but Kate couldn't get that day out her head and remembered how close she was to being alone.

The doctors insisted on re-testing Kyle over and over for months because they could not believe he was cured. Kate was there waiting for him every time. It was always the same routine: Kyle would have to reassure his daughter and show her the latest test results.

Kate still thought of Thomas every day. She missed seeing him at her house, she missed talking with him in her room, and she missed the feeling of knowing he had her back, no matter what she was going through. She would always love him like a brother and she would be forever grateful to him for what he had done.

About a year after Thomas disappeared, Kate started dating Matt Housen. They met him when she started working part time at the local Kmart to make some extra money while she attended college. Matt was the night manager and they hit it off the very first night she started.

Kyle did not approve at all because Matt was much older and he had a place of his own. By the middle of her junior year at Montclair State University, six months into the relationship, Kate was pregnant. Matt convinced her to take a few years off from school and move in with him.

As it was with her first love, Kate fell head over heels for Matt. She blew off all her friends and stopped listening to her father. She was instantly attracted to him because he seemed so different than all of the guys that were her age. He seemed so mature and he had a great personality. He was tall, 6 foot 3, and he was in great shape. He had blonde hair that was long in the front and short in the back. He also had hazel green eyes that would seem to change colors, going from darker to lighter depending on his mood.

All of the female cashiers had the hots for him, but Kate was the one he always hung around with during her shift. Although she lied to her father about dating Matt, she just assumed that he would come around when he found out she was pregnant. One the cat was out of the bag; Kate assured her father that she would go back to school as soon as the baby was old enough.

Kyle fought her every step of the way, but she was over 18 and there was nothing he could do about it. Kyle believed he had lost his daughter to some jerk and now he was living alone.

Kyle wasn't alone for long though, because it was a month and a half later that Kyle had started seeing someone. Even Kyle was surprised at how quickly it became semi-serious. Sharon was unlike anyone Kyle had ever met. They just seemed to click from the beginning.

Sharon was a divorcee with no children of her own who had survived a car wreck on the interstate that killed four other people. She was pronounced dead at the scene and then resuscitated. She spent the next two months in a coma and wasn't expected to make it.

Sharon had read all of the stories about Thomas and the Morgans. She decided one day to write Kyle and tell him how he should now appreciate life more than ever.

She wrote the words to her favorite poem and signed it, "Happy birthday, you've been born again, good luck and God bless, Sharon."

Kyle wrote back and it wasn't long before they were talking on the phone for hours. Eventually they met for dinner and Kyle was smitten the moment he saw her. On the night they met, Kyle waited nervously in front of the restaurant for Sharon to arrive. He was dressed business casual, wearing a pair of brown slacks with a blue long-sleeve button-down shirt.

As every woman approached the restaurant, he felt a knot in his stomach. He hadn't felt like this in a long time and it actually felt really good to him. He wondered if there would be a physical attraction. They had gotten along so well on the phone and they already knew everything about each other. She sent him a picture, but Kyle was afraid it was taken years ago or it was her sister or something. He had seen a lot of daytime talk shows where they surprise people with their secret crushes and it turned out to be someone totally different than they said they were.

Kyle had no need to worry. When Sharon came around the building from the parking lot, she looked exactly like her picture -- even better, Kyle thought to himself as he smiled.

She had long brown hair that was halfway down her back. It looked as if it was a perm, because she had a natural curl. She was 5 foot 1, 125 lbs, and she wore very little makeup because she had a very natural, "girl next door" type of beauty. She stood in front of Kyle smiling, which made her even more attractive to him because her blue eyes seemed to sparkle in the light. She was dressed in a pair of form- fitting black slacks and a red blouse.

Martin was at a loss for words as she reached out to give him a hug. He still refers to that night out as one of the best dates he ever had.

They decided to take things slow and just enjoy each other's company, but instead things turned serious in a hurry. Sharon would tell him often that it was fate that brought them together.

Kyle assumed that the reason the connection was so strong from the start was that they both had come so close to the end. At their age and from what they had endured, neither one wanted to waste time playing games of the heart. Kyle knew that this was something that Kate would have to get used to. She would eventually see what a great woman Sharon was and everything would be fine.

The first time he introduced Sharon to Kate there was some tension. Kyle had dated other women after his wife left, but he never brought any of them around Kate. He had never felt serious enough about any of them to want to bring them into his daughter's life only to have them disappear if things didn't work out.

But now at this point of his life, Kyle didn't want to be alone. He never felt like he needed someone until Sharon came along. He was able to appreciate the gift of life he was given with her because she was the only person who could truly understand what he had been through. She seemed to understand everything about him and he loved her for it.

Kyle still thought about Thomas a lot too and wondered what became of him. He was forever in his debt but he couldn't help but think how much better things got for him after he left. When he would discuss this with Sharon she would always say, "Everything happens for a reason."

"If that were true," Kyle thought, "then what is the reason for Kate meeting that scumbag Matt?"

"At least he makes her happy," Kyle decided.

Sharon taught Kyle that he should always remember to appreciate his life and those who are a part of it, no matter what the circumstances are.

Sometimes it was hard to stick to that rule. When Kate told him she was pregnant and leaving college, he was beyond angry and he was beyond disappointed. The only thing that stopped him from completely losing his cool was the frightened look in his daughter's eyes. He could tell she was confused by everything that was happening so he forced a smile and told her everything would be fine. Shortly after that conversation, Matt and Kate got a place of their own.

It didn't take Kyle long to notice there were problems because he still saw his daughter almost as much as he did when she was living with him. One of the issues was that Kate wanted to be married before the baby was born, but Matt was against it. He said he wanted to wait until after the baby was born because that should be their first priority. Kyle knew it was bullshit, but he was ok with this because he had a feeling that Matt wasn't the marrying kind -- or the fatherly kind, for that matter.

Kate and Sharon's relationship had gotten better after Kate moved out. They would sit for hours at the kitchen table long after Kyle had gotten tired of talking and headed for the TV. They would go shopping together often and to the movies together every other weekend.

Kyle knew there was trouble when Kate started spending the night over his house more and more often. The initial excuse was the Matt was staying out late and she didn't want to be alone, but eventually there wasn't even a reason. She would just bring a bag and stay for a few days.

Kyle became frustrated and he argued often with Kate over how much Matt was going out during the course of her pregnancy. Things would get heated and Sharon would always have to be the referee, stopping things just before one of them said something that they couldn't take back.

Kyle would always end up feeling bad and apologizing because he loved his daughter. The last thing in the world he wanted to do was to upset her. He would wait until after she left then he would complain for hours to Sharon, expressing his concern for the welfare of his daughter and grandchild in a curse-filled tirade. Sharon was great, she was the perfect balance for Kyle and she always made him see things rationally. He respected her and she was his best friend.

Kyle had asked Sharon to move into his big empty house several times, but she always refused. She liked having her own space, and there was Ms. Fluffy to consider. The poodle was her baby, but Kyle hated it. Sharon had Ms. Fluffy groomed regularly, and she cooked the dog meals for dinner. She couldn't count the times where Kyle would be over at her condo and he would watch her do things for the dog then say, "C'mon, you gotta be kiddin' me!"

There was also the fact that Ms. Fluffy didn't care for men, especially Kyle. The dog would bark the whole entire time he was there and this drove him nuts. Kyle thought the dog would stop after she had seen him several times, but it didn't.

Sharon would always say, "Ms. Fluffy is old and set in her ways, she doesn't like change."

Kyle would respond by saying that, "Ms. Fluffy was an old bitch." And he would laugh hysterically. Sharon would be to shake her head and say "Don't you talk that way about Ms. Fluffy."

It had gotten to the point where Ms. Fluffy would have to get locked in a room when Kyle was over. That didn't stop her from barking, though.

It was 9 p.m. on a Saturday night and the three of them were together at Kyle's house watching TV. Kate had started to doze off when the news broke in with a special report: "Thomas Greggs, AKA The Healer, has reappeared!"

Kate, who was now eight months pregnant, suddenly sat straight up, instantly awake. "Dad, get in here now, hurry!" she yelled. Of course Kyle thought the baby was coming early, so he froze for a second and thought of what he would need to do before running into the other room to check on her. When he got there, he was confused to see Sharon and Kate sitting side by side looking at the TV.

"Are you ok, Kate?" Kyle asked.

Kate looked at her father with a big smile on her face and said, "Look, it's Thomas."

"For those of you just tuning in," the reporter said, "Thomas Greggs, AKA The Healer, has come out of seclusion after disappearing over two years ago. Leslie Mcgee is onsite with the details."

The pictured changed and now there was now a blonde field reporter standing outside of a small white church. "That's correct," she said. "Two years after disappearing from a house in West Orange, New Jersey, Thomas Greggs, now 18 and a half years old, has resurfaced in Landstown, Virginia.

"This story broke late yesterday when we received word that Greggs will be part of what is being called 'The Mission'. It will be headed by the Reverend William Johnson."

The camera cut away from the anchor for a moment and a picture of Billy appeared on the screen.

"According to Johnson, there will be a sermon and something referred to as a quote, 'Healing Session' at the Baptist church behind me, which ironically enough is named The Faith and Hope Baptist Church. This will all take place on Sunday, April 21, at 7 p.m.

"As you can imagine, reporters from everywhere are converging on the Reverend William Johnson's property trying to catch a glimpse of Thomas. This story promises to be a big one indeed. We will be back with more details and they come in. Now back to you in the studio."

Kate and Kyle were frozen speechless, staring at the TV. "Are you two ok?" Sharon asked.

There was an awkward silence and then Kyle said, "Wait, I know that guy in the picture! He was at the funeral for Marie, Thomas's mother," Kyle explained. "I saw him talking to Thomas, but when I approached to ask who he was, he got up and walked away before I got too close..."

Kate got up without saying a word and hurried by Sharon to the get the phone.

"What are you doing, honey?" Kyle asked as he stepped out of the way.

"What do you mean, what am I doing?" Kate said as she picked up the receiver. "I'm calling him, what do you think?"

Kate dialed information and asked for the number of Billy Johnson in Landstown, Virginia.

Kate held up one finger and jotted down a phone number on a napkin. She then hung up the phone and looked at her father.

"I want to talk to him Dad," she said. "I just want to know if he's ok, that's it."

Kate stood with the phone to her ear as Kyle watched. She mouthed the word 'answering machine' then spoke, "This message is for Thomas Greggs, please see that he gets it.

"Thomas, this is Kate Morgan, we saw you on the news and we would really like to talk to you. We just want to make sure you are all right and hear your voice. Call us back Thomas, we miss you."

Thomas never called because he didn't get the message. Ever since he contacted the press, Billy started monitoring and screening all of the calls.

Billy didn't want to take the chance this late in the game that Thomas would have a change of heart and go back to New Jersey.

Chapter 17

A few days later back in Virginia, the first day of The Mission was upon them. Thomas sat in a back room of the church, watching TV and biting his nails. Bernie had to change the channel twice because the news kept breaking in with live feeds from outside of the church. Thomas was nervous enough and it was Bernie's job to keep him company and keep him calm.

But even with only a brief glimpse of the news, you could see that it was controlled chaos outside.

The church only seated 200 and filled up in a matter of minutes once the door opened. A thousand or so more people who didn't get in were still lined up outside, hoping that they would be let in at some point. There were several police officers on site, but nowhere near enough so they concentrated their efforts on not letting anyone else in the building.

Thomas peeked out several times while the people were being seated and he was very intimidated by the many faces in the crowd. In his panic, he had trouble breathing and suffered bad stomach cramps.

Thomas had such mixed emotions about what was going to happen. He wanted to get it over with and wondered why he let Billy talk him into this, but there was another part of him that hoped this might be the first step in his redemption.

"Maybe Billy was right," Thomas thought to himself. "Maybe this is what I was meant to do."

Billy seemed to be energized by the size of the crowd and the enthusiasm they were showing. He was so much more animated then usual during his sermon and he involved the crowd more than he had ever done in the past. On top of that, the choir he had assembled was incredible; unlike anything Thomas had ever seen or heard.

Billy's plan was to change everything for The Mission. He didn't use one person from the regular church choir, even though it offended some of the long-time members. It didn't matter to Billy that many of them had been in the choir long before he had joined the church; The Mission was the only thing that mattered. Billy had been planning for this day for years and nothing was going to get in his way.

Thomas moved away from the TV and started to pace back and forth. He had started to sweat through his shirt, so he headed to the fridge to get bottled water. Jerry bumped into him on his way into the room and then put his hands on Thomas's shoulders.

"Hey man, it's crazy out there!" he said. "I ain't never seen nothing like this and Billy is on fire tonight!"

Thomas moved away from him and looked towards to hallway.

"Take a look, there ain't a spot to sit or stand out there!" Jerry said. "Hell, there's even a huge crowd of people outside who couldn't get in. The cops are out there too, but they can barely keep everyone back. Not to mention, I couldn't even count the number of news trucks there are out there!"

Thomas's head began to spin. His only response was a half-hearted "Wow." He wondered if Jerry could pick up on the fact that he wasn't as into this as everyone else seemed to be. Thomas was nervous and he was afraid he'd throw up. Jerry must have picked up on his anxiety a little because he patted Thomas on the back and gave him a big smile. "You'll be fine, Thomas," he said. "I'll come back to get you in a few minutes, so get ready, ok?"

Thomas nodded and forced himself to smile.

Jerry had only been out of the room a few seconds when Thomas heard him yell from the other room. "Holy shit, look at all the people back here too! This is beyond crazy, man!"

Thomas walked down the hallway and found Jerry in the kitchen. They both stared out the back window. There were people everywhere, and three policemen near the back door motioned for them to keep back. A man in the crowd looked in the church window at just that moment and made eye contact with Thomas. He shouted, "Look, there he is! It's him!"

The crowd's reaction was almost instantaneous. The mass of people began to push toward the building and the police were helpless to stop them. Before they even had time to call for help, the back door was pushed open and all hell broke loose inside.

Billy's nephew Michael and two of his friends were nearby when it happened so they rushed to the door and began pushing people back outside. When Michael yelled for help, Bernie, Jerry and several of their other cousins rushed in to help them. It took several minutes, but they managed to get them out and lock the door.

"Holy shit!" Jerry yelled. "They're everywhere now."

Word quickly reached Billy and he immediately took action to make sure things didn't get any more out of hand. He cut his sermon short and had the choir keep singing to try to maintain order in the building while he ran to the back to see what was happening.

When he reached Michael, he was covered in sweat but he was calm. Billy grabbed his arm and looked him in the eye. "Listen to me, you find a room and keep Thomas safe inside until the cops get things under control, you hear me?" Billy said sternly.

Michael was Bernie's son. He was a year older then Thomas and he was what Billy referred to as 'a Big Boy'. Michael was 6 foot 4 and 300 lbs -- most of it was muscle. Billy thought his size alone would be enough to keep people from rushing the stage when Thomas was on, that's why he brought him on board with the mission. The problem was that Michael didn't have a violent bone in his body. He was a big teddy bear. In fact that was Bernie's pet name for him, 'Big Bear'.

"I'm counting on you Big Bear," Billy said. "We're watching the doors now, the cops are out there and I'm sure more are coming. No one's getting in here, you hear me?"

Michael nodded in agreement and Billy playfully tapped him on the cheek twice. "Ya done good kid, you hear me?" Bill said. "Now tell me you can handle this and get Thomas out of here."

"Yeah, yeah uncle, I'm fine, I got this," Michael said, trying to sound confident and tough.

"Good man, Good man," Billy said and patted him on the back as he walked past.

It was another tense hour and 45 minutes before order was restored. It wasn't long before more police cars arrived on the scene and traffic cops were directing cars off the street. News vans and helicopters were everywhere. Billy, Michael, Thomas, Bernie, and Jerry sat alone in the church's basement kitchen. Four of the five men were exhausted by the day's events. But not Billy, he was pouring himself a glass of wine and humming while doing so.

"What a day," he said to Thomas. "How are you holding up, kid?"

"What a mess," Thomas said as he wiped the sweat from his forehead. "We're never going to be able to do this," he said, sounding defeated.

Billy smiled from ear to ear, "Have faith my son."

Thomas gave up trying to read Billy's mind a long time ago, so he just shook his head and smiled back. Billy then sipped his wine while he watched the small TV that was on the counter top.

"Things are pretty clear out there now," he said. "Thomas, I'm going to have Michael take you outta here. Go get some rest, you look beat. The reporters think you slipped out early on, so they're long gone. "I booked you, me and Neesy a couple of nice hotel rooms a few towns over for a few days. We'll lie low for a bit before going home."

Michael pushed his chair out from the table then stood up. "I'm outta here, you ready man?" he said to Thomas.

Thomas nodded and left with Michael, but he couldn't understand why Billy seemed so happy after the first day of The Mission turned into such a fiasco.

Billy walked with them upstairs and watched until they drove away.

When returned to the basement to join his brothers he yelled out, "Whoa, what a day, boys!"

"What the hell are you so happy about?" Bernie asked. "That was clusterfuck, man!"

"A clusterfuck?" Billy yelled as he laughed. "A clusterfuck? That, my dear brothers, was the greatest commercial and advertisement you could ever dream of!"

"I'm lost, man," Jerry said, "did you say commercial?"'

"Boys, boys, boys," Billy said as he walked behind them, crouched down between where they were sitting and put an arm around each of them. "That's why I'm the brains of the operation," he said.

"Look, I knew from the day the story broke about Thomas healing that kid, that this was going to be huge. The media attention he got, the way people started turning out from everywhere? Do you think I really expected this little church would hold all of the people who would come out for this?" Still confused, Jerry and Bernie looked at each other to see if the other was following their older brother's explanation.

"I had a pretty good idea what was going to go down today," Billy said. "I also knew that someone out there would see the potential here to make a lot of money and want to back us as a partner with some capital. By the way, I got that call an hour ago while you guys were down here hiding."

Billy looked at both of his brothers and expected to see the same smile on their faces that he had on his. They still didn't understand his genius, though. Billy poured them each a glass of wine as he continued to explain.

"These backers want to give us enough capital to bring the mission to arenas and stadiums. We can use them to get where we want to get to and to get the things we need for the production. We can use them until we make enough money where we'll be self-sufficient. At that point, my not-too-bright brothers, we will have it made!"

When they didn't react right away Billy said, "This is it boys, the big time!"

He held out his glass and they all toasted, "To the big time!"

The next day Billy sat Thomas down and explained to him that things were changing and growing faster than even he thought they would.

Thomas was concerned and so was Neesy. She had no idea that so many people would come to the church and that it would get out of control so quickly. She knew they were all there for Thomas, but she had no idea how desperate some people were.

Her night started with watching Billy preach while sitting in the front row. When things got out of hand and she heard that people started to rush into the back of the church, Neesy tried to find Thomas to see if he was ok.

She couldn't get to him though because there were wall-to-wall people everywhere.

Billy told her to remain up front in her seat, so she trusted him and did so.

It didn't take long before the police came in and cleared the church because it had become a safety issue. She stayed with Billy until he had another one of his nephews drive her to the hotel.

It wasn't until later that night that she finally got to check on Thomas to make sure he was ok. She stayed with him a while in his room talking to him and trying to explain to him why things went so wrong. She was surprised to see that he wasn't rattled or upset. He just seemed relieved that it was over.

After she left Thomas, she went into her room to express her concerns to Billy. Neesy was surprised at what a good mood Billy was in after witnessing how the whole thing fell apart.

"I don't get it," she said. "Tonight was a disaster, but you seem fine, what gives?"

Billy smiled and kissed Neesy on the lips.

"Yes, it didn't go well today at all," he said, "That ain't no lie. "I knew there was a chance that people would come out of the woodwork because of what Thomas can do, but I had no idea that many would come. But that helped us in a way, too, Neesy. Cause now we know the truth and the truth is we can't do what we need to do in some local church. If we are going to continue on, we are going to have to get organized and move things to a bigger, more secure environment."

Neesy knew Billy only mentioned things when there was already a plan in motion. "Meaning what?" she asked.

Billy flashed that crocked smile again because he knew he couldn't get anything past his wife. He took her hand and he explained everything to her. He told her how several corporate sponsors contacted him and that they all to want to invest in the mission. The mission would travel across the U.S. to various arenas and stadiums. All of the expenses for things like security, travel, food and lodging would be arranged and paid for by the sponsors. They would also take care of planning the dates and all of the bookings.

Billy made sure to stress to Neesy that he would be involved in all mission-related decisions, nothing would happen without his consent and the best part was that the family would be drawing a salary based on attendance as well as merchandising.

"It's a free ride, Neesy," he said. "We will be able to travel across the country spreading the word and helping people. But there is no reason we can't do it in style," he said with a laugh. "We can find jobs for everyone within the mission so the whole family can come on the road."

Billy knew Neesy was a homebody and she didn't care much for traveling, so he followed it up by saying, "It's a sign Neesy, don't you see, this is all happening for a reason. Thomas coming here was no accident, this is my purpose, and this is what I've always dreamed of doing".

Neesy could see the excitement in her husband's eyes and she could hear the passion in his voice. Billy really wanted this and he was going to make it happen come hell or high water. Even though she had her doubts, she loved her husband and she trusted him. She also couldn't deny that there were many signs that something special was happening.

Within days, Billy hired his entire family and gave them all positions within the mission. At first everyone would be traveling together.

Billy had a plan, though. He knew which people would tire quickly of life on the road and return home. His wife was part of that group as well as a four or five others. Billy planned way ahead for how they would be replaced when the time came so they wouldn't miss a beat.

Billy didn't want Neesy to travel with The Mission at least not permanently. It had always been his dream to be one of the well-known preachers that were on TV. He envied them so much because they were rich and known around the country or even the world in some instances. Billy wanted that so much and all of the fringe benefits that came along with it.

He worked with the sponsors so that each quarter there would be a two-week break so everyone involved in the mission could either take a vacation or return home. Neesy wanted more time, but Billy told her for the first year at least that it wasn't possible. He promised that when the mission was more successful and he had more control they would be traveling a lot less. Of course that was a lie. While it was part of Billy's plan to gain total control of The Mission, he also wanted to extend it to the point where they were traveling across the globe.

Chapter 18

They stayed at the hotel for a week while Billy arranged for his sponsors to rent what would soon be referred to everyone as The Mission Compound. Billy pulled no punches with the sponsors because he knew exactly how much money they were going to be making on a regular basis once the mission hit the road. He told everyone who would listen that security and privacy were the most important issues for The Mission Family when they weren't on road. He wanted guarantees that both would be taken seriously before they went on tour. It didn't take long at all before Billy got exactly what he wanted and he knew this was just the first step of what would be The Mission Empire.

The Ferlong Estate, located 30 minutes outside of Washington D.C., was mostly rented to government officials and visiting foreign dignitaries. On occasion it was also rented to very wealthy celebrities who would visit the capital with their families during summer vacations.

The estate was on a private road that didn't appear on any map. The road itself and the house were designed to not visible from the nearby highway. You had to turn at a certain mile marker onto what appeared to be a gravel service road. After driving through the woods for a mile, you approached the large iron gate and the stone wall that surrounded the entire estate.

Two guards were always on duty at the guard station, along with four others that would patrol the grounds when visitors were present. They were all former marines who were trained to handle just about any situation. Billy checked everything out for himself before agreeing to the location.

Once inside the gate you could see the two large mansions up ahead with the two smaller buildings on either side of them. The mansions were to be the living quarters for Billy's entire family, which made up the majority of the mission staff.

The buildings were identical, with eight bedrooms each, seven bathrooms, a fireplace on each floor located in the sitting room, a finished basement with a large secluded apartment, an indoor heated pool and three indoor Jacuzzis. Both kitchens had hired chefs on call from 6 a.m. to 7 p.m. and both houses had fully-staffed cleaning crews.

The two other buildings which were known as Three and Four were both two story rectangular office buildings. Building Three consisted of a conference center on the second floor and an office area on the first floor. Building Four had a complete modern gym on the first floor and a full size movie theater on the second floor.

Neesy was furious because she knew nothing about these plans or negotiations. The last thing on earth she wanted to do was leave behind the house that she was born and raised in. They argued for hours until Neesy told Billy to leave her behind.

Billy quickly countered by turning into the preacher. He told her how many people they would be able to help and how he could now live his dream spreading the word to the masses. He then assured her it was for her and everyone else's safety and that it would only be for a few months until things died down.

But things didn't die down; they only got worse. The Mission was about to take off in a big way and Billy knew things would never be the same. He had no intention of returning to the old hand-me-down house. None of that would be good for him ever again.

For weeks, Billy was hardly ever around. He attended every meeting with anyone who was involved with the production of The Mission, no matter how trivial it was.

He was involved in selecting which charter bus company they would use, which hotels they would be staying in, which vendors they would use for concessions, merchandising, even choosing everyone's wardrobes. During the entire process, Billy was always listening and learning because his main goal was to eliminate the sponsors eventually and take control.

When the first night of The Mission was rescheduled, Billy knew he would have to sit and talk with Thomas the day before their first engagement at the Raddison Arena in Norfolk, Virginia to discuss his preparation for the event.

At the first church event, Thomas showed up wearing a pair of jeans, a white long sleeve button down shirt and a pair of brown shoes. Billy did not say anything because the odds were Thomas wouldn't even make it to the stage.

But this was the real deal and for this, Billy had planned everything to the last detail. This was not some rinky-dink small town church that holds a hundred people or so, this was an arena that seated over 14,000 people. This was the beginning of the big time.

When he heard Thomas was in the building, he searched the arena until he found him. Thomas was wearing jeans again as he paced back and forth on the stage with Bernie. Billy's younger brother was showing Thomas where to enter the stage and where to stand for the "healing." He knew Thomas was nervous, but he was going to have to speak to him about constantly looking down at the taped 'X' marks as he moved around the stage.

Billy watched a little longer before walking up on the stage to approach him. "How's it going?" Billy said to both of them.

"We're doing ok, I guess," Bernie said.

Thomas was pale and sweaty. He seemed out of breath as he said to Billy, "I'm just nervous. This place is huge and I know I'm going to mess up somehow."

"You'll be fine," Billy said. "The first night is always the hardest. I remember watching my daddy for years up there preaching and it seemed so easy. I would remember every word and every motion; I was sure I could do what he did and even do it better.

"Well out of the blue, my chance came when one night he wasn't feeling well and he asked me to perform the service. I was thrilled and I told all my friends to come. I bragged to everyone and told them I would be better than my old man.

"Well, all of my friends came and I was all decked out, looking sharp. I strutted by them all on my way to the stage and tipped my hat as I passed. I gave a wave to the ladies and as I approached the podium… I tripped and fell face first.

"It's like it happened in slow motion, Thomas. All I could hear was my friends laughing and saying, 'Aw man'!"

Billy looked away for a moment and shook his head, but he never stopped smiling. He then turned back and looked Thomas straight in the eye. "You know what happened next?"

Thomas shook his head no and asked.

"Well, I got up, I grabbed the mic and I did it better than my father," Billy said. "That was a sign, too, Thomas. That's when I knew for sure that this was my calling. You fall, you get up. Someone challenges you, you answer that challenge. I have no doubt that you are going to find out tonight that you have found your calling as well; you'll see that for yourself. You'll be fine Thomas, we all believe in you and we're all here for you. You're family, remember that."

Thomas smiled and nodded.

Billy smiled back and then he looked Thomas over from head to toe.

"Now, we need to talk about your clothes and your look, my boy," Billy said.

"What's wrong with the way I look?"

"Well Thomas, if you haven't noticed by watching me all this time, part of this is about showmanship. You have to look the part son, that's an attention getter.

"I dress so I stand out from everyone else on the stage, so I command all the attention.

"You, on the other hand, with your uncombed hair, your blue jeans, and those God awful shoes… you are not going to command any attention looking like that.

"So, to rectify that, I am going to have the tailor come down and fit you for a white suit, one that looks just like mine."

Thomas didn't like the idea of dressing just like Billy, but he did it anyway. If this Mission was about helping people or finding his purpose, it didn't matter how he was dressed. Within a few hours he had his hair cut, his nails done and a brand new suit on that fit him perfectly. He was almost ashamed to admit it to himself, but there was something exciting about all of this.

An hour before show time, Billy came back into Thomas's dressing room where he was hanging out talking with Neesy. He wanted Thomas to go over his lines again, but Thomas protested, saying, "I got it Billy, don't worry."

"You ain't got nothing until I say you got it, ok?" Billy said sharply. "This is my deal and I say we do it again."

Neesy could see that Thomas was getting angry. "If he says he got it honey then he's got it," Neesy said to her husband. "I'm sure there are a million other things you need to look into before we get started. Thomas will be fine."

Billy didn't like Neesy overriding him with Thomas, but he let it go because this was too big of a night to fight this battle. Instead he forced a smile and made a mental note to talk to Neesy about this later.

That first night went off without a hitch, just as Billy has planned it. The place was packed but there was more than enough security to handle anything that could come up. Billy sectioned off a small section to the left and right of the stage for the press. He knew this was another opportunity for a great infomercial for the mission.

Now finally after weeks of planning every detail, the mission was about to go live. The arena had two large silk banners hung from the ceiling to the right and left of the stage. The word 'HEALER' was printed in big letters at the top of the banner and underneath in a smaller font were the words 'Your Mind', 'Your Soul' and 'Your body'. In the center, starting from the front of the arena and going all to way to the back, were hundreds of three-foot crosses hanging with white lights around them. When you looked towards the stage, the only thing you could see was a large magenta curtain that had the words, 'Welcome to The Mission' printed across it in big white letters.

Neesy sat in the front row and she was stunned. Billy had kept her away during the preparation so he could get her unspoiled opinion of the effect. Neesy couldn't help getting caught up in the buzz that was going on inside the building. Even after all this time, she was still amazed at what Billy could accomplish when he put his mind to it.

As she looked around the arena, the house lights went out and all of the chatter stopped as they waited for the show to begin.

Billy had arranged it perfectly so that the lights from the crosses illuminated everything up with a soft glow, almost like candlelight. It created a beautiful effect as the audience members' faces were lit by the soft glow.

Neesy seemed to be the only one looking around at this point. Everyone else's attention was fixed on the spotlight beam focused on the curtain.

Neesy smiled and laughed to herself because she was certain that's just how Billy had planned it. He loved the buildup almost as much as he loved the actual event.

All of the sudden, the choir started singing softly from behind the curtain Gradually their singing got louder and louder, then halfway through the song the curtain opened just as the band started playing.

You could now see the stage in its entirety. A spotlight lit up the chorus on the left side of the stage, all dressed in purple. Another spotlight came on seconds later and lit up the band on the opposite side of the stage, dressed in a lighter shade of purple.

The middle of the stage was dark and remained so while the choir completed two songs.

The crowd was up on their feet. Some sang along, others just clapped their hands along to the music. Neesy just stood there, trying to take everything in.

After the second song, a voice came over the speaker system. Neesy recognized Bernie's deep, sexy voice right away.

"Ladies and gentlemen, thank you all for joining us tonight as we bring the mission to the masses.

God bless you all for your kindness and please tell your friends about us to help spread the word. At this point in the evening I would like to introduce you to the man behind the mission. He is a man of deep faith and conviction. He is a man with a vision to heal the world in spirit, mind and body. Ladies and gentlemen I present to you the Reverend Billy Johnson!"

Neesy was about to stand and applaud but it seemed everyone beat her to it. She got to her feet just as the entire stage lit up so that you could see Billy standing behind a podium at the center. Behind him was a huge neon green cross.

"He always knew how to make a grand entrance," Neesy thought to herself.

When the applause died down, Billy began his sermon. The size of the group and the importance of this night had no effect on Billy at all. He was as calm as if he was in his living room speaking to two people. He worked both ends of the stage and had the choir cued to come in at all the right moments.

Billy spoke for an hour about finding one's purpose. He told the crowd how he had come to be where he is now. He said he always had faith that if he followed the signs and stayed the course, God would show him the way.

Neesy, along with many other people around her, were moved to tears by his honesty and conviction. She had never been more proud of him. At the end of the hour, a standing ovation erupted as Billy said, "Thank you and God Bless".

The stage suddenly went dark again except for the neon green cross. Billy moved to the right side, where a spotlight shone on him. Thomas stood, staring at the sea of people while biting his nails. He knew this was it, his defining moment, his first step towards forgiveness.

"Matthew 4:23 -24," Billy said. "Jesus went throughout Galilee, teaching in their synagogues, preaching the good news of the kingdom, and healing every disease and sickness among the people. News about him spread all over Syria, and people brought to him all who were ill with various diseases, those suffering severe pain, the demon-possessed, those having seizures, and the paralyzed, and he healed them.

"Jesus healed diseases of all sorts, illnesses, fevers, lameness, blindness, leprosy; the list goes on and on. He healed them, letting God's power work through him and through the faith of those who were healed. Well my friend, I am here tonight to tell you that I met a young man about two years ago who had a very special gift.

"When I first met him, he was morning the loss of his dear mother. She was everything to him and all he had in the world. I could tell after speaking with him that her death was something that he might not be able to come back from."

Thomas had no idea how Billy was going to introduce him. He had not heard this introduction before tonight and it made him tear up as Billy continued on.

"I am sure by now you all have read the stories about Thomas Greggs' childhood. Before I met him he had already endured more hardship in 15 years than most people do in a lifetime. Yet for some reason unknown to him, he was given a gift by God.

"When I spoke with him for the first time, we talked about many of the same things that we talked about here tonight. I had known we were connected somehow since the first time that I saw him on the news after he healed a man who was on his death bed. Something called to me and I knew that I had to meet this young man. Then a light came on inside me when I later heard of his mother's passing. Something called out to me again telling me to go to him and I just knew our futures were somehow intertwined.

"In fact I said that exact thing to him during our first meeting when I first spoke to that lost boy about finding his purpose. Together, he and I were meant for something special. I gave him my card and almost a year later he called me. Neither of us knew why, it just seemed the right thing.

"Since then, he has confided in me many times that this was a gift that he didn't want or ask for. In fact, ladies and gentlemen, he thought it was a curse. I am here to tell you all that Thomas Greggs is nothing like the boy you read about or seen on the news. None of those people know the real Thomas Greggs.

"The real Thomas Greggs is one of the kindest, most selfless and giving young men you will ever meet. In fact it was him who came to me and asked if he could use his gift the way it was supposed to be used. He wanted me to help him find his purpose.

"When this whole thing started to take shape, Thomas seemed more at peace and he couldn't wait to get started.

"Ladies and gentlemen at this point I am going to say a prayer to St. Jude and then I am going to ask those of you who would like to participate in the healing session to form a line in the aisles to the left and to the right of the stage. Please don't rush or push others or you will be asked to leave."

When he finished with the prayer, the spotlight that was on Billy went out and just the neon cross was lit on the stage. A moment later, a spotlight came on focused on Thomas at center stage. He fought the urge to run when everyone jumped to their feet and started applauding and calling his name.

Bernie led the first person up to the stage. It was an older woman in her 60s who came up and gave Thomas a big hug. Billy went to push her away, but she let go of Thomas before he did. "I know I'm not supposed to touch him," she said. "I just feel so bad for him for all he's been through."

"It's ok," Thomas said, "What's wrong with you?"

Billy held the microphone to her face as she said, "I have severe arthritis in my hands. I can't lift or grab anything without pain and it's unbearable at times. I feel terrible because I can't even hold my grandson."

Thomas smiled and said, "Just relax, this will only take a minute or two…"

He had her hold her hands out and he placed his on top of them. The crowd was now totally silent as all eyes were on Thomas and the woman. Thomas closed his eyes and held his breath for a minute until he felt the pain in his chest. When it subsided, he held his hands there a moment or two longer and then removed them.

He then smiled at the woman and she said, "Is that it?"

Thomas laughed and asked, "You want to try it out?" Billy got nervous because this was the first person he had seen Thomas try to heal. He didn't know if it worked every time so he stepped in and said, "She can try it out at home, there are a lot of people in line here tonight."

The woman seemed confused and disappointed. Thomas noticed, so he put his arm around her. "No, let's test it out right now," he said.

Thomas walked to the side of the stage and picked up one of the duffel bags he found. He could lift it up with one hand, but it had some weight to it. He walked over to the woman and dropped it at her feet. She heard the thump when the bag hit the floor and she looked at Thomas nervously.

"Go ahead, give it a try," he said.

The woman shook her head no, but the audience started encouraging her to give it a try too. She looked at Thomas as she reached down to grab the bag. Thomas smiled at her again. She closed her eyes, expecting to feel the sharp pain she always felt, but it never came. She lifted the bag all the way up and opened her eyes wide with surprise.

She looked at the bag in disbelief, smiled from ear to ear then put it down. As the audience began to applaud, she reached down and picked up the bag again with ease then placed it back down.

Thomas laughed as she put her hand over her mouth and walked over to hug him again. Thomas felt good about his gift for the first time since he helped Neesy with her back problem when he first arrived in Virginia.

When he turned back to the crowd, he noticed that the lines seemed even bigger. There were so many of them and they came up one by one for two hours.

Eventually, Thomas motioned to Billy and told him that he needed a break. His head was killing him and he felt nauseous. The choir sang two more songs, and Thomas tried to continue. When Billy saw Thomas' nose start to bleed, he called an end to the session. Thomas didn't want to stop. He felt terrible because there were still so many people waiting. Some of them were old and frail, some could barely walk or stand and some had oxygen machines with them. Billy didn't want to hear it. He made the announcement that the session was over and he told everyone where they would be appearing next.

Bernie and Jerry came to get Thomas off the stage and the choir sang one last song. That was the end of the very first mission sermon/healing session.

Chapter 19

After the third Mission event, Billy had to have a sit down with Thomas to discuss knowing when to stop. Billy had Neesy sit in on the conversation for support because he knew Thomas would be more receptive to what she had to say.

Billy was getting tired of arguing with Thomas over how long he would be on the stage healing people. Thomas never wanted to stop until he got to everyone who needed his help, regardless of the consequences to his own well-being. At the second Mission event, Billy knew he wouldn't stop so he had Bernie put the house lights on and escort Thomas off of the stage. Then when it happened again the following night, they began arguing right on stage and Bernie had to intervene because it got so heated.

Thomas thought he would start feeling better about his life after helping so many people, but instead he found it hard to sleep. He kept focusing on the people who looked as if they lost everything when the announcement was made that the healing session was over. It didn't matter, young or old; Thomas knew they were there for a reason and he was that reason. He knew that he was the only hope for some of them.

This time, when Thomas came out he said he would help everyone who needed it tonight.

Billy was mad as hell and he wanted to teach Thomas a lesson. So he let Thomas go on and on hour after hour healing people.

Almost three hours into the healing session, Thomas turned from the old woman who was standing in front of him and grabbed his head. Before Jerry could get to him, Thomas hit the floor.

Thomas woke up in the hospital two hours later still feeling the effects. His head was pounding and his chest was sore. Bernie told him later that his eyes had begun to bleed a little after he passed out.

Billy and Neesy sat down with Thomas the day before the fourth Mission session. "Thomas, Neesy and I are very concerned about you and we want to discuss something with you," he said. "We think that you need to limit the time you are on stage to one hour."

Thomas's eyes opened wide and he started to argue, but Neesy silenced him with a stern look and a shake of her head. He slouched back into his chair as Neesy signaled her husband to continue.

Billy smiled and nodded, because he knew exactly what he was doing when he went to Neesy for assistance. "Now Thomas, I know you want to help everyone in the audience, but that is not possible son," Billy said. "I saw that from the first night. Last night, we let you keep going and you wind up in the hospital. I just don't think you can keep doing it for hours at a time without it affecting you physically.

"Now, I spoke with the neurologist at the hospital and he said there was no damage to the brain. But he did say that these headaches of yours are a concern and that you should be monitored. He thinks there may be some damage initially, but then you may be healing yourself afterwards without even knowing it.

"The doctor is concerned, just as Neesy and I are that if you continue to subject yourself to this for hours at a time that you may cause permanent damage eventually."

While they were both worried about Thomas, Billy's concerns were different from his wife's. Neesy thought of Thomas as a son. Billy thought of him the same way that a baseball coach viewed his star pitcher. You don't want to leave your starter out there for nine innings every game, because you'd wear his arm out and he wouldn't be any good to you long-term. You want to use him in the way that is most advantageous to the team over the long haul.

"I know you feel bad for the people you don't get to help," Billy told Thomas. "I do too. But, the fact of the matter is that the Mission is growing at an even higher rate than even I expected. We will be adding more and more dates. That means we will be back and forth enough to where the people that we missed can come back next time or the time after that."

Thomas stared at the floor during the whole conversation while trying to take in everything that Billy said. When he looked up, he noticed Neesy looking at him with concern.

"Thomas honey, we are just concerned about you and your welfare," she said. "I know how you feel about this ability that you have. I know you want to use it for what you think it was meant for and I know you think you were punished for not doing that in the first place. But honey, you've got people here who care about Thomas Greggs, not The Healer. If you want to continue doing this, I think it's best in moderation for now."

Then Neesy turned her attention towards Billy and she shot him a look. "I'm not so sure adding more dates is the best idea now until we know Thomas is ok with doing this night after night," she said. "Isn't that what moderation means?"

"Those dates are tentative for now, honey. I have already changed the schedule to give him two days off between sessions. We'll see how the hour thing goes and then take it from there. Is that ok with you?"

Neesy smiled back at him then turned back to Thomas, "It's not up to me," she said, "Thomas, the decision is yours. It always will be."

Thomas looked at them both and then put his head down to think. "I want it arranged so that the neediest come up first," he said.

Billy agreed and shook Thomas's hand, knowing full well that he would never keep his word. He already had it worked out that the ones who donated the most generously to The Mission would get preferential treatment during the healing sessions.

Still he smiled and patted Thomas on the back, "That sounds like a good plan to me," Billy said. "I'll have the people questioned as they come in. We'll ask if they will participate in the healing session and if so, what the nature of their illness is. Everything will be confidential; of course, as I'm sure they would prefer it. I'll have Bernie and Jerry send them up to ensure the neediest are addressed first, is that all right?"

Billy looked at Neesy again and she was nodding with approval. Thomas sat thinking quietly for another minute and then he nodded too. "Sounds good," Thomas said. "Thank you both for looking out for me."

Neesy stood up and extended her arms with a smile. Thomas smiled back, got up and gave Neesy a big hug.

After Thomas left, Billy thanked his wife for her help. Neesy hugged him and said, "I know this is your dream, honey, and I know deep down you do really want to help people. But I did that for Thomas. He needs to know someone cares and someone is looking out for him."

Billy thought of a million things he could have said to defend himself, but he just hugged his wife back and gave her a kiss on the lips.

The Mission rolled on for the next six months using the new schedule. It still didn't feel right to Thomas that he was only on stage for an hour, but he took Billy at his word that he was healing the neediest first.

Billy would walk over to Thomas every night and point out to him where the most needy people were while the choir was singing the Amazing Grace intro. What Thomas didn't know was that these people were really the highest bidders. What they got for their money was a guarantee of being healed in exchange for a large donation to the Mission.

As the traveling and Mission sessions became more frequent, Billy and his brothers were missing in action more and more often after the events were over. Neesy would never question it, but when Thomas did, Billy would always say the same thing, "It's business related." According to Billy, he had constant dinner meetings with sponsors and private donors that kept him out most nights until the wee hours of the morning.

Thomas spent all of his time with Neesy and this made life on the road for both of them tolerable. It was just like it was back home: They would play cards together, watch TV together or just sit and talk. But Neesy told Thomas on many occasions that she was getting sick of the road and that it just wasn't her thing.

Thomas didn't like to hear that. He would tell her that if she left, he would miss her and that he wouldn't have anyone to talk to. Neesy worried about Thomas, so she kept trying to stick it out a little longer.

But after 11 months, she had had enough of the road. Neesy just wanted to sleep in her own bed again. She talked privately with Billy first before breaking the news to Thomas. She was sure Billy would make it difficult for her, but instead in was just the opposite. Billy told her how he could see that she was tired and that she wasn't happy.

He asked her if she wanted him to close down the Mission so they could return home for a while (knowing full well she would never ask him to do that) and of course she said no. She was touched by the offer and was pleased that he understood. Neesy made Billy promise to look after Thomas on the road and to spend time with him.

The conversation with Thomas was just as hard as she feared it would be. His look of disappointment almost made her change her mind again. He was crushed and he wished he could return with her. But Thomas knew that wasn't possible. He had chosen a path and he needed to see it through. He had adjusted to losing people who were close to him his entire life and this time would be no different.

Billy soon realized that Thomas was starting to crowd him and follow him around everywhere. He needed time for himself and he definitely wasn't going to get that with Neesy gone. So he decided to hire someone to be Thomas' companion. He actually got the idea from Neesy when he was complained to her over the phone about Thomas being so needy.

Billy knew his wife would approve of the young woman he hired to be Thomas' assistant. Her name was Cheryl and she was fresh out of college. She majored in art and didn't have any real plan for what she wanted to do with her life. She was a light-skinned African-American girl who was very outgoing. When Billy interviewed her and described the job, she almost turned it down. Then when he told her what the salary was, she accepted right on the spot. Her only condition was that she wouldn't always be stuck doing it.

Billy's reply was, "We'll see how it goes, then talk about it at a later date."

That and the money was enough for her. Cheryl came on board and she befriended Thomas from day one. She made sure that on the road Thomas had a refrigerator full of his favorite food and beverages. She had a large TV and Sony Playstation set up in his dressing room everywhere they went. Before Thomas would go on stage, she would sit with him in his dressing room and talk to him while Billy was on stage. They would play video games or watch TV together and Cheryl would keep an eye on the clock so that Thomas would ready for his cue on time.

Then after every session Cheryl would be waiting on the side of the stage with a bottle of water and a towel. They would go back to the dressing room and talk about how the night went. Thomas would take a shower and then they would eat together before getting back on their buses.

Thomas wanted Cheryl to ride on the bus with him, but Billy wouldn't allow it. Billy told Thomas that the big custom-made bus was made exclusively for the four of them and that's the way he preferred it.

All of the buses were basically the same; each had what was called a main suite, which was a single private bedroom in the back of the bus. Connected to that was a section consisting of 12 bunk beds. As you worked your way towards the front, there was a sitting area with a couch, two lounge chairs, a large screen TV with cable and a VCR. In the front of the bus, the first thing you saw was the small kitchen that had a full size refrigerator, a full size stove and a microwave that sat on a small countertop.

The main bus was different in that it contained two main suites with two twin beds in each room and only a very small section outside of it with only two sets of bunk beds. Thomas had no issues at all with allowing Billy and Neesy have one room and Bernie and Jerry have the other. He liked having the time to him at the end of the night to watch some TV. When he felt like he was getting tired, the sounds of the tires on the road at night relaxed him as he lay in his bunk, making it easier to fall asleep.

Even though Cheryl was with Thomas when he asked Billy if she could ride along on the bus, the last thing on earth she wanted was for Billy to say yes.

During the day and throughout the nightly services she was just doing a job, but at the end of the night, when the job was done, she wanted time to herself away from Thomas. Cheryl worked this out with Billy on the first day. She thought Thomas was a nice enough person, but she would never choose to hang out with someone like him. He was too boring and way too needy.

She had a really hard time coping with his constant up and down mood swings. They really bothered her. Thomas seemed to carry his depression around on his shoulders everywhere he went, all day long. He never wanted to go out anywhere or do anything. He just wanted to watch movies, play cards or talk.

She tolerated this for three months until she started dating one of Billy's nephews. That's when Thomas started to notice that she was coming around less and less to hang out. She was just doing her job as an assistant and that was it.

Thomas found out for himself what the deal was when he overheard her talking to Michael and a few other people in one of the dressing rooms before a Mission event. He was looking for her and he was just about to open the door to enter the room when his name mentioned. He placed his ear close to the door and he heard laughter at first.

Michael said, "Did you talk to my uncle about letting you out of your babysitting job?"

Everyone laughed again and Cheryl said, "You have no idea what it's like. He's always talking about his mother and he cries at the drop of a hat. I am so sick of it! And if I have to pretend to like one more game of cards, they are going to find me hanging from the rafters at one of these events."

Thomas backed away from the door just as they were all laughing again.

"Billy paid someone to be my friend," he thought angrily.

Thomas wanted to burst into that room and tell all of them to go to hell, but he just looked for someplace that he could be alone with his thoughts. When he called Neesy later that night, she could tell something was wrong.

Thomas wanted to cry and tell her what had happened. He wanted to tell her he was leaving the Mission and coming back to stay with her. He wanted to tell her that he never felt more alone in his life. But he didn't say any of those things.

The words "cries at the drop of a hat" echoed in his head.

"I'm fine, Neesy, just a little tired," he said. "I just need some time to myself and a good night's sleep, that's all."

Neesy wasn't fooled. "I don't know Thomas, I can tell something's bothering you," she said. "Why don't you see what Cheryl is up to and hang out with her for a while?"

Neesy's innocent question hit Thomas like a punch in the stomach. He knew at that moment that she had known about "the babysitter" and never said anything to him about it. And now it felt like she was pawning him off on her just like Billy had done.

Thomas bit his tongue and held back his anger. "Maybe I will see what she's up to," Thomas said. "Have a good night, Neesy."

He hung up the phone without waiting for her response. "Maybe I was meant to be alone and not have any family at all," he thought to himself before heading back to his dressing room.

From that day on he stayed to himself and no one seemed to care. The Mission continued on and got bigger and bigger. Days turned into months, months turned into years and everything became a blur. For Thomas, it had become less about helping people and more about getting through another day. He continued on because his guilt and his hope of forgiveness wouldn't let him stop. He couldn't live without dreaming of something better.

Chapter 20

Two years passed and Thomas was living on autopilot. Every day felt exactly the same and the only thing he looked forward to was their holiday hiatuses.

Even his birthday had come to be just another day to him. March 14th would have come and gone every year unnoticed to Thomas if it wasn't for Neesy always calling him to wish him a happy birthday. His last birthday was supposed to be one of those rites of passage. He turned 21, but no one involved with The Mission even acknowledged it. Part of him was hoping that Bernie or Jerry would have taken him out for his first drink. But there was another part of him that was afraid of alcohol. He had watched his father turn into a physically and verbally abusive monster too many times after a night of drinking. He was certain he wasn't anything like his father, but there was a part of him that didn't want to take the chance and find out he might be wrong.

Thomas had made himself a promise when he was still just a child that he would never drink, but he was no longer a child and the pressures of life along with the loneliness he was feeling were making it so that the moral lines were starting to blur.

The Mission continued to gain momentum, which meant the planned two-week vacations they were supposed to have every few months went by the wayside. The only times they made it home now were for all the major holidays and for Neesy's birthday.

Neesy was very upset about this. She told Thomas so almost every time they spoke on the phone. But just like Thomas, she went along with it because she felt it was for the greater good. She told Thomas once that if this was God's plan for Billy, and then who was she to try to make him stop doing it?

When the breaks did come, Thomas loved being back in Virginia. Only now he wasn't returning to the house Neesy and Billy lived in when he first came to stay with them - they had taken up permanent residence at the compound.

After The Mission gained national exposure, it was impossible for Neesy to reclaim her normal life in her home. Billy tried to talk her out of going back to the house, but Neesy stood her group and returned to her home anyway.

She wasn't there a full day when people started coming from everywhere to the house. She had to call the police several times over the next two days because people were either wandering around on her property or standing on her porch. Some were just curious to see where Thomas had lived and others thought that if they could speak to Neesy that Thomas would help them.

She tried to deal with it and hold her ground until the death threat came and that was the straw that broke the camel's back. Someone placed a letter in her mailbox stating that if Thomas didn't heal his son that harm may come to her. The man was so desperate that he put his name and phone number in the letter in hopes that Thomas or Billy would contact him. Instead the police showed up at his house and arrested him.

The media was all over the story. It turned out the man bought a ticket to one of The Mission sessions for his son. He couldn't make it to the front before the hour was over, so he was distraught by the thought of waiting another four months before The Mission was back in town again. His son had cancer and he didn't have a lot of time left. He said he explained this to the people at The Mission who handed him the questionnaire, but it still didn't matter.

As a result of this threat, Billy paid 4.2 million dollars to purchase the compound as the corporate headquarters for the mission. Neesy refused to sell the property that had been in her family for years, so Billy hired people to maintain it to keep her happy.

Word quickly spread about the man and his son and soon more stories started to come out from all over the country with similar themes. Desperate people, some of whom who had traveled a good distance with sick loved ones, waited for the chance to meet The Healer only to be turned away after an hour. There were even rumors of preferential treatment for the rich or the select few whom the personnel at the Mission deemed critical.

Billy started doing interviews all over the country defending the practices of The Mission. Much like everything he did, the interviews were coordinated and controlled. He chose outlets that were sympathetic and always knew what the questions would be beforehand. If the interviewer deviated from the script, Billy would thank them for their time, take his microphone off and leave the studio.

At first, Thomas didn't participate in any of the interviews or talk to the media at all. This was an arrangement he made with Billy when they started The Mission. Billy didn't really mind in the beginning because he thought he should be the face of The Mission. However, as the pressure on Billy continued to mount and stories started to surface accusing him of being a con man, he thought that putting Thomas out there with a script may help to cool things down. It would definitely take the attention of off him, at least.

Billy asked Neesy to talk to Thomas about doing the interviews. He promised her several times that he would script everything to protect Thomas and make sure the same stipulations were put in place that he used for his interviews. She was able to convince Thomas, as Billy knew she would, and the strategy seemed to work perfectly at first.

Most of the interviewers were so pleased to have Thomas on their program in any capacity that they agreed to all of the terms without pushing back at all.

Billy was present in the beginning, but eventually Thomas had done so many interviews and said the same things over and again that it almost became routine.

There was one topic that was strictly off-limits for any interview with Thomas – you could not ask him about his parents. The religious programs on the cable networks had no problem at all with any of his stipulations. Thomas' presence increased their donations as well as their viewership. But the mainstream media wasn't so agreeable. Thomas walked off of several live broadcasts because the interviewer didn't follow the rules.

When either of his parents' names came up, Thomas would stand up and look the interviewer right in the eye as he took off his microphone. He would then drop it on the floor and walk off the set. A producer would always chase him down to apologize and beg him to come back, but Thomas would just keep walking and not respond.

Thomas never paid attention to who was interviewing him; he only knew where he had to be and when he had to be there. When someone mentioned the host's name was Robert Van Putten, Thomas didn't even react because he never knew the name of the first reporter who shoved a microphone in his face at the Morgan house. He never really even got a good look at him either, because he was blinded by the light from the camera that day.

Much like Thomas, a lot had changed for Robert since their first meeting. Robert was now an up and coming reporter at the Fox News Network. He made his way up the ranks with the reputation of being a young maverick reporter and Fox loved that about him. They were the highest-rated news program in their market because Robert had a knack for uncovering that extra something that the other networks didn't find.

He also didn't mind asking the hard questions that other reporters wouldn't dare ask. For Robert, having someone storm off during an interview meant that he was doing his job. Fox would always air the entire interview along with whatever extra tidbit Robert had dug up and next thing you knew, the story was everywhere.

After getting a taste of the limelight with The Healer Story, Robert became even more ambitious. He would use tactics that were considered unsavory or unethical by many to obtain a lead or information on a story.

Both Robert and his producer Martin Shulman were fired after he blurted out the name of a then minor Thomas Greggs on the live television. Less than two weeks later, they were working for another station.

A year later, Robert had his next big scoop. Somehow, he found out from a trusted source that Mayor Harold Bertlin of Parsippany, New Jersey had been having an affair with his wife's sister who was now pregnant with his baby. The mayor's wife learned about the affair and hired an uncover cop who she thought was a hit man to kill her husband.

Robert went straight to the station heads and explained that he had the New Jersey story of the year! He demanded that he be promoted to anchor and that he would break the story live on the air at 5 p.m. He assured management that arrests were coming that night and that they could break the story as soon as it was going down. Robert knew this because his source – the undercover cop – informed him that they were arresting the mayor's wife at 5 p.m. when she arrived home from work.

Martin of course backed him, but Robert had to explain to the station managers how he would be the first on the scene of an arrest for what would be a major story. He then guaranteed them that the networks would pick up the story for sure and if they didn't, he would resign.

The managers met privately and gave him the green light. Every local news program was talking about the arrest, but Channel 12 was the first and the only one with video.

Maureen Bertlin was horrified when she surrendered to the police in front of her house. She'd hoped to do it quietly, without any fuss. When she pulled up to her house, Maureen noticed that her lawyer was already out of his car yelling at one of the police officers. To the left of them the other officer was arguing with a cameraman and two other people that were with him.

Unsure of what to do, Maureen rolled down her window her window and yelled to her attorney in order to get his attention. Immediately afterwards, Martin started walking towards her. The policeman grabbed him, but Robert and the cameraman took advantage of the distraction to make a mad dash towards the car.

Maureen sat frozen while she listened to this young man with a microphone describe how he was on site at Mayor Bertlin's house where the mayor's wife Maureen Bertlin was being arrested for attempting to hire a hit man to kill her husband.

When the reporter moved to the left, the light from the camera blinded her so much that she had to cover her eyes.

The light suddenly vanished and when she moved her hand she could see the other police officer pushing the two men back. Her lawyer finally approached her and escorted her over to the unmarked patrol car.

She was just about to get into the back seat when she heard someone yell, "Mrs. Bertlin became aware of an alleged extramarital affair between the mayor and her sister Jacqueline, who is also married. My sources tell me that Jacqueline may also be pregnant with the Mayor's child."

Maureen paused just before lowering herself into the car. Tears welled up in her eyes as she wondered what her mother would think when she found out.

She was just about to close the door when he shouted again, "Do you have a comment Mrs. Bertlin?"

She slammed the door to the cruiser shut, her lawyer got in the other side next to her and then the two officers returned to the car before they pulled away. When Robert asked one of them for a comment, he replied, "Screw you."

Mrs. Bertlin pleaded guilty and received a 15-year sentence for attempted murder. Mayor Bertlin resigned from office. Jacqueline Miles' husband left her and she overdosed on sleeping pills.

The scandal captured national attention, and Robert was asked to do several interviews on several networks about the story. Before long, he became very well known nationally and within months he got a job with the Fox News Network as a lead anchor making ten times his previous salary.

Within months the news program he hosted was number one in its time slot. His claim to fame was that he was 'the interviewer who wasn't afraid to ask the tough questions YOU want answered'. Those words were prominent in the introduction to his nightly show The Van Putten Report.

Chapter 21

Three days away from his 22nd birthday, Thomas sat waiting for his interview with a drink in his hand. As he stared at it, he remembered how he had always been afraid of alcohol because of the way it affected his father. He knew his father's temper and nastiness weren't all because of the alcohol, but it sure did make him worse.

Thomas remembered the promise he made to himself and he remembered the exact day and the circumstances under which he broke it. It was four months ago during their last appearance in Chicago, Illinois.

At a Mission event that evening, Thomas had healed a woman who could have passed for his mother's twin. If that wasn't strange enough, after he healed her she had smiled at him in a way that was eerily similar to the way his mother smiled. He kept his composure the best he could for the rest of the healing session, but a wave of depression came over him.

When he left the stage, Thomas hurried to his dressing room where he started shaking and crying hysterically. He tried to compose himself several times but it just seemed to overwhelm him. It reminded him of how he used to see his mother get at times and this scared him.

He feared he was having a breakdown or that he was suffering from exhaustion, so after he was finally able to compose himself he went to Billy's dressing room. He was going to tell Billy that he was stressed beyond belief and that he needed a break. He wanted to return home and spend a few days with Neesy away from the Mission.

When Thomas opened the door and found an empty room, he suddenly felt nauseous. He tried to get a hold of himself but he started to shake again and cry for no reason. He felt like he was losing his mind.

He closed his eyes and tried to compose himself by saying out loud, "It's ok, and you're ok."

When he opened his eyes again his attention became fixated on a bottle of vodka that was sitting on the counter next to the mirror. The irony of the moment made him laugh for just a second. His father's favorite drink was vodka straight up.

Thomas knew it was poison, but he couldn't stop wondering what his attraction to it was. "Why was it worth drinking it over and over when you know it turned you into a monster?" he asked himself

He grabbed the bottle and studied the liquid inside. His mind drifted from his father back to the woman he healed. He couldn't get over how much she looked like his mother.

He opened the cap of the bottle, closed his eyes and smelled what was inside.

A vision of his mother in her coffin appeared in his head and her voice echoed in Thomas' mind: "How could you do this to me? What have you done?"

Thomas felt the tears stream down his cheek as the depression was replaced by self-loathing and hate. He grabbed the bottle of vodka and took a big gulp. He didn't particularly care for the taste or the way it made his eyes burn, but he kept drinking. He kept drinking until his mind became cloudy and he felt numb. This was a feeling that he appreciated very much. Being able to check out of his life and hide from the demons of the past was a Godsend to him.

There was a knock on the door behind him that made Thomas open his eyes and scan the room. It took him a second to remember where he was before a voice came from the other side of the door behind him, "Mr. Greggs, five minutes until we're on the air."

Thomas rubbed his eyes and tried to focus on the upcoming interview, but he really could care less about it. He looked around the room again and thought, as far as green rooms, or guest waiting rooms were concerned, this was one of the nicest that he had seen. The black leather couch he was stretched out on was very comfortable. Directly in front of him was a big screen TV that was turned off at the moment. To the left of the TV was what looked like a leather barber's chair that sat in front of a small countertop with a large mirror above it. In the furthest corner of the room was a large refrigerator stocked with bottles of ice tea, bottled water, Pepsi and various fruits. Thomas was aware of the contents. The assistant producer escorted him to the green room, she advised him that he could help himself to anything in the fridge. When Thomas refused she asked if there was anything else she could get for him instead, hence the two glasses of vodka he had to calm his nerves.

Thomas attempted to get to his feet but his head was throbbing. He then slumped back down onto the couch and decided he would just sit tight until someone came to get him. After what seemed like a few minutes past he leaned back on the sofa, closed his eyes and started to drift off again.

In a room down the hall, Robert Van Putten was going over some last minute details with his producer. Martin went over the restrictions with Robert knowing full well what Robert's mantra was, 'The Van Putten Report doesn't follow restrictions'.

As Robert was doing his research on what Thomas had been up to since they last met several years ago, he watched one interview in particular over and over again. The Barbara Walters interview with Thomas that aired three months ago fascinated Robert, just as it did everyone else.

Barbara pushed the edge as far as she could with Thomas and it was a riveting interview. She was the first and only person to get away with breaking the cardinal rule by mentioning his parents. Unfortunately, she backed off when she saw he was flustered and angry. What amazed Robert the most was that people were still talking about that interview three months later and he knew why.

Up to that point all of the interviews he watched were all the same, they all followed the instructions set forth by The Healer Camp to the letter or they finished very abruptly. "Barbara Walters danced by the fire, but she was afraid to get burned," Robert told his producer. "That, my friend, will change today. Everyone is going to be talking about us tomorrow, this I am certain of."

Martin smiled and replied, "Can't wait to see what happens next," and left to get Thomas.

Martin knocked on the door twice, and opened it when Thomas didn't respond. He introduced himself, but Thomas didn't acknowledge him except to rub his eyes. He slowly got to his feet, sighed and said, "Ok, let's get this over with."

As the man extended his hand, Thomas blinked several times while he tried to focus.

"Hello Mr. Greggs, my name is Martin Schulman. I'm the executive producer of the Van Putten Report. It's an honor to meet you."

As Thomas shook his hand while tuning out his ramblings, his first impression of Martin was that he looked old enough to be his father. He had green eyes and brown hair that was cut short. It was slicked back, causing Thomas to wonder for a moment why he would do that when he had a receding hairline. Martin looked as though as hadn't shaved in days and he was definitely at least 20 pounds heavier that he should be. Thomas didn't think the man had slept in days. He had black circles under his eyes and just the way he carried himself made him look like he was just going through the motions. That was something Thomas could definitely relate to.

Martin led Thomas down the hallway and onto the set. As Thomas looked around the studio, he thought it looked more like the set of *The Tonight Show* than a news program. The host had the big desk, and the guest sat on a couch next to it. There were two huge monitors behind the desk and the studio audience was about 15 feet from the stage.

As Thomas stared at the crowd from the side of the stage he felt a hand on his shoulder. When he turned around he saw a man with a plastic smile staring at him like he was a long-lost friend.

"Mr. Greggs," Robert said, sounding full of energy. "It is a pleasure indeed! I have been looking forward to this ever since Martin mentioned we had managed to book you for an interview."

Thomas forced a smile even though every bone in his body told him that this guy was not to be trusted. He just gave off a vibe that said, "I'm a phony and a snake, beware."

Thomas couldn't help but notice that this Robert person was the exact opposite of his producer. Robert had blonde hair that was longer in the front then in the back. His hair was parted in the middle and his bangs would touch the corner of his eyes while he would slick back the sides over his ears. He wore squared glasses that had a black thin frame across the top portion and no frame on the bottom portion. Between the bangs and the glasses, it made Robert's blue eyes seem almost fierce in the way he could focus them on you.

He was taller than Thomas, at least 6-foot-2, and he was in great shape. He also had a tan that seemed as if it were sprayed on because the color didn't look quite right. It was a little to orangey, Thomas thought.

"I'm glad to be here," Thomas said, trying to sound enthused. "I've heard so much about you and your show." It was a line that Thomas used with all of his interviewers because it seemed to please them, but he had never once watched The Van Putten Report.

"Ok so, Martin will lead you off to the side of the set, I will do my monologue, and then I will introduce you."

Robert's eyes never left Thomas's the whole time he was speaking. This made Thomas a little uncomfortable. "That's fine," Thomas said and again looked away.

This was a trick the Robert had always used to see if the person he was interviewing was confrontational or not. He believed if he could stare them down, so to speak, then he could control and manipulate the interview to go in any direction he wanted.

"This is it," Robert thought to himself, "I'm about to hit the big time!"

Thomas stood with Martin during the intro and the monologue. Martin tried to have a conversation with him, but Thomas just nodded and yawned.

As Thomas watched the monologue, his impression was that it was nothing special; it was nothing he hadn't seen before a hundred times.

Robert finished the monologue and then introduced Thomas as "the healer, Thomas Greggs."

Thomas walked onto the set and was greeted with a firm handshake. He sat on what was a very comfortable couch and he prepared himself to just get through it like always.

At first, the interview went just as Thomas expected. There were questions about his childhood. Questions about when he first discovered that he could heal people. Questions about his love life, The Mission and all the usual topics. Thomas answered them all in a monotone. Every now and then he glanced up at the digital clock that was in the corner to keep time of the show.

This annoyed Robert to no end. Near the end of the interview, Thomas glanced up at the clock while he was in the middle of answering a mundane question. Robert interrupted, "Let's talk about why you started doing what you do, Thomas."

Thomas seemed surprised to at sudden topic change, but he gave his standard response again. "I started doing this because I was given a gift, I feel the reason I received that gift was to help others."

Robert felt the excitement building up inside him. This was it; he was going to go for it!

"And yet, you couldn't help the two people who mattered to you most," Robert said.

Thomas's mouth closed and his lips were pressed together tightly. "Where was he going with this?" Thomas thought to himself.

When Thomas didn't respond, Robert continued. "We all know about your history with your parents. Your father was an abusive alcoholic and your mother was bipolar. This has all been reported over and over again. Yet no one asks the question: how it is that someone who has healed thousands of people couldn't heal his own parents?"

Robert could see the look of hate in Thomas's eyes. He didn't wait for a response though. He took a quick look up at the clock on the wall and went for the kill. "The truth is you pick and choose who you use this gift to heal, isn't that true Thomas? Tell me, is that how you think that God wanted it?"

Thomas was just about to walk out when Robert raised his voice.

"The most telling instance of all was when you let your father die right in front of you and you chose not to save him!"

Thomas shot up out of his seat and stood in front of Robert with his fist clenched. Robert stood up, met his stare and continued as he pointed his finger in Thomas's face.

"With Mr. Morgan, you ran over to that house as quickly as you could and saved his life. Yet your father died right there in the same room with you and you did nothing! Not to mention what happened to your mother!"

Thomas didn't let him utter another word. He jumped over the chair, pushed Robert to the ground and gave him beating of his life before the stagehands and security guards could pull him away. It was complete madness and pandemonium, but it was also television gold because the cameras caught everything

When the police arrived, Thomas was arrested for assault. By the time Billy and the Mission's lawyer had shown up at the police station, the story was being broadcast all over the world.

Thomas made bail the next morning, but there were dozens of reporters waiting when he left the police station. They were all shouting out questions and Thomas couldn't make out one from another. He just walked alongside the police with his head down as they led him to Billy's car as what seemed like a million flashbulbs went off in his face.

Billy was waiting with the door open. He was aware of the need for some major damage control if the Mission was going to survive. He knew it was for the best if Thomas just lay low back in Virginia with Neesy until this incident was settled, preferably out of court.

Billy, Thomas and the Mission lawyer got into the back of the black Cadillac with black tinted windows, while Michael and two of his friends who came along for the ride sat in front.

"What the hell were you thinking Thomas?" Billy yelled as soon as the car pulled away. "You know how much this is going to cost you? Not to mention what the press is going to say about you? This could really hurt the mission and everything we stand for. What the hell were you thinking, man? That was just plain old dumb and I won't stand for it."

Thomas yelled back and pointed a finger in Billy's face.

"Don't you ever fucking talk at me again! He went way over the fucking line and you know it!"

Billy immediately backed off because he had never seen Thomas like this, "I understand that Thomas, I really do. But you have to understand...."

"I don't have to understand shit," Thomas said. "He said I killed my parents, Billy! My parents!

"Is that ok, Billy?" Thomas shouted. "Maybe you think I'm to blame too? Maybe I should say 'fuck it' to this whole thing and disappear off of the face of the earth. Maybe that is my purpose after all."

"Of course I don't blame you," Billy said calmly, trying to defuse Thomas' rage.

"You know I was there for you. You know I believe in you and I know what kind of person you are. This person is obviously an opportunist, Thomas. He made a name for himself today at your expense.

"Maybe it's my fault Thomas, I should have done my research, and maybe I could have prevented this. I'm sorry, Thomas, I mean that sincerely."

Thomas turned away from Billy and stared out the window without saying another word. As they drove he found himself watching the people as they passed by and wishing he was any one of them. He slept most of the way and didn't speak another word the whole way home. Billy had never seen this side of Thomas and it worried him a great deal. Thomas had never seemed like the violent kind to Billy.

Billy had known about Thomas' father's alcoholic, abusive behavior and he knew that Marie was an emotional wreck. As he stared at Thomas on and off during their trip, he couldn't help but wonder if he was going to be dealing with a little bit of both.

Chapter 22

Billy was forced to keep the mission on hiatus for nine months as a result of the fallout from Thomas's assault on Robert Van Putten. It took the Mission lawyers that long to finally settle out of court with Robert Van Putten for an undisclosed amount of money. They also got the judge to agree to no jail time: instead Thomas was placed on probation and ordered to attended anger management courses.

Thomas didn't mind the time off because he was off of the road and back spending time with Neesy. When he refused to go to anger management, Billy had to pay off several people to fill out the proper documentation to provide the courts as proof of compliance.

The mainstream media followed its usual pattern, trashing Thomas, Billy and the Mission on every possible outlet. The religious sect spoke out about him as well repeating the mantra, "This is not God's way." Billy was concerned that there would be public backlash that would affect ticket sales when the Mission went back on the road, so he carefully planned its return. The first date of The New Mission was to be January 1, 2000, the start of the new millennium. He advertised on every available outlet with the same slogan: A new Century, a New Mission and New Man - Come see for yourself how Faith healed the Healer.

Once the tickets went on sale, Billy quickly learned that desperate people didn't care what the media had to say. The Mission was still selling out everywhere as soon as the new dates were announced. Before long they were back on the road and it was business as usual.

Depression quickly set in and the six months of sobriety Thomas had struggled through went by the wayside. His drinking started slowly, with only one glass of vodka before each session to calm his nerves and it got progressively worse. Although he tried not to think about it, he was well aware that their upcoming schedule was taking them towards New Jersey. He wasn't sure quite when, but he knew Madison Square Garden was coming up in a matter of weeks.

This made him think of the Morgans all of the time when he was sitting alone on the tour bus. He thought about calling Kyle and Kate often, but he would just dial the number, let it ring twice and then hang up.

Even though 6 years had passed, Thomas still remained conflicted about the Morgans and about his entire past in New Jersey. His life there was filled with mostly bad memories with a few good ones sprinkled in here and there. Deep down, he really cared for Kyle and Kate and he wanted to see them again. But ultimately he would think that the Morgans and New Jersey were part of his past, and they were better left behind. It was just like Neesy was so fond of saying, "It's God's plan."

"Still, so much had changed since I left," Thomas thought to himself. He was no longer the naïve boy who left New Jersey in the middle of the night searching for his purpose. He has learned so much about people and the lies they can tell.

Billy, for instance, appeared larger than life when he first met him. If you judged him as Thomas did at first, by the way he carried himself and the way he spoke the word of God, you would believe that Billy was a respectful, God-fearing man who loved his wife more than anything.

The truth, however, was that he was neither of these things. The Billy that Thomas knew now was a selfish, whore-mongering, egotistical liar who wanted to control everything and everyone around him. Never had this been more obvious to Thomas then on this current road trip. Because the curtain was opened, Thomas got a good look at the wizard first hand.

One of the many little secrets Billy kept presented itself at the end of the first week they were back on the road. Thomas had just gotten off stage and Cheryl wasn't there waiting for him with his towel or his water like she was supposed to be. This had been happening more and more often since they went back out on the road and Thomas had reached his limit with her.

She was always off somewhere else and Thomas had to go look for her even though she was supposed to be there waiting for him. Then when he did find her and interrupted her when she was talking with whoever she was with, she would give Thomas an attitude. She'd follow him back to the stage area, hand him his towel and water, then walk away muttering to herself.

On this particular night, Thomas was in a rotten mood and he had had enough. When he walked off stage and saw she wasn't there, he headed straight to Billy's dressing room to tell him he better set Cheryl straight.

When he got there, the door was closed and he could hear Billy and someone else inside. Thomas could barely hear them talking and laughing over the music that was playing. He knocked and waited, but Billy didn't answer. He started to get even angrier as he stood in the hallway dripping with sweat. He pounded on the door harder and waited, still no answer.

Thomas was now pissed so he walked to the other end of the hallway and found one of the maintenance men. When the maintenance man first refused to open the door, Thomas threatened his job if he didn't. This time, the maintenance man unlocked the door, and Thomas pushed it open. He could not believe what he saw. As the door suddenly flew open, a topless young woman jumped off of Billy's lap and crossed her arms to cover herself.

Billy jumped to his feet and yelled, "What the hell is going on here?"

The maintenance man stood behind Thomas with his eyes and mouth wide open until he heard Billy yell; then he took off running down the hall, praying that he'd still have a job in the morning.

Thomas didn't move; he stood there in shock. Billy reacted quickly, tucking his shirt in and escorting Thomas out into the hallway. "C'mon, we got to talk," he said.

Billy put his hand on Thomas's shoulder, but Thomas didn't budge. He looked Billy in the eyes and then down to where his hand was. Billy got the message and removed it. "Please, Thomas, come talk to me for a minute," he said.

Thomas had the urge to hit Billy, but he suppressed it knowing he would probably go to jail this time if he did. Instead, he brushed by Billy and started walking down the hallway.

Billy waited a second until Thomas was a few steps away before he peeked back into his dressing room. "Sorry about this baby," he said, "I'll explain later. You still know the number to my hotel room don't you?" The woman nodded and Billy said, "Ok, see you later then." He closed the door to his dressing room and ran to catch up with Thomas.

Billy followed Thomas down the hallway, down three flights of stairs and out a side entrance in silence. Once outside and the door closed behind them, Thomas let Billy have it. "What the fuck were you doing in there with that woman?" he yelled.

"Thomas, it's complicated," Billy said. "You don't know what it's like, Neesy and I have been together a long time and I have needs that she doesn't attend to anymore."

"You have fucking needs?" Thomas said. "What about Neesy, Billy? Does she know how you take care of these needs of yours that she doesn't attend to?"

"Neesy doesn't know anything," Billy yelled. "Don't think for a minute that I don't love that woman, Thomas, because I do. I can tell you; this ain't about love, Thomas. This is about me having needs because I am a man and Neesy has no interest in taking care of those needs anymore.

"She stopped wanting to be intimate with me years ago, Thomas. I know it's not right to do this, Thomas, but I still have needs. It would kill her if she found out about this, you know that."

At that moment Thomas hated Billy and he wanted to call Neesy and tell her everything that was going on. But something in his mind took him back to when his mother asked about his secret. She asked if he could have saved his father and he told her the truth. It was too much for her to handle. As crazy as it seemed, there was a part of Thomas that knew some secrets are best left untold, no matter how big they are.

He knew Billy was Neesy's world and that this would devastate her. Did Thomas think that she would kill herself? No, he didn't. But what if he was wrong; could he ever forgive himself if she did? Could he ever afford to take that chance again with someone he loved?

Thomas took a breath and looked Billy up and down as he shook his head.

"You need to control your 'needs,'" Thomas said. "I'm not messing around here Billy. If I see that shit again, I am calling Neesy."

Billy had been around a long time and he knew a bluff when he heard one. His gift for reading people told him that if Thomas was going to tell, he would be calling Neesy right after this conversation.

But Billy knew now, that wasn't going to happen. Billy knew that Thomas cared a lot for Neesy and that she cared a lot for him too. He knew that, and that alone, saved his ass that night.

Billy extended his hand out for Thomas to shake and said, "You have my word, Thomas, no more of that nonsense. Thank you for being so understanding."

Thomas really didn't want to, but he took Billy's hand to shake it.

A week later, Thomas heard music and a woman laughing in Billy's dressing room again. This time, he listened for a moment longer, and then walked away down the hall with a sick feeling in his stomach.

Left feeling as if he had lost his faith in everyone around him, Thomas started spending even more of his time alone with the bottle. It was getting to the point where Cheryl had to wake him up in his dressing room and help him to the stage before he was to go on every night.

Everyone could see what was happening and they were waiting for Billy to handle it, but Billy didn't want to push Thomas too far after what had happened between them. Billy insisted "that as long as Thomas was up there doing his thing, there wasn't a problem."

Another night, another bus ride and Thomas drank until he passed out as usual. He woke to the sound of laughter around him. It was now daylight and they were parked behind another arena.

"Hey man, you up?" Jerry asked.

Thomas yawned, rubbed his eyes and sat up.

"Yeah, I guess I am," he said.

"Me and Bernie are going to check out the city, you wanna join us?"

"No, that's ok," Thomas replied. "By the way, what city are we in anyway?"

"Man, we are in THE city, my friend, New York City, performing at the one and only Madison Square Garden tonight!"

Bernie and Jerry were counting their money as they waited for a response so Thomas said, "You guys go ahead. I'm not feeling 100% so I'll catch up with you later."

When they left the bus, Thomas grabbed a pair of pants and hooded sweatshirt then headed outside. He had only seen images of New York City on television, so he wanted to have a look for himself. He pulled the hood over his head and walked towards the front of the arena.

He stood like your typical tourist staring up at all of the skyscrapers as he avoided the rush of people trying to get wherever they were going. He had seen on a lot of movies how they talked about how great the hot dogs were in New York, so he crossed the street to get two hot dogs and a coke.

As he stood eating them, he looked back towards the Garden and he could see the big jumbo screen out in front of the arena playing a commercial for the Mission. Thomas watched as they showed Billy in all of his glory strutting around the stage preaching to the masses. When they showed him, the light from the green neon cross behind him made it appear as if he were glowing as he stood with his hands stretched out to the sides to welcome everyone up to the stage.

The hotdog vendor was watching too and when it finished he stared at Thomas before glancing back at screen. Thomas was afraid that the man would yell out that it was him, so he quickly walked away. He was crossing the street to head back to the Garden when he noticed an electronics store with three TVs in the windows showing footage from what looked like the Morgans' house.

He couldn't hear what they were saying, but the caption on the bottom of the screen read, "Thomas Greggs as close to home as he has been since his disappearance."

The Morgans were nowhere to be seen, but the image of their house and his old house sitting right next to it made his heart start beating faster. He started to have trouble breathing and a feeling of sadness hit him like a wave crashing over him.

He made it back inside the arena, but even Billy was concerned when he saw the state Thomas was in. Thomas just sat in the dark, with his head leaned up against the wall, sobbing the whole time.

Billy called Neesy and asked if she could talk him, and they spoke for over an hour. When she got back on the phone with Billy, she told him that Thomas needed to speak to a therapist immediately and that he may need some Valium just to calm him. Billy, of course, bypassed the therapist and had his brother Bernie get some Valium from a guy he knew in the city.

Thomas took two pills away and washed them down it several gulps of vodka. He was asleep in his dressing room within minutes. He slept through lunch and dinner before Billy sent Bernie into his room to wake him up.

Thomas woke up feeling groggy and unable to focus. He slept for another half hour and finally got off of the couch when Bernie knocked again. The more he tried to walk around the room, the more he felt he needed more time to recuperate. He knew he should be drinking coffee or something with caffeine, but the vodka bottle was right there on the countertop and it was calling to him.

He took a sip and closed his eyes as it went down. Then he took another and another after that. Ten minutes later he was stumbling around the room. He suddenly felt like he was going to vomit, so he scanned the room looking for a garbage can. His eyes stopped instead on a phone that was on a desk in the corner of the room. Suddenly the nausea went away and he carefully made his way over to it.

He stared at it, wondering what Kate and Kyle were doing at that moment. He pictured them sitting together in the kitchen like they used to, eating and talking. Thomas picked up the phone, took a deep breath and dialed the number. It rang twice before Cheryl came into the dressing room and told him he only had ten more minutes to get ready. "It was a sign," he thought. "Things are this way for a reason and this is the way they were meant to be."

Billy finished his preaching and stood on the side of the stage watching Thomas, barely staying on his feet. The Valium seemed to help with the emotional stuff, but he was still a train wreck out there. Cheryl approached him and shook her head as she watched what was going on.

"It's a good thing you didn't tell him about the Morgans trying to contact him this week. He would have been even worse if he knew," Cheryl said. "He can't handle anything at this point; you need to protect him from himself. You're doing the right thing."

Billy looked her up and down with a smug expression on his face.

"Well I'm glad you approve, Cheryl," he said sarcastically. "This coming from someone who couldn't even handle babysitting him and being his pretend friend, which led to the mess you see before you. Just get out of my sight. I've got enough on my mind."

Cheryl walked away in a huff and Billy muttered, "Bitch" to himself as he watched her walk away.

Twenty minutes later Billy was enjoying the company of a young woman who was a devout Mission follower when Bernie knocked on the door. "Ahh what the hell now?" Billy yelled towards the door.

Bernie peaked his head inside the door to make sure everyone was decent and said, "Excuse me but I need to talk to you right now; it's really important."

"You know, Bernie, I am in such a bad mood and I just want some time to myself. What is it that you can't handle yourself?" Billy asked.

"Someone is here to see Thomas, he says he's a close friend and his name is Kyle Morgan."

Bernie could see Billy's demeanor change in front of his eyes. He suddenly had a frown on his face and he looked away as if he was deep in thought.

"I'll take care of this, Bernie. Where is he at?"

"He's in an empty dressing room down the hall," Bernie said. "He asked to see Thomas, but Thomas passed out right after the healing session. He's been popping that Valium like candy since we got here. I'm starting to worry about him."

"Ok good," Billy said, "I'll go talk to Mr. Morgan. Make sure Thomas stays in his room."

Bernie watched as Billy explained to his lady friend that there was "something that needed his attention" and told her that he would see her later. He then followed him down the hall and stood outside of the empty dressing room when Billy went inside.

Bernie knew for certain that his brother was the brains behind the Mission. He appreciated the way his brother always looked out for him and the whole family. He owed Billy a lot, which was the truth. Billy was the reason he could afford a nice house and support his kids. But Bernie didn't always agree with his brother's methods.

Thomas was a good kid and he had become a part of the family. Yet Billy couldn't care less that Thomas sat alone every night drinking. Now he was self-medicating because he couldn't handle being back near where he grew up.

Bernie knew deep down his brother wasn't always like that. The money, the business and the notoriety had consumed him. Bernie knew if he ever confronted his brother, he would be on the outside looking in. He felt bad for Thomas but he wasn't going to risk being "banished," so he stayed quiet and did what he was told.

Billy had thought about something like this might happen, but he never planned for it. As they walked down the hall, he quickly went through in his head how he thought the conversation was going to go and what he wanted to convey. His intention when he entered the room was to stay calm and to get Kyle out of the building as quickly and as quietly as possible.

"Mr. Morgan, it's a pleasure to meet you," Billy said as he offered Kyle his hand.

Kyle shook Billy's hand and looked at him cautiously.

"I know you," Kyle said. "You're the one who was at Marie's funeral sitting and talking to Thomas. I knew it was you the first time I saw you on TV."

Billy smiled and let go of Kyle's hard handshake.

"Yes, Mr. Morgan, that was me," Billy said.

Kyle quickly found himself getting angry at the fact that this person was standing in front of him instead of Thomas. "What were you doing there that day and where is Thomas?" Kyle demanded loudly.

Billy put his hand out, implying that Kyle needed to calm down.

"I was there that day cause my heart went out to that boy and I felt like I had to be there. As I mentioned to Thomas that day, my childhood was filled with its share of pain and hardship as well. Coming from a spiritual upbringing, I was able to find my purpose through the kindness of someone else. I just knew it was God's will that I offer that to Thomas as well."

Billy met Kyle's stare and waited for a response.

"You're a used car salesmen," Kyle said. "Nothing but a two-bit hustler who is taking advantage of a boy who lost everything he ever loved in this world. Yeah, I know all about you Billy Johnson. I've read all the articles and

I've seen all of the interviews with people who know the real you. Now, where is Thomas? I came to talk to him, not you."

Billy looked Kyle in the eye, then smiled and shook his head.

"You think you know, but you don't know," Billy said. "Most of those things you are hearing are all made up lies by people who begged me to be part of the Mission or from those who are looking to make a quick buck. A few things, though, are true. I'm not proud of some parts of my past. Not gonna tell you which ones though, but there are a few.

"The thing is, Mr. Morgan, we can all change. We can all find the path we were meant to be on and right the wrongs, it's never too late. Hey, take you for example. That boy saved your life and you couldn't do the one thing he asked of you in return, keep his secret."

"You son of a bitch!" Kyle shouted. "How dare you judge me! I treated Thomas like he was one of my own. I was there for him when both his father and his mother died! I will not listen to you judge me for a momentary lapse that I have wished every day that I could take back!

"You are using him like he's some kind of circus attraction and you could care less about him! Look at the way you dress, every member of your family is living off of him and you think you can judge me! I am done talking to you, you piece of shit, go get Thomas!"

Billy didn't flinch, he remained perfectly calm and his voice remained the same. "Mr. Morgan," he said.

"My name is fucking Kyle!"

"Kyle," Billy said calmly, "the reason I am here is because Thomas asked me to talk to you and see that you left. He doesn't wish to see you or your daughter ever again."

"That's bullshit," Kyle shouted. "Where is he?"

Kyle acted as if he was going to push his way past Billy to go find Thomas, but Billy stopped him in his tracks.

Kyle was 5-foot-6, 165lbs and gangly. Billy was 6-foot-2, 250lbs and thick; he had no problem grabbing Kyle and holding him against the wall. Both men stared face to face at each other while breathing heavy.

"Kyle, he doesn't want to see you," Billy repeated.

"Why do you think he hasn't responded to any of your calls or letters? He is trying to find his way with the cards he's been dealt and one of those cards was dealt by you. First you told his secret and then he overheard you on the phone complaining about what a burden he was on the family. Is that how you treat one of your own, Kyle?"

"Get the hell out my way," Kyle shouted. "My daughter is sick and she needs Thomas!"

Kyle pushed Billy back with everything he had, and the larger man stumbled backwards and almost fell. Kyle rushed towards him and threw a punch but he missed when Billy ducked. Billy hit Kyle with an uppercut to the stomach and then a punch to the face that sent Kyle crashing to the floor. At this point, both Bernie and Jerry came busting though the door.

The first thing Bernie saw was Billy standing with his fist cocked over Kyle, who was down on the floor and bleeding from his mouth.

"Jesus Christ, Billy, what the hell did you do?" Bernie yelled.

"He came at me, man!" Billy yelled back. "Now get him the hell out of here God dammit!"

Bernie and Jerry approached Kyle and helped him get to his feet. They could see that Kyle wasn't real steady, so they called a cab and then assisted him outside.

As they waited with him, Kyle said nothing the whole time, he just stared straight ahead. Bernie asked if he was ok, and Kyle nodded. When they got him into the cab, Bernie asked where he lived and Kyle mumbled the address through his swollen mouth.

Bernie took all the money he had in his wallet —about $2,000 – and he put it next to Kyle.

"Here man, this is for the ride home and for you to see a doctor if you need to," Bernie said.

Kyle didn't answer; instead he took his arm and bent it so it covered his eyes.

Bernie wanted to apologize for his brother, but he didn't know what good it would do, so he just closed the door and watched the cab pull away.

Bernie returned to find Billy back in his dressing room sitting with the same young female. He again knocked on the door and asked his brother to come into the hallway. He had been listening to Billy's argument with Kyle, and one thing about it bothered him.

Bernie stepped close to his brother and whispered,

"Are you going to tell Thomas about Kate being sick?"

"What? No, man!" Billy replied angrily. "That fool was bullshitting when he said that. He would have said anything to try to get past me and get to Thomas."

"What if he wasn't bullshitting?" Bernie asked. "What if she is really sick and something happens to her? If Thomas was to find out you knew, he would never forgive you, you know that." Billy looked away for a moment while contemplating what his brother had said.

"I make all the decisions and everyone gets rich because of it -- including you. Isn't that right, Bernie?" Billy said coldly. "Don't second guess me or ever go against me again, you hear me?"

When Bernie nodded and looked away, Billy grabbed him by the shoulders and looked him in the eyes. "Listen to me, he was fucking lying, ok?"

Bernie shook his head in agreement again then watched as Billy went back into his dressing room. He stood there for a moment going over the conversation in his head before letting out a long sigh. Even he was ashamed of his brother as he heard him joking and laughing with the woman he was with seconds after he closed the door.

When Kyle returned home, Sharon was waiting on the porch for him.

Kyle tried to walk past her while hiding his face.

"Is everything ok?" Sharon asked.

Kyle just wanted to get in the house and into the bathroom to check if his face was as bad as it felt.

"Everything is fine," he said as he lowered his head and opened the door.

When he heard the way it came out, even he cringed. His lip was completely swollen and he sounded like he just came out of the dentist office.

"Kyle, what's going on?" Sharon shouted, "What's wrong with your mouth?"

Kyle stopped and shook his head.

As he turned around to face Sharon she gasped and said, "Oh my god, what happened?"

She then gently reached up to touch his lip, which caused Kyle to wince and pull away in pain.

"I almost got mugged on my way to the store. "No big deal, I took a punch to the face from some kid but he didn't get my wallet."

Sharon looked at him with concern and disbelief.

"Some kid, huh? Was his name Thomas?" she asked. "Don't lie to me Kyle; I know you went to see him to ask him to help Kate."

Kyle looked away, but not before Sharon saw the pain in his eyes.

"Thomas didn't do this me, he wouldn't even see me. He sent that man, the preacher, to make sure I left the building."

Sharon looked into Kyle's eyes and her eyes began to tear up too.

"Honey, I am so sorry," she said. "We should call the cops. He had no right to assault you!"

"I tried to hit him first," Kyle said, sounding defeated. "He was only defending himself, at least that's the way he'll say it. What hurts the most is that Thomas wouldn't even see me, Sharon.

"I told that asshole Kate was sick and he didn't care. Thomas blames me for his mother dying and telling the world his secret. You know what, Sharon? I blame myself for those things too. Now my daughter is going to die for something I did."

Kyle broke down crying in Sharon arms.

Sharon hugged him tight and said, "This is not your fault, honey, it's nobody's fault."

"But it is my fault," Kyle said. "I wish I would have just died that day, Sharon, I really do. I don't want to live to see my daughter suffer through this."

Sharon couldn't think of anything else to say. She just hugged him and rubbed his back to comfort him.

Meanwhile, Kate had come in through the front door just as Kyle started crying. She stood silently in shock as she heard her father explain what had happened to him. She could not believe Thomas had changed so much and what he was now capable of. At the moment, for the first time in her life, she hated Thomas.

Chapter 23

At 25, Kate was divorced and raising her four and a half year old daughter Marie with a lot of assistance from her father and Sharon. After Matt left her three years ago and moved away with another cashier he met at Kmart, Kyle paid for little Marie to go to daycare while Kate worked at Janet's law firm during the day.

Kyle wanted his daughter to move back in with him, but Kate wanted to continue living on her own instead. This frustrated Kyle, but he still stuck by her and did all that he could to make her life easier.

He even encouraged her to start going to college three nights a week when Janet said the law firm would assist her with her tuition costs. Kyle and Sharon looked forward to those nights because they got to spend time with little Marie. Kyle was amazed at how his granddaughter looked so much like Kate did at the age. She definitely was a blessing to all of them.

Everything seemed to be moving in a positive direction for Kate and she was getting her life on track when she started having symptoms that were all too familiar to Kyle. She would complain a lot of being tired all of time. This normally wouldn't be a red flag for any single parent who worked, went to school and dealt with a young child, but Kyle had a bad feeling that it was just more than being worn out. She also complained of muscle pain and he noticed her taking aspirin several times during the day to try to alleviate it.

When he first approached her about seeing Dr. Strausberg, she refused and dismissed the notion. As the weeks went by, the muscle pain persisted and progressed to the point where she was having a hard time doing things like lifting her daughter out of the tub at night

Kate went to the doctor and Kyle's fears were confirmed. She did in fact have leukemia, but they caught it at an early stage, she was treated and it went into remission. The experience made Kate realize how fragile life was and she started thinking more and more about what would become of little Marie if something happened to her.

Although she was apprehensive about living back home, Kate moved back to her father's house. Her misgivings quickly faded when she saw how happy little Marie was being there with Pop-Pop and Gammy Sharon. Kate was happy too for the first time in a long time.

When Ms. Fluffy died in her sleep, Sharon took it as a sign that she was meant to move in with Kyle. The once too-big house was never happier; it just felt so alive to him now. Kyle had all of the people he loved under the same roof as him and he couldn't ask for anything more.

But things changed a year later when Kate started having symptoms again. When they went back to Dr.Strausberg, they were disappointed to find out that the leukemia had returned and that she would need to go through the treatment again. When the doctor said the prognosis was still good, Kyle was relieved. But he knew the circumstances were the same for Kate as they had been for him. She wasn't going to be able to keep dodging these bullets forever. They eventually caught up to his father and they would have gotten him as well if it weren't for Thomas.

It was at this point that Kyle tried every way he could think of to try to reach Thomas, but none of them worked. Thomas didn't respond to any of the letters or calls.

Kate went into remission, but only six months later she started showing signs again. This time, she wasn't responding favorably to the treatment and the doctor told Kyle that he was becoming concerned.

When Kyle saw the commercial for the Mission appearing in New York City, he knew that it was his chance to speak face-to-face with Thomas. He was certain that if he told Thomas about Kate that he would come with him to heal her. He knew in his heart that Thomas wouldn't let her down. Kyle never imagined that Thomas would refuse to see him.

As he stood in the kitchen with his swollen lip and black eye, Kyle was shocked to see Kate standing there listening as he told Sharon what happened in New York.

"He let this happen to you?" Kate asked, sounding both hurt and angry. When Kyle looked away she walked towards him. "How could he?" she said as tears welled up in her eyes.

Sharon walked towards her and was going to hug her, but Kate moved past her then stood right next to her father. "Does he know, umm about me?" she asked. "Does he know I'm sick?"

Kyle stood up straight, wiped a tear from his daughter's face with his thumb and said, "I don't know if he knew honey. But he knows now. I made sure everyone in the building heard me before they tossed me out. He'll be here honey, you'll see. I feel it in my heart, he'll be here."

Two days later The Mission left the area and they never heard from Thomas. Kate felt worse for her father than she did for herself at that point. He had stayed close to the phone the last two days waiting for it ring, and he almost gave the mailman a heart attack when he ran outside because he heard someone on the porch.

Kate was no longer hurt, now she was just angry. She had been flicking through the channels and she went right past the Van Putten Report like she had done so many times before because she despised him for what he had done to Thomas. As she tapped the channel button a few times a thought entered her head.

She went back to the station and watched the rest of the program until they aired the contact information for the Van Putten Report. As soon as she finished writing down the 800 number, she went to the phone and made the call. She was transferred immediately to a man named Martin Shulman who introduced himself as the producer of the Van Putten Report.

Much to her surprise, Martin came across as a very nice man. Before he even asked her any questions he told her that he grew up in West Caldwell, New Jersey which wasn't far from West Orange at all. It was the sort of ice breaker that Kate had never expected coming from someone who worked with a sleaze ball like Robert Van Putten.

It was almost an hour later before they started discussing the interview and chose a date for her to come in. When Kate hung up the phone, she looked at the clock and was amazed to see that an hour and a half had gone by. She couldn't believe how good it felt to just have a normal conversation with an adult other than Kyle or Sharon. They talked about the local sports teams, the state fair, the Jersey shore and just life in general. Of course she was guarded with some of her answers, but Martin really did seem interested in what she was saying, not like he was going through the motions. She decided after sitting for a while that she would wait to tell Sharon and her father until the week of her interview.

Martin sat at his desk smiling for a moment. Only it wasn't for the reason he thought he would be smiling for at the end of this call. After all, it was mission accomplished on booking one of the biggest guests of the year.

He was smiling because he just had a great conversation with a beautiful woman. For the first time in years and as crazy at it seemed there was a connection somehow. She was so easy to talk to and they had so much in common.

Martin found himself wanting to make up an excuse to call her back tomorrow, so he wrote down a bunch of mock pre-interview questions overnight and went over them with her. Again, the questions took a few minutes to go through, but the conversation lingered on well over an hour again.

He knew the question was coming, so it was no surprise when she finally asked it.

"How in the world did someone like you end up with someone like Robert Van Putten?"

"So we're already getting into life stories, are we?" Martin asked before laughing.

"You just don't strike me as being like him," Kate replied, "you seem different, you're not a..."

"A sleaze ball," Martin said, finishing her sentence for her.

Kate laughed and replied, "You used that word, not me, but now that you mention it, yes, he is a sleaze ball."

"Well, I went to college and I have a degree in both economics and communications," Martin said. "When I was a younger man I was unsure what career path to take, so I tried corporate America. It was way too cutthroat for me. You see, I never had that killer instinct. I just didn't have it in me to step on others to get ahead. It wasn't long before I went back to my first love, which was broadcasting.

"I was looking through the want ads and I noticed there was a position available at the local TV station for an assistant producer. Being a bachelor and having no responsibilities, I could afford to take risks and switch career paths on a whim."

"Oh, so you've always been a bachelor?" Kate asked.

"So far, yes," Martin answered with a laugh.

There was an uncomfortable pause, so Martin continued.

"I was at the station for two years before Robert came on to the scene. I gotta tell you; before he arrived it was just your typical boring local news channel. The station seemed content with the same old news, nothing risky and nothing exciting. When Robert joined the news team, he was young and brash. He would openly mock the old school reporters that were on staff. He was constantly in the lead producer's ear about potential stories and ways to spice things up to get some attention for the network.

"Of course being from the old school, the lead producer wanted no part of it, or Robert. So through the process of elimination, I became Robert's only friend at the station. We've been together ever since, from station to station, on our way to the top."

There was another pause, then Kate asked, "Do you mind if I ask how old you are, Martin?"

Martin dreaded this question more than the questions about Robert. He had seen Kate's picture all over the news and he knew how old she was. He thought for certain he would tell her his age and then she would give him an excuse for why she had to get off of the phone.

Martin had no problems with lying to anyone, especially women. Growing up a wealthy trust fund baby, he had no trouble at all getting women. The lying also worked for him as a producer as well because ultimately it was his job to get the guest to be as comfortable as possible and kill them will kindness before Robert got his hands on them.

Still, there was this voice in the back of his head that said, "Just tell her the truth."

When Martin didn't respond right away Kate apologized for getting too personal.

Martin took a breath and just blurted it out, "No, no, it's no big deal, Kate. I'm 38 years old."

When Kate responded, "Ok, so it is no big deal," Martin exhaled again out loud and they both shared a laugh.

The conversation continued and they agreed to have dinner after the interview was over.

Chapter 24

Two weeks later Mike Tensor walked into Martin's office like he had done so many times before with a yellow folder in one hand and cup of coffee in the other. Martin was on a conference call so he nodded to Mike and motioned for him to have a seat.

Mike smiled then waved him off as he started pacing around the office while humming softly. Martin knew the only time Mike acted like this was when he had something really good on somebody. It was sort of a celebratory thing that he did.

Martin smiled back as he continued listen to the others who were on the line go on and on about budget cuts. His mind started to wander and as he watched Mike go around the room and he thought about how he could be the poster boy for what everyone expected a retired detective to look like. At the age of 54, standing about 5-foot-11, Mike was definitely at least 30 pounds overweight. His hair and his beard were usually dyed black, but you could tell it had been a while because there was more grey than black at this point. His black plastic framed glasses were outdated and he always dressed the same: slacks, black shoes and a solid color polo shirt.

Martin knew between his pension and what the station was paying him, Mike was very well off, but you wouldn't realize it by looking at him. To Martin he looked more like a retired bowler than a retired cop.

Martin listened for a few more minutes before hanging up. As soon as he did, Mike rushed over, sat down in the chair across from Martin and smiled like the cat that swallowed the canary.

"Got something good there?" Martin asked.

"Oh I got something better than good, Marty. Kate Morgan has leukemia and she's been hiding it for some time now. This family doctor of theirs must have kept everything top secret with minimal people involved.

"But you know how it goes, Marty, you keep turning over enough rocks, sooner or later you find what you're looking for. That's something I learned early on during my 23 years of detective work with NYPD. It's all about digging for the right lead and you keep on it like a bloodhound looking into it from every angle. Sooner or later, you always find someone to take the money for the info."

Martin wasn't even listening as he went through page after page of test results and reports.

When he looked up to see Mike looking at him with that same smile his mind raced. He was worried about her health and he knew if Kate went through such lengths to keep this a secret, it would destroy her if Robert ambushed her with it on national television. He knew she would think everything he said during all of their conversations had been a lie and that she would hate him and never speak to him again. They had plans for diner after the interview and Martin was really looking forward to it. He really wanted to get to know her and he couldn't explain why. In his head, he pictured it like one of those sappy Hollywood love stories where two people who were meant to be together find each other by accident. He had never thought his way before and that's why it intrigued him so.

"Well, did I do good or what?" Mike asked, confused by Martin's lack of enthusiasm.

Martin had known Mike for years, and he was going to call upon the friendship now. He took the file, opened his bottom desk drawer, tossed it inside, closed the drawer and then locked it with a key that he had in his wallet.

"I need you to sit on this and not tell anyone about it, especially Robert," Martin said.

Mike looked at him like he had two heads. "Excuse me?"

"Look, I know what I'm asking... but as a friend, you have to do this for me," Martin said. "This woman doesn't deserve this; she's got enough on her plate. Using something like this and ambushing her with it would just be wrong."

"Wrong?" Mike said loudly, "Since when do we concern ourselves with taking the moral high ground, Marty? Have you forgotten who you work with? I mean, c'mon."

"I know who we work with," Martin replied. "I am asking you a favor, Mike. As a friend, please do this for me."

"Just like that, no questions asked?" Mike asked.

"I understand the position I'm putting you in," Martin said. "But you and I both know he's still going to poke and prod her about Thomas. Trust me; the world is still going to get their money's worth from this with or without that folder."

Mike scratched the back of his neck and took a sip of his coffee. He then shook his head from side to side and sighed.

"What are going soft on me now?" Mike asked with a laugh.

"I don't know, maybe I am," Martin said. "Maybe I'm getting a little tired of being alone and working as a wrecking ball."

"I hear ya, pal," Mike replied. "I hear ya, but I don't understand ya," Mike said as he laughed again.

"You got it, ok? I'll bury this one and let the cards fall where they may. I don't feel good about it, though, and if you know who finds out about this somehow later on he will boot your ass out of here himself."

Martin laughed and nodded, "Yeah, I know that's exactly what will happen. Thank you for this, Mike. It means a lot to me that you would do this."

"Hey, it's done ok," Mike said. "Tell you what, tonight you can treat me to a nice steak dinner and pay for the drinks."

"You got it bud, see you later," Martin replied.

Finally, the day came. The taping of the show had been big news all of the world because neither Kyle nor Kate had said a word to the press since Kyle pleaded for information after Thomas had disappeared.

Through the years, both Kyle and Kate had received offers on a regular basis for substantial amounts of money to do a tell all interview and neither ever responded.

When Kate made the call to the offices of the Van Putten Report it was for two reasons.

She knew Thomas hated Van Putten for ambushing him during his interview. She knew it would hurt Thomas almost as much as her father had been hurt that day he went to see him and was confronted by Billy instead.

The other reason was for the money. Kate had insurance, but it did not cover all of the costs for the tests and the prescriptions. She was aware of some experimental treatments, but her insurance wouldn't consider those either. She knew the biggest offer would come from the show. Minutes after she got off the phone with Martin, Robert Van Putten called and offered Kate almost twice as much money as anyone else ever had.

Kate still resented herself for agreeing to do the interview. She hated Robert too after she saw the way he treated Thomas. Not to mention all of the follow up interviews he did with whomever he could get that came into contact with her one-time best friend. Some of Thomas' old teachers, their other neighbors in town, people his mother worked with and even people who waited on him at hotels or restaurants all appeared on the Van Putten Report. Robert was milking his interaction with Thomas for all he could get out of it.

Another thing that troubled her greatly about this interview was Robert's ability to dig up dirt on certain guests and ambush them with it. He seemed to have a knack for finding out secrets; in fact he built a career out of doing so. Kate never said a word to anyone outside her family about her illness. It was a secret kept by the family, Dr. Strausberg and his staff.

She knew that the media would never give her or her family a moment's peace if they found out she was sick and that Thomas wasn't helping her. They had all been through the constant media attention before when Thomas was with them and they were so grateful when it was over.

All of the medical records pertaining to Kate's illness and diagnosis were kept in confidence by the doctor, he personally saw to that. Everyone that was involved in testing or treating her was people he had known for years and people he could trust.

The thing that kept Kate going was that her daughter, she was the world to Marie. She wanted to do everything she could to be there for her as long as possible. Another driving force was her father. She knew he felt helpless. She knew he had given up hope after not being able to bring Thomas back with him to save her just as she had done to save her father years ago. But the truth was that no matter what happened her father was her savior and her hero. She knew when the day did come for her, that little Marie would be raised by a better man than any man she could have ever been with. Kate wished she had taken his advice about staying away from Matt, but if she had done that, she wouldn't have her beautiful daughter.

Chapter 25

Martin made sure Kate got the "A" list treatment. He sent a limo to pick Kate up from her house and take her to the airport, where she flew first class. Another driver was waiting for her to take her by limo to the station. Upon arriving at the studio, Kate was given a makeover that included new clothes, shoes, a haircut, hair coloring and make up.

Once alone inside the green room, Kate sat pondering if she should go through with the interview. She thought of all of time she spent with Thomas and how she thought of herself as his sister for years. She was just starting to lose her nerve when Martin knocked on the door and entered the room to greet her.

"Wow, you look fabulous," he said. "I love what they did with your hair."

Kate smiled. "Thanks, do you really think it looks good this way?"

"You look stunning," Martin said, and Kate laughed. Kate looked at Martin and thought he was very attractive for someone almost twice her age. He didn't fit her image of the producer of a sleaze ball like Robert Van Putten.

Of course Martin went above and beyond to put his best foot forward for Kate. He spent the entire day before the interview shopping for a new suit, getting a haircut, a shave and a manicure. Even Robert was impressed when he ran into Martin that morning, acting like he didn't recognize him as he introduced himself to Martin before laughing and telling him how well he cleaned up.

Martin took a seat next to her, smiled and said. "So, is there anything else I can get for you?"

"Nope, everything has been great so far," Kate said.

They made small talk for a few minutes before Martin wanted to go over some of the questions that Robert would be asking her during the interview. "That's fine," Kate said, "but you and I both know that these are the fluff questions, Martin, I told you, I've watched the show. I have a pretty good idea what's coming."

Martin laughed and nodded, but he thought of the medical report Mike Tensor dug up as he looked at Kate. He knew if Robert had gotten his hands on it, she would have no idea what was about to hit her.

"Ok, let's just skip that then and just talk," Martin said.

"That would be great," Kate said.

They spent the next half-hour just talking about life and their pasts. Kate noticed that Martin seemed to be attracted to her as they spoke. She felt a connection with him, too. They were laughing and having a great time when they were interrupted by another knock on the door. This time, it was the assistant producer letting them know it was show time.

Martin walked Kate to the side of the stage and waited with her through the monologue. She noticed that he seemed just as nervous as she did. She gave Martin a look of concern and he responded with an uneasy smile. The assistant producer walked towards them and told them it was time.

Kate leaned and grabbed Martin's arm to pull him towards her, "I don't want this edited to make Thomas look bad, I want you to air exactly what I say in the context I say it."

Martin nodded, looked away and said, "Ok."

"No, Martin, I want you to promise me," Kate insisted. "This is important."

Martin nodded again and looked into her eyes, "Ok, I promise," he said.

"Great, see you for dinner when this is over, right?" Kate asked.

"I'm looking forward to it," Martin replied.

The assistant producer then walked Kate to the side of the stage and waited with her until Robert finished his introduction.

"Ladies and Gentlemen for years people in the media, myself included have done story after story on the phenom that is Thomas Greggs, aka The Healer," Robert said. "I'm sure you all are aware of the incident that took place when Thomas was on this very stage. For those of you who didn't see it, here it is again."

Everyone's attention turned to the monitors as they replayed the end of Thomas' old interview When the video reached the point that Thomas was beating Robert, everyone in the audience cringed at the same time. Most shook their heads in disgust or shouted at the monitors.

As the replay ended, Robert stared at the monitor for a moment before turning around. "I spent six hours in the emergency room and it took three weeks before I was in good enough condition to return to work," Robert said.

"Since that interview, I have spoken with many people that knew Thomas briefly or people he had worked with on the Mission. Up until now, I have never interviewed anyone who has had a close relationship with the Greggs family or with Thomas in particular.

"That is until tonight, ladies and gentlemen. Tonight's guest and her father have been pursued by every media outlet in the world. They have been offered substantial amounts of money time and time again to discuss Thomas Greggs, aka The Healer, but they have refused over and over. As a result, the puzzle that is Thomas Greggs' past has been put together using mostly hearsay and rumors. That will all change after tonight, ladies and gentleman.

"So, without further ado, I would like to introduce to you one of the few people who knew the real Thomas Greggs and she is here to tell all about him. She is one of his closest friends and as a child; she was healed by Thomas after breaking her arm. Ladies and gentlemen, please welcome Kate Morgan."

Everyone in the studio audience got to their feet and applauded when Kate walked onto the set. Scalpers were selling the freely-distributed tickets to be in the studio audience for up to $500 apiece. People wanted to be the first to hear what she was going to say about Thomas. They didn't want to have to wait until later that night like everyone else.

Robert greeted Kate and shook her hand, but she saw through Robert's fake plastic smile. Kate tried to mentally prepare herself for whatever was about to come her way.

Robert began the interview by discussing Thomas's childhood and how they met. Kate told him that they were neighbors, but they weren't close friends until after he healed her broken arm.

She explained how Thomas's father was an abusive drunk who beat his wife and son often. When Robert asked about the night that Thomas' father died, Kate tried to explain that she believed that Thomas did try to heal his father, but something went wrong.

"I don't know for certain what happened that night, Thomas never wanted to talk about it," Kate said. "But I know if it was possible, he would have saved him."

"Now hold a minute Kate," Robert said. "Thomas has healed thousands of people with many different illnesses or afflictions. He saved your father from certain death, how was it that he couldn't save his own father?"

Robert didn't wait for a response before continuing.

"You just said his father abused both him and his mother, do you think maybe when given the choice, and Thomas didn't want to save his father?"

Kate was more flustered then she thought she would be. She looked to the side of the stage, wishing that Martin would come out and put a stop to this for her.

"Kate, did you hear my question?" Robert asked.

"I know that he tried and that he gave up at some point," Kate said. "It must not have been working because he told me he reached the point where it was in God's hands."

When the crowd let out a collective gasp Kate paused for a second to scan the audience.

She didn't realize the repercussions of what she said until Robert smiled and repeated the words, "In God's hands, huh?"

"So we can, in fact, speculate that Thomas chose not to save his father," Robert said coldly as he looked straight into the camera.

"Now wait a minute!" Kate insisted. "I did not say that Thomas *chose* not to save him! I only tried to explain the circumstances surrounding his father's death and what Thomas went through while trying to save him, so don't put words in my mouth! You have no idea what his life was like as a child, or the things he's seen!"

Robert sensed that she was close to walking off, so he pulled it back for the moment.

This interview was too important to have her get up and leave halfway through it. So instead of pursuing that line of questioning, Robert moved on from Thomas' father's death and talked about his mother's suicide, calling it another tragic day in Thomas's life.

Kate wouldn't talk about that at all. She just said that Thomas loved his mother more than anything. She explained that even though Marie dealt with her widely-reported issues, she was still a caring and loving mother.

Robert kept prodding Kate for details about where Thomas was when he found out his mother was dead and if he tried to use his ability to bring her back after they found her in the lake.

"Thomas was devastated, he loved his mother," Kate said, ignoring the other questions.

Since Kate wasn't giving him much to work with, Robert changed subjects again. He asked what she knew about Thomas' abilities.

Thomas could not bring someone back from death, she thought. Nor could he heal someone whose "time had come." Kate explained that she was raised to believe that we all have our time and when it's your time to go, that's it. "Not even Thomas can interfere with God's plan," she said.

Robert asked if Thomas had come from a religious family. Kate told him that Thomas always seemed to shy away from talking about God or religion.

"How do you suppose that someone who you say isn't very religious ended up becoming the poster boy for the biggest traveling congregation in the country?" Robert asked.

"I think Thomas became involved in this Mission for his own reasons," Kate said. "He liked the idea of using his gift to help others."

"Something he should have started doing with his father," Robert remarked, which drew a cold stare from Kate.

The conversation went on focusing more about Thomas as a person. There were several filler questions about his relationship with Kate and Kyle, but nothing that hadn't been reported before. Robert was just trying to fill out the show, so he kept it cordial. When he looked up at the clock and noticed time was running out, he took it up a notch.

"Let's talk about the day Thomas left," Robert said. "You said you were close friends? You said you and Thomas stayed up many nights talking and crying together. You said your father treated him like he was one of his own. Was that before or after Thomas saved his life, by the way?"

Kate shook her head in disgust and said, "My father was always good to Thomas."

Robert laughed and replied, "Always good to Thomas, huh? Is that why he left in the middle of the night without saying a word to either of you?

"Let me ask you something, Kate. Do you think Thomas would have disappeared and joined up with some preacher of questionable values if your father hadn't told a secret you had promised to keep?"

"You son of a bitch," Kate shouted, "don't you dare!"

"Oh, I *do* dare Kate! The world believes that Thomas Greggs is some kind of gift from the heavens! But this man stood by and watched his father die right in front of him! This man made millions touring the world with a 'religious mission' carnival when he doesn't even believe in God!"

"I never said that!" Kate got up and started to walk off the set.

Robert got to his feet and shouted over her.

"So here is a man who chose when to use his 'gift' at an early age! He got rid of his father -- who you say he hated – but he healed both you and your father.

"And dear, innocent Kate, how do you repay him? By telling the world his secret -- the one thing he asked you not you tell. As a result of this, what does he do?"

Robert now stood face to face with Kate

"He takes the gift and uses it to his benefit making millions with a used car salesman who calls himself a preacher. He selectively heals again and again while using God and Religion as his reasons for doing so when in reality; he could give a rat's ass about either."

Kate had enough; she slapped Robert across the face and ran off stage crying. Martin tried to talk to her, but she pushed past him and ran down the hallway. Feeling helpless and ashamed, Martin called the limo driver and told him to pull around to the front of the building to pick Kate up.

Meanwhile, on stage Robert was in his glory. "Sometimes the truth hurts, ladies and gentlemen; but it is the truth nonetheless," he said. "For the Van Putten Report I am Robert Van Putten, good night and God bless."

Chapter 26

When the Van Putten Report finished taping, the stage went dark and the audience erupted with applause for several minutes, continuing long after Robert had left the set. Robert was greeted with high fives from everyone backstage. Everyone from the station seemed to be there smiling and patting him on the back, everyone except for Martin.

Robert's producer was standing in the front lobby, watching helplessly as Kate ran away from the building. He saw the limo drive up the street after her. The driver got out of the car and spoke with Kate for several minutes. He must have convinced her that the airport was too far to walk, because she got into the car and they drove away.

When Martin went back inside, he immediately got word that Robert was looking for him. He took a few minutes to gather his thoughts before going back upstairs to meet Robert.

Martin entered the editing room, where Robert stood standing side by side with the lead editor as they discussed how to put the show together. He lit up with a big smile when he saw Martin.

"There is the man of the hour!" he shouted. "I owe you big for this one, buddy. That was better than I ever thought it would be."

Martin didn't say anything as Robert laughed and patted him on the back. He felt ashamed so he just looked down at the floor and nodded.

"Wait to you see the final edit of this thing. It is going to be amazing," Robert said.

Martin suddenly remembered the promise he made to Kate, and he felt even worse as he realized he had no way of keeping it. Even if he asked Robert to go easy, he would just throw a fit and find a way to make Kate and Thomas look worse.

The guilt must have been written all over Martin's face. Robert's expression turned from elation to confusion. "What's going on, man? You are usually thrilled when a show comes together like this, are you all right?"

Martin looked past Robert to the monitor on the wall. He watched the recorded images of Kate crying as she walked off stage and it broke his heart.

Robert didn't like being ignored so he turned to see what had gotten Martin's attention.

"Hey, you're not getting soft on me now?" Robert asked with a smug smile. "I thought we were past this shit years ago."

Martin knew they had built an empire on doing things a lot worse than this. He understood what he signed up for when he followed Robert from place to place.

But as Martin stared at Robert, he remembered Kate referring to him as a sleaze ball. He wondered if that was all he was too.

"I don't know, maybe I am getting soft in my old age," Martin said. "Maybe I don't feel good about what we're doing, or what I'm doing with my life anymore."

"What the hell are you talking about?" Robert asked "Look, you're not making sense and you're certainly not thinking clearly. Go out, have a few drinks and get laid. You'll feel better. Lord knows it's always worked before when you thought you were growing a conscience."

Martin laughed for a second, but took another good hard look at Robert. "Sure, he was famous and wealthy; but what did he really have?" Martin thought.

"I could say the same about myself," Martin realized.

He wasn't getting any younger and the window for having the things that he always put off was closing. Things like a wife and a family. At the least, he wanted someone to love and someone who would love him.

Martin took a deep breath and then just came out said it, "I can't do this anymore, Robert."

"Is this about money again?" Robert asked.

"You know, Robert, she was right. You are nothing but a rat bastard. I quit."

Martin wasn't going to wait for a rebuttal. He turned and headed straight for the door without even looking in Robert's direction again.

"Fine then, get the fuck outta here!" Robert yelled. "I'm a fucking rat bastard, is that what you called me? This fucking rat bastard made you, Martin; you wouldn't be shit without me!

"You were right there with me all through the years, Martin. Don't act all holier than thou now!"

Without saying another word, Martin opened the door and left to clean out his office. Within a half-hour he was out of the building and it was over.

Kate didn't say a word to anyone about the interview when she finally got home. She just went into her daughter's room and watched her while little Marie slept. She was so lost in her thoughts that didn't notice when Sharon opened the door.

"Someone named Martin Shulman called from the station and told us what happened. Are you ok?"

Kate got up from the chair and walked into the hallway with Sharon. It was no surprise to her that her father was there too. She motioned for them to follow her into the living room where they sat and talked.

"Martin had the nerve to call here?" Kate sounded tired, angry and hurt.

"He called right after you left, he said he was sorry and he apologized to your father too," Sharon said. "He even said something about quitting the show."

"Yeah right," Kate said. "I bet he pulls that bull with every one of his guests. He treats them like they are something special, talks to them on the phone, gives them a makeover and then gives his friend Robert the dagger to drive into their hearts."

Sharon looked at her with compassion.

"I'm madder at myself though," Kate said. "I've seen the show, I feel like an idiot."

"Why did you do it then?" Sharon asked. "Your father and I warned you, and you yourself knew what kind of person you were dealing with."

"I thought I could control what happened," Kate said "I thought I could control what was said, and I was…"

"And you were what?" Sharon asked.

"And, I was angry at Thomas for what happened to you, Dad," Kate said. "Angry that Thomas didn't come to help me," she said as a tear formed in her eye. "But when I got there and I saw that smug look on that arrogant sleaze ball's face, I changed my mind. I decided that I would explain about the person that Thomas really was and what made him that way.

"But he turned it around on me and I gave him all he needed to crucify Thomas. You know, part of me thinks Thomas deserves it. But another part of me thinks he's already been through more than enough in his life."

Kate started to cry and Sharon tried to comfort her while Kyle looked on with concern.

"What about you?" Sharon asked. "Haven't you been through enough too? Maybe you need to give yourself a break too, honey. Lord knows if anyone deserves a break or a miracle it's you. That's why your father went to see Thomas.

"I told him at the time it might not be such a good idea, and you know what he told me? He told me that he got a chance once to start over and change his life for the better because of you. He said he was going to do everything he could to see that you got that chance as well."

Kyle's eyes started to well up with tears and he reached for his daughter's hand.

"You know I can't even tell you how frustrated he was that you would subject yourself to an interview with Robert Van Putten because you needed money for medicine and experimental treatments. You know he would have mortgaged the house in a second and I would have done all that I could to help you too."

Kyle moved over to sit on the other side of his daughter and he put his arm around her.

"It's ok to be angry, Kate. You wanted to hurt someone back for all of the hurt you've been through. You were angry you were left to raise your daughter alone. Angry you inherited a disease from your father and that the person who saved him isn't here to save you.

"I understand these things Kate, you know that. I hoped with everything in me that you would never experience the things that I had been through; it was my job to protect you from them. What I learned through everything I've been through, Kate, is that as long as you have people who love you in your life, there's always hope. You are not alone and you never will be. We love you and that little beautiful girl in the other room loves you too.

"Snakes like this Martin guy and his boss Robert will never know this kind of love. They will die alone, I can assure you of that, because karma will find them."

Kate leaned into him and Kyle hugged her tight with his one arm while kissing her on the forehead.

"We will do whatever it takes to help you, you hear me, whatever it takes."

Kate nodded and they both started to cry.

Chapter 27

An hour later, they all sat and watched the interview together. It was even worse than Kate feared. She could tell right away that Robert and Martin had edited it so that there was very little of her explanation about Dan Greggs being an abusive father. Gone too were all of the nice things she said about Marie.

Instead, it was cut up to show her talking about the night Thomas' father died and how he said "Let God decide," along with so many other things taken out of context. She knew Robert was capable of this, but she was furious with Martin. He seemed so honest and sincere, how could she let herself be taken like that? As Kate watched the show, she imagined that Thomas was sitting and watching it too. She knew he was; she could feel it within every fiber of her.

In a show of sympathy, Kyle would rub his daughter's back from time to time as he sighed while watching. He was mad at Thomas, but this was painful to watch.

They had reached the end of the interview when Robert launched into his tirade and Kate slapped him when someone knocked on the door. Everyone was still glued to the screen, so no one got up after the first knock. After the second knock, Sharon went to answer the door but didn't recognize the person standing there.

"Hello," the man said, "I sincerely apologize for disturbing you at this time of night but I was wondering if I could please speak to Kate Morgan."

Sharon immediately assumed that this was a bloodsucking reporter looking for a quote right after the interview aired, so she started to close the door.

"I'm sorry," Sharon said, "Kate is busy at the moment and she won't be commenting on any of this."

"Please, my name is Martin Shulman; I'm Robert Van Putten's producer."

Sharon didn't need to hear anymore, she slammed the door hard in the man's face and headed back to the living room.

"Please ma'am," Martin yelled from outside the door, "I owe her an apology and I need to speak with her, please, I am so very sorry!"

Sharon paused for a moment before shaking her head and walking into the living room.

As she entered the room she could see that the interview was over. Kyle and Kate were now just sitting and talking with the TV off. "What's wrong?" Kyle asked. "Who was that at the door?"

"I think you're going to have to call the police," Sharon replied.

"There is a Martin Shulman on the porch from the Van Putten Report. He says he wants to talk to Kate and apologize, do you believe the nerve of these people?"

Kyle was furious; he got to his feet and headed for the door, but Kate stopped him.

"Wait," she shouted, "did you say Martin Shulman?"

"Yes," Sharon said.

"I'll take care of this, dad," Kate said, "I have a lot I want to say to Mr. Shulman."

Kate opened the door to find Martin sitting on the steps with his head down.

Gone were the jacket and tie he was wearing earlier. He was now dressed only in the white button-down shirt and a pair of grey slacks. His hair was no longer neatly combed and he looked very sad to her as he stared out into the street ahead.

She thought about just telling him to get the hell out of here, but she didn't see Robert or a camera crew and that made her curious.

"What are you doing here Martin?" Kate asked coldly.

Martin lifted his head as if surprised and looked at Kate.

He quickly got to his feet. "I um, I wanted to apologize," he said, "I'm so sorry for what happened."

"You're sorry!" Kate yelled. "You've got a lot of nerve coming here, Martin. Who the hell do you people think you are?"

Kate turned to go back inside, but Martin stopped her.

"I know you're sick," he said

Kate turned around. "What did you just say?"

"We have a private eye we use," Martin said. "His name is Mike Tensor. I've known him for years and he is very good at what he does. He's had a hand in almost every story we've broken since we began the Van Putten Report."

"What does this have to do with me?" Kate asked

"Robert asked me to find out any deep dark secrets that you may have so he could ambush you during the interview," Martin said. "Mike somehow got his hands on your hospital records and he gave them to me to pass on to Robert."

"Wait, if you had them why didn't Robert mention anything about it or about Thomas not helping me?" Kate asked.

"Because I never gave Robert the records and I asked Mike to keep his mouth shut about it," Martin said. "I had a feeling it was going to be bad enough out there for you with Robert and his usual banter."

"When I found out you were sick, the thought of him using that on the show and blindsiding you with it. Well, I had to do all I could to prevent that. You see, Kate, I can't control what he says when he's out there, but I can control what he knows and what he doesn't. Well, I could before today anyway."

"What's that supposed to mean?"

"I quit the show," Martin said. "I reached the point where I couldn't look myself in the mirror anymore.

"Then when I met you and something just clicked. The way we spoke on the phone, we just talked like two people who knew each other for a while and it's never like that for me. Don't get me wrong, I am good at what I do, but I'm just going through the motions when I make those calls, almost like it's scripted, the same thing every time.

"I know the answer to the question and even the reaction to every question I ever ask. Yet there I was, talking to you, the pre-interview was over, the scripted version was done and we were still talking about nothing that was show-related. Just like two regular people. I guess I had forgotten what that was like and how much I missed it.

"Then when I met you in person and I got to talk to you face to face," Martin blushed, "I wanted to spend even more time with you and I wanted to see that smile over and over again."

Martin lost himself in the moment and he found himself looking right into Kate's eyes.

When he snapped out of it and regained his composure, he was embarrassed by all he had said.

"Look," he said trying to do some damage control while still blushing. "I just wanted you to know how sorry I am, very truly sincerely sorry."

Martin smiled and nodded before walking down the stairs.

"Wait," Kate said just as he reached the bottom step. "Would you like to come inside for some coffee or tea?"

Martin stopped dead in his tracks then turned and smiled, "I would love to," he said. They went back inside and talked for hours.

Before Martin left, he and Kate kissed on the steps.

Chapter 28

Thomas had just walked off the stage at the Philips Arena in Atlanta, Georgia. He noticed Cheryl was standing there with his water and a towel as usual. As he reached to grab the items and walk away, she stopped him.

"Billy wants to see you in his dressing room; he said it's kind of urgent."

Thomas wiped the sweat from his forehead and took a long sip of the water. "This can't wait until later?" he asked.

"Billy said that I should get you as soon as you came off stage."

Thomas tried to read Cheryl's expression as he toweled off his neck. He didn't say anything, but motioned for her to lead the way as they started walking down the hall towards Billy's dressing room.

When they got to the door, Thomas heard several voices inside and the TV was really loud.

Cheryl let Thomas inside, then left and closed the door behind her.

Thomas saw Billy, Bernie and Jerry all watching TV together on the couch. They did not even acknowledge that he had entered the room.

Thomas approached them from behind and said, "What's up?"

Just as Billy stood up to approach him, something on the TV caught Thomas's eye: It was the Van Putten Report.

"What the hell are you watching this trash for?" Thomas asked.

"There's something going on that I didn't tell you about cause I knew it would really upset you," Billy said. "But all of the networks are talking about this now and there is no way I was going to able keep this from you."

"Billy, what the hell are you talking about and what does this have to do with him?" Thomas asked as he gestured towards the TV.

Billy didn't even have a chance to respond. Thomas's eyes were fixated on the screen once he saw Kate Morgan walk on stage. Thomas felt as if he had been kicked in the stomach. Even more disgusting was that fact that she smiled and shook hands with the devil before sitting down.

He stared at the TV and didn't say a word until after the final credit scrolled off the screen.

Bernie and Jerry looked at Billy for direction, not knowing what to say or do. Billy asked Thomas if he was ok, even though he could tell that Thomas wasn't. Billy watched as Thomas raised his hands up near his face and looked at them. Then he closed them into fists.

"I need a minute, he said coldly. "Get out."

Billy thought about staying to talk to Thomas, but instead he said, "Ok man, I'm here if you need me." Billy motioned for his brothers and they all left the room.

As soon as he closed the door, Billy heard the first crash. "Damn it," Billy said, "That was my TV!" They heard another crash and another, followed by the sounds of Thomas shouting, "God damn you, God damn you!"

Billy held his brothers at bay until the room went silent. Three minutes later, Thomas opened the door and came out. He was covered in sweat and his hands were bleeding. Billy's room was completely trashed. Billy was mad, but he didn't want to push Thomas. He forced a look of concern and he put his hand on Thomas's shoulder.

"Are you ok, Thomas?" Billy asked. "Is there anything I can do?"

"No, I'm not ok," Thomas shot back, "but there is something you can do for me."

"Sure man, just name it," Billy said.

"Tell everyone and make sure they understand," Thomas growled.

"They are to accept no correspondence at all from Kyle or Kate Morgan or anyone affiliated with them ever again. SHE IS DEAD TO ME!" Thomas shouted.

"I don't want to see or hear anything to do with them and if anyone screws up --I don't care who they are -- I will fire their ass, you got that Billy?"

Billy had only seen Thomas like this one other time, after he beat Robert Van Putten into a bloody mess during his TV interview. Billy knew Thomas was in a very fragile state and worried that he could just walk away from this whole thing like he did from Morgans. Billy wasn't going to take that chance.

"I'll make sure everyone gets it, Thomas," Billy said.

"Now please, Thomas, let's go see the nurse and get those hands looked at."

Thomas looked down at his hands as though he just noticed that they were cut and bleeding, then he started to walk away.

He stopped for a moment halfway down the hall and yelled, "I don't need anyone to look at my hands, I'm the fucking Healer, remember? Bernie, have someone bring two bottles of vodka to my room ASAP, don't make me wait."

"Sure thing man," Billy yelled back.

When Thomas was gone, Bernie looked over to find his brother smiling again. "What should I do, Billy, and what the hell are you smiling about?"

"You get his drink and let him drink himself calm, that's what you do," Billy answered.

"I am smiling because Kate Morgan did us a favor tonight. He ain't never going back there again, so we just have to maintain control and the money train keeps rolling along for a good long time. That's why I'm smiling, my brother."

Six months had passed since Kate's interview, and it was a few days after Thanksgiving. Thomas had just walked off stage after a healing session and he was beyond tired. He couldn't remember the last time he'd slept more than an hour or two at a time. Even with the alcohol and pills in his system, he would still wake up several times during the night.

Cheryl handed him a bottle of water just like she always did, and Thomas didn't even acknowledge her. He walked down the long hallway, past his dressing room and out an exit door located in the back of the building.

He sat on a railing with his eyes closed and enjoyed the quiet. He tilted his head upward to feel the cold wind on his face as he breathed the clean air. When he opened his eyes, all he could see was a sea of red lights as the cars left the arena.

Thomas felt no sense of accomplishment or gratification. He had helped more people than he could remember, but they did nothing to fill his feelings of emptiness or assuage the guilt he felt over his mother's death. Everything had become a blur. The people he saw each night looked more like cattle then those in need. He had no friends, no family and no one to love. Not for the first time, Thomas felt pathetic because he had never had a girlfriend. He would watch as every man on the Mission staff spent time with one woman after another, city after city, but Thomas remained a loner.

It wasn't as if Thomas didn't want a girlfriend. He was considered a geek and a loser in school, so the opportunity never presented itself. Once the Mission took off, it seemed the only women that approached him were religious fanatics who scared the crap out of him.

Thomas focused on the cars again and his mind drifted to thoughts of the upcoming holidays. Neesy always made such a big deal of Christmas and it was really nice being around her, but something was missing. When he would sit and watch husbands and wives, and boyfriends and girlfriends exchange gifts at the compound, Thomas always felt more like a guest than a member of the family. When the day turned to night and everyone else paired off together, Neesy would spend as much time as she could with Thomas before Billy came down and asked her to come to bed.

The sound of the door opening behind him snapped Thomas back into the present. He was certain that it was just Cheryl coming to tell him how long he had to shower and change before the bus left, so Thomas didn't even turn around. But it wasn't Cheryl; it was a woman he didn't recognize.

"Oh, I'm sorry. I didn't mean to startle you or disturb you, I saw you come out here and I thought it might be a good opportunity to introduce myself, I'm Kelly Taylor. I've been with The Mission a little over a week, but I don't think we've ever been introduced."

When Thomas turned around, his mouth opened and suddenly he was at a loss for words as he stared at the gorgeous redhead who was standing in front of him smiling. As she stood under the light that hung over the metal door, Thomas thought she looked like an angel.

Her hair was long and straight, her eyes were a sexy green color that he had never seen before, her skin was pale and she had freckles on either side of her nose. She had big pouty lips and a perfect smile.

She dressed very stylishly and it was easy to see that she spent a lot of time getting her hair, makeup and nails done.

"Hi umm Kelly, nice to meet you," Thomas said while trying to clear his voice and without making eye contact. He felt very awkward because, as Billy pointed out to him on many occasions, "He had no game."

"I think it's great what you do," Kelly said, trying to alleviate the uncomfortable pause. "I think we should all try to give a little back in some way to try to make a difference, that's why I'm here."

Thomas still wouldn't make eye contact or acknowledge Kelly in any way. She quickly regrouped because she thought she would only get one chance to make an impression.

"Hey Thomas, what do you like to do for fun?" Kelly asked. "If you don't mind me saying, I've noticed that everyone here kinda pairs up and you go off by yourself a lot. I don't have anyone to pair up with so we can hang out or go do something if you want."

A thought suddenly occurred to Thomas, and he asked Kelly, "Why are you here?"

"Well, I wanted to get my foot in the door with The Mission so when there was a temp position available, I jumped at the opportunity," Kelly answered. "It's only supposed to be for five events, but I'm hoping I make enough of an impression that they keep me on. I've never been far from home and I've always wanted to travel."

Thomas shook his head and then looked her in the eye, "What I meant was did Billy hire you to be my pretend friend?"

Kelly looked confused and shook her head. "No of course not, Thomas. I don't even have any idea what that even means. Why would anyone hire a friend for you?"

Kelly had the same gift as Billy when it came to reading people, so when she saw the look of embarrassment on Thomas' face, she quickly changed gears again.

"By the way," she said, "between you and me, I think that Billy is a pompous control freak. I mean all I did was introduce myself to him then try to tell him some of the ideas that I had for The Mission and he got a big-time attitude with me. He started referring to me as 'Missy.' 'Listen Missy, I don't need any advice from some green college girl on how to run The Mission, we're doing just fine.'

"When I told him that he graduated with honors in both business management and economics, he started again saying, 'we are doing just fine, now do your job and maybe we'll keep you around for more than a day.' I know he's your friend or mentor, but the guy can be a real jerk, you know?"

Thomas laughed out loud, something he hadn't done for a long time. "Billy, my friend or mentor?" he said, still laughing. "No, I really don't think he was ever either of those things."

Kelly smiled and made a mental note that this was definitely a chink in the armor that she could exploit.

They sat outside and talked for over an hour before Cheryl came out to get him. Thomas found Kelly to be very easy to talk to because she did all of the talking. By the time he held the door open for her and they went back inside, Thomas knew her whole life story. Like him, she was an only child. Unlike him, she was very popular in both junior high and high school. She was also on the high honor roll throughout and this intimidated a lot of guys so she didn't date a lot.

She received a full scholarship to a state college where she graduated with honors. Her goal at this point was to just travel for a while before deciding on a career path. Eventually she wanted to start her own business.

Thomas thought that meeting Kelly was one of those signs that Neesy always talked about.

After he showered, she came back to his dressing room and hung out with him until it was time to get on the bus. Billy noticed them talking as he passed by. He made eye contact with Thomas as he walked up the stairs and gave him a disapproving head shake as he went inside.

Thomas said goodbye to Kelly and watched as she made her way down the sidewalk to board one of the other buses. He had a big smile on his face as he made his way up the stairs to his bus.

Billy was waiting for him. "Hey, before you go messing with that, I have to tell you I got a bad vibe from her, Thomas," he said.

"Do you know we were barely through with shaking hands when she started talking to me about wanting to discuss some ideas she has to promote The Mission? I mean, can you believe that shit, on her first day, during our first meeting?"

Thomas was in too good of a mood to listen to Billy's paranoid nonsense, so he blew him off. "Whatever," Thomas said. "I like her and I want her promoted to take Cheryl's job."

"Wait a minute, you want what?" Billy said.

Bernie could see that his brother was getting upset, so he tried to defuse the situation. He grabbed his brother from behind and whispered, "Leave this alone for now; he might be sweet on her."

Billy shook his head and then backed off.

"Look, Thomas, we'll talk about this later ok?" Billy said in an effort to be diplomatic, but Thomas wouldn't have it.

"There's nothing else to talk about," Thomas replied coldly. "This is what I want, give Cheryl another job."

Thomas didn't wait for a response, he turned and walked away, leaving Billy to wonder what kind of an impression that girl made on Thomas.

Although it was against every instinct he had, Billy did as Thomas requested. Cheryl didn't put up a fight at all. Billy knew she would be thrilled that she didn't have to deal with Thomas anymore, so in that respect it worked out. But he still thought it was a mistake, even though he wasn't willing to risk losing Thomas over something so trivial.

After the transition Thomas started to spend more time with Kelly and it blossomed into a relationship within weeks. Thomas had never been in love, so he fell hard and fast for Kelly. He wanted to spend all of his time with her and they were seldom apart. When he started having her travel with him on the bus, Billy made a big fuss about it, but Thomas wouldn't back down. Billy reluctantly agreed because he wanted to be able to keep an eye on Kelly as much as possible. He was constantly in Thomas' ear telling him, "This girl was nothing but trouble." According to Billy, "She was nothing but a gold digger." Thomas wouldn't listen to a word he said, which frustrated Billy to no end.

Billy knew he had lost control and had a big problem on his hands about a month into their steady relationship. He was just about to go on stage one night when he noticed Thomas hanging around backstage, joking and laughing with Bernie. The miserable, depressed, self-loathing boy Billy first met at a New Jersey funeral home was long gone, replaced by a smiling, relaxed, outwardly confident young man.

"Hey man, what's up?" Billy asked Thomas.

"Nothing man, just hanging out waiting to do my thing," Thomas said and laughed.

"Your thing, huh?" Billy said as he studied him. "You smoking something, man? Did you give him some of your shit, Bernie?"

"Nah Billy, it's nothing like that. It's a different kind of drug entirely," Bernie said with a big grin.

"Oh shit, you weren't kidding when you said doing your thing, then, huh?" Billy said and they all laughed. "My little Thomas, all grown up now and getting some! Good for you, man."

Thomas didn't like the comment and he quickly turned serious. "Don't make it sound all sleazy like what you do, 'cause it ain't like that. I love this girl," Thomas said.

"Oh, you love her now?" Billy said, staring Thomas in the eye. "You've known this girl how long? And just because she gives you some, now you're in love? You think you're her first, Thomas? You better be careful, hear?"

"No, *you* better be careful," Thomas said angrily. "She means a lot to me and I don't want you talking about her like she's one of the floozies that you associate with, you got that?"

"Easy man," Billy said, knowing now that he had to tread lightly. "I'm just looking out for you man, telling you to take it slow and see where it goes, ok?"

"Huh, I stopped believing you were looking out for me a long time ago, Billy," Thomas said. "I can look after myself just fine, thanks anyway."

Bernie interrupted before the confrontation could become more heated. "Hey Billy, you've only got a second or two before they announce you. You should get out there."

Thomas and Billy stood eye to eye for a moment without saying a word. Much to Bernie's surprise, it was Billy who broke away from the staring contest first.

Two and a half months into their relationship, Kelly persuaded Thomas that he should start looking into the business side of the Mission. She was beginning to drill it into his head that he should have more money than he could spend. Kelly also started to introduce the idea that there was no need for Thomas to live with Billy and his wife when he could afford a house ten times nicer then the place they were currently living in.

Kelly wanted to get Thomas away from Billy's competing influence, and the compound was a big bone of contention for her. She kept pointing out that all of Billy's relatives were under the employ of the Mission in some respect and that their housing, food and other expenses were being supported by Thomas' talent.

Thomas had never concerned himself with any of that before because none of it mattered to him. When he needed spending money, Billy gave it him. He lived in a great big mansion with a theater room, bowling alley, pool and tennis court. In the furnished basement there was a pool table, air hockey, a pinball machine and skeet ball. When he wanted time to himself, he had a great big room with the biggest TV you could buy and a private bathroom with a Jacuzzi as well as a wall in shower. On the rare instances when he wanted to go someplace, Bernie or Michael would drive him. It was simple and it worked well for him up until now.

The only time Thomas had approached Billy about spending thousands of dollars was when he wanted to put two really nice headstones on his parents' graves. He also wanted Billy to hire someone to put flowers on them once a month and keep the area around them maintained. Billy agreed with no questions asked and Thomas was happy. Of course he had seen Billy and the others buying things and spending money, but it didn't matter to him.

With Kelly now pulling Thomas's strings, Billy had a real problem on his hands. The 16-year-old boy who just wanted family and forgiveness was gone; now the winds of change were blowing. When Billy frustrated Kelly's attempts to learn more about the Mission's inner workings by ignoring her questions, she began to use Thomas to filter her ideas to Billy. Thomas kept encouraging him to sit down with Kelly to discuss her ideas – like that was going to happen.

Just when Billy thought things couldn't get much worse, Kelly moved into the compound. Now he couldn't even use Neesy to get through to Thomas because Kelly was spending every waking moment with. She lived with him, traveled with him on the road, and they were even taking vacations together.

The happy couple had been together for six months when Thomas told Neesy he was marrying Kelly. Billy was at a loss for what to do. He tried again and again to talk Thomas out of it, but nothing worked. Even when Neesy tried to have a "heart to heart" with him about it, Thomas politely dismissed her. He told her that it really didn't matter to him that no one else understood the love they had. "As long as I feel it in my heart, I know it is meant to be," he said

Neesy begged Thomas to get a prenuptial agreement, but he was certain they would be together forever, so he didn't need one.

Kelly wanted an extravagant wedding and that's what Thomas gave her. The wedding took place on June 25th, 2001. Thomas was 24 years old.

The entire ceremony cost well over a million dollars. After the ceremony, Thomas told Billy that the original two- week honeymoon hiatus they had agreed to was going to be extended to a month. Kelly wanted to travel to several different locations and they needed more time.

Two days after the newlyweds left, Billy received a letter from an attorney representing Mr. and Mrs. Greggs requesting a meeting for the day after they returned from their honeymoon. The letter stated that he had to be prepared to show all current assets and revenue of the Mission at the request of Thomas Greggs, co-owner of the Mission. Billy almost fell over when he read it. He knew without a doubt now that the battle for the Mission was coming and the first shot had just been fired.

Before the meeting even took place, Billy learned that he was between a rock in a hard place. He had met with his lawyers several times over the course of the month and the results were always the same.

The Mission attorneys explained to Billy that he was the sole owner of the enterprise. As such he was entitled to any and all revenue generated by their marketing, merchandising and their events. But there was one big catch: Thomas never signed a contract with the Mission. There was nothing to stop him from walking away and starting his own venture that would crush the Mission.

Billy had the lawyers put together several compensation packages that he would present to Kelly in hopes that he could get her to settle for money without the control. He had to get Thomas under contract before Kelly persuaded him to cut his family out of the picture entirely.

The meeting lasted four hours. As expected, Kelly and their lawyers did all of the talking while Thomas occupied himself. The net worth of Mission was in the hundreds of millions on paper. Kelly agreed that Thomas would stay on as a "contractor" for ten years for $150 million, half of which would be paid up front after the contract was signed.

Billy reluctantly agreed and he stared at Thomas as he signed the contract, but Thomas never looked back. Kelly didn't want Thomas anywhere near Billy, so she brought the contract over to him and he signed it. She whispered something in his ear and he left the office without saying a word. The meeting concluded with the lawyers shaking hands and Billy and Kelly standing face to face. She extended her hand, gave him a crooked smile and said, "Pleasure doing business with you. Oh and by the way, Thomas and I bought a place about an hour from you while we were away. I'll have someone stop by to pick up his personal things tomorrow, if that's ok with you?"

Billy looked at her hand and shook his head. He saw this coming a mile away and he was helpless to do anything about it. "Yeah, that would be fine," he said coldly. Tell Thomas we start back up again in a week."

"Great," Kelly replied, "just send me the schedule and I will coordinate everything for him."

"I'm sure you will," Billy said.

Chapter 29

Thomas had no idea how big the house they were moving into was. As the iron gates opened and they drove up the long driveway, it finally came into view and Thomas's jaw dropped. "All of this for two people?" he wondered.

He hadn't paid attention when Kelly was showing him picture after picture of houses during their honeymoon. He just nodded along and told her that he trusted her to pick the best one. She said something about hiring her friend to go along with a real estate agent, but the money didn't matter to Thomas. He just wanted Kelly to be happy and judging by the look on her face as they parked in the front of the house, she was ecstatic.

Kelly wasn't kidding about them owning a better place than the compound, Thomas thought as he got out of the car. It was really a mansion, and Kelly still hadn't finished furnishing and decorating it by the time the Mission went back on the road on July 4th 2001. Everything was specially ordered and handmade so Kelly decided that she would stay behind and catch up with Thomas when everything was done. Thomas hated the idea because this was going to be the first time they were apart, but Kelly convinced him it would just be a matter of days.

Thomas felt alienated from everyone at the Mission. Now that there was a contract in place forcing him to be there, no one had to pretend anymore, he thought. Jerry and Bernie avoided him and Billy was never around. Thomas only saw him when they were rehearsing, or when Billy came off stage.

Thomas decided to keep traveling in the limo even though Kelly wasn't with him. He figured he would be just like them; there was no reason to pretend anymore. If they didn't accept him with Kelly, then they didn't accept him at all.

Kelly didn't return to Thomas for three weeks and when she did she didn't stay long. "There were issues with the house," she said and she had to be there to make sure they were corrected "the right way." Thomas missed her terribly, and with nothing else to occupy his time he started drinking heavily again. When Kelly was with him everything was right in the world, but when she was gone, the demons would return.

Over the next four months, Thomas had only been together with his wife for six weeks total. The house was perfect, or so Thomas was told, because he hadn't been there since just after they returned from their honeymoon. With that squared away, Kelly started spending a lot of her time traveling to do research for what type of business she wanted to own. Thomas knew it was her dream to own and run a business, so he tolerated the time apart.

Kelly assured him that once everything was settled, someone else would handle the day-to-day stuff and she would just oversee the operations remotely.

As they spent more time apart, the rumors started to spread throughout the Mission about what Kelly was really up to. During a sponsor function, Thomas finally became aware of them when he overheard a very drunk Michael say, "Kelly was a gold-digging puppet master who was spending Thomas's money and out doing God knows what with God knows who." Bernie noticed that Thomas was standing nearby, so he grabbed Michael by the shoulder then pulled him to the other side of the room. The damage was done, though.

Thomas went straight to Billy and told him he was suffering from exhaustion. He said he needed two weeks off for the holidays before the Mission Christmas Eve event and that he was heading home to spend some time with his wife. Billy argued and cussed, but Thomas didn't react. He told Billy he was going home and that was that. Billy even tried to use the contract agreement, but Thomas told him to shove the contract up his ass and left the building.

He returned home to find there was a holiday party going on. It was a semi-formal get together with 40 or 50 people that Thomas didn't know. He didn't want to be noticed by any of them, so Thomas asked the man working security to take him another way up to his bedroom. As they walked around the building and entered a side door, Thomas thought how pathetic it was that he didn't know the way around his own house. Once upstairs, he asked the security man to find Kelly and ask her to join him.

Almost an hour later, Kelly entered the bedroom with a big smile on her face and hugged Thomas. All of his anger and frustration were gone. He no longer even cared that he didn't like anything about his new house because he was together with his wife and everything was right in the world again.

The two weeks went by in a blink and Thomas was scheduled to return to the Mission for their upcoming Christmas events. He asked Kelly to come back with him so that they could be together for their first Christmas, but she apologized and said that she needed to meet with the lawyers to finalize the details of her new business. With tears in her eyes Kelly promised Thomas husband that it would take "two weeks, max" and then she would join up with him for a few weeks before the company "went live." Then they would celebrate both events together, and the dates didn't matter.

Four weeks passed, and Kelly still hadn't caught up with Thomas. Every day or two, she'd call and apologize profusely while telling her husband how much she missed him. When Kelly told him she would give up her dream if he wanted her to be by his side, Thomas gave in again, telling her that he didn't want her to ever regret being with him.

"If this is that important to you, then it's that important to me," he said. "Like you told me, we just have to get through this startup period, and then we'll be good."

Four weeks turned into eight and on Valentine's Day when he couldn't reach Kelly, he remembered what Michael had said about his wife months earlier. As the time passed, so did the drinks until he reached the point where he couldn't take it anymore.

It was the middle of night, when Thomas knocked on Billy's hotel door to tell him that he was leaving again for another few weeks. Billy was with another woman, so he didn't put up much of an argument at all. He saw how drunken Thomas was and when he was like this; there was no reasoning with him at all. Besides, Billy knew no matter how many cancellations they had, desperate people kept showing up and they kept selling out night after night. He would work his magic, make something up and the show would go on as always.

"You do what you gotta do, but this is the last time, you hear me?" Billy said, his disgust for Thomas evident. "I will use the terms of that contract as leverage if I have to, Thomas. Make sure you're back in two weeks."

As far as Billy could tell, Thomas didn't even hear him. Billy watched as he staggered down the hall and into the elevator before going back into his room. He called and woke up Bernie to tell him to cancel all of the Mission events for the next two weeks. When Bernie asked why, Billy replied, "Because Thomas is messed up again, why else?"

Thomas made it down to the lobby and had the desk clerk arrange for a car to take him to the airport. Once there he paid an absurd amount of money to charter a private plane to take him home.

At 7:20 a.m., the limo pulled into his driveway. Thomas was still drunk, but the expression of one of the cleaning staff workers immediately put up a red flag. It wasn't the "Oh my, that's Thomas Greggs, The Healer" face. It was more like a "Oh boy, I didn't expect to see you" face.

Thomas said hello and staggered up the stairs, trying to be as quiet as possible so he could surprise Kelly. The bedroom door was closed, so he pushed it open. What he saw made his entire world collapse in an instant. Kelly was lying on the bed, naked, with her head resting on the chest of a naked man that Thomas had never seen before.

Thomas felt rage. Kelly woke up when he stomped his foot. She cried out, "Oh my God!" and grabbed a blanket to cover herself. The man shook awake and quickly got to his feet to search for his clothes on the side of the bed.

The room remained eerily quiet for about ten seconds while Thomas stared at them. Kelly broke the silence when she demanded to know what Thomas was doing there. Thomas didn't respond; he just watched as the man hurried to pull up his pants and grab the rest of his belongings.

Thomas was overcome by tears as he shouted, "How could you do this to me?"

Kelly offered no sign of guilt or sympathy for her husband. She knew this was a way to get out of this relationship for good with a large chunk of Thomas's money if she played her cards right. All she had to do was manipulate the situation so that she was the victim.

Kelly yelled back at him, "I'm neglected, Thomas! You're never home, I'm always alone because you're first love is that damn Mission. I've put up with it for too long because of your issues with needing forgiveness, but I have needs too, Thomas!"

"Are you fucking kidding me?" Thomas yelled back. "I would have given all of that up in a second if you asked me, and you know it!"

Thomas walked closer to Kelly, so he was almost face to face with her. The mystery man didn't like that, so he came over and grabbed Thomas from behind to pull him away from her.

"Ok, that's enough!" he said.

Thomas lost control. Without thinking, he turned and punched Kelly's lover in the face as hard as he could. The man staggered backwards and Thomas punched him over and over again. The man tried to block Thomas' fists, without much success. Thomas only paused the attack when he heard Kelly yell, "Leave him alone, it's not his fault!"

Thomas looked at his wife, but he didn't see the woman he loved more than life. He just felt anger, guilt and disgust. While Thomas was distracted, Kelly's lover got to his feet and tried to approach him again. Thomas hit him in the face again, hard enough to break several bones in his own hand in the process. The man fell to the ground unconscious and Thomas stood over him, breathing heavy.

He turned around to see Kelly holding the phone. "Hello Police, this is an emergency, my husband Thomas Greggs has just assaulted a man in our house and he's unconscious, can you please come to my residence right away?

"Yes, he is still here, please hurry, I fear for my safety because he is intoxicated and acting crazy." Kelly gave the address and hung up the phone.

Thomas started to cry when looked at her again as she went to check on her lover. He looked down at his own bloody, broken hand before closing his eyes and tilting his head towards the heavens. "How could this be happening to me?" he thought. "I've tried to do all of the right things and still, this is what I get?"

"They are coming to arrest you, you son of a bitch," Kelly told Thomas before she locked herself in the bathroom. He felt completely sober now and almost as sad as he had been on the day his mother died.

He left the room, went outside, and sat on the porch to wait for the police.

Thomas pleaded no contest to the assault charge, but the judge threw the book at him. The list of injuries that Kelly's lover sustained made matters much worse for Thomas.

"A broken jaw, a broken nose, three cracked ribs, a cracked eye socket and several missing teeth." The Mission lawyer cringed when he heard the list of injuries read out loud by the prosecutor, but Thomas never blinked or showed any type of emotion. He certainly didn't reflect an inkling of regret and that angered the judge.

Thomas served six months in a minimal security facility. From there he was sent to rehab for another six months where he received anger management therapy five days a week. Thomas was released on February 21st, 2003, three weeks before his 26th birthday.

Billy and The Mission lawyers were granted power of attorney over Thomas' affairs while he was in jail. Billy settled out of court with Ken Turley, the man Thomas beat up, for two million dollars. He also represented Thomas during the divorce negotiations. Kelly agreed to twenty million dollars and the house. Kelly told her attorney to accept the deal, because she just wanted to be done with the whole thing, even though she could have fought and gotten more.

The Mission was essentially shut down for more than a year. Billy tried as always to do damage control by telling the reporters every so often how great Thomas was doing with his intensive counseling program. How he had accepted God again in his life and he was now a new man ready to start over forsaking the things of the Devil such as violence and liquor. Whether it would matter or not remained to be seen. For now the Mission was in ruins.

Billy spent that entire year Thomas was gone putting together a marketing plan that would repair the image of both Thomas and the Mission. He was confident that it would work, but it would take some time for things to get back to normal.

The plan would have to wait, though. After Thomas left rehab, he packed up some of his things, got on a plane and disappeared. There was no word at all from him for months.

Chapter 30

Neesy begged Billy to try to find Thomas. After three months, Billy agreed it was time and hired a team of private detectives to begin searching for Thomas. Of course, Billy's motive was more self-serving that his wife's reason, but she didn't need to know that.

Billy had been keeping the media at bay with a story that Thomas was in a private facility outside of the United States to get additional treatment. Thomas was making tremendous progress and that he would return when he was ready, Billy said.

Billy had tried to revive the Mission on his own, but it failed miserably. A big theatrical Baptist ceremony just wasn't enough on its own. He needed Thomas and he knew it more than ever. After a month of searching, Billy's detectives hadn't found a sign of Thomas. Billy was beginning to think that Thomas may have done harm to himself -- or worse.

When Billy saw a news story about patients in a children's hospital in a small town in Mexico being miraculously healed, he knew Thomas was out there. The story was unconfirmed, and there were rumors of another person of Mexican descent with the same abilities as Thomas. The eyewitness accounts all described a person who looked nothing like Thomas, but Billy was certain it was him. Thomas always wanted to be a do-gooder, and now he was.

Billy called his team of investigators and sent them to Mexico. Two days later, they reported back to Billy that they had located Thomas in a rundown motel, not far from the children's hospital.

Their initial report said, "Thomas was an emotional, drunken mess." Billy had no idea how to handle him in that state, so he brought Neesy with him to Mexico.

When they got to the motel, both Neesy and Billy took turns pounding on the door for ten minutes, but no one answered. Billy finally got fed up and paid the man at the desk $100 to open the door for him. When they went inside, the first thing they noticed was the smell. It was a combination of rotting food and body odor. Neesy opened the curtains to let some light in the room, and they saw vodka bottles everywhere: on the floor, on the otherwise empty bed and scattered on the dresser.

Neesy covered her mouth and nose with her hand and Billy yelled out, "God damn, smells like a dead body in here."

Neesy she shot him a look of disgust and shook her head. "Sorry honey," Billy said, "I didn't mean it as if to say Thomas was dead."

The bathroom door was closed, Neesy slowly pushed it open. She immediately covered her mouth again because the smell was even stronger in there.

"Oh my God!" Neesy shouted when she saw Thomas lying face down with half-dried vomit all around him. "Is he alive, Billy?" she asked as she kneeled down beside him.

Billy turned on the light and saw that Thomas was breathing, so he sighed with relief. "He's fine Neesy, just passed out drunk is all."

Neesy searched for something to use to clean him up while Billy went back into the other room and found the phone. "I'll be in there in a second, Neesy, I'm gonna call someone to help us out."

Neesy started to cry as she brushed Thomas's greasy hair away from his face.

"You poor thing," she whispered. "I'm gonna take you back home with us and everything will be all right. You'll be back with family, no one's gonna hurt you anymore, you hear me?"

After a few minutes, Billy came back into the bathroom to tell Neesy that an ambulance was on the way. He was going to have Thomas admitted into a hospital under an alias. Neesy made him promise that this would all be kept quiet; she didn't want Thomas to suffer any more, no matter the cost.

Thomas woke up in the hospital the following day to see Neesy sleeping in the chair beside him. Even though his head hurt so much that he couldn't blink his eyes without feeling it, he still smiled when he saw her.

After he was discharged, they went back home. Thomas returned to his old room at the compound, but he was no better off then when he left Mexico. Neesy pleaded with him to spend time with the family, but he preferred to be alone. He only came out of his room to get something to eat. There was too much of a rift between him and everyone else involved in the Mission to just go back to the way it was before Kelly.

Whenever Thomas tried to get a drink, Neesy would reprimand him. He tried to respect her wishes and the rules of the house, but his mind just wouldn't stop torturing him. The nights were long and painful, as he relived every bad thing he had been through.

Thomas stayed at the compound for two weeks before he decided to leave. He rented a small house about thirty minutes away in a town called Falls Church. He still wanted to be close enough to see Neesy, but he wanted to get away from everyone else. The house had a great view that was filled with trees and wildlife. Thomas thought that the move and the change of scenery would give him some peace, but it didn't last.

While flipping through the channels one night, Thomas saw a picture of himself so he paused for a moment. He didn't realize that it was the Van Putten Report. When his ex-wife was introduced Thomas shouted, "You gotta be kidding me!"

He knew he should change the channel, but he sat and watched what turned out to be an uninterrupted hour of the former love of his life bashing him while telling every detail of his private life. Nothing was off limits: she talked about how she met him, what it was like dating him, their sex life and their marriage. Then they discussed his temper in a segment complete with a clip of Thomas beating Robert years ago.

Kelly followed that up with a lengthy explanation of how Thomas couldn't get close to anyone. She said he was great at first, but for the most part she felt unloved and unappreciated through most of their relationship. She described Thomas as disconnected and robot-like in his feelings for others.

When Robert asked if she thought Thomas was upset about the divorce, Kelly said, "No, not at all, because people were disposable to Thomas." She used Thomas's relationship with Kate and Kyle as an example, saying that at one time they were the most important people in the world to him, but now he hated them both.

When Robert questioned her next about Thomas' relationship with Billy, Kelly said that her ex-husband could not stand the preacher. She went on a tirade about how Billy committed adultery in every city in the country, calling him the most "unethical man I ever met."

When it was over, Thomas drank until he passed out. Everyone he knew had betrayed and lied to him. Being numb was the only way to survive at this point.

The interview was the highest rated show that Robert had ever done, surpassing Kate's interview by leaps and bounds. Billy went to the press and told anyone who would listen that Kelly had lied. He said that he and Thomas were as close as ever. He also said that he and his family would remain by Thomas' side, no matter what the outcome meant to the Mission.

Billy really was hurt by what he heard during that interview. He knew he and Thomas didn't get along so well, but he had no idea that Thomas hated him that much. Even worse than that, Neesy wasn't speaking to him because of what Kelly had said. He knew that despite the contract Thomas had signed, the Mission was probably over.

Thomas started to wander when he had gone beyond his limit. He would call a cab and just have them drive until he saw something that caught his eye. At first it was bars, then strip clubs. It had been so long since the Mission had gotten mainstream media attention that most people didn't recognize him anymore.

Thomas would always find an out-of-the-way table and sit by himself just watching people as he drank. Watching normal people living their normal, everyday lives had become one of his favorite things to do. When he went to strip clubs, he would pick out a dancer he liked and he would give her tip after tip, but he never went to the same club twice. Thomas didn't pay attention to how much money he spent, but those evenings always ended with him having sex with the stripper at a motel near the club after it closed. He decided that this was the only kind of interaction he wanted to have with women: no talking, no feelings, just a good time where everyone leaves happy with no regrets.

One night, Thomas found himself more intoxicated than usual as he wandered the streets near one of these short stay motels. He had called a cab for his new friend, "Star," and just started walking. By the time he started to sober up, he was lost in a rundown neighborhood. With a pocket full of money but no phone, he started to panic when a group of men yelled something to him from across the street and then began to follow him.

Thomas walked quickly to the corner and made a right turn before starting to run. He heard the voices behind him and they seemed to be getting closer, so he scanned the street for a store or anyplace else he could run into.

He spotted a rundown brick church up the street on the other side of the road. Thomas ran toward it as fast as he could and hid behind the lit stone-encased sign that stood on the church lawn. He tried to catch his breath as he listened for the sounds of people approaching, but the street was quiet. He waited a few minutes before coming out from his hiding spot to look around. The men hadn't left; they were talking amongst themselves several houses down on the opposite side of the street.

Thomas was too scared to run, but he didn't want to stay out in the open either. At a loss for what to do next, Thomas closed his eyes and rested his head against the sign. He cursed his stupid luck for putting him in this position. When he opened his eyes, he noticed the writing on the sign. It read, "In memory of Sister Marie, may she rest in peace."

Thomas backed away from it and read it twice before being overcome by a wave of sadness.

"What have I become, mother?" he said softly.

Thomas was startled when a shadow appeared by the side of the sign. Thomas stumbled as he tried to turn and run. He expected to be beaten and a robbed, but the man behind him just asked a question.

"Do you need some help, son?" the man asked kindly. A skinny white gentleman who appeared to be in this late 60s or early 70s, with a full head of gray hair and a short white beard, held his hand out to Thomas.

When Thomas looked at his wrinkled face and into his brown eyes, he could see a look of concern on the man's face. The man only stood about 5foot 7 and he there wasn't much to him. Thomas was afraid that if the men following him were close, both he and this old man would get hurt badly.

He tried to get to his feet, but Thomas staggered and almost fell again. The man quickly grabbed his arm to steady him. "Easy there, fella," he said, "let me get you inside for a second to sober you up a bit. It's not safe for you to be walking around in the state you're in."

Thomas looked again and saw that the men were watching him talk to the priest. He knew his best choice was to go inside, find a phone and call someone to get him the hell out of there.

By the time Thomas turned around, the old priest was already at the top of the stairs holding the door open. "Those aren't the types of fellas you want to be messing with my friend, let's get you inside and figure out how to get you home."

Thomas nodded, thanked him and then followed him inside the church.

Thomas was surprised to see that the church looked much different on the inside. The wood on the floors and in the pew was in perfect condition, beautifully polished. The designs on the stained glass windows were amazing, the detail was perfect. Although many viewed him as a religious figure, Thomas had only been in a few churches and it was under tragic circumstances. He had never taken the time to actually look around any of the buildings, until now. He had a sense of peace inside of this building. It was nothing like nothing like the big concert halls and arenas he had gotten used to.

The old priest helped Thomas sit down on one of the benches. "Wait here a sec, I'll be back with a cup of coffee for ya," he said before leaving for his office.

As Thomas continued to look around the building, he felt like he didn't belong there. He wondered if God was looking down at him and thinking, "What the heck is here doing here?" Thomas became lost inside his head until he felt a hand on his shoulder.

"Here you go," then priest said as he handed Thomas the cup. "Careful, it's hot. But it'll do the job and wake you up a bit."

Thomas took a careful sip and the priest smiled at him.

"My name is Father McBride," he said.

Thomas didn't respond, instead he took another sip of his coffee and lowered his head.

"I'm assuming you're not from around here," the priest said. "Most folks know better than to go walking around these streets at night."

Thomas shot him a quick look and nodded. He didn't feel much like talking. He just wanted to get some caffeine in him and get to a phone.

Father McBride smiled again and studied Thomas. "You look so familiar to me. Have we met before? I have one of those photographic memories. I never forget a face and I know I have seen yours more than once before."

"No, I don't live around here," Thomas said, "I was just visiting someone."

"Well, heck, I know everyone around here," Father McBride replied. "Who was it that you were visiting?"

Thomas was quickly becoming annoyed by how nosy this man was, so he cut him off.

"Look, do you have a phone I could use? I just want to get out of here, ok?"

Father McBride looked surprised, but said, "Let me get you the portable phone in my office, just sit tight and finish your coffee."

As he walked back from his office, recognition hit the old priest like a bolt of lightning to the brain: "The Healer!"

"I know you," Father McBride said, "You're him, aren't you?"

Thomas didn't answer; he just lifted his cup and took another sip before reaching for the phone.

"I should have known," Father McBride said with a hint of sarcasm to his voice. "Drunk, wandering around the neighborhood, what were you doing, looking for drugs or something?"

Thomas said nothing. He wanted to give this priest a piece of his mind but he fought to control his anger.

Father McBride wasn't finished, though. He pointed his finger at Thomas and continued on, "I will never understand it, why you? Out of all people, He chose to give a gift like this to you. There are people who believe the Word and live their lives true to it... so many others who are more deserving. Yet you use it for your own gain like you were a magician who learned a trick that no one else could do."

Thomas slammed the cup down and stood up. He wanted to tell this priest where he could stick his opinion, but he managed to calm himself. He met the priest's stare before looking away and then down at the ground.

Father McBride had read all about Thomas's famous anger streaks. He fully expected this young man to launch into a tirade or maybe even hit him, but that didn't happen.

Thomas cleared his throat and said, "Thank you for sobering me up, I'll be leaving now."

The priest noticed the sadness in the young man's face and heard the defeated tone in his voice. Father McBride remembered something else that he had read about Thomas: that he had lost both his parents at a young age. In that instant, Thomas didn't look like some savior for hire, arrogant millionaire drunk to him.

Instead Father McBride saw a broken and lost man walking towards the door even though he knew what was probably waiting for him outside.

A feeling of shame overcame the priest for judging this young man who needed help. This was not the Lord's way and he knew it. "I'm sorry, Thomas," Father McBride said. "I should have never said those things, I was wrong to do so."

Thomas stopped as he reached the church door, but didn't turn around. "It's ok, Father," he said. "Everything you said was the truth, every word. "You're a man of God and I'm just ... me."

Father McBride jogged towards Thomas and put his arm on his shoulder. "Please come back inside for a moment, Thomas. I would really like to talk to you. Just for a moment, you can use the phone and we can talk while we wait for someone to pick you up."

Thomas nodded and joined Father McBride; they sat and talked for two hours. Thomas was cautious at first, but after a while he felt at ease and opened up to old priest. "There was something very sincere about this man," Thomas thought to himself, "something very calming. He seemed so genuine, he had very caring eyes and you could tell that he listened to every word you said carefully."

Thomas told Father McBride about everything he had been through. He told him the real story about his father and mother, about Kate, his wife Kelly, and about Billy. He never did call anyone to come pick him up. Instead, Father McBride drove Thomas home and they talked about God and faith.

The priest told Thomas that there is a reason for everything. He told him that he didn't need to worry about his parents' forgiveness. "You will see them again someday, Thomas, this I promise you and you will see for yourself that they never blamed you."

Father McBride answered all of Thomas's questions about God and faith. Even though he still didn't fully understand the big picture, Thomas listened closely to what the old priest said. Father McBride didn't seem like he was following a script or preaching like Billy did. Father McBride was clearly speaking about what he believed, about what he had faith in. There was no money involved, no women or fancy cars, it was just about his faith.

When they got to Thomas' house, Father McBride got out of the car, walked around to Thomas and gave him a hug. He then reached into his pocket and pulled out a business card. "If you ever need someone to talk to, you can either come by the church or call me, ok? Lay off of that booze, Thomas, you don't need to rely on it as a crutch, you're better than that."

Thomas nodded and smiled.

"Hopewell, is that where your church is Father?" Thomas asked as he squinted to read the card.

"Yes, Thomas and the name used to fit way back when I started at the church. Isn't it ironic that our church is in Hopewell and here you live in a town calls Falls Church? I would say it might have been some kind of sign that we met, wouldn't you?"

When Thomas shrugged his shoulders Father McBride continued on, "I wouldn't recommend walking the streets alone again if you decide to pay me another visit. The neighborhood has changed a lot since I started at that church 30 years ago."

Thomas nodded and smiled then headed for his house. Father McBride stayed and watched until he was at the door before he beeped his horn and waved. "Thanks for everything, Father," Thomas yelled before opening the door and going inside.

As he drove back to the church, Father McBride was again amazed by the Lord's ways. He knew Thomas was put in front of him for a reason, and he hoped it was to make a difference in his life.

He promised himself that he would never again judge anyone. Thomas didn't deserve that. In reality he was just a sad young man who had a gift that he didn't ask for, a gift he didn't want, nothing more. He really was just Thomas Greggs.

Thomas went back inside then laughed to himself when he thought about the night's events. He wanted to believe that this was a sign and that what the priest had said about his parents was the truth. But the last sign he followed led him to believe that a woman loved him even though she turned out to be a heartless gold digger.

"There were so many questions and so few answers," Thomas thought to himself.

The thought of seeing his parents again stayed with him and he found himself getting really down again. As much as he didn't want to let Father McBride down, there really was only one way for him to cope. He went to the kitchen cabinet, grabbed a bottle and went into his bedroom.

As his cares drifted away and the thoughts in his head faded, he closed his eyes. Visions of the church filled his head as he finally drifted off to sleep.

Chapter 31

Over the next few months, Thomas spent a couple of days a week with Father McBride at the church in Hopewell. As they got to know each other better, the priest would repeat again and again how Thomas needed to forgive others as well as himself if he ever wanted to be at peace.

"The anger and the pain lead to the booze," Father McBride would say. "Just let go and trust that He has a plan for Thomas."

Thomas took his advice and the first person he reached out to was Neesy. He apologized to her for cutting ties with her after he returned from Mexico and everything that was said during Kelly's interview.

It wasn't long before he was spending a lot of time with her again, only now it was at his place in Falls Church. Neesy liked coming to Thomas's rented house because she thought it suited him well. It was a one story ranch with a one car garage attached to it. There was one living room, two small bedrooms, one bathroom and a small kitchen. The house was white with a grey shingled roof secluded on an acre of land with his nearest neighbor far enough away where he could have what he craved, which was privacy.

Thomas hired an attorney who assisted him in renting the house under a corporation's name. The attorneys also arranged it so that he could call the closest supermarket with an order for groceries. The cost for the food and the delivery was paid directly to the store by the attorneys with the stipulation that the food was to be left on the front porch and that the occupant never is disturbed. There were a few occasions where the high school kids who were making the deliveries would try to look in the windows, but Thomas would scream at them at the top of his lungs to scare them. He would then have a good laugh to himself as he watched them run down the steps and back to their car.

What Neesy liked most about his small house beside the tranquil surroundings was that it had a beautiful wrap-around front porch. She and Thomas would spend hours out there sitting on the swing together, sipping iced tea while talking about everything under the sun.

When he told her he didn't want to step foot anywhere near the compound or Billy again, Neesy understood and didn't make an issue of it. It was mostly because she was very pleased with the influence Father McBride had on Thomas. He was still drinking, but he didn't seem as angry at the world anymore.

Neesy went out to lunch with Thomas and Father McBride several times. Because she was raised in the church, Neesy loved to hear him talk about the lessons of the Bible. She found it to be refreshing to hear someone speak the words of Lord without all of the flash or pizzazz her husband used. She told

Thomas that he was right about him, Father McBride wasn't doing it for any other reason other than that it was his faith, there was no profit at all in it for him.

When she would return home to Billy and he would question her about what they discussed Neesy would just tell him that Thomas was not ready to come back yet. When Billy would become agitated, she would tell him about Father McBride and ask him if the Mission was just all about the money. Billy would respond by acting surprised and hurt by the question. He would then mutter something and walk away.

A few more months passed and Thomas couldn't help but become inspired by Father McBride's actions and his selflessness.

Two days before Christmas, Thomas decided to perform another selfless act of his own. First he took a taxi to the closest toy store. He paid the manager $20,000 to load up a trailer full of toys for kids of all ages and deliver them to Brighton Children's Hospital on Christmas Eve. He didn't want to media to think it was a publicity stunt to improve his image, so he made sure everything was anonymous again through his attorneys.

Thomas knew that this hospital had a special place in Father McBride's heart because he spent a lot of time there with the children. Every Christmas Eve, the priest even dressed up as Santa to hand out presents that were donated at the church.

Thomas watched with a bottle in his hand and a huge smile on his face as the news broadcast from the hospital. Every child had a present and Father McBride was visibly overcome with emotion by this act of generosity. Even though he was alone on Christmas, Thomas was as happy as he had been in a long time. Thomas finished watching the report then he watched "It's A Wonderful Life." He was plenty drunk, but he couldn't get to the point where he could shut down. He kept thinking about those kids and how terrible it must be waking up in the hospital on Christmas morning.

Just then it occurred to him. He could give them a gift better than any store-bought item. Thomas put on a pair of sweatpants and hooded sweatshirt then called a taxi. The rest of the night was a blur, but somehow he woke up in his bed the next morning. He immediately put the TV on. One of the things Thomas hated most was the sound of silence. He was just about to get up to go to the bathroom when he heard the report.

"Just to recap on what is being referred to as 'The Miracle at Brighton Children's Hospital,'" said a reporter, "It all started yesterday afternoon when a Toys R Us tractor trailer arrived with hundreds of presents from an anonymous donor for all of the children in the hospital.

"If that wasn't enough of a miracle, Mr. Miracle himself, Thomas Greggs, apparently sneaked into the hospital during the night and healed all of the children. Parents have been arriving here this morning to pick up their children and take them home for Christmas. All of them seemingly throwing caution to the wind against the doctors' recommendations to wait until further tests are done."

The screen then switched to several parents crying while thanking God for Thomas and wishing him a very Merry Christmas. One after another they conveyed their heartfelt thanks to him. Thomas felt the tears run down his cheek as he saw the parents holding their smiling children as they walked out of the hospital. He knew Father McBride would be proud of him.

He was right. A half-hour later, Father McBride was at his house with a present in hand. When Thomas opened the door, the emotional priest reached out and hugged him tight. "I told you there's good in you, son. Thank you so much for what you did, it was the best present I ever got."

When they let go, both men had tears in their eyes and they both laughed simultaneously as they watched the other wipe them away. Father McBride told Thomas he had a morning service so he couldn't stay, he just wanted to come by to thank him, give him his gift and invite him to Christmas dinner later at his house. Thomas accepted and thanked him, and then Father McBride left, humming "Jingle Bells" the whole way back to the car.

A few hours later Thomas received a call from Neesy wishing him a merry Christmas. She knew he wouldn't come to the compound for dinner, but she asked him anyway. She was just starting to tell him what a great thing it was that he did at the hospital when Billy got on the line.

He didn't say hello or even wish Thomas a merry Christmas, he just started right in with a lecture. "Look Thomas, while it was a good thing what he did for the children, I don't think it is a good idea to continue doing things like that.

"There are very real, very possible legal ramifications from doing that sort of healing. If for any reason, any of those children weren't healed, the Mission would be liable and it could jeopardize everything. Neesy and I could wind up in the poor house, Thomas.

"When you heal people at our events, it's very structured and we are protected by asking people to sign waivers before they get anywhere near you. If they aren't satisfied or if it didn't work, they know that's a risk they are willing to take. There is no recourse except to complain to the media."

"Are you sure this isn't just about you not getting paid for his one, Billy?" Thomas asked.

Billy's tone changed and he sounded like he meant business, "Look, whether you believe it or not, I have been protecting you for a long time. There are people out there, not a lot of them, but some who you couldn't fix.

"Now the first one cost me a ton of money to settle up with, but I only made that mistake once. The lawyers came up with an ironclad protection waiver the day after we settled and it hasn't been an issue since, except in the press.

"If you want to help people again, Thomas, why don't you come with me? Hey, it's Christmas, what better day than Jesus' birthday to give this gift back to the world?"

"There it was," Thomas thought to himself, the difference between Billy and Father McBride. Billy used words like tools to build an empire and promote himself while Father McBride used them to encourage and give faith.

"No thanks," Thomas replied. "You and the family have yourselves a merry Christmas, Billy, I gotta go."

Thomas didn't wait for a response; he just hung up the phone. He didn't want to dwell on the past or on Billy's bullshit, he just wanted to enjoy his Christmas with Father McBride and savor this moment when he felt good about something.

When Billy hung up the phone, Neesy could see a big smile on his face.

"It feels good to clear the air on Christmas and just let things go for a day, doesn't it honey?" she said.

Billy laughed and gave her a big hug. "It sure does, honey, it sure does."

Neesy had no idea that the reason Billy was smiling was because he actually believed that The Mission might be back someday. Thomas still had that desire in him to do well with his gift in order to find forgiveness. That might just be enough to bring him back.

Just after New Years, Robert Van Putten had a one-hour special featuring one of the children at the hospital that Thomas healed. Billy called Thomas to tell him to watch the show because The Mission had been served with court papers as a result. He might as well have called to say "I told you so."

The interview opened with Robert sitting on a couch next two a man and a woman. As the camera focused on him, he stared into it with a very serious look on his face.

"Ladies and gentlemen, my guests tonight are Mr. and Mrs. Scalone. They are the parents of young Michael Scalone, Jr., who passed away four days ago. Michael was one of the children that Thomas Greggs healed during what many called 'The Miracle at St. Joseph's.'

"As you can see, my friends, this was not a miracle for everyone. In fact it turned out to be tragic for a boy and his parents who assumed that Thomas Greggs healed him just like all of the other children on Christmas Eve.

"Both Mike and Peggy has asked me to speak for them tonight. As you can imagine, they are still dealing with their grief, but they felt compelled to be here when I reported on their story.

"Michael Scalone, Jr. was in intensive care at the time Thomas arrived at the hospital. He suffered from cancer in its advanced stages and he was brought to the hospital via ambulance two weeks before Christmas. The Scalones were told that prognosis was not good and that they should prepare for the worst.

"Mike Sr. and Peggy said that their first impression of Thomas when they saw him enter their son's hospital room was that, "He was off a little off.""

"When I asked her to clarify that description, Peggy said that he was staggering a little when he walked and that he would hold onto things from time to time to steady himself. Peggy told me how she ran right over to Thomas and told him all about her son. She said she thought her prayers had been answered as Thomas followed her over to her son, Michael."

"I know it's hard, but please share with us what happened next, Peggy," Robert said.

The grieving mother cleared her throat and took a deep breath, "Well, he closed his eyes and he put his hands on Michael, just like he did with all of the other children. I could tell something was wrong because he opened his eyes and just stared at my son like he was confused.

"He put his hands on little Mike as if he was going to try again, only to up and walk away when other parents started calling out to him. I didn't say a word to him because I thought my son was healed.

"We took him home the next morning like all of the other kids' parents did and little Mike was happy as could be."

Peggy started to get emotional so Robert placed his hand on her shoulder and said, "I understand."

He then turned to look back into the camera and said, "It must be said that the Scalones left the hospital against the advice of the doctors that we on duty that morning. They are in no way, shape or form responsible for what happened next.

"The Scalones' only mistake, if you could call it that, was that they assumed that a Christmas miracle was bestowed upon them by The Healer. Unfortunately that was not the case; Michael died in the middle of the night three days later. He was gone by the time Michael Sr. went to wake him for breakfast."

When Peggy and Michael Sr. started to cry, Thomas cried too. He didn't remember anything about that night and he started to feel sick to his stomach. He went to the bathroom and threw up. A wave of depression hit him like a slap in the face, so he hurried to the kitchen to get a bottle.

Thomas cried as he took gulp after gulp until he felt sick again. He threw up again, and grabbed another bottle as soon as he came out of the bathroom. He woke up the next morning to find Father McBride sitting in a kitchen chair beside his bed.

The priest had been watching the TV broadcast too, and got worried when Thomas wouldn't answer his phone. He let himself in to Thomas' house and found him lying passed out in a pool of his own vomit.

Thomas made eye contact with Father McBride before he rolled over and pulled the covers over his head.

"You can't blame yourself for what happened to that boy, Thomas," Father McBride said. "There are things in this world even The Healer can't do. There is someone who we all answer to and He has a plan for us all, including you, Thomas. That boy's destiny was decided long before he ever came into contact with you, no matter how unfair it might seem."

"Thank you for coming, Father," Thomas said, "but I really don't want to hear about this right now."

Father McBride stood up, pulled the covers off of Thomas's head and said, "I want you to come with me to visit that boy's parents."

Thomas looked at Father McBride, but was at a loss for how to respond.

"Thomas, you did what you could, and that was all that you could do. You have nothing to be ashamed of or to be sorry about. For some reason beyond your control, you could not help this one child, but there were so many others you *did* help that day. So many parents who had their prayers answered when you walked into that hospital. Not to mention the tens of thousands around the country who you've helped before."

Thomas sat up, but didn't say anything as he thought about what the priest said.

"I wouldn't even know what to say to them," Thomas finally said.

Father McBride sat next to Thomas on the bed and put his arm around him. "You let me do the talking and if you feel you have something to add, then by all means say what you feel."

Thomas got cleaned up, shaved and dressed in a suit. They arrived at the Scalones house two hours later.

Father McBride rang the bell three times before Peggy answered the door. When she saw Thomas and a priest standing there she said hello and forced a smile.

Father McBride introduced himself and said he was a good friend of Thomas. He asked Peggy if she would mind if they came in for a moment to talk.

Peggy looked like she hadn't slept in days. "I appreciate you both coming here, she said, but it's not a good time. We have been through a lot these last few weeks and we just need some time now to recover now, if that's possible. We finally got rid of the media and now we just want to be left alone to grieve for our son."

As she slowly closed the door, she noticed that Thomas was crying. When he made eye contact with her he said, "I am so very sorry," as the tears rolled down his cheeks. Peggy nodded and closed the door.

She closed her eyes and the tears started coming. She just wanted it all to be over, but she had to know. So she pulled open the door just as they were stepping off of the bottom step. "Why couldn't you help him?" she asked.

Thomas stopped and turned around to face her.

"Why did it work for all of those other children and not my Michael?" Peggy said as her bottom lip began to quiver.

"Can we please come inside to speak to you for a moment? Mrs. Scalone?" Father McBride asked. "We've come here to explain the best we could, that's all I can offer you."

Peggy let them in and they followed her into the kitchen.

Michael Sr. was sipping a cup of coffee with a confused look on his face as his wife entered the room with a priest and another man behind her.

When he noticed it was Thomas, he put the coffee down and yelled, "What the hell?"

Father McBride immediately stepped forward and offered Mr. Scalone his hand.

"Please sir, you have our deepest sympathies for your loss. Thomas wanted more than anything to talk to you both after hearing about the loss of your son. Please just hear him out and then we will leave."

When he saw Mr. Scalone shaking his head in anger, Father McBride approached him and placed both of his hands on his shoulders while looking him in the eye. "We look for blame in times like these, but there is no one to blame. It was God's will and no one, not even Thomas, could prevent that even though he tried the best he could.

"I have been a priest for many years and I have many times questioned why things happen, especially to children. Sometimes even for me, maintaining my faith is a struggle with some of the things that I have seen.

"But I do believe there is no higher power then our Lord. He created all of us, even Thomas, and it is He who allows Thomas to do what he does. I have known Thomas for some time now and just like you, before meeting him, I had heard all of the stories about him.

"But the honest truth is the person I have known is nothing like what they say. He is very kind and very caring. The media didn't report this, but it was Thomas who purchased all of those presents for the children. He personally went to the store, paid for the items and then had them delivered.

"If that wasn't enough, he started to try to heal everyone in the hospital. He did it with no cameras around and with no one collecting donations in the hallways. He did it because he wanted to give those kids and their families something that no one else could, hope.

"All but one of the children got their Christmas miracle and yes, I said miracle, but not just because of what Thomas can do. The real miracle is the gift itself.

"That gift was given to Thomas by a higher power that has a plan for us all, even the children. But what all of you fail to see, including Thomas, is that there are limits to what he can do, limits that even he doesn't know or understand.

"From what I can see, Thomas cannot interfere with His plan," Father McBride said as he pointed upward. "If it's your time, as they say, even Thomas can't stop it."

Michael put his head down and he began to cry, so Father McBride hugged him.

"Don't blame Thomas for this, Michael," Father McBride whispered to him. "He just wanted to heal your son as well as your family."

Michael nodded then let go of the priest and hugged his wife. They both stood there crying while Thomas stood silently next to them.

Father McBride then motioned to Thomas that it was time to go and they headed out.

He paused for a moment before they left the room and said, "We are so very sorry for your loss. Please know that Michael is with the Lord now and he is no longer in pain."

They were just about to open the door when Peggy called out to Thomas.

"I said all of those things out of hurt and anger for what happened to my son. Mr. Van Putten kept talking about what kind of person you really are and how you cared for no one but yourself before we went out onto the set. He got me all worked up and then he started filming.

"I don't hate you, Thomas, I just miss my son. I know you can relate because you lost your parents, it's hard you know? Just don't stop using that gift of yours, there are people out there who could really use a miracle and you are that miracle."

When Michael started to cry again Peggy came up from behind him and they hugged again.

Father McBride touched Thomas's shoulder and said, "Let's go."

On the drive back, Thomas asked Father McBride if he meant everything he said about him.

"You gave me the best Christmas gift I have ever gotten, Thomas," Father McBride said. "I didn't say anything tonight that I didn't mean. I consider you a good friend and if you need me, I will always be there for you."

"Well, how can I help people without returning to the Mission?" Thomas asked.

"I'm not sure about that one, Thomas, I wish I could help you but my little church could never handle the masses that come out to see you," Father McBride replied.

Upon arriving home Thomas thanked Father McBride and gave him a hug. Thomas was able to sleep that night without any pills or alcohol.

Chapter 32

After months of talking on the phone about it with both Neesy and Father McBride, Thomas did some major soul searching and decided to return to the Mission. He knew he wasn't helping anyone by drinking alone in his apartment and that he was wasting what Father McBride referred to as his gift.

Billy was thrilled when Thomas reached out to him. Both he and Neesy took Thomas out to dinner and Thomas actually had a good time with them. It reminded him of the family atmosphere he enjoyed when he first came to live with them. He was even able to talk to Billy without getting lectured or having anything about the Mission's past being brought up.

When Billy made the announcement that Thomas was coming back to the Mission on his 27th birthday, March 14, 2004, people rushed to buy tickets for events just the same as they did after every hiatus. Thomas' assault conviction, ugly divorce and absence from the public spotlight didn't dissuade the faithful. If anything, it made them more determined to buy tickets before the Mission went away again, perhaps for the final time.

Once back on the road, Thomas was surprised that he was actually enjoying himself. Neesy decided to come out with them for a few months and everyone was getting along again. But as soon as Neesy returned home, things went right back to the way they were before. Billy started making up for lost time with a different woman every night, Bernie and Jerry started to avoid Thomas again and Thomas spent most of his nights alone with a bottle.

Now that Thomas knew "Billy's system," he could clearly see that the people coming up first weren't the worst of the bunch. Billy must have coached them to say they had severe ailments, but there always seemed to be a pattern of the same three ailments repeated over and over. Thomas tried to counter this by staying on stage to heal everyone. He only could until his body made him stop.

Thomas asked Father McBride over and over again for guidance over the phone but all he could to tell him was that his resolve was being tested.

"You are doing this for the right reasons," Father McBride would say. "You are still helping people and that's the main thing."

But the faces of those he couldn't get to and the little boy from the hospital who died still haunted Thomas every night.

What it all got to be too much for him, Thomas started drinking from the time he woke up in the morning until he passed out drunk. He needed help getting to the stage, where he would stagger around and mumble into the microphone. Eventually Billy just turned his mic off, because most of it was about him.

Billy tried to get both Neesy and Father McBride to talk sense into him but he was too far gone. Thomas started passing out during the show, and sometimes he couldn't even make it to the stage. After Billy had to cancel several events and refund the ticket price, he finally had enough and decided to confront Thomas.

Only now, Thomas was no longer the meek and mild boy he met in New Jersey. When Billy got in his face, Thomas stood his ground and didn't back down.

"You don't tell me what to do," Thomas said while pointing in Billy's face. "No one tells me what to do. I am the damn Mission, you hear me? Without me, you have nothing and you know it. You are still the same piece of crap that you were before. You know nothing about God or what his words really mean. You really are just a two-bit car salesman and nothing more. So go back to your skanks, you adulteress scumbag, and leave me alone."

Billy just wanted to kick Thomas' ass, but he forced himself to keep his temper. He knew Thomas was right, that the Mission couldn't go on if left again. Everything Billy had was tied into the Mission. With all of the money it cost to settle the lawsuits, pay back the sponsors after they shut down last time and the Mission's high overhead, Billy needed to keep it going to maintain his lifestyle. His empire had taken some major hits over the last few years and he needed more than anything to right the ship, whatever the cost.

Billy met Thomas' glare. He knew that if looks truly could kill, he'd be dead ten times over.

Billy looked away and shook his head. "Whatever, you do what you want to do man, it's your life."

"I *am* doing what I want, Billy," Thomas said. "Screw you and everyone else if they have a problem with it 'cause I don't care anymore."

Bernie had seen enough so he got between them, whispered something in Billy's ear and they left together. Thomas went back to his dressing room and drank until he passed out again.

As The Mission continued, both the mainstream media and various religious groups spoke out against Thomas every chance they got. Even though Billy had a strict policy in place to keep people from recording Mission events, there were images of Thomas drunk on stage on every channel.

Father McBride came out to visit on several occasions and even he was surprised at the state Thomas was in. He told Billy again and again that Thomas needed to go back into rehab for counseling, but still Billy did nothing.

A few weeks before Christmas, Billy told everyone about a new Christmas day event in Charlotte, North Carolina that was going to be televised around the world via satellite. At first, many objected to the Christmas Day Miracle Mission Event because they were usually off for a week after the Christmas

Eve event every year. Now they would have to work on Christmas day as well and many of the staff members complained.

Billy changed their minds when he offered them a big bonus and told them that he would be flying all of their families out and putting them up in a five star hotel after which they quickly agreed. The Mission was going to make a fortune off of sponsors so Billy could afford to splurge.

Thomas was the only one who still fought against it because he wanted to spend his Christmas with Father McBride. Rather than risk the boat load of money that was at stake, Billy promised to fly Thomas back on a chartered plane right after the event was over. Thomas held out until Billy also agreed to shut down the Mission for an additional week before he agreed.

The event was a huge success, with ratings through the roof. As everyone celebrated on the three floors of the hotel that Billy reserved, Thomas slipped away by himself because he was angry. He found out after the show that Billy's idea of 'right after the show' was three hours later.

It was after 9 p.m. and he was feeling good, but not drunk. He wanted to change that, so he hailed a cab and asked to be taken to the nearest bar that was open. They drove past several bars and all of them had closed early or didn't open at all on Christmas day.

Thomas' buzz was starting to wear off and depression was started to set in. He started to think about what he did last Christmas and what happened to that boy, Michael. At that exact moment the cab stopped right in front of a hospital. Thomas stared at it while the cabbie waited for the light to change.

"Jesus, this light is taking forever," the driver said. "I could go through it, but with my luck I would get caught."

The light finally changed, but when they started to pull away Thomas told the driver to stop. He got out of the cab and walked towards the emergency room entrance. He had never done this sober, so was really nervous about getting caught.

When the security guard stopped him, Thomas lied and said his wife was waiting for him inside. He walked directly into the waiting area and sat next to a pair of women, one close to his own age and one who was quite frail and elderly. The younger woman made eye contact with him and smiled.

"What's wrong with her?" Thomas asked.

"This is my grandmother," the woman said. "She had this hacking cough for a few days and she's wheezing when she breathes."

The older woman looked so fragile to him. She was pale white and she looked as if she hadn't slept in days.

"Heck of a way to spend Christmas, huh," the woman said. "Is everything ok with you?"

The elder woman had been staring at Thomas since he sat down. He was just about to answer the younger woman's question when her grandmother chimed in.

"It's him," she said before coughing uncontrollably again.

"Easy grandma," the other woman said as she rubbed her back.

"I apologize," she said to Thomas, "my grandma sometimes has a hard time remembering things. She thinks she recognizes a lot of people she's never seen before."

Grandma started coughing again and then cleared her throat.

"He's that healer fella from the TV, Thomas Greggs, right?"

Thomas smiled as she pointed at him and nodded to her. Her granddaughter stared at Thomas with her hand covering her mouth.

She was a very attractive woman, but not the high-maintenance kind of attractive like Kelly. She had more of a girl next door quality. She was dressed in a pair of jeans, a tee shirt and a white pair of sneakers, with not a lot of makeup and straight brown hair.

"Oh my God," the granddaughter said, "what are you doing here?"

"What is your name?" Thomas asked.

"Oh, I'm sorry, my name is Pam and this is my grandmother Abigail."

"I'm pleased to meet you both," Thomas said and shook both of their hands. "The reason I am here it to...."

He didn't get to finish the sentence before Abigail chimed in, "He's going to heal everyone on Christmas, just like he did at that children's hospital."

She started to cough again and Thomas got up to sit beside her. "That's right, Abigail, and I'm going to start with you."

He asked Pam to keep a lookout and he placed both of his hands on Abigail's shoulders. He closed his eyes, took a deep breath and waited for the pain in his chest, but it didn't come. He closed his eyes again, repeated the process and still he felt nothing.

Suddenly Father McBride's words about God's plan popped into his head and Thomas panicked.

"Is there something else wrong with her besides the bad cough?" Thomas asked.

"Yes, she had lung cancer from smoking for most of her life, that's why it's a miracle that you're here to help her. She had been getting progressively worse and I was afraid she didn't have much time left."

Thomas looked at Abigail and she was smiling at him. "Thank you so much dear," she said to him. "I just want you to know, I didn't believe any of that nonsense that they said about you in the news. I know you hard life and still you go out and try to help people. That's a sign of a good young man and of a strong young man."

Thomas put his hands on her again, and again nothing happened. He got up and walked away, swearing under his breath.

Pam knew something was wrong. "It didn't work, did it? Just like it didn't work for that one boy at the children's hospital, right?"

Thomas turned to face her and shook his head. Abigail saw the tears in his eyes and went over to hug him. He was amazed when she repeated the words that Father McBride had said to him.

"It's ok Thomas; it's just God's way. I've lived a long and happy life. If He says it's my time to move on, then I'm ok with that. Besides, there are a lot of people that I am looking forward to seeing again that I've missed for a long time."

She let go of Thomas and wiped a tear from his cheek before smiling at him.

"I'm not afraid of dying, Thomas; I just don't want to leave my little Pammie all alone in the world without me. I'm all she's got."

Pam was now crying too as she hug her grandmother. Thomas felt like he had made a huge mistake. He decided to go back out the way he came, call another cab and drink until the memory of his failure faded. While Pam and her grandmother were still hugging, Thomas made his exit. He was just about to go through the automatic door when someone called out to him.

"Thomas Greggs, is that really you?"

Thomas froze for a second, then lowered his head and walked through the door. He had reached the parking lot when he heard the voice again.

"I thought you were coming in to heal people on Christmas, like you did last year. There are a lot of people here who could use your help, several in the emergency room alone."

Thomas stopped and turned around.

"It doesn't work all of the time," Thomas said, sounding dejected. "I couldn't help that old woman in the waiting room."

"Even if it's the majority of the people, isn't that enough?" the woman asked. "You can make such a difference in their lives tonight, isn't that why you came here?"

Thomas sighed, but nodded his head in agreement.

"I can get you around the emergency room and get you access to anywhere else you want to go. I'm assuming you want to visit the most critical first to see what you might be able to do there. I'll notify the nurses I know on each floor that you are coming. I promise they will keep it quiet until after you've gone."

Thomas followed her into the emergency room and healed everyone there, except Abigail. When he came to her he just held her hand for a few moments.

"You're doing a great thing Thomas, keep it up," she said before a deep hacking cough overtook her.

Thomas and Pam both rubbed her back and Abigail smiled as she looked back and forth between them.

"You know, she thinks you're very handsome, she told me so after you left us," Abigail said with a laugh.

"Jesus Grandma," Pam said while turning a bright shade of red, "did you have to go and tell him that?"

"Is that right?" Thomas replied and they all laughed together.

He looked over and the nurse was waving her hand for him to come join her.

"Do you have a pen and some paper on you?" he asked Pam.

She dug into her pocket book and found a pen, then a business card.

"This is my home number and the number at the hotel I'm staying at. I will be in town until we go back on the road after the New Year. If you're feeling up to it, Abigail, I would like to take you and your beautiful granddaughter out to a nice dinner or have something catered at your house. You name it, anything you want, and I'll get it for you."

Abigail smiled from ear to ear as she held the card in her hand.

"That would be fantastic, Thomas, thank you so much for everything and Merry Christmas."

Thomas leaned over, kissed her on the forehead and wished them both a merry Christmas before joining up with the nurse.

Before he left, Thomas healed everyone in the hospital with the exception of eight other people. They were all in the intensive care unit suffering from some terminal illness or accident. None of them were conscious while Thomas was trying, but he apologized to them anyway before he left.

By the time he was through, Abigail had been admitted and she was in her own room. Both Pam and Abigail were asleep when he looked in on them, so he left without waking them. Before he left, Thomas told the nurse that Abigail was to get the best treatment available and that he would pay for it. She advised him to call the administrator in the morning and that's exactly what Thomas did. It was the first morning in as long as he could remember that he woke up sober and clear-headed. The thoughts or images of those he couldn't heal weren't tormenting him as they had before. All he could think about was Pam and how he couldn't wait to see her again.

Chapter 33

When Thomas woke up late the next morning, the first thing he thought of was getting in the shower and going back to the hospital. He was humming on his way to the bathroom when a thought occurred to him. "I was supposed to be on a plane last night so that I could celebrate Christmas and the New Years with Father McBride."

He rushed to the phone and called Father McBride at home. "This had better be you," the priest said when he picked up the phone. Thomas laughed and replied, "Yes, it's me."

"Oh you're laughing, that's good," Father McBride said with an attitude. "I see you got yourself drunk enough last night to the point of healing a bunch of people that may or may not sue you. Also, judging by the area code you're calling from, you never made it on a plane so we will not be spending any time together.

"Thomas, I preach to you time and time again about what alcohol does to you."

"I was not *that* drunk and I met someone last night," Thomas said. "Not someone in the sense that you're thinking, I met an older woman who I tried to heal. It didn't work and she's pretty bad off.

"Anyway, she's an amazing woman and she has an amazing granddaughter. We seemed to have some kind of connection right away, the three of us. I can't explain it but it almost felt as if I was supposed to meet them. I know it sounds crazy but I can't wait to see this woman again, she's just different."

Father McBride laughed and said, "Listen to you, you sound smitten, good for you!"

"It's not like that," Thomas insisted. "It's more like the connection I used to have with Kate; it's sorta on a deeper level, not just physical attraction."

"That's wonderful Thomas," Father McBride said. "It sounds like you got a nice Christmas present this year for all that you have done for others."

"Would you hate me if I didn't come back to Virginia, Father?" Thomas asked.

"You follow your heart, Thomas and your instincts and trust that He has a plan for you as well. You don't have to worry about me being mad, Thomas. You are my friend. The fact that you called to share all of this with me just strengthens that friendship. Follow your heart, Thomas, and you have yourself a great time."

"Thank you Father, you do the same, I'll see you soon."

Thomas took a quick shower, got dressed and then notified the front desk that he would be staying longer. He was barely there, though, because he wound up spending most of his time off from the Mission with Abigail and Pam.

When Thomas returned to the hospital, he couldn't find them right away. After he had left the hospital, Abigail took a turn for the worse. She started coughing up blood and she was having trouble breathing so they put her on a ventilator. They had moved her into intensive care with all of the other people Thomas couldn't save.

When he finally did locate them, Thomas was upset to see Abigail attached to so many machines after he had left her sleeping peacefully the night before.

Pam didn't know what to think when she saw Thomas walk into the room wearing a maintenance uniform and a black baseball cap. She was surprised but happy to see him once she recognized him. She got up from her chair and greeted him with a hug and a kiss on the cheek. Thomas was taken off guard and just stood there with a dumb smile on his face.

"What the heck is this get up you got on here?" Pam asked with a laugh.

"Well after last night, I knew the media would be all over the place today so I met with the hospital administrator before I came to see you. I made a very large donation to the hospital, anonymously of course, and I made arrangements to pay for the best care for Abigail.

"When I told him I needed a way to get in and out without drawing attention, this is what he came up with. I made sure the nurses on this floor are all on board as well -- they will all receive a large holiday bonus after I'm gone."

"Why would you do all of this for us?" Pam asked.

"I wish I could have done so much more." Thomas felt so helpless when he looked at Abigail. "Here I have this ability that can cure sick people, but there's nothing I can do to help this woman," he thought to himself.

Pam noticed the change in his demeanor. She put her hand on Thomas' shoulder and said, "Don't blame yourself for this. From what I hear, you helped pretty much everyone in this place last night and they all went home this morning.

"She doesn't blame you and I don't blame you, there is no reason for to blame yourself. You would have helped her if you could have and that's all that matters."

Thomas turned to face Pam and they stared into each other's eyes. "She is not only beautiful," Thomas thought, "but she has the kindest eyes I have ever seen."

When the orderlies came to move Abigail to a private room, Thomas and Pam followed them onto the elevator, up to the second floor. The private room had a second bed, a reclining chair and a large screen TV. There were also several different floral arrangements along the windowsill.

"I don't know what to say Thomas. Thank you is all I can think of but it doesn't come close to expressing my appreciation," Pam said as she started to tear up. When she hugged Thomas again, he felt better than he did after taking any drug or drink. Her hair smelled like strawberries and her body was so soft to the touch.

"I want to do this for her," Thomas said, "she shouldn't be in this room."

Thomas stayed and talked with Pam until visiting hours were over. Abigail woke up for short periods of time and she looked around room and smiled at Thomas through her oxygen mask.

The next three days went the same way until Abigail was finally stable enough to eat and drink on her own. Thomas felt an instant connection to Pam -- he thought she was amazing and when he talked to her it seemed like seven hours went by in five minutes. He found that he could make her laugh so easily and she could do the same for him. Still, Thomas didn't pursue anything more than friendship with her. It all felt so perfect to him, but it seemed that way with Kelly in the beginning, too.

Abigail's doctors released her on the fourth day, since they couldn't do much more for her in the hospital. Thomas stayed in the guestroom of Abigail's house, where he slept soundly without any assistance. At night, Abigail would watch her shows while Thomas and Pam either took a long walk in the cold or hung out in the guestroom telling each other their life stories. It made him think of how he used to stay up all night talking with Kate when he was a boy. Pam reminded him of his old friend; Thomas assumed that was reason he got along so well with her.

On New Year's Eve, Abigail turned in early so Thomas and Pam stayed up to watch Dick Clark until the ball dropped. It was Thomas' last night in Charlotte; he had to fly on to the next Mission stop the next afternoon. He had their dinner catered and he ordered some liquor, but Pam wouldn't let him drink it. She was aware of his issues with alcohol and she wanted to spend her time with the real Thomas, not the staggering mess she had seen on TV.

When the ball dropped, they hugged each other and said "Happy New Year" to each other at the same time, which made them laugh. Thomas leaned in to kiss her on the cheek but Pam turned her head and kissed him on the lips.

Thomas stepped back. He wasn't sure what to do or say next.

"I don't understand, Thomas, we get along so well and we're obviously attracted to each other," Pam said.

"I think you're great and yes, I am very attracted to you, but with what I do, I'm always on the road. I don't want any attachments, they just complicate things and it all ends the same way."

Pam grabbed both of Thomas' hands. "I know all about her," she said. "I am nothing like her, can't you see that? I've lived in this town my whole with my grandmother. She raised me from the time I was three when my teenage meth head mother took off one night and didn't ever come back. I love it here and I am dedicated to two things: my grandma and my bagel store.

"I worked there from the time I was a little girl, when it belonged to my grandma. I helped her out when I could, and when she couldn't handle the store anymore, I took it over. I'm just a simple woman who loves the simple, sappy things that are in all of those romance novels - walking on the beach, holding hands in the park, stuff like that. I don't need your money and I never will."

Thomas let go of her hands and walked away from her.

"I'm sorry, Pam, but I just can't," he said. "I am a walking disaster and everything I love turns bad. I don't want to go through that again. If you're cool with being my friend, I would love keep in touch with you and Abigail."

Judging from the look on his face, Pam knew she couldn't change his mind. He really was too damaged and nothing she said was going to change that. She could see his mood change because he suddenly looked so sad.

"Well, if we're not going to suck face would you at least hang out with me for a little while longer and talk before you leave?" Pam teased.

Thomas laughed and agreed. Before long, they were talking as if there had never been a "weird moment" between them.

The next day, Thomas disappeared out of their lives almost as fast as he came. But before he left, he promised that he'd keep in touch and told Pam that if there was anything at all she needed for Abigail to call him and he would make it happen.

The first month he was back on the road, Thomas called Pam every day and talked to her for hours at a time. As the months went on, the calls became shorter and further apart. They stopped completely when Pam told Thomas that she had started seeing someone that her friend had introduced her to.

Left behind again, Thomas went back to the only friend that would never leave him, the bottle. He had reached the point where he no longer cared about anything. When Thomas missed a few Mission events because he was too drunk to go on stage, Father McBride tried to get involved. Thomas stopped taking his calls too.

Seven months into the current Mission tour, Thomas staggered back to his dressing room in a drunken haze to find a familiar face there waiting for him one night. At first he thought he reached a new level of intoxication and was hallucinating.

Pam was standing in the corner of his dressing room. She reached to hug Thomas, but he put out his hand to stop her.

"What the hell are you doing here?" he said in a barely coherent tone. "Why aren't you back enjoying your simple life with your new boyfriend?"

"I came to see you, Thomas. I was worried after seeing you pass out again and again on the news. You just cut me off and stopped taking my calls," she said.

"Worried about me? No one worries about me because I don't have a friend in the world. The great healer man with the gift from God doesn't have a friggin' friend in the world!"

"I am your friend," Pam said, "and I'm here to help you."

"Help me, huh?" Thomas said.

"I don't need another two-face back-stabbing woman in my life! How's that saying go, 'fool me once, shame on you, fool me twice, shame on me'? Now go back to your grandmother and your perfect life, ok?"

"My grandmother died three months ago, you asshole. If you hadn't stopped taking my calls, you would have known that. She saw you spiraling out of control on the TV too and she always asked about you. She would have come to see you herself if she could have."

Pam stormed out of the room in tears. The door had already slammed shut before the meaning of her words reached Thomas' brain.

"Abigail's dead?" he said out loud to the empty room. He staggered to the door but by the time he got out into the hall, Pam was already gone.

Thomas went back inside his dressing room and trashed it. When he was exhausted, he sat on the floor and looked at his swollen, bloody hands. He forced himself to get back up so he could look for another bottle to dull his pain.

When he opened his eyes again, Thomas found himself in bed in a hotel room surrounded by Father McBride, Neesy, Pam, Billy and a man he had never seen before. He introduced himself as Dr. Henry Crawford, an addiction specialist at the Phoenix treatment center in Arizona.

"You know these people here with me," he said. "They are people who care about and feel you are spiraling out of control. Now I'm going to let them each read a statement they prepared for you and I want you to listen."

Thomas had seen a few interventions on TV, so he knew how it would go down. He listened as they took turns telling him how he wasn't the same person and that he was destroying himself. He noticed that Pam wouldn't even look at him during this whole process. She kept her head down and nodded in agreement as everyone spoke. When it was her turn, Thomas recalled what he had said to her the night before. There were so many nights when he was so drunk that he didn't remember anything, yet recalled each hurtful word he said last night.

As Pam looked down at the paper she was holding and cleared her throat, Thomas said, "Pam, I just want you to know that I am so sorry for what I said last night. I am so sorry that Abigail passed. I shouldn't have been so stupid after you told me you were seeing someone, I should have kept in touch."

A tear came down his cheek and he said, "I am so sorry, I just want you to know that. I hear what everyone is saying and you're all right when you say I am not the same person when I drink.

"It's not an excuse, but there are things going on in my head all the time that most times make me wish I was dead. The drinks... they're the only things that make those thoughts go away."

Thomas lifted his hand to cover his eyes as he started to cry and Pam rushed over to his side.

"I've seen the real you," Pam said. "I know that wasn't you last night. But you do need to go away and get some help, Thomas. You are in a free fall, sooner or later the liquor won't work like it used to and you will be dead. I don't think that's what you really want at all. I think you just want to be happy."

Thomas nodded. The look in Pam's eyes made him think everything would be ok. It was the same look his mother had.

Thomas leaned towards her and kissed her on the forehead. He cleared his throat and asked, "So are you still going to read your speech or is that it?" He laughed and everyone else joined in, but then there was an awkward silence in the room.

"Are we leaving tonight, Dr. Crawford?" Thomas asked.

"There's a car waiting outside, Thomas," he replied. "Pack a bag and we'll be on our way. Keep in mind that you will be there for at least 90 days."

The first 30 days were some of the toughest days of Thomas' life. Even with the ability to heal himself, the physical effects of the detox process were terrible. His body ached and he would get the cold chills at night while somehow sweating through all of his clothes.

From the first day he arrived, Thomas went into a three- a-day therapy session schedule with the center psychiatrist. He was put on Prozac the first day and given a low-grade sedative to help him sleep.

He wasn't allowed to have visitors at all for first 30 days, but the time alone was good for him. Pam called him every night and they talked for an hour before lights out. It was almost like a fourth therapy session with him because he found it so easy to open up to her. Even though his head told him that he shouldn't let their relationship go past a friendship, his heart started to tell him otherwise.

Pam was very open and very honest, unlike anyone Thomas had met before. She had a way of speaking her mind and speaking from her heart at the same time that Thomas didn't really understand. Pam knew almost by instinct how to broach certain subjects with Thomas without making him angry.

One night, Thomas was talking to Pam about the events of the day and somehow the subject of parents came up. Thomas, as usual, tried to change the subject, but Pam wouldn't let him.

"You know, Abigail was great to me and I never felt like I wasn't loved, but not having a mother affects you," Pam said. When there was nothing but silence on the other end of the line, she continued on. "I have sporadic memories of my mother coming in and out of my life, but that's about it. I have no idea who my father is, because from what Abigail told me when I got old enough to understand, my father could be any guy in the neighborhood."

Pam laughed and Thomas laughed along with her, but then apologized for doing so. "That's ok," Pam said. "All I'm saying is that I know losing your mom and dad was really tragic. I know it changed you and you think about them every day. But you were lucky to have them in your life, especially your mother.

"After all you've been through, you still have a heart and you want to save others from feeling the loss that you felt. That is amazing to me and from what I can tell, you must have gotten that quality from your mother. I remember you telling me at the house how she would always come to your rescue when your father was… well, being your father. How she would always make you feel better about the things he did or said. How she made you feel that you weren't such an outcast or a loser because you didn't have a lot of friends or any girlfriends."

"Boy, you make me sound really pathetic," Thomas said.

"No, not pathetic at all Thomas just different, maybe. Your mother saw how special you really were and I see it too, even if everyone else can't or they choose not to. I have never felt a connection with anyone before like I felt with you when you stayed at the house. It was as if we had known each other for years because we just got each other and the only word I can use to describe it was comfortable. I've had more than a few relationships, but I have never felt comfortable before.

"Your mother was your healer, Thomas. She taught you how important it is for people to have someone they can turn to when all hope seems to be lost and the world isn't there for them. *That's* what you are Thomas, not some healer for hire. You're the face of hope and goodness for a lot of people, including me. I see beyond the pain and struggle. I see what your mother saw: someone who could be great even if the world just gave him a break."

Thomas was quiet at first and all she could hear was him breathing on the other end of the line. "Are you ok?" Pam asked "I hope I didn't say anything to upset you because that wasn't my intention."

"What you said was great," Thomas replied in a soft voice. "It was really great and I have felt you're special since we first met. Trust is so hard for me after all I've been through. I struggle with the feelings I have for you all of the time, especially at night after I get off the phone with you. It's just like you said. I feel like I have known you forever and that comfortable feeling you mention is that same for me, but it scares me.

"I am afraid to love anyone or anything at this point because love eventually leads to a great deal of pain…the kind of pain that knocks you down as low as you can get and takes a little bit of your soul with it each time you fall until there is nothing left but a shell of a man that used to be you."

"So that's what we'll work on," Pam said. "I'll show you that you were wrong about love and that you can trust someone without being hurt."

"Is that right?" Thomas asked and laughed half-heartedly.

"Yes, that is right," Pam replied. "You need someone else to help heal you. I would like to be the person if you'll let me."

Thomas felt a sense of calm as Pam's words echoed in his head. "I think I would like that very much."

They talked for another few minutes before it was time for lights out. That night, while lying in bed staring up at the ceiling, Thomas thought about his mother. Instead of his usual tears, he smiled instead. Instead of remembering the last time he saw her, Thomas remembered good times and happy memories.

With his mind clear of alcohol along with the intense therapy he was receiving, Thomas started to feel normal towards the end of the month. He was now comfortable enough to speak at length about his parents and the Morgans. The conversation with Pam and the doctor's insights helped him finally start to put things in perspective.

The Prozac had a lot to do with his outlook as well. After the doctors worked out the proper dosage and the drug was in his system for a while, Thomas actually became much calmer. When Thomas would find himself thinking of something sad, his mind would drift and the sadness would pass. He found that he could be more sociable and that he wasn't so caught up in how people viewed him.

On day number 31, Thomas watched as all of the other people who had entered the facility on the same day as him met up with family members, wives or girlfriends. Thomas knew that Neesy and Father McBride were coming. He was really looking forward to seeing them and letting them see the progress he had made. When his name was called over the intercom system Thomas smiled and made his way to the cafeteria.

When he opened to door to go inside, Thomas saw Neesy and Father McBride talking with someone on the other side of the room. At first he thought it was one of the other patients, but as he got closer he felt both nervous and excited at the same time.

"Hey guys," he said as he approached. When Pam turned around and smiled, Thomas felt like his heart stopped beating for a moment. She rushed right over to him and hugged him tight.

"You look so good," she said. At that moment, as far as Thomas was concerned, they were the only two people in the world. He closed his eyes and he took in a long sniff of her hair as he rubbed her back. Neesy and

Father McBride stood looked at each other and smiled until the reunited couple separated.

"Hey guys, thanks for coming," Thomas said as he hugged Neesy and then Father McBride.

They ate and talked while catching up. Thomas told them about all that he had been through and that he was doing much better. Throughout the meal, he was focused on Pam. He couldn't believe that she had come and he couldn't believe how happy he was that she did. They walked the grounds and spent the entire day together. When it was time for visitors to leave, Thomas thought he would be upset but he wasn't. Instead he was grateful that he had people in life that cared enough to be here for him.

Neesy and Father McBride hugged him, told him how well he was doing then went out to the car that was waiting for them. Pam stayed behind, and Thomas was confused about why she didn't leave with them.

"Neesy rented an apartment for me nearby so I can come see you every day," Pam said. "I hope don't mind, I just wanted to help you get through this and be here if you need someone to talk to."

"What about the bagel store?" Thomas asked.

"I got it covered," Pam said. "My two very best friends, one of whom has been working with me at the store for three years, are taking care of it for me. There are no other people in the world that I would trust with that store except for my grandma."

"Why would you do that for me?" Thomas asked.

Pam looked into his eyes and took both of his hands in hers like she did the last night he was in her house in Charlotte. "Trust starts with being there for someone when they could use some support," she said. "Besides, helping you become the person you were meant to be is worth two months of my life. I'm here for Thomas, unless you don't want me here?"

Without thinking, Thomas leaned in and kissed her. The kiss went on and on until an orderly came out to tell Thomas it was time to go back inside for therapy.

The rest of the time at the center was something that Thomas would remember always. It was a time in his life that the world was right and everything suddenly made sense. Pam stayed in Phoenix until Thomas was discharged, and when she flew back home to North Carolina, Thomas went with her.

Chapter 34

Thomas enjoyed his new chance at a normal life with Pam in Charlotte. He thought there would be an adjustment period, but that wasn't the case at all. With The Mission behind him for good, Thomas was ready to start over. He grew a goatee and Pam helped him to bleach his hair blonde. Her two best friends knew who he was, but to everyone else he was just Wayne, a guy who had moved to Charlotte about a year ago that Pam had been secretly dating, waiting until she was sure it was serious before telling everyone.

Thomas worked with Pam all day at her bagel store, learning everything there was to know about the job. When they got home at night, they would spend hours sitting on the swing on Pam's front porch and talking. They got engaged on August 24th, 2006; Thomas had never been happier in all of his 29 years.

Thomas invited Father McBride to spend a few days with them. The more time he spent with Pam, the more he was certain that she was the best thing to ever happen to him. No one smiled more at their engagement party than Father McBride. He believed his prayers had finally been answered and Thomas had finally found peace.

Later that year, a few days after Thanksgiving, Thomas and Pam were heading home from the store when Thomas noticed there were people standing on their porch. As they got closer, he could see Neesy smiling from ear to ear as she waved to him. "My lord, is that you with that blonde hair and beard?"

She ran down the stairs and hugged Thomas. "Look at you! You look so calm and happy! You know how long I've been waiting to see that look again on you?"

Thomas kissed her on the cheek and said, "You look great too, Neesy, it's good to see you." When he let her go, Billy came over to join the reunion. For a moment, Thomas thought he'd try to hug him too, but Billy settled on a handshake.

"She's right man, you look great and congratulations to you both, we were so happy when we got the news."

"Thanks," Thomas said. He noticed they both had suitcases. "So you just show up and you're staying?" he said with a laugh. "What? No, we would never do that," Neesy said as she laughed too. "Pam invited us to come down for a few days. We knew that we couldn't come to your engagement party, but Thomas honey, people are going to find out who you are at some point. You can't keep you a secret forever."

Thomas asked them to come inside and showed them to the guestroom. While they were settling in, he cornered Pam and asked, "What the heck is going on? Why would you do something like this and not tell me? When I was ready to see them again I would have said so."

Pam stepped up close to her fiancée, so that their bodies were touching. She looked in his eyes and smiled at him. "It's going to fine," she said. "Things are different now. We have each other and you are not the same person you were when you last saw them. You are stronger, your mind is clear of clutter and you are in love. Let's just take it as it comes and have a good time."

Thomas reluctantly agreed and was surprised to find that Pam was right. He enjoyed spending time with Neesy and Billy over the next three days. They all went out to dinner together and played cards or watched movies at night. Thomas and Billy even disappeared onto the porch a few times together when the dishes were supposed to be done.

Billy seemed different to Thomas too, he couldn't put his finger on it, and he just seemed more humble. They talked about marriage, kids and family. Billy seemed genuinely happy for Thomas and looked at him with something akin to fatherly pride.

As they sat eating dinner on the night before Billy and Neesy were to leave, Thomas sensed a different atmosphere in the room. He wasn't getting the 'gosh we're going to miss you' type of vibe, it was something different. The conversation was stilted and awkward, not like it had been the other nights. As Thomas ate, he watched as Neesy looked at Billy and Billy looked at Pam and Pam looked down at her plate, as if each was waiting for the others to say something.

Thomas grew more and more uncomfortable until he finally spoke up. "Can someone please tell me what the heck is going on here? Is there something that I don't know about because you three are acting really weird?"

Billy put his napkin down, sighed and was just about to speak when Neesy put her hand on his shoulder to stop him.

"I'm sorry, Thomas, but you're right, there is more to us being here than just a visit," Neesy said. She tried to compose herself to continue. When Thomas noticed a tear come from her eye, he became concerned.

"You're ok, Neesy, right? There's nothing wrong with you, is there?"

"Oh you dear boy," Neesy said as she wiped her eyes with her napkin. "There is nothing wrong with me, I'm just fine. But I'm afraid we put Pam here in a bad position by forcing her to lie so that we could talk to you face to face."

"Lie to me?" Thomas asked in surprise and anger. "What the hell is going on here?"

"Thomas, we're going broke," Neesy said and looked away in shame

"Broke?" Thomas asked sarcastically. "How in the world could you be broke?"

"We lost a ton of money on overhead, bad investments, lawsuits, cancellations and other ventures," Billy said. "Everything we have in tied into The Mission and The Mission is underwater. The sponsors are threatening to liquidate whatever's left and take it to settle up, but even that won't be enough."

Thomas closed his eyes and rubbed his forehead with his fingers. "Look if you need some money, I can loan you some to try to get you through this," Thomas said.

"It ain't gonna be enough, Thomas," Billy said sadly.

"Well than, what do you want from me?" Thomas shouted.

Pam shot him a look of disgust and Neesy lowered her head to cry. Thomas felt like a heel for a moment, but that gave way to anger when he realized that Billy and Neesy must have already spoken to Pam about this. They had convinced her to help them and Thomas knew exactly what that entailed. He felt like an animal trapped in a cage.

"You want me to go back with The Mission," Thomas said quietly while looking down at the table. "That's what you want, isn't it?"

"I'm so sorry that we have to ask you to do this, Thomas," Neesy said. "But Billy tells me we should be all right with everything in two years, and then you can be done for good. I promise."

"Two years," Thomas said. He looked at Pam and repeated it, "Two years?" She reached across the table and held his hands, "I know, babe, but I'm going with you and I'll be there the whole time," she said.

"What about your business?" Thomas asked. "I already spoke to Bridget about it. She wants to buy into the business and become partners, so it will be in good hands until I get back," Pam replied.

Thomas shook his head and gave Billy a look of disdain. He realized the weekend had just been an act and he was mad at himself for falling for Billy's manipulations again. But when he saw Neesy crying in shame, he thought, "How in the world can I say no to her?"

"When do you want to start again," Thomas asked as he stared at Billy.

"The best way to kick this thing off in a real positive direction financially would be to start with the Christmas Eve Mission Event.

"I can get big sponsor dollars and that will help Neesy and me to start paying of our creditors and the lawyers. Between that and the fact that I can tell them that we have a two year commitment from you, it should be enough to keep them off our backs."

Thomas looked at Neesy again and then over to Pam before shaking his head side to side and looking away off into the distance.

"Let me take the night to think about it," Thomas said before letting out a sigh. "I'll let you know in the morning before you guys head out."

Thomas spent the night telling Pam why it was a bad idea for him to go back to the Mission.

"How did you get involved in this?" he asked her. "Why did you keep this from me?"

Pam sat next to Thomas and held his hand. "Neesy called about a week ago and she was very upset," Pam said. "She was ashamed to ask you to come back, but she didn't know what else to do. Some of the property she owns has been in her family for generations and Billy tied it all in with the Mission. It would kill her if she lost it. I didn't want to take it upon myself to make any kind of decision, but I know the way you feel about her so I told her to come here and talk to you herself.

"I want you to trust me, Thomas, and I didn't keep anything from you. I just thought they should come directly to you."

"You still should have told me, Pam," Thomas said as he looked her. "Now if I say no, I have to see her face as she's about to lose everything."

"So, you're not doing it?" Pam asked.

Thomas put his head down and closed his eyes. He knew he couldn't let Neesy lose everything when he could help. The guilt would eat him up inside.

"I'm here for you either way. Whatever you decide, I will support you," Pam said.

"You don't know what it's like out there, Pam," Thomas said. "It drains the life out of you and turns you into a robot as the days all blend together. I get no joy out of it at all anymore, I haven't for years."

Pam kissed on the cheek then smiled, "Well, that's because you haven't been out there with me before," she said. "I've always wanted to see different places because I've lived in this town my whole life. Plus you probably didn't even get to see any of the sights before because of the state of mind you were in. This could really be a fun experience for both of us and we can enjoy it together. It might even make you appreciate that gift you have again."

Thomas considered what she said and he smiled. She was right, he had been to so many places around the country but he never stopped to see or do any of the things that a normal person would have. When he thought about it, it did seem like such a waste. The idea of experiencing it all for the first time with Pam just felt right to him.

"I'll do it on one condition and I won't take no for an answer," he said as he stared into her eyes.

"Ok, what is it?" Pam asked, with no idea what Thomas was hoping for.

"I want you to marry me before we go," Thomas said with a nervous smile.

Pam screamed out, "Oh my God! Really?"

When Thomas nodded and repeated, "really." Pam hugged him and kissed him all over his face.

Thomas laughed and asked, "Is that a yes?"

"Yes, yes, of course it's a yes," Pam yelled as she jumped up and down.

Neesy came running into the room with Billy right behind her. "Is everything all right with you two? What's going on?" she asked while looking concerned

"Thomas and I are getting married!" Pam shouted before she hugged Neesy.

"Oh my God, that's wonderful," Neesy said as she teared up and hugged Pam back.

Billy's eyes opened wide and he looked shocked. He approached Thomas and extended his hand. "Hey congratulations man, she's a great gal and we're so happy for you."

Thomas shook Billy's hand and replied, "Thanks Billy, I know she's great."

"Yea, she is," Billy said while looking around the room nervously. He scratched his head and looked at Thomas. "So um, are you uh going to help us out or not?"

Thomas looked over at Neesy and Pam. They were both teary-eyed now as they stood talking in the corner of the room with great big smiles on their faces. Thomas thought about how they had become the two most important women in his life. Neesy had come to his aid now on several occasions when he was at his lowest. It was time for him to do the same for her.

Thomas agreed to go return to the Mission and the four of them celebrated together into the early morning hours.

A week later in a small church outside of Charlotte, Father McBride performed the ceremony for a small gathering consisting of Pam's closest friends, along with Neesy and Billy, who stayed in Charlotte until the ceremony.

Pam and Thomas then went away to Hawaii for their honeymoon before joining up with the Mission in Colorado. When Billy saw Thomas again, he had dyed his hair back to black and shaved his goatee.

Things were different this time for Thomas because Pam was there to support him. Just having someone to talk to before and after healing sessions made all of the difference in the world to Thomas. He was able share the anxiety he felt, and he didn't turn back to the bottle to escape it. Pam always had a big smile on her face when she saw her husband, because she was so proud of him.

Thomas tried something new in an effort to heal as many people as he could. He would heal until he felt a little pressure in his head and then he would take a 15-minute break. This seemed to work well for a few weeks, but eventually the breaks got longer and his tolerance got shorter. It seemed no matter what he tried, he couldn't heal everyone.

Pam was aware of the mental toll that Thomas paid because people who paid to seek his help had to be turned away each night. She tried her best to take his mind off of the Mission once he stepped off of the stage. Most nights, it was a romantic encounter but when that didn't happen they would both watch a funny movie together or just stay up and talk. They would also wear different disguises and go sightseeing. It seemed to work because Thomas was able to fall asleep without turning to alcohol or pills and he was able to stay calm and content.

The Mission was making money again and Thomas checked off the days on his calendar in anticipation of his return to anonymity. Therapy made him realize that his life was his own, no matter what kind of gift he had received and although he didn't completely forgive himself for what happened to his parents, he was able to accept it. He had totally embraced the 'God's Plan' theory and he had found peace because of it.

One of the happiest days of his life was April 20th, 2007. The Mission had just finished an event in Dallas, Texas. Pam was waiting by the side of the stage as usual however this time, she was holding something else instead of the usual towel and bottle water, but she was smiling from ear to ear.

"Whatcha got there?" Thomas asked before giving her a kiss.

"Oh you mean this thing?" Pam smiled. Thomas waited until she stopped waving it and took a good look at the unfamiliar object. He had a hunch about what it was and what it meant.

"Is that what I think it is?" he asked nervously and smiled.

Pam nodded and burst out laughing.

"Oh my God, you're pregnant!"

"Yes, Thomas," she shouted, "we're having a baby!"

Thomas hugged Pam and picked her up in his arms. "Attention everyone!" shouted the 30-year-old father-to-be. "Me and my lovely wife are having a baby!"

Bernie was standing on the other side of the stage talking to one of his nephews when Thomas yelled his news. He hurried over to Thomas to congratulate him and before long the entire Mission congregation joined him. It turned into a big celebration with everyone wishing the parents-to-be the best.

Everyone except for Billy, that is. When Jerry told his brother the good news, Billy pounded his fist down onto the countertop in his dressing room and shouted, "God damn it, why did this have to happen now!"

"I thought you would be happy for him, bro," Jerry said. "Pam's good for him and this baby will make sure he stays on the straight and narrow, no more of that booze bullshit."

Billy turned and stared at his brother before shaking his head. "Do you honestly think that Thomas is going to stay on with us after this baby is born?" Billy asked sarcastically. "I thought I would get two years out of this deal, and now it's going to be over in a little over one! Do you have any idea the people I have lined up and the money they're ready to spend knowing that this is Thomas' farewell tour? God dammit!"

Jerry watched his brother. He could tell that the wheels of Billy's mind were already spinning, formulating his next move.

"Look man, you're the only one who hasn't got there and congratulated the happy couple," Jerry said. "He's gonna notice and if you piss Thomas off, this thing may end a lot sooner than you think it will. You need to get out there and do what you gotta do, whether you're happy about it or not."

Billy shook his head again then let out a breath that he felt like he was holding in from the time Jerry told him the news. "You're right, Jerry, you're right," Billy said sounding exhausted and frustrated.

He made his way down the hall and to the stage area where music was playing and everyone was gathered around the happy couple. There were bottles of champagne everywhere and it appeared as if someone had poured a bottle over Pam's head because her hair was soaking wet.

Billy took a deep breath and put on a plastic smile before making his way through the crowd. "There they are!" he shouted as he approached the happy couple. "I just heard the news, congratulations you two."

He shook Thomas' hand and hugged Pam. He stayed to have a glass of champagne and talk a bit before leaving to handle so business. He said congratulations again before leaving with another handshake and another hug.

Thomas watched him leave. Bernie stopped his brother and whispered something in his ear before he left the room. Billy's smile slipped and he appeared as if he was mad at the world as he listened to Bernie. Billy shook his head in disgust and glanced over in Thomas' direction. He looked surprised to see Thomas staring back at him and immediately put the plastic smile back on his face.

Thomas realized that Billy was probably upset because he knew Thomas have to leave the Mission before his two-year commitment was up if he didn't want the baby to be born on the road. He felt bad about breaking his promise to Neesy, but as Thomas looked at his wife and rubbed her stomach, he knew he would be leaving the Mission towards the end of the pregnancy no matter what.

Chapter 35

As soon as Neesy got the news, she took a plane out to join up with the Mission in Las Vegas the next morning. Thomas also invited Father McBride and flew him out first class.

Everyone was in the mood for a big celebration. Billy reserved two floors at Caesar's Oasis and they partied until the early morning hours in one of the conference rooms. After everyone went to their separate ways to gamble, Thomas, Pam, Father McBride and Neesy went back to Thomas' suite to talk.

Thomas broke the news to Neesy that he was leaving The Mission for good when it was time for the baby to be born and apologized for not being able to keep his promise. Neesy looked upset but he knew she understood.

"Tell Billy to line up the richest people in the next six or seven months and I'll heal them all," Thomas said. "I will make sure that you guys are ok financially when this is all said and done, even if I have to give you some of my own money."

Father McBride gave him a disapproving look, but held his tongue. Thomas knew what was on the priest's mind anyway. "Healing for the right reasons is what separates you from Billy," Father McBride always said.

Now Thomas was willing to cast his morals to the side to give Billy and Neesy financial stability. It didn't sit well with the priest and it was written all over his face. Rather than argue about it or discuss it any further, Pam changed the subject back to the baby and everyone was smiling again.

The next day, Neesy talked to her husband about what Thomas had said and Billy quickly became agitated.

"Line up the richest people, he actually said that?" Billy said with a mocking laugh. "What the hell does he think I've been doing since we started this thing again? Listen, even if he leaves in six or seven months, that will have given us a year and a half on the road. We will be fine even if he doesn't come back, don't you worry about that."

Neesy shook her head as she stared Billy in the eyes.

"You don't care about that boy at all do you?" she asked.

When Billy stared back at her and didn't answer she became upset as well.

"You never cared for him at all throughout this whole thing. What was he to you, just the goose that laid the golden eggs?"

Billy could see that Neesy was getting angrier by the second so he backed off.

"Of course I care for that boy," Billy fired back. "I have done nothing but protect that man from himself and look after him. He would be face down drunk in some Mexican ditch if it wasn't for me, so don't tell me I don't care about him!

"My number one priority has been and always will be my family. I admit, a lot of the times I have tunnel vision when it comes to my family but at the end of the day when all of this is gone, it will just be us again, in our home, in Virginia. I want to be able to get old with you and not have to worry about nothing ever again. That's what all of this is about, honey."

When Neesy started to tear up, he knew she bought the whole thing hook line and sinker. He let out a big sigh as he hugged her while he mind raced. He needed to make sure that there were no more surprises. He needed to be certain that he could line up everything he needed and that there wouldn't be any more issues that could jeopardize the potential millions he could make.

Billy still had tens of millions of dollars in several banks. But it was like he always told his brothers when they would ask about money, "How much is enough?" He was going to do everything in his power to ensure that by the end of this tour, there would definitely be enough.

The following evening, Billy asked Thomas, Pam, Neesy and Father McBride to join him in his suite before the Father left for the airport. He wanted to make it clear to everyone that he supported Thomas's decision "one hundred percent" and that he wanted nothing but the best for their growing family.

He surprised everyone when he suggested that Pam should find a doctor to join them on the road, telling her that "the Mission would spare no expense."

"Family always come first," Billy said, "and you two are definitely family."

Judging by the stunned expressions on their faces, Billy felt as if he just delivered a performance worthy of an Academy Award. Neesy was the first to get up and hug him, and Pam followed right after. Thomas shook his hand and thanked him while Father McBride patted him on the back.

"You stick to your word Billy, you hear me?" Father McBride whispered into his ear as he continued to pat him.

Billy made eye contact with him and mouthed the words, "I will."

Billy kept his word and everything was fine throughout the next eight months.

In late December of 2007, the Mission arrived in New York City for its big Christmas event at Madison Square Garden. Billy had filled the arena with the neediest richest people in the Tri-State Area. Not only would they receive the gift of being healed, the whole world would see it because it was being televised across the globe in several different languages. People called him months in advance to be part of this event because they thought they had more of a chance to be healed on Christmas Eve.

Pam had not been feeling well for the past several days. Her morning sickness wasn't subsiding and she was having a difficult time dealing with it. Pam's doctor had gone home to be with her family, but she gave Thomas the names of several doctors in the city to call if the need arose. Pam knew it was just normal pregnancy stuff so she didn't bother anyone.

On Christmas Eve morning, Pam threw up several times and she felt exhausted. She knew Thomas meant what he said when he offered to cancel the event, but she couldn't let him do that. She relaxed the whole day at the hotel and the nausea eventually passed for a while. She decided to take advantage of it by showering and putting on a green dress she had bought for the event. When it was time to leave, she was right by Thomas's side as they headed to the Garden.

She wasn't there long though. As soon as they got to the dressing room she felt sick again and vomited into a wastebasket. Thomas was going to leave with her but she told him that wasn't necessary.

"I'll just go back to the hotel and lie down again," she told him. "It will only be for a couple of hours and you'll be back, no big deal."

Thomas wanted to stay with his wife, but she insisted.

"Just go do your thing and I'll be fine," Pam said as she caressed his cheek with her hand. "Those people out there are counting on for six more months and then it's over. Now go give them a Christmas miracle that only you can give."

Thomas looked deep into her eyes and then kissed her on the lips.

"Are you sure you'll be ok without me?" Thomas asked.

"I can be alone for a few hours, Thomas, I'm a big girl," Pam said, "in fact I'm getting bigger by the day."

They both laughed together and then Thomas shook his head.

"You won't be alone, hold on a second," he said and ran out of the room. He came back a minute later with Billy's nephew Michael.

"Michael here is going to see that you get back to the hotel and he's going to wait with you until I get back. If anything happens, he is going to call me on my cell phone and I will drop everything to get to you. You can't say no to this because if you do, I'm not going out there."

Pam looked at Michael and he shrugged his shoulders before smiling.

"He's the boss," Michael said. "What he says goes right?"

Pam laughed and then gave Thomas a hug.

"I'll be fine, don't worry," she whispered in his ear. She let go of him and then fixed his hair with her hands. "Now go do some good out there and make mama proud."

Thomas smiled and said, "Will do honey, see you later."

As he watched them leave the room all he could he think of was how he couldn't wait until this was all over and the Mission was behind him for good.

As Pam and Michael walked down the hall, he asked her if she would mind if he invited someone along for the ride.

Pam just wanted to get back to the hotel so that she could lie down so she said, "Sure, no big deal."

She followed Michael down another hallway where a very attractive, tall and thin black woman was waiting for him. "Pam, this is Cynthia. She's a big fan of Billy's and your husband, of course."

Pam shook her hand and tried to be gracious but her stomach was very unsettled again.

"Michael, I need to get going now. My stomach isn't going to hold out to much longer."

They left the building, parked the car in the garage and entered The Palace Hotel together. The lobby was packed with people who were coming and going. As they made their way through the crowd, Michael noticed what appeared to be a party going on in one of the lounges. There was Christmas music blasting as the crowded room was alive with people celebrating.

When Michael and Cynthia stopped to take a look, Pam became agitated.

"Hey, why don't you do go and enjoy yourselves while I go upstairs and lie down?" she said.

Cynthia whispered something in Michael's ear, but he shook his head no.

"Thomas told me to stay with you, Pam, and make sure you were ok," Michael said, but he was still looking in the direction of the party. Finally, he turned back to Pam. "I am not going to do anything to get myself fired on Christmas Day."

"It's fine Michael, really. I'm just going to change and get into bed. I'll probably sleep straight through until Thomas gets back 'cause I'm wiped out."

Cynthia whispered into his ear again and laughed.

"I'll come up in a little while to check on you to make sure you're ok," Michael said. "We won't be long."

Pam forced a smile and Michael was gone with Cynthia by his side.

When Pam got onto the elevator, there were several people inside. They all got off one after the other as the elevator went up. Only one tall and thin older gentleman wearing the thick eye glasses stayed on. Pam thought it was a little odd when she noticed that he hadn't pressed any button for a specific floor. The only button still lit was the one she pressed for one of the private floors that were booked exclusively for the Mission.

As they got within two floors she made eye contact with the gentleman and smiled. When he smiled back, she could see that his forehead was covered in sweat. It made her nervous. Pam's stomach reacted, and as the elevator door opened she quickly got out.

Without looking back, she headed straight for her suite and hoped she'd make it before she vomited all over the hallway carpet. When she stopped to reach into her purse to get the key card, she heard footsteps come from behind her and her heart dropped.

Pam turned to find the man from the elevator standing behind her with a gun in his hand. Her knees got weak and she thought she was going to pass out so she held onto the wall to steady herself.

"Where is your husband?" the man asked as he nervously looked back and forth to see if anyone was coming.

Fighting her fear and nausea, Pam turned to face the wall and rested her head against it.

"Don't turn your back from me, Goddammit!" the man shouted. "Where the hell is he?"

Pam held her stomach for a moment before vomiting all over the wall in front of her. She started to hyperventilate in between dry heaves.

"Jesus Christ, take it easy lady," the man said as he placed his hand on her back.

When she turned to face him, she could see there was kindness in his eyes and a look of concern on his face. She didn't know what to make of this person at all, but she could see that he was very nervous and very unstable.

"Thank you sir, I'm ok now," Pam said as she straightened up.

"We need to get inside right now," he said

The man grabbed the key card away from her. He let them in and he told her to sit down. When the man disappeared into the bathroom for a moment, Pam didn't know what he was planning and she was scared. She thought about running, but the moment was gone. He came out with a small glass of water in one hand and a towel in the other.

He gave the water to Pam and sat down on the couch across from her and used the towel to wipe the sweat off his forehead and then clean of the lenses of his glasses.

Under the lights on the hotel room, Pam could see that the man had dark bags under his eyes as if he hadn't slept in days. He had short grey hair that he slicked back and it looked like he hadn't shaved in three or four days at least. He was wearing brown slacks and a white short-sleeve button down shirt. The thick glasses had even thicker black plastic frames which took up half of his face.

Pam didn't know what to do as he tapped the gun lightly against his leg while talking to himself. She hoped that if she could stay calm that she might be able to reason with the man and get him to let her go. Her mind raced trying to find a possible reason the man would try to see Thomas armed with a gun. She thought of two possibilities: either he wanted Thomas to heal him or he wanted Thomas to heal a loved one.

"Umm sir, I don't know why you're doing this, but I'm sure you feel there is a good reason," Pam said. "Thomas is a good man and I'm sure he can help you, but please don't do it this way."

The man became agitated and turned his attention towards her.

"Did you say he was a good man?" he demanded, the anger and bitterness in his voice impossible to ignore.

"Yes, sir, I did say that," Pam replied nervously. "I know him a lot better than most do and I can say for certain that he is a very good man. He's had a hard life and made some mistakes along the way, but he does try to help as many people as he can."

The man laughed for a moment and then pointed at Pam.

"You may protect him because of his millions and the lifestyle he provides for you, but Thomas is nothing but a lousy drunk who is probably responsible for his parents' deaths along with the death of countless others who waited on line for hours for their chance at a miracle only to have him pass out drunk right in front of them."

Pam's jaw dropped in shock and she covered her open mouth with her hand. "This man is here for revenge," she realized. She closed her eyes and started to cry.

The man handed her the towel and asked in she'd like some more water. Pam tried to compose herself and told him that she was fine while silently praying that she would be.

The man started to talk to himself again. "What am I doing here, Margaret? I am so lost without you. I just want the pain to stop."

He started to cry and raised the gun to his temple.

Pam jumped out of her chair and shouted, "No, please, you don't have to do that, sir!"

The man stared at her in surprise, but still held the gun to his head.

"Please, just put the gun down sir, let's just talk. I know you're in pain; I lost someone very close to me once too. She was like a mother to me and when she died, I lost a part of me, but life goes on. I'm sure whomever you lost would want you to go on."

The man lowered the gun and extended his hand.

"My name is Roger," he said. "Can I please have the towel?"

Pam gave it to him, but her eyes never left the gun. When he thanked her, she extended her hand and said, "It's nice to meet you, Roger."

Pam knew she had to keep this man calm and she had to keep Thomas away. There was little doubt in her mind that if he saw Thomas standing in front of him whatever hurt was eating Roger up inside would take over and it would end badly.

Pam had watched plenty of television programs about hostage situations and they all said the same thing. The hostage should always try to make their captor see them as a real person.

"I'm sorry about the mess I made out in the hallway, I'm pregnant and the morning sickness has been brutal. That's why I came back her tonight because I have been throwing up all day."

Roger stared out into the distance, and Pam realized that he hadn't heard a word she had said. His thumb went back and forth across the handle of the gun as he sat lost inside his head.

"Are you ok over there?" Pam asked politely

"I had known Margaret since I was 16 years old," Roger said. He continued to stare at the hotel room's wall as he spoke. "We were high school sweethearts who got married and stayed together for over 40 years. I had just retired from the NYPD three years ago with when she found noticed the lump in her neck.

"The doctors said the cancer was already in her lymph nodes and that she had less than a year and that was 'a generous estimate.' I was so upset and depressed, but she was calm about the whole thing. She told me Thomas the healer was coming to coming back to New York soon and that everything was going to be all right.

"I tried to schedule to chemotherapy, but she wouldn't do it. My wife was a woman of very strong faith and she believed in her heart that Thomas would heal her. She even had me buying into it as we stood in line for hours waiting to get into the Garden with all of the other people.

"I remember it was a cold day and there was a light rain that wouldn't let up. It didn't dampen Margaret's spirits at all though. She passed the time by talking to everyone around her in line, telling them that they were going to get their miracle today. We finally got inside and she loved the whole show," Roger said with a bitter laugh.

"She sang along with the choir and she gave several big ole 'Halleluiah and Amen's' throughout Billy's sermon. When Thomas came out, she screamed and hollered his name as she lifted her hands towards to heavens. As we lined up and waited she was filled with excitement, telling me over and over, 'This is it, honey.' I could tell right away that he was off, but I prayed he would make it until the end.

"But your husband – your 'good man' – was already staggering back and forth on the stage after healing just a few people. Someone in the crowd started shouting at him and he was cussing them on mic so everyone could hear it. That's when Margaret started worrying and it was written all over her face. I tried to tell her everything was going to be ok, but I knew it was just a matter of time.

"Sure enough, Thomas got into an argument with Billy on the stage. He healed a few more people before turning his attention back to the heckler in the audience. I thought your husband was going to jump right down into the audience to confront the guy, but one of the stagehands grabbed him first. Thomas broke free, but took two steps and passed out cold right there on the stage."

Roger chewed on his bottom lip as it started to quiver while a tear ran down his cheek before he continued on.

"Billy rushed over to him and cussed at him before two other fellas dragged him off stage. Then the lights came on and Billy made the announcement that the event was over. He said everyone would get a full refund mailed to them within a few weeks. Within seconds, the stage was empty and dozens of security personnel were in the aisles herding people towards the exits where The Mission attendants were waiting with pre-stamped cards that were to be used for the refund.

"You know, I think I lost my wife at that very moment. I tried my best to keep things positive by telling her we would drive to the next event, but she didn't care. She told me that it wasn't meant to be and that this was a sign that it was her time.

"I begged her for weeks afterwards to change her mind, I even bought the tickets for the healing session in Washington D.C., but she wouldn't do it. Every day I had to sit and watch her suffer until the end, I thought of Thomas.

"Your 'good man' took her from me and I haven't been the same since. My hatred has been the only thing that has kept me alive all of this time, waiting for the moment when I could confront him face to face so he can see firsthand the damage he has done."

Pam faked like her stomach took a turn for the worse again and she put her hand to her mouth. "I think I'm going to be sick again, Roger," she said. "Would you mind if I run to the bathroom?"

Roger looked at her sympathetically and nodded. "Don't take too long," he said, "and please don't try to make a run for the door."

Pam nodded back to him and rushed into the bathroom. She turned on the water while she coughed loudly a few times. Then she pulled her cell phone out of her pocket and called 9-1-1. She told them what had occurred and that she couldn't stay on the phone or he would get suspicious. She thought about her husband. Thomas would be on the stage now healing and would be coming back to the hotel suite as soon as the show was finished. She worried what would happen if Thomas came back before the police came. She knew if that occurred, Roger would lose control and shoot Thomas dead.

Her mind continued to race until she heard Roger call out from the other room, "Are you ok in there?" She started coughing again and yelling back, "Be out in a second Roger, my stomach is a mess."

She watched the ribbon of light under the door to see if he was approaching, but it was clear so she assumed he was still on the couch waiting for her. She decided to push her luck and call Billy, who sounded annoyed when he picked up.

"Billy, listen to me because I don't have much time," Pam whispered. "There is a man holding me hostage in my hotel room. He has a gun and he blames Thomas for his wife dying. I already called the police but I don't want Thomas here. This man will kill him if he gets the chance."

Billy's mouth dropped as the words registered in his head.

"Billy, are you there?" Pam asked desperately.

"Yeah, I'm here," Billy said as he tried to process what was happening.

Roger banged on the door and said, "I think you need to come out of there now."

"I have to go," Pam whispered and hit disconnect

Billy stared at his phone in shock.

"Hey man, what the hell is going on?" Bernie asked. Billy ignored him and walked down to the other end of the hall to make a call.

When Michael picked up, there was loud music in the background and it was very hard to hear him over the sound of everyone talking over it around him.

"What's up Uncle Billy?" Michael said when he picked up.

Billy was irate at his nephew's carefree tone.

"Where are you, you stupid fuck? I thought Thomas fucking told you to stay with Pam the whole time."

"Oh man, sorry Uncle but she was ok, just a little stomach ache is all," Michael said.

"You listen to me, stupid," Billy growled, "There is a man with a gun up in her room waiting for Thomas to get there so he can kill him. Now don't you say a word and let me finish. The police should be there any second. What I want you to do is meet them at the door and tell them what room she's in, that's it.

"You are not to go anywhere near that room or even on that floor, you understand me? This is hard enough to deal with without having to worry about my dumbass brother's kid's blood being on my hands too."

Michael was quiet for a moment. "Oh my God, I'm so sorry uncle."

"It's just as well that you're down there, Michael," Billy said. "He probably would have shot you first before taking Pam hostage. Now you just stay put and I'll be in touch and don't call your father yet 'cause he don't know nothing."

Bernie waited until his brother came back down the hall

Billy hung up the phone and walked back over to Bernie, "I need you to come with me," he said, more serious than usual.

They walked to the side of the stage and they watched as Thomas healed two different people. Billy scanned the people that were left in line and he could immediately tell that there were still at least 10 millionaires at the front. Their money was already in the bank.

"Are you going to tell me what's going on here, Billy?" Bernie asked.

Billy ran his hand across his bald head and looked towards the ceiling. "You're going to have to forgive me for this one," he said.

"What are you talking about, man?" Bernie asked

Billy grabbed his brother and held onto him by both shoulders. "Look man, when this is done and he comes off that stage, this whole thing is over for good, you hear me? Not like the other times when he came back either, it is done without a doubt.

"So we're going to let him finish, then pray for our souls when this is all said and done. Just remember, everything I did since this thing started, I did for all of our families so that we'll be taken care of."

Bernie pushed his brother off of him and studied him. "Jesus, Billy, what the hell did you do?"

Billy looked at the ground and then back at his brother, "I did what I had to, same as I've done since our father went to jail. I made sure you, Jerry and your families would be taken care of for the rest of your lives. This was my creation, my idea and if it's gonna burn down, then I'm gonna light the match."

Bernie was at a loss for what to say or do next. He knew whatever it was; it was big because as he stood next to his brother watching Thomas finish up, Billy's bottom lip quivered from time to time and when Thomas took a bow before saying good night to the crowd Billy started to tear up.

As Thomas came off the stage, he noticed immediately that something was wrong. Billy and Bernie never waited for him--if Billy needed to see him, he sent someone to tell him to come to his dressing room. He was certain it was bad news and his thoughts immediately went to Pam.

"What happened?" Thomas asked before they could say a word. "Is it Pam? Is she ok? Is the baby ok?"

Billy put his hand on Thomas' shoulder and let out a deep breath, "There's a situation back at the hotel."

When he noticed that Bernie and Thomas looked at him the same way, he was overcome by guilt.

"A gunman is holding your wife hostage in your hotel suite. He blames you for his wife's death."

"This is some kind of sick joke, right?" Thomas asked even though he knew Billy wouldn't do something like that. "Tell me this isn't real!"

"Pam called me herself from the hotel, Thomas. She didn't want me to tell you because she's afraid this man will kill you if you go there."

"How long ago was this?" Thomas demanded. "I've got to get over there!"

Billy grabbed Thomas by the arm before he could run away. "She called a while ago, the cops are there now and they'll talk this guy into letting her go. You can't go anywhere near there, Thomas, or you'll just agitate the man into doing something stupid."

Thomas stared at Billy with a look of pure hatred in his eyes. "You take your damn hands off of me," he said.

Billy let go and Thomas turned his attention to Bernie.

"Please take me over there right now, Bernie, I'm begging you!"

Bernie looked over at Billy and Billy shook his head no.

Bernie pulled his keys out of his pocket and told Thomas, "Come on," before running down the hall.

"Damn it," Billy said as he ran to catch up with them.

Chapter 36

The seven minute ride to the hotel was quiet. Bernie drove and Thomas sat in the front with his fists clenched in his lap as he stared out the window. When they turned the corner to 5th Avenue, they could see police lights everywhere. They were still blocks away from The Palace Hotel when they encountered police officers directing traffic away from the site.

When Bernie stopped at the police barricade, Thomas opened the car door and bolted from the car. One of the patrolmen tried to grab him as he went by, but Thomas eluded him and ran as fast as he could towards the hotel. Bernie knew the least he could do for Thomas at this point was to give him every chance to get to the hotel, so he quickly got out of the car and approached the police. Billy followed him and they stalled the officers as Thomas tried to get to his wife.

Thomas made it as far as the entrance to The Palace Hotel before he was stopped by more uniformed officers who were standing guard. "Please, you have to let me in," he begged as he tried to catch his breath. "I'm Thomas Greggs, my wife is being held hostage."

One of the policemen stepped in closer and looked down at him. "I don't care who are you are pal, you ain't gettin' in there." He pointed to a man who was wearing a cheap suit and tie. "That's the man in charge, go over and talk to him."

Thomas ran over to the man the cop pointed to. For once, fame worked in his favor – Thomas was recognized right away. The man introduced himself as Ron Dowsing, the hostage negotiation team lead.

"We are trying to get the man to release your wife, but he keeps demanding that you go up and talk to him. We're doing all we can, Thomas. The best thing is for you to just let us do our job."

Thomas was stunned, but asked what the hostage taker wanted and how to get up to see him.

"Our opinion is that this is someone who either wants you to heal him or someone who blames you for not healing someone close to them," Dowsing said. "I would not recommend going up there at this time, Thomas. Odds are if he wanted you to heal him, he would have mentioned that as part of his demands. Instead the only thing we can get out of him is that he wants to see you face to face."

Thomas looked towards the entrance; the urge to make a break for the door was becoming stronger and stronger. "We do not want to agitate this guy any more than he already is. Something tells me putting you in front of him will do just that," Dowsing said.

Thomas bowed his head as he bent over with his hands on his knees. He started to have trouble breathing. He felt a hand on his back and heard a sympathetic voice, "Don't worry, Thomas, we'll get her out of there, ok?"

Thomas looked up and saw an officer in uniform who appeared to be around his age. "You don't remember, do you? I didn't think you would, not with all of the people you've helped. I took my mom to a Mission event two years ago in Connecticut. She had been in a car accident and was in a wheelchair for years. You put your hands on her and three minutes later she was back to her old self. You have no idea the good you've done for so many people."

Thomas looked the officer in the eyes and he could see the gratitude the man felt. "I appreciate you saying that, but I could use your help just as bad as you needed mine. I need to get in that building to help my wife. You have to help me, please."

The officer looked around for a moment and then looked back at Thomas before nodding his head. "Head around through the parking lot to the back of the building, I'll let you in through one of the back doors. Just keep an eye out for my flashlight and get to me as fast as you can."

Thomas did as he was told and made in through one of the back doors. He thanked the police officer and headed up the stairs.

When Pam came out of the bathroom, Roger was staring at the television news coverage of the hostage situation. He still had the gun in his hand. Pam considered trying to make it to the door quietly, but there was just too much of a risk that Roger would turn around.

She cleared her throat and Roger turned quickly with the gun raised. "It's ok, Roger, it's just me," Pam said.

When he saw her nervously rubbing her stomach, he asked, "How far along are you?"

"I'm a little over three months," Pam replied while walking back over to the recliner chair. As she eased into she asked Roger, "Did you and Margaret have any children?"

Roger made his way back over to the couch and let out a deep breath, "No, we don't have any of our own. We tried for years but it never happened for us. It's a real shame too because Margaret would have been a great mother. She was an amazing woman. I was damn lucky she stuck by someone like me for all those years."

Pam could see the internal struggle Roger was going through written all over his face. "Are you going to work with the police to try to resolve this, Roger?" she asked. "You seem like such a nice man and if you were to tell them that this was just an emotional overreaction to the loss of your wife, I'm sure they will be lenient. It's Christmas, Roger, please forgive Thomas and don't hurt him. Be the man I think you are -- the better man and end this. I'm sure Margaret is with you and she doesn't want this for you at all."

Roger put his head in his hand and he started crying. "I've lost everything that was great in my life the day she passed. I died the same day she did, only I am still here in this miserable place."

Pam went to sit next to Roger. She was scared to death of how he would react to what she would do next, but she had to calm him down.

Pam put her hand on Roger's shoulder and rubbed it lightly. Roger tensed up at first before leaning towards her and crying harder. His hand was off the gun as he hugged her and for a second she thought about grabbing it, but instead she hugged him back tightly and told him that everything would be ok.

Thomas had reached the 10th floor, but as soon as the elevator door opened, he could see two police officers standing on either side of the door that led into his suite. When he approached them, they told him to stop and go back. Thomas told them who he was and that Mr. Dowsing had told him to go upstairs. When one of the officers radioed to verify his story, Thomas lunged toward him and knocked him down. By the time the other officer could react, Thomas was pounding on the door yelling for Pam.

Inside the suite, the sound of Thomas' voice made Roger grab for his gun and quickly get to his feet. He approached the door and looked out the peephole to find Thomas struggling with two police officers that Roger had no idea were even out there.

"Let him go, you hear me?" Roger shouted. "I want to talk to him now!"

Both officers looked at each other, than back at Thomas. Thomas looked back at them and mouthed the word, "please."

When the first officer let go; the other one followed suit. As Thomas approached the door, one of them grabbed him. "You are not going in there, you hear me?" he said. Thomas nodded in agreement and leaned on the door.

"I'm here now; whatever you want from me doesn't involve my wife. Please let her go and I will come inside and talk to you for as long as you like."

"You want to talk, Thomas?" Roger asked coldly. "Is that what you want to do? I didn't come here to *talk* to you, Thomas. I came here to show you what it's like to have no control over whether the person you love most in the world lives or dies. You have to rely on someone who is unstable and cares about nothing, just like my Margaret relied on you. Tell me, how does that feel, Thomas?"

"Please don't hurt her," Thomas begged. "I love her more than life itself." He started to cry. "If my sins made you to lose someone dear to you then I will pay for them myself. She does not deserve this. Take me instead 'cause I don't want to live without her."

There was a short silence where all Thomas could hear was his own breathing.

"You know, Thomas, I said almost the exact same thing when you passed out on stage and sentenced my wife to die. She didn't deserve it either and I truly can't live without her! Do you have any idea how that feels, Thomas? Do you?" Roger screamed.

Thomas grabbed for the handle of the door before realizing he didn't have the card key. He pounded on it and cried out, "Please, I am so sorry for what I did to you, I am so sorry!"

Roger looked out the peephole one more time at the man who took everything from him then said, "No, you're not sorry, Thomas, not yet, but you will be."

Pam suddenly shouted, "No! Roger, please don't!" and a shot rang out, followed by two more. Thomas screamed as he drove his shoulder into the door. Another shot rang out from inside the room before one of the officers pulled Thomas away from the door and radioed for backup. The other shot out the lock.

The officers pushed their way inside, but something was making it difficult for them to open the door. When they finally got it open, Thomas saw the body of an old man sprawled on the floor near the door. There was a pool of blood around his head. Thomas saw a black handgun on the floor near the man's body, as well as a broken pair of thick glasses.

"Pam, where are you?" Thomas shouted as he ran into the room.

He didn't get far before he saw a pair of legs sticking out from behind the couch. He stood frozen as the one of the officers crouched down near the old man. The other officer approached Thomas with his gun still drawn before he noticed what Thomas was staring at. Thomas watched as the officer walked around the couch and stared at Pam. His eyes told Thomas all that he needed to know.

Thomas rushed over to her to find her bleeding from her head and chest. He dropped to his knees and leaned down to listen for a heartbeat. He thought that he heard something, so Thomas put his hands on her chest and closed his eyes. When the tension in his chest didn't come, Thomas screamed out loud, "God damn it, don't you do this to me, not now!"

He closed his eyes tight and pushed his hands down into her chest while concentrating as hard as he could. When the pain came on, it was stronger than he had ever experienced it before. So much so that he screamed out in pain because it felt like someone had reached inside his chest and squeezed his heart. He held on until he couldn't take it anymore and then he listened again for her heartbeat. It was still faint, so he assumed the position again.

The room had filled with policemen and two separate teams of EMTs. The first team tended to Roger, while the other team approached Pam. "You stay back, you hear me?" Thomas yelled. "There is nothing you can do for her."

The officer standing next to Thomas signaled that they should stay back. Thomas closed his eyes again and this time the pain was even worse. He screamed out as his chest and arms burned and the room started to spin. The last thing he heard before everything went black was a voice saying, "Oh my God, his eyes are starting to bleed."

When Thomas opened his eyes, he found himself in a hospital room. He was in pain throughout his whole body, something he'd never experienced. The only light coming into the room was from the hallway. The clock said it was 1:15 a.m.

He looked towards the other bed hoping to see Pam lying there, but it was empty. Thomas felt around on his bed searching for the nurse's call button, and he felt jolts of pain in his shoulder and neck. He found the button and pressed it until he heard a voice through the speaker behind him.

"I will be there in one moment, Mr. Greggs," the nurse said.

Thomas lifted his hands up and looked at them while he waited. Someone had washed Pam's blood off of his hands, but it was still around his nails. He started to cry uncontrollably. "Oh please let her be alive," he prayed. "I will do anything you want, I will learn to use this gift the right way, I promise. Please just don't take her away from me, I beg of you."

He cried and cried until he heard a woman's voice from the doorway. "Mr. Greggs, I'm the nurse on duty tonight, my name is Karen. How are you feeling?"

Thomas wiped his eyes and tried to compose himself. He was still finding it hard to breath, but he had to know. "Where is my wife Pam?" Thomas asked. "Did she make it? Did I save her?"

Karen approached him without answering and checked the heart monitors that were connected to him. The readings were off the charts when he was rushed into the emergency room, but they quickly had settled into a normal range. She pulled out a pocket light and checked both of his eyes. They looked normal now too.

"Please Karen, I need to know. Is she ok?" Thomas asked. His bottom lip quivered, and he was likely to start sobbing again at any moment.

Karen cleared her throat and reached for her stethoscope. She placed it on his chest and said, "I called the doctor as soon as I knew you were awake. He should be here soon."

On some level, Thomas already understood that the worst had happened, but he held on tightly to what little hope he had until the doctor came into his room. When he saw the look on the doctor's face, he knew that he had lost his wife.

"Mr. Greggs, I'm Doctor Gensil," he said as he approached his patient and extended his hand. Thomas just stared at it for a moment before he asked softly, "Is she gone?"

Dr. Gensil looked towards the window and answered without looked at Thomas. "I'm afraid so, Mr. Greggs. We did all we could but she was gone before she even got here. I'm very sorry for your loss."

Thomas covered his eyes with both of his hands and broke down into hysterics. "Please don't do this to me, please don't take her from me," he begged of God, or fate or anyone else who might be listening. "I am so sorry for all that I've done, please take me, not her, not her."

Dr. Gensil attempted to put his hand on Thomas's shoulder and he pushed him away. "Stay away from me damn it," he shouted. "Can't you see that I am fucking cursed?"

The doctor looked for a way to escape from the room Thomas cried out and pounded his fists on the gates of the hospital bed. "Your friends are downstairs Thomas. I will send them right up."

Dr. Gensil told the nurse to give Thomas a sedative and then call the psych ward. He had seen a lot of suicidal people since he started working at the hospital 12 years ago. He felt that Thomas was definitely someone who needed to be monitored.

As soon as the doctor stepped outside, Thomas wiped his eyes and ripped all of the devices off of him. As the alarms sounded, Thomas waited by the door for the doctor to come back. As soon as he came into through the doorway, Thomas grabbed him and threw him across the room where he slammed into a wall. Thomas ran down the hall as fast as he could as the nurse screamed and called security.

He found a stairwell and ran down the stairs as fast as he could. Along the way, he ran into a security guard. Thomas tripped the guard before he could react. He fell down half a flight of stairs and grabbed his ankle. Thomas started to continue his escape, but glanced back at the injured guard.

The heavyset man was struggling to get back on his feet and he was in a great deal of pain. When Thomas looked at the man's injured ankle, he could see that it was purple and swollen. Thomas first opened the basement door to see if anyone was coming before turning back to help the man

When his leg returned to normal and the pain subsided, the man thanked him. Thomas didn't respond. Instead he ran towards the door to the basement and disappeared. As the door closed behind him, Thomas could hear the security guard on the radio reporting Thomas' location. Thomas wanted to go back and re-break his ankle, but the need to get out of there was stronger.

He was halfway down the hallway when he noticed a big opening coming up on the right. He could also hear traffic in the distance, so he assumed that this was a way out. When he got there he could see a garbage compactor on the left side of the room and stacks of broken down boxes everywhere else on pallets. Towards the back of the room there was an overhead door that was left open, so Thomas approached it cautiously. When he stepped outside he could see to his right that there were two men talking near a dumpster. He waited until he was certain they weren't watching before running away as fast as he could in the opposite direction.

Thomas kept on running until his side was aching with pain and he was out of breath. The cold didn't affect him at all; he felt nothing. His feet would hurt from time to time, but it wouldn't last. Lots of cars passed him, but no one stopped, they only honked their horn or shouted things through the window at him.

Thomas continued walking with his head down with his mind in a fog until he saw headlights in front of him and heard tires screech. He stayed there while the woman driving the car screamed at him and told him to move. She inched the car closer and closer to him, but Thomas stood his ground. As she honked her horn several times, Thomas got down on the ground and lay in front of her car.

She put the car in reverse, and then went around him. As she drove away, she rolled down the window and said, "Go kill yourself someplace else, you crazy bastard!"

Thomas sat up and watched as she drove down the road and made a right hand turn onto a bridge. He got to his feet and stood looking at the bridge. It wasn't long before another car came up behind him and started beeping. When Thomas looked back he could see the driver with his arms up in the air as if to say, "What the hell are you doing?"

Thomas moved out of the way and as the man rolled down the window to yell at him, Thomas said, "Don't worry; I'm going to go someplace else to kill myself."

Chapter 37

The bridge was separated into two lanes heading north and two lanes heading south with a divider in the middle. A cement walkway for pedestrians and bike riders ran along both sides of the bridge. Thomas followed the sidewalk and stopped at the middle of the bridge.

He leaned over the metal railing and stared into the darkness below. All the painful memories of his life played out in his mind like a movie. He was overcome with emotion and he collapsed to the ground. He shivered as the cold wind stung his face.

"I've done everything I thought I needed to do with what you gave me, yet you still punish me over and over again. If Father McBride was right, then giving me this curse was your plan for me and that's just cruel."

Thomas got to his feet and grabbed the railing to climb up on top of it. He was just about to thrust himself over the edge when he heard the sound of screeching tires and a crash behind him.

Thomas turned around he saw that a car had slammed into the divider on the other side of the bridge. Its headlights seemed to be focused on him as he stood with the wind blowing his hospital gown.

Thomas turned back to the railing again, but he stopped. He cursed under his breath and ran towards the crash as fast as he could. He checked the driver's side door and saw a woman who appeared to be in her 30s screaming as she tried to free herself from her safety belt. Thomas pounded on her window, but she screamed and cried out, "Please help my daughter. I think she hit her head because she wasn't wearing her seatbelt."

Thomas tried to see where her daughter was but it was too dark inside the car. The woman panicked as she struggled to get free. "Please help her," she begged.

Thomas knew he couldn't open the doors on driver's side, so he went over to the passenger side and tried the front door first. It was locked, but he was relieved when the back door popped open. He reached up towards the ceiling searching for the dome light. When he located the switch to turn it on, he noticed the little girl who couldn't have been more than four years old lying unconscious on the floor of the car. She had a large lump on her forehead. Thomas lifted her and gently placed her on the back seat before putting his hands on her to try to heal her.

The girl's mother couldn't turn around, but she could see the back seat reflected in the rearview mirror. When she noticed the strange man wearing only a hospital gown touching her daughter, she screamed and tried to free herself from her seat again.

Thomas jerked back and held up his hands. "It's ok, I'm not going to hurt her, and I'm going to help her."

The woman screamed, "Get away from my daughter, you damn pervert!" She tried to reach back with her free arm to stop him, but she couldn't really reach. Thomas put his hands on the girl again and closed his eyes. When he opened them, he saw the prettiest blue eyes staring wide open back at him.

After doing what he could for the little girl, Thomas struggled to help the woman get out of the car, too. Once she was free, she grabbed him. She started to yell, "What the hell do you think you're...."

She didn't finish, though; once she got a better look at his face, recognition dawned on her. She let Thomas go and stared at him with her mouth open. "It's you, isn't it?" she said. "That would explain the hospital gown because I heard on the news that this is where they brought you after...." There was a brief moment of silence before the woman said, "I am so sorry about what happened to your wife, Thomas."

He closed his eyes for a moment before nodding. "You daughter will be fine now," he said. The woman thanked him, but he said nothing more. He left them there, walked over to the other side of the bridge and jumped over the edge. The woman was stunned as she searched the car for her cell phone. She dialed 9-1-1, which led to the famous call that was played on every news station the following day.

"Operator, 9-1-1 what's your emergency?"

"Please send someone as fast as you can to the Dewhauser Bridge, Thomas Greggs just jumped, I think he's dead."

Within minutes after that call, the bridge was shut down with police, media and curiosity seekers everywhere. Thomas's death was being reported all over the world within an hour of the incident.

The following morning, Neesy, Billy and Father McBride were on site as the police used boats, helicopters and divers to search for any sign of Thomas' body.

When Father McBride saw Robert Van Putten reporting from the spot where Thomas was said to have jumped, he lost his composure and confronted him. He stepped right in between Robert and the cameraman without any regard for how others would view his actions.

"You should be ashamed of yourself," he said as he pointed a finger in Robert's face. "You and all of the others like you should be ashamed for what you did to that poor man. He just wanted to help people and make some sense of a gift that he didn't ask for, but you wouldn't let up. You used him to build a career for yourself and to line your pockets. You're no better than..."

Father McBride stopped because he knew Billy and Neesy were standing a few feet away. He knew everyone was grieving in their own way, even Billy, and he didn't want to make things worse for them.

But Robert knew exactly what he was going to say and he used it. "No better than whom, the Reverend Billy Johnson, founder of the Mission? Is that what you were going to say, Father? Everyone knows he was the puppet master and the he used Thomas. So if you're going to point that finger at anyone, I would start there first."

When the cameraman panned over to Billy and Neesy, Billy grabbed Neesy's hand and quickly walked her away in the opposite direction.

Father McBride could not believe what he was seeing and he lost his cool. "You bottom-feeding, soulless coward. One day, you will be judged too, my son, and when that day comes you may finally see the consequences for the damage you've done."

He walked away as Robert continued to shout questions at him and tried to catch up to Billy and Neesy. When he finally reached them, a very angry Billy lashed out at the priest.

"Who are you to say those things about me?" Billy said angrily. "I'm the one who looked after that boy when he had no one else to turn to. I'm the one who showed him how to use his gift to help people. I tried to show him what his purpose from God was. We were doing just fine until that gold digger and you came long."

Father McBride stood there with his mouth open, shocked by what he was hearing. "What you did, Reverend Billy Johnson, was mess up that boy beyond the point of repair. His mind was already a mess when he met you, but you tore apart his soul as well, using his guilt for your financial benefit and the benefit of your entire family. He trusted you, looked to you as a spiritual mentor and you used him. Thank God for your lovely wife because she was his only salvation during the whole time he was involved with you. He told me everything, Billy, and I mean everything, so don't push me."

Billy wasn't sure what exactly the older man meant by that remark, but he didn't want to take any chances. "Ok look, we're all very upset but now's not the time to be going back and forth at each other. I'm sorry for the things I said Father, I'm just finding it hard to believe that all of this is happening."

When Father McBride looked Billy in the eye he could see the tears forming. He knew that this wasn't an act and those were actual tears from someone who was in pain.

"Let's just stop all of this nonsense," Neesy said as she rubbed her husband's shoulder. "We are all in shock and hurting in our way. I can't believe he's gone."

Billy hugged his wife and they cried together. Father McBride walked a few feet away from them and cried alone as he looked over the edge of the bridge into the water below. About 30 feet away from them, Robert's cameraman was filming the whole thing.

The police searched the muddy river waters for three days but were unable to locate Thomas' body. Because he had the ability to heal himself, they waited another week before they held a press conference stating that they were confident that he didn't survive the fall.

In Virginia, a funeral was held with an empty coffin. Father McBride started the memorial service and spoke for 20 minutes, followed by Billy who spoke for a half hour. The funeral ceremony itself was more like a Baptist funeral; everyone had a chance to get up and speak in between songs that were sung by the choir.

Outside of the church, thousands of people from different parts of the world waited in the cold rain to pay their respects to Thomas. Only when the news helicopters showed the overhead view could you see the magnitude of the event that was taking place. The entire town was shut down and people were everywhere.

In light of all of the events that led up to his death, most of the media outlets handled Thomas's apparent suicide with respect, especially after they witnessed firsthand the public outcry. Their phone lines, email inboxes and websites were inundated with messages from people wanting to express their grief over what had happened to Thomas immediately after the story broke.

Most stations aired the memorial service live, and it was the most-watched event of the year. The reporters spoke softly and only talked about the positive things Thomas had done as they added their commentary to the live feed.

Only Robert Van Putten was different. He compared Thomas to the many celebrities and rock stars that overindulged themselves before reaching a tragic end. He offered his condolences to Pam's friends and family, but that was as sympathetic as he got. The memorial video he aired before the service was more of a worst of video consisting of Thomas passing out on stage, Thomas beating him up live on television and Thomas getting arrested.

After the service, the empty coffin was flown to New Jersey and buried alongside Thomas' parents. It was only a matter of days before crowds of people were coming to the gravesite to either take pictures or to pray. The same people who had lined up to see Thomas in the hopes that he would save them were now traveling to his gravesite to pray for a miracle.

After a week that included constant updates and interviews with everyone from the Mission except for Neesy, the media turned their attention to the next big story.

When Thomas leapt from the bridge, he was surprised at how long the fall was – it lasted long enough for his whole life to play out like a movie in his head, just like the old cliché.

When he hit the water, it felt like hitting a concrete wall and then everything went black. He wasn't sure how long he was in the dark nothingness before a light appeared. At first it faint and way off in the distance, but it gradually got closer and brighter. He could tell that something was in front of him, but it was blurry and out of focus. He thought he heard voices, but they seemed too far away to make out what they were saying.

Things remained that way for what seemed like hours until the blurriness started to clear and the figures started to come into focus. Thomas' first thought was that he was in Heaven and that whoever this was; it had to be someone he knew. But eventually he realized that he'd never seen either of the two men standing over him with a clear blue sky behind them.

"See, he ain't dead, I told you so," the skinny old bald man who smelled as if he hadn't showered in weeks said to his friend. "From the looks of him, he's probably some nutso who got loose from the hospital and jumped from the bridge."

"Leave him alone," the second man said.

He was heavyset and appeared to be in his 60s as well. He wasn't as dirty as the other fellow, but Thomas could smell them both from a few feet away. This heavier man had a full grey beard along with a full head of grey hair that he wore in a ponytail. They both wore old tattered jeans, brown work boots and winter coats that looked as old as they were.

When the heavyset man extended his hand to help Thomas up, he pushed it away. He felt a sharp pain shoot through his neck and straight down his arm. Thomas tried to roll over on his side so he could get to his feet, but he screamed when he felt another jolt of pain in his ribs.

The heavyset man tried to help him again, but Thomas pushed him away a second time. "Keep your friggin' hands off of me!" he shouted.

Even though his body was wracked with more pain then he had ever experienced, Thomas got to his feet. He was covered in sweat and breathing heavy as he looked around to try to get his bearings. He tried to turn around, but fell after experiencing a jolt of pain in his right leg.

Both men started at each other as he laid face down in the dirt. When the heavyset man heard Thomas start to cry, he grabbed him and rolled him over on his back. Thomas screamed in pain again.

"I'll stay here with him, you go get him some help," the heavyset man said to the other guy.

"The hell with that," the skinny one replied. "Leave him be, this ain't our concern."

Thomas panicked; the last thing he wanted was to be found and to live as Thomas Greggs the Healer again. That man died with Pam, as far as he was concerned. All that he needed now was to be numb.

"Please don't get anyone, I'll be fine," Thomas begged. "I don't want anyone to come looking for me, you hear me? Just leave me be and I'll manage, forget you saw me."

"See, I told you he was some escaped nut job from the mental ward at the hospital," the skinny man said. "Let's leave him be, Eddie, that's what he wants."

"Would you shut your mouth for one second, Sam?" Eddie shouted. "You ain't all right and I ain't gonna leave you here. You wouldn't last ten minutes in place at night in the condition you're in. You think you're crazy, there are serious crazy people who hang out here at night, dangerous crazy people. Sam and I will take you to my spot for a while, is that ok?"

Thomas looked at Eddie and then over at Sam. That's when he noticed that Sam had a bottle sticking out of his side pocket.

"I need something for the pain," Thomas said. "Can I have some of that to dull it while we get wherever we're going?"

Sam looked to where Thomas was pointing and noticed it was at his pocket.

"Hell if I'm going to share my stuff with you!" he yelled.

Eddie approached Sam and looked him in the eye. "Give it to him and I'll give you two bottles when we get to my spot, ok?"

"Here we go again with you," Sam replied. "You are always a sucker for the sad sack stories, always taking the strays, you'll never learn."

"Just give him the damn bottle so we can be on our way, ok?" Eddie said.

"Unbelievable," Sam muttered as he reached into his pocket and handed the bottle to Thomas.

When the cap came off, the strong smell of the liquor almost made Thomas dry heave. It had been so long since he had taken a drink and it felt wrong to him. He turned to look off into the distance and he noticed the bridge. Everything came back to him as a sharp pain cut through his rib cage. He lifted the bottle and took gulp after gulp until there was nothing left before tossing it away. As he sat feeling the numbness slowly overtake him he heard Sam complaining, "Are you friggin' kidding me, did you see that? This guy is seriously messed up in the head, Eddie. We gotta just leave him be."

Thomas was able to tune him and everything else out as he lay back down onto the ground and stared up at the sky. His mind drifted to thoughts of Heaven, wondering if his mother would meet Pam and the baby up there. He closed his eyes and the next time he opened them he was in an alleyway lying on a piece of cardboard with two old jackets covering him.

Chapter 38

As Thomas examined his surroundings, he noticed that his neck and back were still throbbing. He wasn't used to pain like this He could tell it was daytime, but he had no idea what time it was. When he tried to lift his hands to rub his eyes, a pain shot through his right arm as well. A voice from behind him startled him and he instinctively froze.

"So you're alive after all," Eddie said. "You've been out for two days. You spent one of 'em yelling in pain every so often. When you finally got quiet, I thought maybe that fall you had taken finally got you. I'm still not sure how you survived that one."

Thomas rolled over, taking his time and cataloging all of his body's aches. By the time he got situated, his forehead was covered in sweat and he was breathing heavy. "I didn't fall from anything," he said. "I wandered down here after leaving the hospital and I got beat up by a couple of thugs. They must have thrown me in the water afterwards, that's why I was near the shore."

Eddie stared at him for a moment before smiling at him. "You know, as you were lying near me passed out for the last two days, I had this feeling like I had seen you somewhere before. It bothered the hell out of me that I couldn't remember where.

"As me and Stan were walking to the liquor store a few blocks over, I saw a news report about Thomas Greggs. It said he jumped to his death a few weeks ago from that bridge over yonder. That's when it hit me that I had seen you on TV a few times during the last few years.

"I know what you're thinking, how does this guy get to watch TV, right? Stan and I are buds with Maxie from the liquor store. Every now and then he lets us hang out with him. He orders a pizza and we watch a football game or baseball game together. We kept seeing commercials for the Mission's Christmas event.

"Can you really do what they say you can do?" Eddie asked.

Thomas was silent for a moment before he spoke. "You're wrong, Eddie, Thomas Greggs is dead. I'm just some crazy nobody with no family or friends. As soon as I can get on my feet, you won't ever see me again."

Eddie walked towards Thomas and sat beside him. "If that's what you say, then that's ok with me," Eddie said. "It's a darn shame what happened to that Thomas fella. I know all about loss myself, that's how I wound up here," Eddie said as he looked around while scratching his beard. "But you don't want to hear my sob story, do ya?"

Thomas looked down towards the ground and away from Eddie. He just wanted to disappear from everyone and everything. The last thing he wanted was to hear some homeless guy's life story. As he struggled to get to his feet, his arm gave out on him as he tried to use it for leverage.

Thomas shouted out, "God damn you" before collapsing into tears. He kept his hands over his face as he cried because he was ashamed for anyone to see him this way. He stopped for a moment only when he felt a hand on his shoulder. When he lowered his hands, he saw that there was a clear bottle in front of him filled with peppermint schnapps.

"I've been where you are, friend," Eddie said. "I know better than anyone what it takes to get through certain things in your life. If you think this will help with the pain, then help yourself. But go slow this time, don't..."

Before Eddie could finish his sentence, Thomas was gulping it down. "Hey, take it easy there friend," Eddie said. "You haven't eaten in days so it will do what you need it to do, even if you take it slow."

When Thomas didn't listen, Eddie reached to grab the bottle from him. Thomas instinctively pulled it back and raised his fist. "You don't want to be doing that, friend," Eddie warned. "I'll let you get away with that once, but you do it again and I will hurt you."

Thomas took another look at Eddie, who was now on his feet and standing in the light. Thomas could see that underneath the worn clothing, Eddie was a big, powerfully-built man. As he stood with both of his fists clenched, Thomas knew he meant what he said.

Thomas sighed and handed back the half-empty bottle. "Could you please just help me to another alley or something so I can be alone?" he asked before starting to cry again.

Eddie looked at him with sympathy and shook his head. "You keep it," he said as he lightly pushed the bottle back at Thomas. He watching quietly as Thomas turned away and sipped from the bottle until it was empty. By then, both the bottle and one of the world's most famous alcoholics had dropped to the ground.

When Thomas woke up again, it was just starting to get dark. When he moved slowly to see if everything was still hurting, he was glad that the pain in his shoulder and back were gone. He assumed that his body had healed itself, so he tried to sit all the way up. A jolt of pain shot through his ribs, pointing out to Thomas that he wasn't quite there yet. He was starting to worry because this kind of lasting pain was a new experience.

Thomas noticed that his gown was soaking wet. He threw off the two jackets that had been covering him and the smell of urine was overwhelming. "Oh you've got to be kidding me," Thomas shouted as he looked down at himself. He thought about taking the gown off and using the jackets to cover himself, but they reeked of urine as well.

As the cold wind blew around him, Thomas searched for the bottle. When he couldn't find it, he decided that freezing to death may be the best option,

"Surely being soaking wet would speak up the process," he thought and almost laughed out loud.

He sat there with his eyes closed and his head in his hands, shivering. Thomas' face was numb, his fingers and toes were tingling and his stomach was growling. He thought about getting up and jumping into the river, but when he managed to get to his feet another jolt of pain went through his right leg. He leaned against the wall before sliding back down to the ground.

"Haven't I been through enough?" he said as he looked towards the sky visible between the buildings. "I don't care if it's a mortal sin, I just want to die. I just want to be with Pam and my mother."

He stopped talking and listened to the two voices that were approaching. Eddie and Stan were coming down the alleyway together.

"Hey were you talking to somebody?" Eddie shouted as they got closer.

When they were close enough to see him, Stan stopped dead in his tracks. "Holy crap man, that nut job of yours is covered in his own piss! This ain't right man; you gotta get rid of him. He probably eats his own poo too, the crazy ass."

When Thomas grabbed for one of the jackets, Eddie scolded Stan, "Jesus, man leave him alone ok? There ain't nothing wrong with this fella except that he's in a world of hurt. We've both been there so cut him so slack.

"Now help me get him over to the park so he can clean himself up in the restroom. I got a bag of clothes here from the drop box. I'm sure I can find something that almost fits him, at least it will be dry."

"I ain't helping this nut ball!" Stan said. "You take care of this, I'm outta here."

As Stan walked away, Eddie threw his hands up in the air. "Thanks a lot, you good for nothing son of a..."

Thomas watched as Eddie's shoulders dropped and he ran his fingers through his hair. The older man stood there for a moment talking to himself before turning around and walking towards Thomas.

"Ok, look, I have half a sandwich in my pocket that Maxie gave me and some chips. Let's go get you cleaned up and something warm on you, then you can eat, ok?"

When Thomas shook his head no, Eddie got angry. "Why the hell not?" he yelled. "Do you enjoy lying in your own urine?"

Thomas looked down at the ground and met Eddie's eyes with a defeated expression on his face. "I can't walk," he said. "I tried while you were gone and there's something wrong with my leg."

Eddie leaned down towards him and put his hand on Thomas's shoulder. "Well then I'll just have to carry you over my shoulder then."

"You're going to do what?" Thomas exclaimed.

"C'mon, it's no big deal," Eddie said. "You ain't that heavy and besides, I can't even count the number of guys or bodies I carried over my shoulder in 'Nam."

"I'm covered in piss, Eddie," Thomas argued, sounding ashamed.

"Yeah, so I'll wash up after you're done," Eddie said. He smelled under his own arms and said, "I'm about due anyway, I think." They both laughed.

"Look, you were out for two days the first time you passed out, then a day and half the second time. You need to eat something and you need to get some real liquids in you, ok?"

Thomas nodded in agreement then forced a smile before Eddie reached down and hoisted him over his shoulder. "Jeez Louise, you are ripe," Eddie said as they walked away. They had walked for almost 15 minutes before Eddie stopped and said, "We're here."

Thomas was embarrassed that he was on the shoulders of homeless man so he kept his head down and his eyes closed the entire trip. He could tell that everyone in the neighborhood must have known Eddie because every so often a different voice would say hello to him and ask him, "Who's the dead guy?"

Eddie carried Thomas into the restroom and left him by the sink. He reached into his jacket and pulled out a plastic shopping bag. He placed it on the sink then patted it with his hand while looking at Thomas. "There's a dry pair pants, a pair of under drawers, a long sleeve shirt and some socks in there," he said. "I don't imagine that they're all gonna fit you perfect, but they're dry and they'll keep warm. I also put some twine in there that you can use as a belt, along with a bar of soap and small tube of toothpaste.

"Just because we're homeless, don't mean we have to live like animals, right? Good old Maxie hooks me up with this stuff every so often to get me by."

As Thomas looked through the bag, Eddie headed for the door. "I'll be right outside making sure no one comes in. Stan and I usually do this for each other 'cause some shady stuff goes on in this bathroom from time to time. Lots of crack heads and other types use it for whatever. Anyway, you're totally safe, so take your time and don't worry about nothing, ok?"

It took Thomas quite a while to clean himself up and get dressed. The pain forced him to stop every so often. He just closed his eyes and listened to the sound of his breathing until it subsided enough to let him continue. When he finished, Eddie put him back on his shoulder and he walked back to the alleyway.

Thomas kept his head up this time and looked around. He was surprised at how bad this section of the city was. There were so many two- and three-story apartment buildings that had been boarded up and abandoned. Thomas was curious so he asked to Eddie, "Why don't you stay in one of these? You would be indoors and away from the elements."

"Remember those crack heads I told you about?" Eddie answered. "Well those buildings are full of 'em. You will never catch me in one of those buildings. I met lots of people over the years that got mixed up going into those places that disappeared and were never heard from again."

When they reached the downtown section of town, there were mostly empty storefronts. It seemed to Thomas that the only businesses they had were liquor stores, pharmacies, laundromats and convenience stores. Even though it was cold out, there were small groups of people hanging out in front of empty buildings huddled together talking. Thomas assumed that they were either homeless or just really poor because they were dressed the same way he was. The whole trip back, Thomas couldn't get over how there was such a feeling of hopeless and despair in this entire area. In some bizarre way, it seemed almost fitting to him that this is where he ended up. Since he was little he had heard people talk about karma and what goes around comes around.

As they approached the two buildings that looked familiar, Thomas thought, "Welcome to Eddie's Alley, located at 114 and a half Karmaville, New York.

Thomas ate his sandwich and watched Eddie rearrange his duffel bag. He wished that he still had access to all of his money so he could give enough to Eddie to get him out of this place for good. When he took another bite of the turkey and swiss sandwich, a glob of mayo oozed out all over his cheek. He wiped it with his right hand and when he looked at it, the smear of mayo reminded him of Pam's blood being all over his hands. He started to shake and he dropped what was left of his sandwich. After he started to cry, Eddie came to sit beside him.

Eddie reached into his right pocket, pulled out another bottle of schnapps that was a little less than half full and placed it into Thomas's lap. Thomas didn't even look to see what it was as he reached down, unscrewed the top and lifted it to his mouth.

Eddie watched him down the whole thing in a matter of minutes as he scratched his beard. "You know, that stuff has gotten me through some pretty tough times too," Eddie said. "It stops your brain as well as the pain, that's what I always used to say."

"See, I know all about the pain that someone like that Thomas fella was feeling. I was just a stupid kid a year removed from high school when they sent me away to Vietnam. I was drafted six months after my oldest brother went. A lot of my friends had already gone and I didn't want to end up in jail, so I went.

"No movie or documentary will ever give you more than a hint of what I saw over there... kids younger than me who were afraid of their own shadows in basic training turned into some of the worst killers you could ever imagine. There is no way these guys just turned that off when they got home.

"At least they made it, though. It's hard to explain how you could become so close to these guys as you go through all of this stuff together only to see them die around you one after the other. Hell, my brother was killed in combat three months before he was supposed to come home."

Thomas had just started to feel the effects of the schnapps but he could still hear every word Eddie was saying. When he looked over at the older man, Eddie was just staring forward with a blank expression on his face as he spoke.

"When I got back home to Ohio, none of my friends could relate to what I had been through. I wasn't used to sleeping in a bed, so I slept on the floor at my mother's house for months. I was drinking every day, getting into fights all the time and disrespecting my mother, so she gave me an ultimatum, go into rehab, get some counseling or get the hell out of her house.

"Deep down I knew I was like a zombie, dead on the inside but still walking around with the living. But my mom wouldn't give up on me; she kept in my ear until I gave up and went to rehab.

"I gotta tell you, I was amazed by how many people there were who were just like me. I mean, the place was full of vets. The 90 days I spent there probably saved my life. That's where I also met my wife Darlene. She was a nurse at the facility and we hit it off right away. Of course I couldn't 'officially' date her until after I finished my inpatient treatment, but there were ways around that, if you know what I mean?

"We were so happy together for about two or three years. I look back and I wish I could have savored those moments so much more than I did. But how was I supposed to know that those would be the happiest moments of my life?"

"You see, the things that I saw and that I did over there just don't go away. I lived through hell and saw the worst that man can do. There ain't no way that 90 days can erase that."

"So I struggled with it and kept it buried while we were trying to make a life together and start a family. I stared drinking again a few months before my little girl was born. The pressure of being someone's father and supporting a family was getting to me. Mentally, I wasn't prepared for it and I knew it. Darlene could tell I was off, but I guess she was hoping I would straighten out once the baby was born.

"When Samantha was born, I didn't feel that attachment that they say people feel right after their child comes into the world. I didn't really feel anything.

"In fact when I went home from the hospital that night, I cried myself to sleep because I thought something was wrong with me. All I could think about was the guys I saw die in front of me in Nam. Why was I one of the ones who made it? I was no better than any of those guys, yet here I was breathing air, living in suburbia and having a baby.

"Well, after little Sammie came home my depression got worse. Darlene spent all of her time with the baby and I had no one talk to. I assumed she had more than enough on her plate and she didn't need to hear about how I felt alone.

"One night she went out to the store and left me with little Sammie. I was already pretty buzzed because I went to the bar after work, but that's no excuse because I continued to drink as soon as Darlene walked out the door. I remember feeding Sammie some baby food and she got it all over her, but I don't remember ever putting her in the tub."

As Eddie scratched his beard and cleared his throat, Thomas looked at him with sympathy because he had a feeling what he was going to hear next.

"Darlene's screams woke me up. I must have nodded out when Sammie was in tub and she....drowned. Darlene stayed at a friend's house until the wake and funeral were over. Then she packed up her things and moved back home with her parents in Texas. I never saw her again."

Eddie bit his lip and fought to hold back his own tears. He closed his eyes as a tear ran down his cheek. He let out a breath he was holding and shook his head back and forth to regain his composure.

"I'm so sorry for what happened to you, Eddie. I don't know what else to say."

"Thanks Thomas," Eddie said as he looked over at him. "Look, I knew who you were the second I laid eyes on you. The reason I shared that with you is because I wanted you to know that you ain't alone. You're not the only person who's lived through hell and had everything taken from him."

"After Darlene left, I lost the house and what friends I thought I did have abandoned me. My family blamed me for what happened to Sammie so I had no one to turn to. I sold what I could and I hit the road. I met Stan in Boston and we've traveled together since, watching each other's backs.

"What I'm saying is I know what you're going through, all of it. The booze ain't gonna take it away though, you know that. Use it to get you through the rough spots and that's it. Those two bottles you drank of mine would have lasted me for weeks or maybe even months.

"Believe it or not, talking helps and I'm here for ya Stan had been through some heavy stuff too and we helped each other that way, sorta like a support group. We're here for you, too, if you need us. I just want you to know that."

"How long have you been...this way?" Thomas asked.

"What you do mean homeless?" Eddie replied "I've been on the streets for about seven years, I guess."

"Do you ever think about trying to find Darlene? A lot of time has passed and maybe she'd be open to talking to you now. I would give anything to talk to Pam again, no matter what the circumstance was."

"I think about it a lot," Eddie said, "almost every day. But look at me, Thomas. Besides, I have no idea where she is and even if I did, I couldn't afford to get to her. She wouldn't talk to me anyway, I'm sure she still hates me."

"If I was you, Eddie, I'd do everything I could to get close to her again. I'd never give up, no matter what. When things are that important to you, you can't turn your back on them, otherwise you are just a walking corpse, like me. I don't exist in the world anymore, yet I'm still here.

"Why am I still here?" Thomas asked angrily.

"That's the question for us all, ain't it Thomas?" Eddie said. "Maybe there's something else we're supposed to do before it's our time. That's one thing my mama used to always say to me when I was young, 'when it's your time to go, you're gonna go.' She made it seem like God had a clock for all of us, young and old, part of his 'big plan,' I guess."

Thomas and Eddie sat and talked for another hour before the schnapps kicked it. A couple of days later, Eddie was able to get a set of used crutches from Maxie. Eddie was definitely the most popular guy in the area, which made things easier for Thomas to be accepted within the community. Eddie told everyone his name was Brian and that he escaped from the mental ward of the hospital. Thomas was amazed that no one else even noticed that he looked like The Healer TV.

By the time spring arrived, Thomas's hair had grown longer and he had a full-grown beard. If Neesy or Billy ran across him, they *might* still recognize him as Thomas Greggs, but people who had just seen "The Healer" on stage or on a television screen never would. His leg never fully healed. Even though he tried time and time again, it never responded to his attempts to fix it. He was concerned because he had always been able to heal himself, and he wondered if he'd finally lost his unasked-for gift.

He got his answer on a sweltering hot night in July. Stan had caught a summer flu and he was constantly coughing. Eddie was so concerned about him that he made him stay with him and Thomas in their alley. It was the middle of the night and they were all asleep when Thomas heard Eddie yelling. "Breathe, you son of a bitch, breathe!"

When Thomas sat up to see what was happening, Eddie was switching back and forth between giving Stan mouth to mouth and pressing his chest down.

"What's going on?" Thomas asked, "Is Stan ok?"

"Jesus, Thomas I forgot all about you being here. Stan stopped breathing, please come over here and do whatever you do to make him better!"

When Thomas didn't rush right over Eddie started to panic. "What the hell are you waiting for?" he shouted. "Stan needs you, get the hell over here!"

Thomas made his way over to Stan and kneeled beside him. He looked at Eddie, who was out of breath and covered in sweat. "I think maybe that fall did something to me Eddie, I don't know if I can…"

"He is not breathing, Thomas!" Eddie shouted as he pointed to Stan "He's going to die unless you help him! What are you waiting for?"

Thomas nodded and then placed his hands on Stan's chest. He closed his eyes and hoped for the familiar sensation that came every time he healed someone, but Thomas knew instantly that nothing was happening.

He felt a sinking feeling in his stomach. When he opened his eyes, Thomas saw Eddie frantically looking back and forth between him and Stan. Thomas closed his eyes again and tried as hard as he could to focus, but again nothing happened. When he opened his eyes again and looked at Stan, he knew he was gone.

When Thomas removed his hands from Stan's chest, Eddie shouted at him, "What the hell are you doing, why aren't you healing him anymore?"

"I couldn't do it... I can't do it anymore, Eddie," Thomas said as he looked him in the eyes.

"What the hell do you mean you can't do it anymore? You gotta help him! Stan can't go like this!"

"I mean, I can't do it anymore," Thomas said as he put his hand on Eddie's shoulder. "Look at my leg; don't you think that I would have been fine by now if I could still heal someone? It just doesn't work anymore. I think it was the fell from the bridge, it did something to me, took it away. I can't explain it, Eddie, but I can't help him."

"No, no, no, Goddamn it!" Eddie yelled as he got up. "Stan told me all that they said about you on the news and I didn't believe it, but it must be true. You ain't getting paid so you can't help folks like us, ain't that right?"

Thomas got to his feet and stood toe to toe with Eddie. "Don't you dare," he said as he stared into his eyes. "I would have helped him in a second if I could, now you take that back."

Eddie pushed Thomas to the ground then stood over him with his fist clenched. "I'm going to get help, you better not be here when I get back, and you hear me? I don't know if I'll be able to control myself if I keep seeing your face."

As Eddie walked away Thomas slowly got to his feet and limped over to his crutches. He put one under each arm then made his way over to Eddie's belongings. He used one of the crutches to move things from side to side, open up bags and look inside his cooler. It was inside one of those bags that Thomas found what he was searching for. There were four full bottles of schnapps and a half-full bottle of vodka. Thomas eased himself down far enough to grab the bag and put it around his neck so that it hung from his side.

As he passed his Stan on his way out of the alley, he paused for a moment to say a prayer. After saying the words, "Amen," Thomas apologized to Stan then was on his way. He walked on his crutches as far as he could until the pain in his arms and his leg was too much for him to bear. He made it about

20 blocks from Eddie's alley in the dark before he searched for a place to rest. He walked into three separate alleyways where the occupants told him, "Get the hell out before he got himself killed" before finding a small empty alleyway of his own.

Thomas remained there drinking every day for the next two weeks.

Chapter 39

At the age of 33, Kate's health was quickly reaching a critical state. After years of recurrences followed by remissions, her leukemia wasn't responding to the treatments this time. She could tell that Martin was stressed beyond his limits but he was still her rock. It made her wish that she had listened to him all those times that he wanted to bring her to a Mission event to see Thomas. Every time they scheduled one anywhere near New Jersey, Martin would plead with Kate and even try to trick her into going, but she wouldn't do it.

Every time Kate thought about Thomas and The Mission, she remembered her father's bruised and swollen face after his altercation with Billy. It made her furious all over again, but what hurt most was the way Thomas had just shut her out. She knew that both her husband and her father had tried to contact Thomas several times unsuccessfully.

Kate always believed that if she or her father needed him, Thomas would come with no questions asked. But as she went through the treatment time after time without seeing or hearing from someone she once thought of as a brother, Kate knew that he wasn't the same Thomas she had known. Now that he was gone, she wished every day that she had swallowed her pride so that she could see her daughter grow up.

Little Marie was now 13 and half years old and Martin was the best father she could ever hope for. When he wasn't taking care of Kate, he was making sure that Marie had everything she needed. Looking back, Kate knew that marrying Martin was one of the smartest things she had done in her life. When he entered their bedroom with a breakfast tray, she smiled through the pain and kissed him on the forehead as he placed the tray down near her.

"You are too good to me, you know," Kate said before she kissed his lips.

"You're pretty good to me, too," Martin answered with a smile.

Kate pushed her food around the plate with her fork and called to Martin before he left the room.

"I know you don't want to think about this, but the treatment isn't working and we should discuss the what ifs in case it comes to that," Kate said.

Martin paused in the doorway, stunned. He had no idea what to say because up to now there had always been hope. When Kate didn't respond to the treatment, he had flown her all over the world for months in hopes of finding some miracle treatment in another country. He had needed the help of Kyle and Sharon to talk her into going. Kyle begged her while reassuring her that Marie would be fine while she was gone.

"The what ifs are not something that I will ever accept," Martin said. "You and that little girl are my life; I don't want to ever be without either of you.

"Ever since the day I showed up on your porch after the Thomas interview and we kissed, I knew something had changed in my life. I saw everything I ever wanted in your eyes."

Martin sat next to Kate on the bed and took her hand.

"My whole life living by myself, I never felt alone. But now, without you in my life, I would be alone forever. I need you and your daughter needs you, we will keep hoping until all hope is gone. Then and only then will we discuss the what ifs.

He kissed her again on the head and said, "But I am nowhere near the point where I believe there is no hope. Something is going to change soon; I believe it with everything in me. People like us don't just find each other to have it end this way."

"It does happen that way sometimes, you know," Kate said. "From what I've read and seen on TV, Thomas found the love of his life and now they're both gone. He finally had the things I know he wanted in life, someone to love him without condition and a baby on the way. Life can be cruel sometimes, Martin, and the happy endings are just in the movies."

"Hey, stop talking like that," Martin said. "I need you to remain hopeful and stay positive -- giving up is not an option, you hear me? Your daughter needs you. I need you."

"Maybe if I hadn't told his secret, none of this would have happened," Kate said as she started to tear up. "I caused the whole thing, his mother, the drinking, The Mission and Pam. If I had just kept my mouth shut like I promised him, he would still be living next door with his mother, don't you get that?

"He would have been there to heal me like he did for my father. I would be able to see my little girl grow up, get married and enjoy my grandchildren someday. It's my fault and now I am being judged and punished for what I caused."

Martin stared at his wife. "Do you actually believe that?" he asked.

Just then, Marie came in the room with a bouquet of flowers. She kissed her mother on the forehead and held her hand. "These are for you," she said. "I thought they would help brighten up the room and cheer you up a bit. They're your favorites, dandelions."

When she noticed that her mother was crying, she wiped away her tear and kissed her again. "You're going to be fine mom, I just know it. Grandpa got a miracle and you will too, I know it."

Martin watched as Kate reached up to hug Marie and rather than allowing himself to break down in front of both of them, he left them alone in the room to talk while he went downstairs to make a call. When Kyle answered, Martin explained what had happened and what Kate had said, then asked him if he would come over.

The blue two story townhouse that Martin and Kate had bought was about 20 minutes away from Kyle's house in West Caldwell. Martin was actually looking for something in the same neighborhood, but Kate wanted some space in between them.

Being a trust fund baby, Martin had enough so that he didn't have to work another day of his life. Even after spending hundreds of thousands of dollars on experimental treatments, he was still very well off.

When it came time to buy a house, Martin's choice was a three-story building in Livingston, with five bedrooms, three baths, a Jacuzzi, a swimming pool and a tennis court. He was on his way to show it to Kate when he got off at the wrong exit. He drove around for a while, refusing to ask for directions no matter how many times Kate asked him to. He passed a sign to get back on the highway so he drove to the next street so he could turn around. He had just finished his K turn and was about to go onto the main road when Kate shouted, "Wait a minute, look at that house!"

Martin didn't hate the house Kate picked, but it wasn't what he expected to be living in. When he noticed how excited Kate and Marie were when they saw the big back yard with the different color trees, he walked around to the front of the house and called the real estate agent.

He knew for certain that he would be living there as Kate and Marie held hands with big smiles on their faces as they walked through the house. The room that would be Marie's was already painted pink and she loved it. Kate loved the hard wood floors and she said the kitchen was perfect. Martin compromised by having a Jacuzzi and pool installed soon after they moved in.

Martin waited on the porch until Kyle's car pulled into the driveway. He walked down the steps to meet him and Sharon at the car. "Thank you both for coming," Martin said. "She's not doing well and I'm really getting concerned. She's been so depressed and now all of this talk about being punished for telling Thomas's secret? I'm afraid she's starting to give up and from what I've heard when that happens, people usually get worse in a hurry."

Kate's mood didn't improve, despite the visit, so Sharon and Kyle spent the night to help look after her. Sharon took Marie to see a movie and go shopping get her mind off of worrying about her mother, while Kyle stayed with Martin to talk to Kate. Nothing they said changed her mind. She didn't get upset or cry at all as she talked to them both about life after she was gone.

"Martin, the best thing I did, besides marrying you, was to allow you to adopt my daughter. You will always be her father no matter what and I always want you in her life."

Kyle tried to change the subject, but Kate wouldn't have it.

"Dad, I want you to remain as close to Martin as you are now, that's very important to me to know that he still has you and Sharon in his life. He's going to need you both to get through this and still take care of Marie. I know how strong you are dad. You raised me all by yourself and Martin is going to need your advice from time to time. Having Sharon and Aunt Janet around will help with all of the 'woman things' that you two might not be comfortable with. I couldn't ask for two better role models for her than those two."

"You're acting like…" Kyle started to say.

"Like I'm going to die, Dad?" Kate asked. "Is that what you were going to say? I *am* dying, Dad, I can feel it. I don't want to be one of those people who didn't say everything they wanted to say to everyone they cared about before it was too late, I want you all to know that I…"

When Kate started to cry, Kyle rushed to her side to hug her tight. Martin stood and watched, feeling more helpless then he ever had before. There were no other options and he knew it. He had exhausted every lead and now all he could do was wait for the inevitable. He was going to lose Kate for sure; it was just a matter of when.

By the time Sharon and Marie got home, it was after 9. Marie was exhausted so she took a shower, gave her mother a kiss goodnight and went to bed.

Since her mother had taken a turn for the worse, Marie would stay close to home. She didn't hang out with her friends anymore, she didn't talk on her cell phone as much and she didn't touch her computer much at all. She would go to school, come straight home and do her homework, then help Martin with whatever chores there were around the house. When all of that was done she would spend time with her mother. Sometimes they would talk, other times they would just sit quietly and watch TV together. Marie just wanted to be with her for as long as could, because she knew from all of the whispering she had heard between her father, Sharon and Kyle that things were really bad and time was running out.

She too knew all about Thomas and she hated him as much as her step father did for not helping her mother. Marie would find herself getting so angry at her mother when she would speak so highly of Thomas and their childhood together. She herself had made several calls to The Mission before Thomas died and tried to reach someone through email and the Mission website, but no one ever responded.

She wanted to shake her mother and tell her to wake up and see what a selfish bastard Thomas was, but she didn't have the heart to and she didn't want to upset her mother.

Sharon remained in the room with Kate and they talked most of the night while Kyle and Martin stayed downstairs in the living room, sharing of bottle of Jack Daniels while talking about what happens next.

After a few hours Kyle fell asleep, leaving Martin alone with his thoughts in a quiet house. He imagined that it was going to be like this all the time once

Kate was gone. He grabbed the half-finished bottle and went into the kitchen to continue drinking alone while watching the Late Late Show.

Before he finished off the bottle, Martin noticed the blinking display on the answering machine showing one new message. With the alcohol taking its effect, Martin leaned against the wall and stared down at the number in a sort of trance. He finally decided to hit the button.

"Hey Martin, it's Mike Tensor, I've been calling your cell all night but it goes straight to voicemail. Listen, I'm in the neighborhood following up on something for Robert and I thought maybe we could meet up for lunch or something tomorrow to catch up. Give me a call in the morning and we'll make some plans, take care."

Martin's first thought was that Mike had finally decided to come clean to Robert about Kate's condition and now he wanted to see how bad she was for himself so he could report back to Robert. But he dismissed that thought because Mike had every chance to do that on several occasions through the years. Instead, he had kept his promise, like a true friend.

Martin reached into his pocket, pulled out his cell and then scrolled through the numbers until he found Mike's. They arranged to meet at noon at a local pub.

The private investigator arrived first and was already seated at the bar having a Heineken when Martin walked in. When he spotted his old friend, Mike got up from his stool and walked over to hug him. "It's been to long buddy, how the hell have you been?"

When he released Martin and took a good look at him, Mike's smile quickly faded. "What the hell is going on, you look like shit? Is everyone all right?" Mike didn't wait for a response before it dawned on him, "Oh my God, it's not Kate again is it?"

Martin looked him in the eye and nodded. "Grab your drink and let's sit at that table in the corner so we can talk."

Martin explained about the different experimental treatments they'd tried without success and said that Kate had already started planning for what would happen after she was gone. "I've lost all hope Mike, there's nothing left for me to try," Martin said as he stared down at the table. "All I can do now is cherish the time I have left and wait for her to…"

Mike got up from his seat across from Martin and took the seat right next to him. He placed his hand on his friend's shoulder and stared helplessly as Martin started to cry. "I'm so sorry, I wish there was something I could do."

Martin wiped his eyes and nodded, not trusting himself to say anything without breaking down in tears again.

"It makes me wish the theory Robert had about Thomas was true," Mike said before taking another sip of his beer.

It took Martin a moment to process his friend's words, but once he did he sat upright and stared into Mike's eyes. "Theory? What theory is that?"

"Ah, it's nothing," Mike said as he put his drink down. "You know how he was with Thomas; he was always looking for ways to keep that story going."

"So what was the theory?" Martin asked again.

Mike could tell by the look on Martin's face that he probably just said the wrong thing to a very desperate man. He also knew that Martin wouldn't let it go, so he told him.

"Robert had this theory that Thomas didn't die when jumped off that bridge," Mike said. "He believes that Thomas healed himself and that he's still in the area living anonymously somewhere.

"His whole theory is based on the fact that the authorities never found a body. Now you and I both know that his body could be trapped somewhere in the muck of that river or that he floated miles away and is lying somewhere toe tagged as a John Doe. The guy had no money on him when he jumped, hell he was wearing a friggin' hospital gown! So for Robert's theory to be true, he would have to be living somewhere amongst the...."

"Homeless!" Martin yelled before Mike could finish.

Mike grabbed Martin's hand when he stood up to leave. "Whoa whoa, where do you think you're going?" he asked.

"I know whereabouts he fell, so I'm going to drive around searching every God damn alleyway to see if it's true!"

When Martin pulled away from him and headed for the door, Mike followed right behind until they got to the parking lot. He grabbed Martin and pushed him against his car.

"Listen to me, Martin, this is crazy, Robert didn't know what the hell he was talking about." Mike said. "He was just searching for an angle to keep beating that dead horse long after it had become glue, you gotta believe me."

Martin began to shake his head from side to side as the tears streamed down his face. "I have to *try*, Mike can't you see that? I have to try. If by some miracle he is down there, I can tell him that Kate needs him and I'm sure he'll come. She was like a sister to him."

"Martin, Martin, please get a hold of yourself," Mike pleaded. "You're just setting yourself up for heartbreak and more pain. I can't let you do this."

Martin looked Mike in the eyes with a cold stare and slowly pushed him away. "I am not asking you to let me do anything, Mike. I have to be able to live with myself. When this is over and knowing there was one more chance, no matter how farfetched or ridiculous it seems, I have to try."

Martin tried to get in his car, but again Mike stopped him.

"Ok, you got it," Mike said as he matched his friend's stare. "But you are not going into those neighborhoods, you hear me? Some of the people down there will cut your throat if you even approach them. Most of those homeless people are crazy and they keep to themselves. What good what it do Kate or that little girl of yours if you went and got yourself killed in some alley? Did you consider that as part of your plan?"

Martin's head sunk down, but he looked back up at Mike and said, "I have no choice, I've got to go."

Mike then put his hand on Martin's shoulder again and looked at him. "Listen, you and I have been friends for a long time. To see you dealing with this breaks my heart. So if this is something you really want to do, then I will go look for you. I'll dig up a couple of the pics we have of Thomas from before he vanished and I'll ask around."

"I can't ask you to do that, Mike" Martin said as another tear rolled down his cheek.

"You didn't ask me," Mike replied. "I'm your friend and I offered, because that's what friends do. I just don't want you to get your hopes up too much. It's a one in a million chance at best."

Martin hugged his friend and cried on his shoulder. "Whatever it takes Mike, you hear me, if someone knows something offer them enough money to make them talk, whatever it takes."

"I'll do all that I can Martin, I promise," Mike replied.

He then let go of Martin and reached in his pocket for his cell phone. "Now I gotta call Robert and tell him I'm taking some of the vacation time that I've never used."

After getting off of the phone with Roger, Mike made a few more calls to get an idea of where exactly eyewitnesses placed Thomas on the bridge when he jumped. Once he had the information, he went back to the hotel he was originally staying at, packed his bags and headed for the Holy Grace Hospital.

Mike retraced Thomas's route that last night the best he could based on statements gathered from witnesses who may or may not have seen Thomas, starting at the hospital. He drove until he could see the entrance of the bridge approaching. Knowing that Thomas had walked across it, Mike parked his car on a side street and proceeded on foot.

He looked through his notes as he walked and before long he was approaching the center of the bridge where Thomas was said to have jumped. After walking a little further, Mike found exactly what he was looking for: the remains of a makeshift memorial that he assumed had marked the spot where Thomas jumped.

As he looked at several burned-down candles and two weather beaten teddy bears, Mike asked himself, "What the hell am I doing here?" After contemplating the question, the answer came quickly: "Keeping a promise to a friend," he thought.

He let out a breath he was holding and pulling out his digital camera. He leaned over the railing to see just how far down it was. "Geez, I don't think anyone, including Thomas, could survive that," he thought. "Even if he survived the fall, the hypothermia definitely would have killed him."

Still, he did as he promised and started taking pictures of the water and the surrounding areas. When he was through, he opened his notebook as he watched the flow of the water while trying to guesstimate the places where Thomas may have washed up on shore. "From the looks of the current," he thought, "the odds were that Thomas's body was taken way down stream into the deeper water."

But there was a chance, no matter how slim it was, that the wind was blowing in a different direction that cold night and Thomas's body somehow went straight across the river to wind up on one of those embankments. That was a big area, so Mike decided to start on the left and work his way across the section the best he could.

He went back to the hotel and researched the area further on his laptop. It was definitely a high crime neighborhood with a large homeless population. As he scrolled through the pictures he took, he decided that he would take it easy tonight and rest up for what was surely to be a very interesting couple of weeks.

Mike spent the next week and a half in urine-soaked alleyways getting threatened by every vagrant under the sun as he asked everyone he could find if they recognized the man in the picture he was carrying. Mike had a program on his computer that he used often that allowed him to change the features on a photo. He could age enhance someone, change their hair or eye color, shorten or lengthen their hair, add or remove weight to their face and even change the color of their skin.

He used this program to create a picture of Thomas the way he thought he'd look if he was living among the homeless. He had given him a dirty black beard and long dirty dark hair.

After a day or two, including a couple instances where he almost had to use the concealed revolver he carried, Mike learned the best way to approach these people was to keep his distance and offer them cash for their time. This technique worked 98% of the time. The only time it didn't work was when he was dealing with some crazy person who didn't want to be approached for any reason.

Another trick he learned was to find the one or two guys who knew everyone in the area and in turn were known by everyone else. But even as efficient as he had become, he was running out of time. He knew there was no way he was going to cover the entire in the next three days. This weighed heavily on his mind as he headed back to his car. He went over in his head what he was going to say to Martin when they spoke later in the evening.

It had gotten progressively tougher each night they talked to try remain focused when he could hear the disappointment in Martin's voice. As each night passed, Mike could hear the hope fading in Martin and it killed him that he had nothing new to report to his friend.

Mike fumbled with his car keys and cursed when he dropped them. He had just picked them up when he heard someone approach him from behind.

"I hear you're looking for a fella with long black hair and a black beard, is that true?" the man asked

Mike stood upright, shoved the keys back into his pocket and turned the face the man.

"Yes I am," Mike said as he reached into his other pocket and pulled out a folded picture of Thomas that he handed to the man.

When the man smiled and nodded, Mike's heart felt like it skipped a beat.

"You've seen this man?" Mike asked anxiously.

"Eddie, my name's Eddie," he replied, "and yes I've seen him."

The words didn't register in Mike's head for a moment because he couldn't believe this was possible. When he didn't respond Eddie looked at the picture again and said, "I hear from others around here that you are offering money for anyone with information about him. Hell, we both know his name is Thomas so let's just call that, all right?"

Mike's jaw dropped and he said, "How did you…"

"Let's not worry about that, ok? 'Cause I'm the only one who knows who he really is around here," Eddie said.

"Now let's get back to the money. I'm gonna tell you what I want, and if you agree then I'll lead you right to where he is staying, you ok with that?"

"Uh, sure Eddie, I'm fine with that," Mike said. "What is it that you want?"

"First I want you to contact someone for me," Eddie said. "If you can get her to agree to see me, I want you to provide me with a first class ticket to wherever she is, a makeover and one hundred thousand dollars in cash. I want a chance at starting my life over and that's what it will take to put me on the right path. If you can do that, then we got a deal."

Mike agreed on the spot and asked Eddie for the name of the person he wanted him to contact.

"Her name is Darlene Hacksdon, she's my ex-wife," Eddie said. He told Mike his life story and begged him to get her to agree to see him. Mike promised him that he would do all that he could as soon as he got back to the hotel.

Mike thanked Eddie and told him he would meet him at the same location tomorrow morning at 9 a.m. to which Eddie replied, "I'll be here."

As Mike turned to unlock the car door a thought entered his mind, "What if he's not here tomorrow, what if he changes his mind?"

Mike quickly turned around and yelled to Eddie, who was walking down the street away from him. "Hey Eddie, how would you like to get some news clothes tonight, followed by a nice hot shower, a warm meal and then you could sleep in a nice comfortable bed?" When Eddie turned around and started walking towards him, Mike continued on, "This way you'll know exactly how it went with Darlene, then in the morning after you take me to Thomas, we'll go take care of that makeover and get your money."

Eddie stood in front of him scratching his beard while he thought about what Mike had said. "Are we going to be sharing a room or will I just get the room next to yours?" Eddie asked.

"Whichever you prefer Eddie. This is the beginning of that new life you wanted, so you decide."

Eddie scratched his beard again then said, "I think I want my own room, no offense."

"None taken," Mike said, "just give me your sizes and I'll pay someone from the hotel to go shopping for a few things for you, just to get you by until tomorrow."

"Sounds like a plan," Eddie said and then they both got in the car.

When they arrived at the hotel, Mike kept his word and got Eddie checked in to the room right next to his. He told Eddie to go take a shower while he went down stairs to find someone to shop for him. He listened by the door to Eddie's room until he heard the bathroom door shut before he took out his cell to call Martin.

Martin screamed so loud when he heard the news that it almost made Mike drop his phone. Martin agreed to every one of Eddie's conditions and even told Mike to offer him more if that's what it took.

Mike told Martin to get the money and meet him at the hotel by 8:30 a.m. Martin cried and thanked Mike over and over while repeating, "I can't believe this, it's a miracle!"

An hour and a half later, Mike was sitting in Eddie's room having a steak dinner with him. Eddie remarked about how great it felt to be clean again. He also loved the clothes that the bellhop picked out, especially the loose fitting jeans and the black leather work boots.

When it came time to make the call to Darlene, Eddie stood at the opposite side of the room staring out of the window while he bit his nails. Mike didn't know what to expect, but he knew everything hinged on the outcome of the call.

He was very surprised to find that the woman was very pleasant and that she wondered for years what became of Eddie. It only took but a few minutes before he was on the call with her crying like a baby and begging for forgiveness.

Mike sat and watched TV as they talked for almost an hour before Eddie handed him back the phone and said, "All right then, you got yourself a deal."

Chapter 40

Martin arrived at the hotel at 8:15 carrying a leather duffel bag containing one first class ticket to Cleveland, Ohio and one hundred thousand dollars in cash. He should have felt exhausted after not sleeping at all the night before, but he had something he hadn't had for months: hope.

Even though there was a good chance that this homeless person was a crazy loon and that he was chasing a ghost, Martin still felt it in his gut that this was his miracle.

During his drive, Martin thought that Kate must have felt the exact same way before she ran over to Thomas' house all of the years ago to get him to heal her father. One moment, all hope was lost; the next, she realized she had the one person in the world that could help her within reach.

Martin took the elevator up to the third floor and walked down to the end of the hall. When he got to room 331 he paused, took a deep breath and exhaled before knocking on the door. He was surprised when a man who towered over him opened the door and said, "You must be Martin. Is that my money?"

The man grabbed the bag from Martin's hand and went back into the room as Mike approached the door. "Hey buddy, how are you holding up?" he asked.

"I'm doing well now," Martin said, "I can't wait to get started. How far is Thomas from here?"

"He's only about 10 minutes or so," Mike replied. "It won't take long at all to get to him. I just don't know how he's gonna react when you approach him, so be careful.

"If it is really him, then he's checked out of society for a reason and being found isn't something he wants."

"When I tell him about Kate, I'm sure he'll come along with us," Martin said. "Besides, seeing Kate and Kyle may do him a world of good, it may actually help him. But either way, I'm not going back without him, that's just not an option."

Mike was just about to question Martin to find out what he meant by that when Eddie came up behind them. "Got my ticket and the money's all there. Are you guys ready to go?" he asked.

"Sure, let's go," Martin said as he turned from Mike and headed out the door.

The ten minute ride was quiet. Martin looked out the window the whole time, checking out the surroundings as Mike and Eddie made small talk. When the car stopped, Martin looked at Mike before turning to Eddie in the back seat.

As if sensing what Martin was going to say, Eddie smiled and said, "Yep, this is it, we're here." He pointed to an alley to the right that didn't appear to get much sunlight, "He's right down there, probably drunk as can be from last night. From what I hear, he's like that all the time now. I hear he gets the money from begging for change a few blocks over."

Martin was the first one out of the car. He headed straight towards the alley, but Mike yelled for him to wait. Martin stopped just as he reached the entrance to the alley. As he heard the car door shut behind him, Martin squinted to try to see if anyone was down there. All he could see were full garbage cans with garbage bags piled on top of them.

"He's back behind them," Mike said as he ran over to Martin. "Eddie says he's got some cardboard on the ground that he sleeps on a few feet back from the garbage, towards the corner."

"So Eddie's not coming, I take it," Martin said as he looked back at the car.

"According to him, something happened with Thomas that he can't forgive and he'd rather not have to see him again," Mike replied.

Martin nodded and then put his hand on Mike's shoulder. "Listen, I need to go in there alone to talk to him. If I explain that I am Kate's husband and that she is dying, I'm almost certain that's all it will take for him to come with us.

"If that's not enough, I'll tell him she has a young daughter who needs her. No way he would let her die if he can help it, I know it."

"Look Martin, *if* that is him -- and that's a really big *if* -- from what Eddie says he's drunk all the time. Now, from what I've seen, he can be a mean cuss when he wants to be. Let me go with you, just in case.

"Besides, if that isn't him and you go walking up on some nut job by yourself, you could get stabbed or something. Some of these people don't play well with others, believe me, I found that out the hard way.

"What good are you going to be to Kate if you get hurt or something worse happens down here?"

Martin nodded in agreement and motioned for his friend to lead the way. Mike was happy to see that he finally was able to get through to Martin before he got hurt.

Mike proceeded cautiously down the alley. He stopped suddenly and put up his hand to signal Martin to do the same as he heard a noise come from behind the garbage cans. Martin whispered, "What's going on?"

"I could hear those fancy shoes coming from a mile away," someone shouted out from the corner in a slurred tone. "Now get the hell back to where you came from or you're going to get hurt, you understand me? I've killed before and I will do it again in a second, now get outta here!"

The voice echoed through the alley. The unseen man kicked one of the garbage cans, sending several trash bags falling to the ground.

Martin took a step backwards, but Mike grabbed onto his arm to stop him from going any further.

"Thomas Greggs, we know it's you over there!" Mike shouted. "Eddie told us you were alive and he told us where to find you!"

The alley was completely silent for several moments.

"Do you hear me Thomas? I'm with a man who is married to Kate Morgan. Kate is very sick now, in fact she's dying. Her husband Martin desperately needs you to come and help her -- you're the only one who can at this point."

As Thomas' mind processed those words, he closed his eyes and threw his head back against the wall. "Why is this happening again?" he whispered before the tears came. "I have nothing more to give, please don't do this to her."

As the men came closer, Thomas staggered to his feet and pushed over another one of the garbage cans. Both Martin and Mike backed away this time.

"I said leave me the hell alone!" Thomas shouted as he stepped out from the shadows.

He looked over at the first man standing in front of him without having any idea of who he was. There was something familiar about the other man. Thomas tried to recall where he had seen him, but his mind was still feeling the effects of the alcohol.

"My name is Martin Shulman, I'm Kate's husband," the familiar-looking man said. "She has leukemia just like Kyle and just like he was when you healed him, he is beyond help from any treatment or medicine."

Martin reached into his pocket and took out his wallet. "Here is a picture of her daughter," he said as he slowly approached Thomas and extended his hand.

When Thomas took the picture and stared at it, Martin continued, "Her name is Marie. Kate said she named her after your mother."

As Martin watched this homeless man study the picture and then start to cry at the mention of Marie, he knew for certain he was looking at Thomas Greggs.

"Oh my God, Thomas, it is you!" Martin said as he started to cry as well.

Thomas touched the picture with his finger as he outlined Marie's hair and face. It was remarkable to him how much Kate's daughter looked just like her mother at that age. It brought back a lot of memories all at once of how close they were.

"She's beautiful," Thomas said as he handed the picture back to Martin. "She looks exactly the way her mother did."

Mike's jaw dropped in disbelief and without thinking he blurted out, "Holy crap, it *is* him! I can't believe this, Robert was right, if he only knew!"

Thomas suddenly turned cold. "What did he just say? Did he mean that snake Robert Van Putten?"

Martin could see exactly when Thomas remembered who he was; he watched as Thomas bit down on his lip and he clenched his fist.

"What the hell is this, some kind of sick ploy to get me out into the open so that sadistic bastard can get yet another exclusive? Is there no level you won't sink to, you bottom feeders! Telling me that Kate is dying and showing me a picture of some little girl that looks like her?

"I know who you are now, Martin. You're his producer and this must be another of his lackeys behind you."

"Thomas, that's not it at all!" Martin shouted as he approached him. "I really *am* married to Kate, that really *is* her daughter Marie and she really *is* sick."

"Do not say my mother's name again!" Thomas screamed as he pushed Martin away.

"Hey, that's enough!" Mike yelled as he got in between Thomas and Martin, who had fallen on the pavement.

"He's telling the truth, Thomas! All of it is true. If you come with us back to Jersey, you'll see for yourself."

"I'm not going anywhere with you two," Thomas growled. "You'll have to drag my limp body out of here and I promise you, you won't walk away from this unscathed."

Mike reached down to help Martin get to his feet and stopped him before he could approach Thomas again.

He pushed Martin back several feet away from Thomas while he whispered to him. "You trust me, don't you?" Martin looked past him towards Thomas before nodding yes to Mike.

"Good. I have a plan that I think will work, I just need to go along with it."

Mike let Martin go and motioned for him to stay where he was before turning back to Thomas. When he got close enough to Thomas that he could speak without yelling, Mike said, "Ok Thomas, I can understand why you don't believe us and why you wouldn't trust us.

"So to prove to you that what we are saying is the truth, we are going to go back to New Jersey and bring Kate here so that you can see for yourself how dire the situation is. Would you agree to stay in the area long enough for us to do that?"

Thomas stared at the ground, not making eye contact, but when Mike was finished Thomas responded with one word, "sure."

"Ok, so we'll take at your word and we'll back in a few hours. Kate will be counting on you to be here Thomas, so please don't let her down."

"Whatever you say," Thomas replied, "I'll be here, ok."

Mike turned around walked over to Martin and put his arm around him before they walked off together. "What the hell are you doing?" Martin whispered. "You know damn well that he won't be here when we get back and then we won't ever find him again."

"Yes Martin, I am well aware of that," Mike said. "That's why we're going to get into the car together and you are going to drop me off around the corner so that I can tail him wherever he goes until you get back here with Kate."

"I know she's not in any shape to travel, but you will probably have to get her here for this to happen because there is no way in hell Thomas is going to agree to go anywhere with the two of us.

"Make the arrangement with the hospital across town, Martin. Do what you have to do; this may be your only chance."

When Martin looked at him uncertain of what to say next, Mike put his hand on his shoulder and looked him in the eyes.

"I won't let Thomas out of my sight Martin, I promise you that."

"After you let me off, take Eddie to Penn Station. Give him some more cash and he can find his way to either Newark or LaGuardia.

"On your way there you can call that priest who was friends with Thomas. Maybe you can arrange for him to fly out and meet us at the hospital. We can use all of the help we can get with Thomas."

After Martin drove off, Mike doubled back quickly and watched the alley knowing that any minute Thomas was going to emerge. It took a little longer than he thought it would, but Thomas showed himself. As Mike watched him steady himself, it was easy to see what had taken Thomas so long. Not only was the alcohol affecting him, but he was also limping badly, almost dragging his right leg as he walked.

Thomas made it down the street and around the corner before he had to stop. Mike continued to watch from behind a parked car as Thomas rubbed the leg with the palm of his hand while he winced in pain. Mike wondered "why hasn't he healed that leg if it's that bad?"

Thomas checked to see if he was being followed before continuing on, but he didn't spot Mike. He forced himself to ignore the throbbing pain in his leg because he knew he had to get as far away as he could before they came back. He made it eight blocks before his leg gave out completely, sending him crashing down onto the pavement.

Thomas cursed out loud as he grabbed his leg with both hands. Mike considered helping him, but before he had a chance to react two men came around the corner and assisted Thomas in getting to his feet.

"Are you ok my friend?" one of the men asked Thomas.

"Yeah, I'm fine, thank you."

"Are you sure?" the man asked. "If you need some money for some food or if you need to know where the nearest shelter is, I can help you out."

"Some money for food would be great," Thomas said. "I haven't eaten in days." He didn't like lying to this nice man, but he knew he was going to take his money and find the nearest liquor store.

The man opened his wallet, pulled out a ten dollar bill and placed it inside a flyer he took from his companion. "Come join us if can," the man said as he handed it to Thomas with a smile. "Donations are accepted, but you can get in for free."

Thomas took the money without looking at the flyer, but the man was undeterred.

"You see my friend, The Mission has helped so many people in the past and it's still going strong. They don't do the healing sessions anymore, but the message is still there."

Thomas opened the flyer in his hand and couldn't believe his eyes. Smiling on the front page was the Reverend Billy Johnson with his arms spread apart like Jesus. On either side of him was a picture of Thomas healing someone.

Thomas scanned the page to see where they were and he found it at the bottom of the page.

"Where is this?" he asked as he pointed to the address.

"So you *do* what to check it out!" the man said enthusiastically. "That's great, my friend."

"The Ardon Theater is one street over to the right and five blocks down in that direction," the man's companion said while pointing south. "They've got a big banner out front that says 'The Mission.' You can't miss it."

Thomas jammed the ten dollars into his pocket and started walking again without saying another word. He left the two men looking at each other and wondering what just happened.

As Thomas turned the corner, Mike approached them. "Hey guys, what did you just hand that gentleman you were talking to a minute ago?"

"We gave him some money for food and one of our flyers before he stormed off without even thanking us," the short man said.

"Really?" Mike replied, trying to act surprised. "Can I have one of those flyers please?"

"Sure can, here ya go."

Mike opened it up and scanned the page. "Holy crap!" he said out loud, "where did you say this was?"

After giving Mike the same directions they had just given Thomas, they watched as he too hurried away without saying a word.

When Mike turned the corner, Thomas was nowhere to be found. He jogged down to the next street over and looked down the road, but still there was no sign of Thomas. "There was no way he could have gotten far from me with that leg," Mike thought.

He waited a few more minutes before deciding to go to the Mission. He was certain Thomas was heading there and he was pretty sure he knew why.

Thomas had to assume Billy was using him still, even in death, but that wasn't the case.

Robert had planned to do a story months ago when The Mission announced it was starting up again. He, too, assumed that Billy was trying to squeeze every last drop out of the remaining faithful using the memory of Thomas as a gimmick to get people in the seats.

When he found out that it was going to be held in much smaller theaters and that it was operating on donations alone, he had Mike check it out. After Mike reported back that it was more of a Baptist service in honor of all Thomas had done, Robert lost interest and didn't bother with it.

Thomas couldn't know any of this, so he had to be thinking the same way Robert did at first. Mike knew for sure he would be there; he just had to wait for him. He checked the brochure again and noticed it didn't start until 7 p.m. He decided he would wave down a taxi so he could head back to the hotel to eat; shower and rest before heading back out.

Thomas emerged from the liquor store still fuming. "The frigging nerve of that man," he said out loud.

He walked until he reached the theater, pausing as he noticed the digital sign out front showing pictures of himself and Billy followed by the words, "He's gone, but The Mission lives on. Join us at 7 p.m. tonight as we continue to preach the word. Heal your mind, heal your body, and heal yourself."

Thomas watched in cycle three times before crossing the street and walking a short distance. He found an alley directly across from a bank that also had a digital sign that displayed the time and temperature. He decided he would stay there and drink until show time. Then it would be time to confront Billy for all that he had done.

Chapter 41

The first thing Martin did after getting in the car with Eddie was to get the number for Father McBride's church. At first Father McBride thought it was a cruel joke and almost hung up on Martin, but after he started to break down and cry, Father McBride started to listen. By the end of the 10 minute conversation, Father McBride agreed to get some things together and take the next available flight out to New York. Martin told him he would arrange for a car to meet him at the airport and bring him straight to the hospital.

After hanging up with Father McBride, Martin was a little relieved. He knew he still had to call the hospital and then call Kyle, but he felt he owed something more to Eddie then just the money so he spent the next 20 minutes talking with him until they arrived at Penn Station. Eddie went on and on about how this one thing probably saved his life. He said all he ever wanted was the chance to start over again with Darlene.

When Martin dropped Eddie off, he shook his hand than thanked him for the chance at a new beginning for at least the eighth time. With his passenger on the way to catch a cab to the airport, Martin flipped open his cell phone and called the hospital. It took several transfers to several administrators, but Martin was able to make all of the arrangements.

During the 25 minute call, his phone had beeped several times to alert him that someone else was trying to get through and he heard the chime of a message being left at least three times as well. He couldn't stop to answer it for fear that he would have to call the hospital back and start all over again with the arrangements.

When he checked his voicemail, the first message was from Sharon, "Martin, if you get this please call me right back. Kate is not doing well at all. Kyle is in with her now, but I don't think it will be much longer before she might have to take a trip to the hospital. Please call me as soon as you get this."

Martin was about to hang up and call Sharon when the second message started. This time is was Kyle and he sounded out of breath and panicked. "Martin. This is Kyle. Where the hell are you and why aren't you answering your phone? Kate passed out on her way to the bathroom and she's not responding. I have an ambulance on the way. Sharon's going to stay with Marie while I ride to the hospital with Kate, call me back right away!"

Before the third message played, Martin whispered, "Please, let her be ok."

"Martin it's me again," Kyle said, sounding even more exhausted. "We're in the ICU and she's not doing well. My poor little girl is hooked up to a machine to help her breathe. I hope you found him and you're on your way here, because she needs him more than ever."

Martin felt the panic set in as he sat frozen unsure of what to do next. He closed his eyes and placed both hands over his face, "Please God, help me, what do I do", he cried.

Just then Martin had a thought as his eyes popped open and he reached for his cell phone again. After several more transfers and an agreement on payment, Martin was able to get the hospital to agree to pick up Kate, Kyle, Sharon and Marie by medevac helicopter and bring them to New York. He then tried to call Kyle's cell and when he didn't answer he called the hospital and had the nurse get him on the phone.

He explained everything to Kyle and told him he would meet him at the hospital with Thomas. Kyle thought he was crazy when he mentioned Thomas's name but Martin assured him that he would be there and that he would explain everything when he saw him.

Martin hit the call end button and started to cry. He felt like the world was against him as he caught red light after red light. He decided he was going to ask Mike to hold Thomas wherever he was and not let him leave. There was no time to try to reason with Thomas now. If he wouldn't come voluntarily, Martin would just have to convince Mike to help bring him by force.

When he called Mike, he could barely hear him because the connection wasn't good. "Hey Mike, can you hear me? It's Martin"

"I can barely hear you Martin, are you on your way back already?" Mike asked.

"Yes, I'm heading back to you, Kate is being Med-evaced to the hospital and we need to get Thomas there as soon as possible whether he comes along voluntarily or not."

"I didn't get all of that," Mike yelled as he tried to make out what Martin had said.

"The Mission is on Conway Street in some small theater. Thomas is waiting across the street. I think he means to confront Billy."

"The Mission, how could there still be a Mission?" Martin asked "Anyway, just stay with him and I'll be there as soon as I can. I need him to come back with me one way or another, Mike."

"Martin, I'm catching every other word, I heard you say something about coming here so I'm assuming you're on your way. I'll see when you get here."

"Mike did you hear me, Kate is in the hospital, she might be dying" Martin yelled. "Mike, are you there? Can you hear me? We need to bring Thomas back with us no matter what it takes!"

Martin looked down at his cell and he saw that the call had ended. When he tried to call back, it went straight to voicemail. He tried again with the same result. Martin drove the rest of the way in silence, gripping the steering wheel tightly with his fingers.

Across the street from the Ardon Theater, Thomas leaned against the wall of an empty store and sipped a bottle of vodka. He watched the side street to the left of the building, because that's where he expected the Mission staff to drive up to access the building's back entrance.

He knew Billy liked to arrive at all of the events early to coordinate every detail himself, so it would just be a matter of time. When he saw two buses and a tractor trailer turn onto the street an hour and a half later, he knew it was the Mission. It was definitely a scaled-down version of what he was used to, but it was them none the less.

Thomas crossed the street just as the first bus was turning into the parking lot. He waited until the tractor trailer turned in before walking behind it to the back of the building.

The driver must have seen him and warned the others because one of the bus doors opened and out came Michael and Bernie.

Thomas kept his head down as they walked towards him.

"Hey man, I don't know what you're on, but you don't belong back here," Bernie said. "If you want to come inside at seven that's fine, but you're not supposed to be back here."

When Thomas didn't stop, Michael stepped out in front of Bernie and yelled to him. "What part of 'get the hell outta here' don't you understand, man? Don't make me remove you from this area myself, friend, cause I won't do it nicely."

Thomas kept walking, so Michael grabbed him by the front of his shirt. "What's the matter; can't you understand what I'm saying you crack head?"

Thomas lifted his head to make eye contact with Michael, and the bigger man's jaw dropped in recognition. He immediately let Thomas go.

"Holy shit!" Michael said in disbelief "It can't be, no way, it just can't be?"

"What the hell is going on over there?" Bernie said as he walked over toward them. "Is this fool going to get outta here or wh…?"

Bernie blinked his eyes and shook his head like he was trying to forget what he thought he was seeing.

"It can't be!" he said as he squinted to look at Thomas. "Thomas, is that really you?"

Thomas looked away from them and seemed to be talking to himself as he stared off in the distance.

"Nah, you ain't him," Bernie said with a laugh. "There is no way you could be him."

Thomas turned towards Bernie and walked over to stand right in front of him. "It's me, Bernie," Thomas said. "I don't want to get into the hows and the whys; I just want to talk to Billy."

"Oh my God Thomas!" Michael shouted, "Is that really you? I don't believe this, it's a miracle!"

Thomas turned his attention to Michael and the rage started to build inside him. "You were supposed to watch her that night, Michael." he said. "I trusted that she would be safe with you and…."

Michael's head dropped as he looked at the ground in shame. Bernie could see that this was about to get ugly, so he intervened. "Look Thomas, none of us have forgotten what happened that day."

Thomas was surprised by what happened next. Michael placed his hand on Bernie's shoulder and gently moved him to the side. "I got this," he said. "You don't need to speak for me."

Michael faced Thomas and it wasn't long before his eyes started to tear up. He tried to compose himself and said, "Not a day has gone by that I don't go over the events of that night, Thomas. I can never convey to you how sorry I am for not being there for Pam. I wish it could have been me in that room that night and I would give anything to go back to change it.

"Something was taken from you and there is nothing I could ever say or does that will make you ever want to forgive me. You have no idea how I have struggled with that and how it tears me up inside. For a while I didn't want to live and I almost drank myself into an early grave.

"Night after night I was unable to sleep. Every time I closed my eyes, all I could see is Pam being taken out through the lobby with a sheet over her head. Then they wheeled you out, you had blood spewing from your eyes and you were covered in Pam's blood. I felt so much guilt, it was overwhelming me."

"But through therapy and counseling, I was at least able to function again eventually. When The Mission started again, I knew it was a chance for me to help others and try to earn my forgiveness for what I'd done.

"I don't ask for your forgiveness, Thomas, because if I were you I would never forgive me either. I just ask that you try to understand that I made a very bad decision one night without ever thinking something as terrible as that would happen."

As Michael cried, Thomas hated himself for feeling sympathy for him. He could relate to bad decisions and tragic circumstances better than anyone. He knew Michael never thought that something would happen to Pam that night – just as he knew that it was his own curse that led to her death.

Thomas patted Michael on the shoulder. "I appreciate you saying that, I really do. I don't blame you for what happened to her, Michael. I blame me. I blame me for all of it."

"What the hell is going out on over there?" a voice shouted from the distance.

Thomas knew it was Billy, so he took a deep breath to prepare for what was going to happen next.

"I said what the heck is going on over here and who the hell is this?"

Billy's attention was focused on his brother; he never took a good look at Thomas. When Bernie grabbed him by the shoulders and turned his brother towards Thomas, Billy stumbled backwards as he saw the familiar face.

"Are you guys messing with me? Cause this ain't funny," Billy said as he stared at Thomas.

"It's really him," Bernie said.

"It can't be him," Billy said. "Thomas is dead, Bernie. He's been dead for a while now." Turning his attention towards Thomas, Billy continued, "I don't know what you're up to here friend, but posing as a man who was near and dear to us is just wrong."

Thomas met Billy's eyes and he could tell that his one-time mentor recognized him.

"I ask you, Billy, can The Healer ever die? I mean think about it, can a person who has this gift kill himself without this gift bringing him back to continue his life of suffering?

"You were right about one thing though, I did find my purpose after all. My purpose was to suffer and to lose everyone who means anything to me while helping people I could care less about and making others rich beyond their wildest dreams."

When Billy moved to try to comfort Thomas, he got shoved back into Bernie's arms.

"You all took everything from me!" Thomas yelled, "Everything! And here you are still feeding off of my memory while lining your pockets. I'll tell you one thing that I know for sure, when I get to hell for what I've done, I won't be alone."

Soon people started to come off of the bus one after the other when they heard the commotion. Bernie and Michael tried to get them to keep their distance, but they kept making their way closer. Whispers of Thomas' reappearance spread quickly and they all wanted to see for themselves if it was him or not.

Thomas noticed the people coming, so he glared at Billy one last time and turned around. He walked as fast as he could out of the alley, but he heard footsteps behind him when he got to the street.

"Thomas, please, just hear me out for one minute," Billy pleaded before grabbing Thomas by the arm.

"Don't you dare touch me, you hear me?" Thomas said with his fist raised.

"Ok, ok, no problem," Billy said as he released his grip. "I still can't believe it's you, where have you been all this time?"

"Have you no soul at all, you bottom feeding son of a bitch?" Thomas asked. "Even in death you're using me! You were there the day my wife and child died. You thought I was dead too and what do you do? How long did you wait before you took the Mission back out on the road with videos of me playing in the background?

"I knew you were low, but that whole damn family of yours is filled with nothing but vultures and opportunists. How the hell could Neesy let this happen? She was the only decent one among you, how could she let this happen?"

When Bernie peeked his head around the corner, Billy said, "It's all right, we're ok. Just make sure nobody gets out here and tell Michael not to tell anyone that this is Thomas. Just tell everyone that it's some drunk trying to get money from us."

Thomas shook his head and began to walk way when Billy ran around in front of him.

"I'm standing right here, you say whatever you want," Billy said. "I won't interrupt and I won't walk away. Just say whatever you want, don't hold back."

Billy kept his word and let Thomas finish without saying a word. He didn't even react when Thomas pointed in his face or got so close to him that he could smell the vodka and feel the spit hitting him in the face. He just let Thomas get it out and he listened to everything he had to say.

When Thomas was finished, his hands were shaking and his face was strained. Billy had seen that look many times and he knew one of two things were about to happen. Either Thomas was going to hit him, or Thomas was about to have a breakdown.

When he leaned over and started to cry, Billy lifted his hand to place it on Thomas' shoulder but stopped just short of doing it. Instead he walked up next to him and leaned down so Thomas could hear him.

"I admit that I have done a lot of wrong in my life to a lot of people," Billy said, "a lot of people. You're right about what happened. At first after I thought you were gone, I admit it, I thought of myself and my family.

"I came up with a plan days after your death for how we could continue on without you even though Neesy was dead set against it, and she *was* dead set against it, Thomas. Hell we fought about it almost every day and we even separated. She actually moved out of the compound and went back into the house we used to live in.

"But you know what, Thomas? Even that didn't stop me. My only thought was that I built this great thing and I didn't want it to end. To tell you the truth, there was no way I was going to let it end.

"Well, things were going fine for a few months, people were still coming out and the money was still coming in like before. But I started to miss Neesy. I tried to reconcile with her but she thought the same way about me that you do now.

"I tried to talk to you her on the phone, but all she would say was that she prayed every day for me the change.

"The one night she did stay on the phone, she let me have it good. She told she believed in me up until I decided to bring The Mission back out for a memorial tour. She said she thought that deep down inside I just wanted to do right by people in spite of all my misdoings.

"She said her faith in me was completely gone when she realized it was just all about the money and the notoriety. She thought it was disgusting that I would make a mockery of the deaths of you, your wife and your unborn child all in the name of a dollar.

"But you know me, Thomas. I continued on anyway.

"Then one day about six months ago, I'm on the road in Memphis and I got a call from Neesy's sister Annabelle. She told me Neesy had a massive heart attack and that she was in the hospital.

"She said Neesy was in surgery as we were speaking and the doctors didn't think she was going to survive the procedure.

"Well, Thomas, I dropped everything and left for the hospital with the clothes on my back, nothing more. By the time I got there, she was in intensive care in a coma. She had barely survived the surgery and she was on life support. There were tubes and hoses in every part of her body; one of them was keeping her breathing."

Billy paused for a moment to compose himself and Thomas didn't know what to think. As he watched Billy wipe the tears from his eyes he couldn't help but wonder if it was an act.

"I stayed at that hospital alone for seven days and seven nights thinking about all the wrongs I've done." Billy's voice cracked. "Thinking about how I always talked to you about forgiveness, knowing that it was what you wanted more than anything.

"I didn't get it then, to tell you the truth, and I really didn't care to either. But in that hospital alone night after night, alone with my demons, as you used to call them, I got it.

"I prayed to God, Thomas that Neesy would not have to suffer for my sins as I'm sure you had done so many times before. I told God it was all me and that she was an angel on earth. I even talked to you, Thomas.

"I knew in my heart that you were up there and I asked for your forgiveness too. I asked that you somehow reach out and heal her from the heavens, not for me, but for her, because she always loved you."

Thomas turned away from Billy because hearing those words about Neesy touched a chord in him that made the anger dissipate and the depression take over.

"Is she dead?" Thomas asked, not sure he wanted to know the answer.

"No, that's just it," Billy said while sniffling and wiping his eyes again. "I got my miracle and Neesy came to me on the eighth day!"

When Thomas turned to face him again, Billy put both of his hands on his shoulders. "It was a sign, Thomas," he said with a smile.

"A sign for me to change and to be the man she hoped that I would be. The doctors thought she would never come out of the coma and that she would eventually have to be taken off of life support. When she opened her eyes and looked at me, I knew it was you, Thomas.

"I knew God heard me and he let you heal her for me. From that moment on, Thomas, the Billy that you knew ceased to exist. I stopped the Mission and I stayed with Neesy until she was better.

"We even got married again on our anniversary and I've devoted my life to the woman I love. Believe it or not, it was her idea to start the Mission up again, but under a different premise this time.

"She was the one who insisted we keep the pictures of you up during the ceremonies. She wanted your memory and your spirit to live on. It's all about giving back now, Thomas, and being a better man."

"That's really what it's all about now?" Thomas asked, still suspicious of Billy's motives.

"We made more than enough with you to be able to support several generations of Johnsons," Billy said with a smile.

"All of this money goes directly to shelters, hospitals, the Make-A-Wish foundation and so many other places."

Thomas stared at the man in the white suit standing before him and didn't know what to think. Thomas was well aware that Billy was a great bullshitter, the best of the best, but this seemed so genuine, he was so humble. None of the ego and brashness that was "Billy" was coming through now.

Billy could see the confusion written all over Thomas' face so he smiled again and said, "Look Thomas, I owe you so much and you being here is just another sign for me to right another wrong. Come back to the compound with me. Neesy would be so happy to see you, she won't believe it.

"She still talks about you all the time; you know she's always loved you like a son. I swear to you, we wouldn't tell anyone you were back. You know my family, if I tell them to keep their mouths shut, no one will talk. We could whip up a new disguise and it will be like when you first came to live with us.

"I read somewhere a few years ago in an article that you said those were some of the happiest days of your life living with us before The Mission started. You said that you liked being unknown and living with my family, being 'normal,' you said.

"Well the least I can do is offer you that again, Thomas. For all that you've given me and my family that is surely the least I can do."

Thomas looked at Billy for a long time amazed by the transformation he saw before him. As much as he hated to admit to himself, he wasn't angry with Billy anymore.

"I didn't save Neesy," Thomas said softly. "I've never saved anyone close to me except for Kyle Morgan and look where that got me."

When Thomas turned away Billy stepped in front of him again.

"Look, when Neesy had the heart attack and I was in the hospital alone, all I could think of was you and the talks that we had when we first met."

"Specifically the conversation we had at your mother's funeral played over and over in my head. You said all you wanted was forgiveness. You talked about how you thought God would never forgive you for you not using your ability to save your father. Then you said you felt your mom's death was punishment for not saving your father.

"I felt the same exact way when Nessy was lying near death in front of me. I believed I was going to be punished for all of my past sins too, Thomas. All of the lying, cheating and manipulating were finally going to catch up with me.

"He was going take Neesy from to punish me for all that I had done. I used Him just as much as I used you Thomas and I was scared to death that He was going to make me pay in the worst way.

"I prayed and prayed with all of my heart for the first time in years. I begged for forgiveness and asked the Neesy be spared, I promised I would change. Then on that eighth day, when Neesy opened her eyes, my eyes were opened too, for the very first time, they were wide open and I was seeing clearly.

"I knew I was given a warning to open my eyes and see what is really important. Now just like you Thomas, I seek forgiveness for the things I've done or didn't do. So, to answer your question, yes you did save someone, you saved *me*.

"Everything happens for a reason Thomas. Our true purpose is to see the signs and to change to be the best us we can be, cause if we don't? Then in the end when we are judged, we will already know the outcome because we earned it and did nothing to change it."

Thomas smiled because he knew in his heart that Billy meant everything he was saying. He didn't know how or why, he just believed him.

He patted him on the shoulder before clearing his throat, "Thanks for the offer Billy, I'm really happy to hear Neesy is ok, please give her my love.

"But I can't go back with you. I've been alone for a while now and that's how I want it. Maybe it is me, I don't know, but tragedy follows me and affects those around me everywhere I go. If I am alone, only I can suffer. It seems that's the way it was meant to be."

Thomas turned to leave and Billy called to him. "Thomas, please, just come back for a few days, you'll see it can get better."

Thomas took a few steps before turning around. "I haven't had that life-affirming revelation that you've had Billy. There are no signs for me, there is only pain. That's all I have to offer, just pain.

"This is the last time you'll see me, Billy. I wish nothing but the best you and Neesy. Don't ever forget what brought on the change. I like you much better this way."

Thomas turned the corner and headed down the street. Billy wanted to chase after him and ask him again to come with him, but he knew he wouldn't come.

He was just about to go back into the parking lot to join the others when he heard the screech of car tires screech from the direction that Thomas had gone. He immediately feared the worst, thinking Thomas had said his last good byes before walking into traffic but that wasn't the case.

As he turned the corner he saw a man grabbing Thomas and trying to force him in a car while another man was running across the street towards them yelling something.

Chapter 42

Martin had been on the phone with Mike and heard the play-by-play of Thomas' encounter with Billy as he raced to the scene. Mike had waited until Thomas walked into the parking lot and was out of sight before he headed in that direction. When he saw Thomas talking to one of the men who had gotten off of the bus, he hid behind a dumpster at the edge of the lot and watched from a distance.

He stayed there until Thomas left and Billy followed behind him. He waited a few minutes before leaving his hiding spot, passing Billy as he headed for the street. They had both heard the car screech at the same time and they both rushed to see what had caused it.

When Mike saw that it was Martin who had stopped in the middle of the road to confront Thomas, he ran over to assist him, racing past Billy as he did so.

Billy saw them try to force Thomas into the car, and he knew he had to help him. He hurried back to the parking lot and yelled to his brothers, and they ran towards the struggle together.

As Thomas tried to pull away, Martin pleaded with him. "Please Thomas, she needs you, she will die without your help, don't you see that?

"I am telling the truth! I called Kyle and he is making arrangements for me to have Kate transported via medical helicopter to Holy Grace Hospital. We can be waiting for her when she gets there."

"I told you Martin, I cannot do it anymore!" Thomas yelled. "Why do you think I walk with a limp? I lost it, it's gone for good. I can't go there and watch her die, I won't."

"You let him go right now or there will be trouble," Billy shouted as he approached with his brothers.

Martin let go of Thomas and turned towards Billy, while Mike made sure the former healer didn't wander away.

"Look, this doesn't concern you. My wife, Kate Morgan, who Thomas knows very well, is deathly ill. I need him to come with me or she will die."

"You're married to Kyle Morgan's daughter?" Billy asked.

"Yes, Billy," Martin said with an angry tone, "The same Kyle Morgan you beat to a bloody pulp when he came to ask Thomas for help years ago. Did Thomas even know that happened?"

When Billy looked away Martin shook his head in disgust, "I didn't think so," he said.

"You are the biggest sleaze ball on the face of this earth and you will get yours one day. It's a shame I won't be around to see it. Now get out of my way 'cause you're not going to beat me like you did Kyle."

When Martin grabbed Thomas again, Billy reached for Martin and pulled him away. Martin punched Billy in the mouth and wrestled him to the ground. When Mike tried to rush to his aid, Billy's nephew grabbed the private investigator and they began to fight. Bernie joined in to help his brother and all of a sudden there was a melee in the middle of the road.

Thomas used the confusion to slip away. He turned down the first corner he approached, walked down that street a bit and then turned down the next corner. He kept doing that until his leg started to give out. He hid behind a dumpster in an alley. He listened, expecting to hear Martin or Billy approach him, but they never came.

The police arrived within minutes of the start of the fight. They were all arrested and taken to the police station, but they were released on their own recognizance a few hours later. When Martin called Kyle to let him know what happened, Kyle told him that Kate made it through the trip without incident and that she was currently in the ICU of Holy Grace Hospital. He said he spoke to Father McBride and that he should be arriving there soon.

Martin tried to hold back the tears as he told Kyle he had no idea where Thomas was, but Kyle just said, "I know in my heart he will be there for my daughter now that he knows how bad things are for her, I just know it."

Thomas set out walking without any destination in mind. He just wanted to get as far away from this location as he could in case they came back looking for him. As he walked his mind was filled with thoughts of Kate and the times he spent with the Morgans. He kept picturing the image of little Marie in his head while thinking how sad it was that she was going to have to grow up without her mother. He remembered standing in front of his own mother's coffin, staring at her face and knowing it was the last time he would see it.

He thought about how he would have been able to save Kate if Billy had told him that she was ill. Even though Billy seemed to have changed, he was still the cause of so much damage, Thomas thought.

He walked through the night for hours lost in these thoughts while his whole life played out in his head like a movie. His leg was no longer throbbing, or maybe it was and he was just too numb inside to feel it.

As the birds began to chirp, Thomas saw the first glimmer of daylight approaching. As he looked around, he recognized where he had ended up. He was standing at the base of the bridge that he had jumped off of years ago.

He felt a sinking feeling in his stomach as thoughts of signs crept into his head. So many people had told him through the years that things happen for a reason and that the signs were there if you chose to see them. "If that were true, then being back on this bridge was surely a sign as well," he thought. "If the first jump took my ability away, then another jump would surely end this."

One by one, the images of all the people he had lost appeared in his head, joined by the picture of Kate lying in a coffin with her little girl standing over her that his imagination provided.

"I don't want to be here anymore," he whispered as he started to cry. "I just want to be see you all again and stop the pain."

Thomas looked for the same spot he had jumped from last time, intending to make one final leap and end his suffering forever. As he walked, the sun rose and when he looked down from the bridge this time he could clearly the see the water beneath him. There were two seagulls directly below him, so Thomas moved down a few more feet to avoid hurting them.

When he looked towards the sky he saw how blue it was -- there wasn't a cloud in sight and a cool breeze blew across his face as he closed his eyes.

He didn't know why, but he thought back to when Pam told him she was pregnant. He smiled to himself and he recalled how happy the both were. Again he thought this must be sign that she was waiting for him on the other side and that's what brought him there.

"So that's what all of this was for?" he said as he opened his eyes and looked towards the heavens. "Why couldn't You just let me die the last time then? You gave me this ability and You never once told me what to do with it. It was wasted on someone like me and You knew it, so why did You choose me at all? Is this how it's supposed to end?" he shouted. "Please, can't You at least tell me that?!"

At that exact moment, Thomas heard an ambulance approaching in the distance. He watched as it got closer and sped past him on its way up the hill towards the hospital. As he watched it, he noticed something he hadn't seen the night he jumped from the bridge. Above the tree line at the top of the hill, he could see roof of the hospital. He stood there staring its huge cross, and he felt like the cross was staring back at him somehow.

"Somewhere in there, Kate is dying," Thomas thought to himself.

When he turned from the cross and grabbed for the railing, several cars began to honk their horns behind him as they passed. Someone even shouted out, "Why don't you jump already?"

Thomas was just about to do just that when he heard the sounds of tires screeching behind him. He thought of the accident that occurred last time he was on the bridge. When he turned to see if everything was all right, he saw that one person had stopped their car right behind him and they were blocking traffic.

As he titled his head and peered into the windshield, he saw an older woman, well into her 70s staring back at him while motioning for him to go to the passenger side window. Thomas turned to look towards the water again, but she honked her horn and continued to point to the passenger side window.

Thomas shook his head in disbelief before walking over to the window. He watched as it slowly came down before staring at the woman. "Hey there, are you ok?" she asked

Thomas looked to the left at the oncoming traffic and without even looking back at the woman, he said, "I'm fine, you need to get out of here before someone hits you in the back."

He was surprised when the woman rolled down her driver's side window and started waving the oncoming traffic around her. When the road was clear again she leaned towards him with a look of sincere concern.

"Whatever it is, it can't be that bad," she said sympathetically, "Trust me, I know. I was once where you were, at my lowest. Years ago, I had cancer, I was riddled with it."

Thomas watched as two cars again approached her and again she waved them around without losing her train of thought.

"My doctor had given me six months and I was pretty much dead inside when he told me that. I had stopped living and started watching the calendar. Each day that passed, I could literally see the sand going through the hourglass of what was left of my life.

"My family was there for me, of course, but they started to look at me differently after I got the news. It was almost as if they could see the clock ticking down on my head as well and they were preparing for it all around me. I had given up and accepted that it was my time and then I got my miracle."

Thomas stepped back away from the car and stared at the woman. "Does she recognize me too?" he wondered

She waved three more cars around while shouting, "Geez Louise, just go," but the she could see that the road was filling up.

"A young man with a gift from God put his hands on me and saved my life one day. I knew there would come a time when I would do something to help someone in return for that gift, but I never imagined it would be anything like this.

"He works in strange ways," she said as she pointed up. "I was running late on my way to meet my granddaughter. We haven't seen each other in over a year; every time we set something up she had to cancel for whatever reason."

"So I can't find my keys, I miss my turn and I wind up on this bridge with you. Maybe I was sent here to save your life, maybe I'm supposed to be your miracle?"

Thomas looked at the cross again in the distance and he knew what he had to do.

"It was a sign," he thought. "It had to be. I'm supposed to be there for her, Kate's my dear friend, and she's my sister."

As the woman in the car tried to wave cars around the traffic jam that was behind her, Thomas walked around to the driver's side window, gently grabbed her hand and kissed it.

"Thank you so much for what you did," he said. "I know what I have to do now and it's not on this bridge."

Thomas walked away before the woman could say another word. Fifteen minutes later, he was standing in the hospital parking lot looking for a way in.

Chapter 43

Thomas walked around the back of the building, trying to stay out of sight as he looked for a way into the hospital. It would have been easier if he was able to go to the front desk and ask for Martin or Kyle, but that wasn't an option. He was afraid hospital security wouldn't let him anywhere near the front entrance looking the way he did. He thought about going in through the emergency room, but he figured that security would be watching him the whole time if he did.

As he walked along the road behind the hospital, Thomas saw a sign that read, "All deliveries 500ft on left." When he got closer, he saw the exact bay door that he had walked out of. Only one of the hospital's loading docks was ground level; the other three were made so that tractor trailers could pull up to them. To the left of the docks there was a small cement stairwell that led to a brown steel door with a key card entry system. To that left of that was a small parking lot that could only fit ten cars.

Thomas hid behind the car that was furthest from the door while he waited for a chance to get inside. The minutes felt like hours as he stared at the camera that was above the door. Because it was one of those cameras that were shaped like a ball with a tinted shell around it, he was certain that it could rotate back and forth. When a car sped by he got nervous and started to walk away. He had only gotten a few feet away when the sound of the bay door opening behind him stopped him in his tracks.

Thomas ducked down and watched through the driver's side door of the car he was hiding behind as two men came walked out with a large grey container full of industrial size garbage bags. It really was déjà vu, but this time he was heading in instead of running out.

Once inside, Thomas knew he had little time to find his way back to the ICU on the third floor. He was certain someone had to have seen him sneak in and that people would be coming for him soon, so he limped down the hall to the nearest stairwell as fast as he could.

He had just reached the first level when he heard to door above him open.

"Leave two people in the stairwells and have everyone else start searching the floors," he heard a man say. "Make sure the police are on the way too."

Thomas reached for the door labeled first floor and opened it as quietly as he could.

"Roger that," someone replied over a walkie-talkie. "You never know with these homeless types, so I'll advise everyone to approach with caution and wait for backup."

Thomas went through the door and closed it as gently as he could behind him. When he turned around he could see that he was at the far end of the first floor. Without any other options, he started to look for an elevator. He came across a sign and followed it left down another hallway before he heard a voice yell in the distance. "Someone said they saw him on one of the first floor cameras, keep an eye out."

Thomas was in a panic as he looked for a place to hide. He entered the chapel and was relieved to find that it empty. He walked to the front and sat in the pew on the right side. Thomas rubbed his forehead as he tried to catch his breath. "What am I doing here?" he said out loud. He thought that if he was arrested in the chapel and people found out who he really was that they would never leave him alone.

Thomas stared up at the cross on the altar before closing his eyes and bowing his head. "Please tell me what I'm supposed to do," he prayed. "I have no idea how to even get near her."

Just then, Thomas felt a hand on his shoulder that made his entire body tense up. He expected to hear a member of the security voice say, "Come with me, sir," but instead he heard a familiar voice.

"He's not going to answer you, son," Father McBride said from behind him. "It doesn't work that way. You should know in your heart what the right thing to do is and the way to get to her will present itself to you. He's listening, though. You can have in faith in that."

When Thomas didn't respond, Father McBride walked around the pew to stand beside him. The priest extended his hand and introduced himself. When Thomas didn't react, Father McBride withdrew his hand and sighed. "I don't mean to bother you, sir. You just look like someone who may be in need.

"Hey, I could use some company, why don't you join me in the cafeteria?" the priest asked. "I'm sure you could use a hot beverage and something to eat, it will be my treat. I might be able to put you in touch with a few really good shelters around here where you can get some help, too."

Thomas smiled and stood up. Even though everything else in the world had changed since the night Pam died, Father McBride was the exact same man he had always known - a good man, who he could trust.

Father McBride's look of kindness quickly changed shock when he recognized Thomas.

"Oh my God, it is true!" the priest said as he embraced his friend. "When Kyle called me and told me that you were alive I couldn't believe it, yet here you are. It truly is a miracle and I couldn't be happier to see you again, my friend."

Thomas hugged Father McBride as tightly as he could and they both cried together. As he withdrew from the embrace and wiped his eyes, Father McBride said, "I am so sorry for your loss Thomas. Pam was an incredible person. I know you're not a believer, Thomas, but you have to believe me, you will see them again. I promise you this."

Thomas wiped his eyes again then cleared his throat, "I don't know what to believe anymore Father," he said. "I've been through too much and I just want it to end. I wish it were me up there in that bed instead of Kate.

"She has Kyle and a family of her own now. It doesn't make sense that I would remain here while someone like her is taken, leaving a good family in shambles. None of it makes any sense at all."

"I wish I could tell you that I know why things happen the way they do Thomas," Father McBride said. "To tell you the truth, my faith was tested as well the night that Pam died and you jumped from that bridge. I cried out loud as I prayed for understanding for weeks while I tried to deal with the tragedy in my head. There just weren't any answers that made sense and trying to have faith that there was a reason for everything just didn't seem right.

"Then one night I was watching one of the memorials that were televised and they showed a montage of all of these healing sessions that you had done. At one point they actually did a split screen where they showed you healing people on one side of the screen while on the other side, name after name scrolled by of those you had healed. It seemed like it was endless and I knew at that moment that you were where you were meant to be, back with your family. I could feel it in my heart that it was your reward for all of the good you had done and it helped me deal with what had happened a lot better.

"We are all put through tests while we are here, Thomas, and some are tested a lot more than others for some reason. What I do believe in my heart is that the reward is much better in the end for those who were tested the hardest and came through it with their faith still intact while making the world a better place in their own way. That's the code I live my life by.

"I could see you in my dreams, reunited with your family, smiling as you held your child and I would always wake up with such a good feeling in my heart."

"Even with what's happening here now, you being here just feels right, no matter what the outcome. It feels like it's as if this is the way it was meant to happen.

"How about we go up now to see Kate, you and me together? I'm sure seeing you again will do wonders for her. She had a lot to say to me about the guilt she holds onto when it comes to how things turned out for you. She's in and out of consciousness, so you might have to stick around for a while before she wakes up again. Believe it or not, she really missed you, Thomas. They both did."

Father McBride headed for the doorway with Thomas right behind him. When Thomas stopped just before leaving the chapel, Father McBride put his hand on his shoulder to comfort him. "It's ok," he said.

"Did Martin tell you I can't do it anymore?" Thomas asked, unable to meet his friend's eyes.

"He did say something about that to me, but I get the feeling he doesn't believe it," Father McBride replied. "So it is true then, you can no longer heal anyone?"

"It was taken from me the day I jumped from that bridge," Thomas answered. "That's when He took it from me for good."

Father McBride looked Thomas in the eye and shook his head. He forced a smile and said, "You still don't understand after all this time, do you Thomas? It's His plan, not yours. You have done many amazing and wonderful things while making a huge difference in so many people's lives. But like I have said to you a hundred times, it's His plan. You just have to believe and have faith in it, Thomas, no matter what happens."

"You know I don't believe as you do," Thomas said angrily.

"I know you don't," Father McBride said as he opened the door. "Let's just leave it be and get you up there so you can see an old dear friend of yours who is looking forward to seeing you again."

Thomas followed Father McBride to the elevator and they were just about to get on when someone shouted for them to stop. Two security guards stood behind them, but they appeared confused by the sight of the homeless man standing with the priest.

"He entered the hospital through the loading area," one of the guards said. "The police have been called and everyone has been looking for him. What is going on here, Father?"

"He is a relative of Kate Shulman, who is on the third floor in the ICU. As you can see, he has some mental issues and we have been wondering where he was since we heard he was on his way here. I'm sure he has no idea that he even came in through the wrong entrance. He probably just walked around until he found an open door and went through it.

"I can assure you his harmless. He heard his cousin was fading and he somehow found his way here. Both Mr. Shulman and Mr. Morgan can vouch for him if you ask them to come down."

Despite Father McBride's effort, the guards made them both wait in the security office until the police arrived. The police asked Martin and Kyle to come down and confirm Father McBride's story.

When Martin heard that a homeless man had entered the building claiming to be Kate's mentally disturbed cousin, he knew for certain that it was Thomas. He was ecstatic as he accompanied Kyle down to the first floor while filling him in on what had occurred.

Martin lit up like a Christmas tree when he saw Thomas sitting next to Father McBride. A feeling deep inside him told him that everything was going to be ok now and that Kate would be returning home soon.

Kyle came in after Martin and he stood frozen in place when he looked at the person everyone was claiming was Thomas. The eyes were the same, but with the full beard and the long hair, Kyle couldn't be sure it was really him.

"Thank you officers for locating our cousin Thomas," Martin said before they could ask him any questions. "I'm sure you can see for yourself that's he's not, um, all together. The last thing we needed was for him to come up missing on his way here. Kate's aunt called and said he was coming, but he was already on his way before we could tell him not to."

After a brief conversation they all left the room together and walked to the elevator. Once inside, Martin couldn't control himself. He hugged Thomas and said, "Thank you for coming, thank God you're here."

Thomas stood with his hands at his side until Kate's husband released him. "I'm here for her," he said, "I just wanted to be here for her."

When he saw the way Martin was staring at him, Thomas felt like he had to let him know for certain that there was no miracle coming. No matter how much it hurt to hear, he didn't want to give anyone false hope.

"Listen, I know you are all hoping that I could help her," Thomas said softly. "Believe me, I wish I could help her too, I want to be able to do that more than anything right now.

"But I wasn't lying when I told you I couldn't do it any more, Martin. When I jumped off of that bridge, it was gone." Thomas paused for a second then said, "It was taken from me."

When Thomas looked over at Kyle and saw his eyes welling up with tears, he approached him. "I would give anything to be able to help her, but I can't, I just can't. I would trade places with her in a minute if I could. I just … can't, I'm so sorry."

Martin still didn't believe Thomas. "You will try to help her whether you think you can or not!" he shouted. "You are all we have left and you will *try*, damn it, do you hear me!"

When Martin pointed his finger in Thomas' face, Father McBride grabbed him from behind and pulled him away from Thomas. "Leave him alone, Martin," the priest shouted. "You don't think that this man understands pain, desperation and loss after all he's been through?"

"He can't do it any more, Martin. I'm sorry, but it's true. He wants to be here for Kate now and you for you as well, Kyle. You were his family at one time and you are still very dear to him, no matter what has occurred since he left your home. If you want him to leave, then we will respect your wishes and leave together. But Kate confided in me earlier when she was conscious. She wants to see Thomas again very badly. There is so much she wants to say to him before…"

Martin was hysterical when the elevator door opened. Father McBride knew he wouldn't want Kate to see him that way, so he put his arm around him and led him away from her room. Kyle and Thomas stood side by side watching them walk away before Kyle turned to face Thomas. There was so much that Thomas wanted to say, but the only words that came out of his mouth were, "I'm so sorry Kyle."

Chapter 44

Kyle seemed very angry to Thomas, who assumed it was because he couldn't help Kate. He was reluctant to meet the older man's eyes.

"I need you to come with me so we can talk, Thomas," Kyle said and walked down the hallway without waiting for a response.

Thomas followed him until he ducked into an empty room with two hospital beds. Kyle waited until Thomas was inside before turning on the light and closing the door behind him.

"First of all, I am really sorry for what happened to your wife and child," Kyle said. Thomas could here sincere sympathy warring with anger in Kyle's voice, so he didn't interrupt. "I tried to contact you several times when you were on the road with the Mission about Kate's condition and you never responded. I even went to see you when you were in New York City and I was beaten up by Billy Johnson. Please tell me you didn't know anything about that?"

"Kyle, I swear, I never knew that happened. No one ever said anything to me about it, but that doesn't surprise me," Thomas said sadly. "You met Billy, you've seen him on the news -- he controlled everything back then and he used me for all I was worth. If I had known, I would have...."

Just then Thomas remembered watching the interview Kate did with Robert Van Putten. He also remembered telling everyone on the Mission staff to not accept any type of correspondence from any of the Morgans, threatening to fire them if they did.

The realization hit him like a fist to the face. He could have saved Kate if he hadn't done that. "Yet one more horrible choice that had dire consequences," he thought to himself.

Before he could say anything to Kyle, the man who was once his father figure reached out and hugged Thomas. "I knew that he didn't tell you, you would never leave her like that," Kyle said. "I told Martin that was the reason you never came."

When he let Thomas go, Kyle looked him over from head to toe. "Jesus Thomas, look at you, I wish you would have come to us after.... We could have helped you and been there for you just like after your mother..."

Thomas and Kyle stayed in that room for another half-hour catching up. Thomas told him about everything that had happened since he left New Jersey all those years ago, and Kyle filled Thomas in about Kate's first marriage, little Marie and Sharon. Kyle also confessed the horrible guilt he lived with after Thomas' mother committed suicide. Kyle admitted that he also suffered from depression and alcohol abuse.

"There were nights after your mother died that I wished you would have never healed me," he said to Thomas. "It just wasn't fair that I should live and your mother was taken. She was a good woman, Thomas, and she loved you very much."

When they finished talking, they walked back to the ICU together. Sharon was waiting outside and she greeted Kyle with a kiss. Thomas smiled because he could see for himself immediately how good they were together and he was happy for Kyle.

Kyle introduced Sharon to Thomas and she gave him a hug. "It's so nice to meet you finally", she said. "I'm so sorry for all of your loss."

They spoke for a little while longer out in the hall before heading inside to see Kate.

Kyle went in first and when Thomas hesitated, he looked back at him, forced a smile and said, "Take your time."

Thomas stood outside the doorway for several minutes trying to prepare him for seeing Kate for the first time in years.

When Thomas entered the room, he saw Kyle talking to Father McBride in the middle of room. He noticed Martin pacing back and forth near Kate's bed, and a teenage girl standing beside it holding her mother's hand. Kate was just lying in her bed, but Thomas couldn't be sure if she was unconscious or just sleeping.

When Marie noticed Thomas, she let go of her mother's hand and stared at him in disgust.

Thomas met her stare and thought that she was indeed the mirror image of her mother at that age. In that instant his mind was filled with a montage of memories of his childhood with Kate.

"If you can't help her then you shouldn't be here," Marie said with nothing but anger in her voice.

"You could have saved her. She said you were like a brother to her and you let this happen to her. What kind of monster are you?"

Father McBride couldn't stand to hear any more, so he had to intervene. "Young lady, I know you're upset and you have right to be. I know you love your mother and you are hurting, but this is not the time or the place to be saying such things.

"Regardless of what you may think of him, he is here for your mother now because he loves her. Both she and your grandfather are the only family he has left in the world. As you can see, he is hurting very much too and I know him well enough to say that I know he would give anything in this world to be able to save your mother."

When Marie started to cry, both Martin and Kyle rushed over to comfort her. They walked with her out to the hallway leaving Thomas alone standing by the bed staring at Kate.

As he looked at her, he was overcome with sadness. She was connected to tubes, wires and various devices that were beeping at different intervals. She was pale as a ghost and she looked as if she had aged fifty years since he saw her last. Thomas reached for her hand and whispered, "I am so sorry Kate," before he started to cry.

When Thomas lifted her hand to kiss it, he noticed the intravenous tube coming from a clear bag labeled morphine. He knew then that she was really near the end.

Thomas placed her hand down at her side. He lowered his head and closed his eyes as the tears ran down his cheeks. "Why would You do this?" he whispered. "Your plan is a cruel one that makes no sense at all. She does not deserve this."

When Thomas opened his eyes, he was surprised to see Kate smiling as she looked up at him.

"Hello Thomas," she said softly. A tear formed in the corner of her eye as she said, "I knew you would come. When Martin told me he found you, I knew you would come."

Thomas leaned over and kissed her on the forehead before taking her hand again.

"I'm so sorry, Kate," he said as he sniffled. "I was stupid and arrogant; I could have done something before it was too…"

Kate grabbed his hand tightly and held it against her face.

"Thomas, it's ok, none of that matters now."

"It *does* matter," Thomas said as his eyes filled with tears. "I can't do it anymore, Kate. I can't save you, oh God, I'm so sorry, but I can't save you."

Kate closed her eyes and nodded in understanding. "I know that, Thomas. Martin told me yesterday," she said. "I don't blame you, Thomas, none of us do."

"I prayed many times that I would get to see you again," Kate said. "Even after I thought you died, I just wanted to see you one more time just to tell you how sorry I am."

"There's no need for that Kate," he said. "You didn't do anything wrong, all you did was react to me ignoring your cries for help. I know that's why you did that show."

"You're wrong, Thomas. There is one thing that I *do* need to apologize for," Kate said. "I should have asked my father to keep your secret, Thomas. I should have made him promise like you made me promise."

Kate started to cry as she tried to sit up, "I'm the one who's to blame for the horrible life you have had, Thomas. It's my fault you had to go into hiding, it's my fault you turned to alcohol and it's my fault you lost Pam and your baby."

"No, Kate, it's not your fault at all, it's mine," Thomas said as her took his hand and gently guided her back down into the lying position in her bed.

"You don't understand," Kate said. "I have been carrying this guilt around with me for years, Thomas. I believed my first marriage and my sickness was a punishment for what I had caused you. I let it consume my life to the point where I couldn't even be there for my husband or my daughter."

Thomas didn't noticed but everyone had come back into the room and they were standing behind him and as Martin heard what Kate said he shook his head to show he disagreed with her.

"But it makes sense now, Thomas, it's come full circle," Kate said. "Finally at the end, I can say I'm sorry to you like I should have done years ago and be at peace with things. Thank you for letting me do that, Thomas."

A tear rolled down Thomas's cheek as he squeezed Kate's hand, nodded and forced a smile.

"I want you to promise me something Thomas and I want you to mean it."

"Anything, just name it," Thomas replied.

"When this is...over, I want you to promise that you'll go back home with my father and Sharon. I want you to come back to the family that always loved you and I want you to be in my daughter's life. I know with all of you there for her, she will have a great life surrounded by people who will protect her and love her. My father has always thought of you as a son and having you around will make things easier for him too, after...."

Thomas looked over towards Kyle and Kyle walked over and stood beside him. He placed his hand on Thomas's shoulder and nodded while his lip quivered.

"She's right Thomas, you should come home with us; it's time. You have always been one of the family and it's where you belong."

As the tears streamed down his face Thomas nodded then said, "Ok" softly.

Kate smiled before moving his hand towards her mouth and kissing it gently. "Thank you Thomas, you've made me very happy," she said as she closed her eyes.

Kate's monitors suddenly started to beep and she seemed to be having a problem catching her breath.

"Kate! Are you ok?" Thomas shouted before two nurses rushed into the room and ordered everyone out. They waited for what seemed like an eternity not saying a word to each other. Martin hugged Marie tight while Kyle held onto to Sharon. Thomas felt alone and like an outsider until Father McBride came over to him and placed his arm around him.

After a few minutes the alarms went silent and the nurses came out of the room.

One of the nurses walked away down the hall while the other approached Martin and Kyle.

"Can I talk to you both over here in private for a second, please?" she said.

Martin motioned to Kyle and they both joined the nurse for a walk down the hall.

"She's stable now, but I don't know for how long," she said softly. "The situation is not good and it would be best if you didn't do anything to upset her or get her worked up. I'm sorry to have to tell you this, Mr. Shulman and Mr. Morgan, but it really is just a matter of time. All we can do at this point is to make her as comfortable as possible until…"

"She's going to die!" Marie cried out as Sharon hugged her.

"She's going to die and it will be all your fault!" she shouted at Thomas.

The pain on Thomas's face was obvious as he turned and walked away, stopping just before he reached the elevators.

Father McBride approached Marie and looked at her sympathetically. "I don't know what's going to happen to your mother, but I know it's not Thomas's fault that she is the way she is now. The truth, whether you chose to believe it or not, is that it's in God's hands at this point. He has a plan for your mother and for all us. The only thing that any of us can take comfort in is that either way she will be at peace and she won't be in pain ever again."

Thomas stood alone until Martin and Kyle returned, then they all went back into the room together. Again there was an uncomfortable silence as everyone sat quietly just staring at the bed.

Thomas watched as Sharon comforted Kyle and Martin hugged Marie while he repeated over and over that everything would be all right.

When Father McBride put his hand on his shoulder, Thomas shook his head from side to side before leaning over and whispering in his ear. "How could this happen? How could this perfect family be torn apart and why was I meant to be here to see it without the ability to heal? How can I believe there is a God after all of this?"

When Father McBride turned to face him, Thomas met his stare. "No God would do something like this, not to these people, not like this," he insisted to the priest.

Kate's whole body suddenly shook while the monitors went crazy with noise again. Thomas stood and was frozen in place as he watched her body shake again and then go limp.

Martin quickly got to his feet and looked over towards Sharon. "Get her out of here now, please," he said as he pointed to Marie.

"No, I'm not leaving", Marie cried out. "I won't leave her, not now!"

As Kyle made his way over to comfort Marie, Thomas approached Kate.

His heart dropped when he could see that she wasn't breathing and that she was starting to turn blue.

Martin pushed him to the side and yelled, "Oh no, Kate, wake up, please wake up honey!"

Another nurse came running into the room with an oxygen bag that she immediately applied to Kate's mouth and started pumping it. The heart monitor flat lined and the other monitors just beeped steadily.

"Damn it, c'mon breathe Kate!" one of the nurses said before the other yelled, "Get the crash cart!"

Martin started to reach down to try to get her to wake up while crying hysterically. "Please stay back Mr. Shulman," one of the nurses said as she gently pushed him away. Kyle grabbed him from behind and held onto him. "Let them do what they have to," he said as he too started to cry uncontrollably.

Thomas stood off to the side watching this entire surreal scene.

When medical team shocked Kate over and over without any response, Martin broke free of Kyle's arms. Two of the three nurses tried to hold him back as he screamed out Kate's name over and over. Father McBride did his best to assist them, but Martin had lost all control.

Marie cried out, "Dad please stop, please stop" before Martin dropped to his knees, lowered his head and broke down crying.

The remaining nurse continued with the CPR long after Kate flat lined even though she knew there was no hope of resuscitating her. She had seen the way this family interacted together and the last thing she wanted to do was to see her daughter's face when she found out her mother was gone.

When the nurse finally did stop and lower her head, the sound of the machine flat lining was the only noise in the room until Marie cried out, "Oh no, oh no, please don't say she's gone."

"Oh God, she can't be gone!"

Thomas didn't even think as he rushed over to Kate and pushed the nurse to the side.

"What the hell are you doing?" the nurse yelled.

Thomas ignored her; instead he looked back at Kyle and Martin. "Keep everyone back!" he yelled.

Kyle got to his feet. "You said you couldn't..."

"I have to try," Thomas answered. "Now keep everyone back."

Martin didn't need to hear another word. He grabbed onto both nurses and pushed them against the wall. "I need you to stay right here and let him do what he needs to do."

His then stepped away from the nurses and held his arms out as if he were creating an invisible barrier that they couldn't cross.

Kyle went over to the other nurse that Thomas had pushed and said, "Believe it or not, that is Thomas Greggs, The Healer, please, just let him try."

The nurse looked at Thomas and then back to Kyle, "She's gone sir, there's nothing that he or anybody else could do now, I'm sorry."

Thomas ignored her and placed both of his hands on Kate's stomach and closed his eyes. He felt nothing, so he backed a way for just a second and he started again. When nothing happened again, he closed his eyes and dropped his head. He could hear Kyle crying behind him so he opened his eyes and turned towards him.

"She's gone isn't she?" Kyle said, "She's really gone?"

Thomas felt anger and rage building inside him.

"C'mon," he yelled as he tried again while looking up towards the heavens. "I've given everything I have and lost everyone I have ever loved! She does not deserve this and you know it! This family doesn't deserve this and that little girl doesn't deserve this! You want to take someone, take me! Take me!"

Just then Thomas felt a sharp pain in his chest and a surge of energy through his hands. He let go and stepped back because the feeling was no longer familiar to him. He stared at his hands in disbelief before looking at Kate again.

He touched her face with his hand and he whispered to her, "You either come back or we're going together," he said.

He placed his hands back on her and concentrated as hard as he could. The room remained silent until Thomas shouted out in pain.

Martin turned away from the nurses and nobody moved. Everyone's attention was on Thomas.

"Is it working?" Martin said.

"Just stay back!" Thomas yelled through the pain. "Whatever happens, don't let me let go, you hear me, no matter what happens!"

No one said a word as they gathered around him to watch.

Thomas cried out in pain again and again as his body convulsed. After that blood started to come from his eyes. At first, it was mixed with tears but then it became a steady stream of pure blood.

His hands began to shake and Thomas started to cough up blood, but still he held on.

"I will not let go! You hear me, I will not let go until she comes back!"

"I have to stop him," Kyle shouted, "he'll die!"

Kyle stepped forward, but Martin tackled him before he could reach Thomas.

"Let go of me, Martin!" Kyle shouted as both men lay on the floor. They both struggled until one of the nurses suddenly yelled out, "Oh my God!"

Thomas stumbled backwards and collapsed to the floor. As the nurses rushed over to him a familiar voice came from the bed.

"What happened? Is Thomas all right?" Kate asked.

The room was silent for a moment. Martin rushed over to Kate with Kyle right behind him. "She's alive!" Martin shouted. "Oh my God, she's alive!"

Everyone rushed over to her as Thomas sat in total darkness listening to what was going on around him. He couldn't move and he could hear his heart beating slower as the feeling of numbness overtook him.

He felt someone take his hand and a familiar comforting voice spoke to him. "Thomas it's me, Father McBride, can you hear me?"

"She's ok Father," Thomas whispered.

"Yes, she's ok Thomas, you saved her, you saved the whole family."

Thomas smiled, even as the blood poured out of his eyes.

"I'm scared, Father," he said. "It's dark and there is no light, where am I going?"

"There is nothing to be scared of Thomas, the light will come and they will be waiting for you, all of them, I know this in my heart. "I told you a long time ago my friend that none of this was your doing. His plans for your journey were set from the time you were born. I don't claim to understand any of it, but I have faith that the journey had meaning and had a purpose. You helped so many, Thomas, and you've suffered for your sins. I feel in my heart that the world is a better place because Thomas Greggs made it so. So many lives you've changed, so many families you've saved even up to the very....end."

As Thomas coughed up blood then gasped for breath, Father McBride pulled him towards his chest and hugged him while petting his head.

"Shhhh, it's ok now Thomas, you've done all you can. It's ok to let go now, go be with them, where you belong."

Thomas listened as Kate told her daughter she loved her and they all cried together.

This made him smile again one last time before he heard the last few beats of his heart and everything went black with no sound at all.

The darkness remained for what seemed like several minutes until a small light appeared in the distance that was slowly moving closer and closer towards him.

It got bigger and bigger in size as it drew closer until it encompassed everything. At its closest it was like looking into the sun for a moment where everything becomes just light then a blur.

Then slowly the light rescinded and two people appeared in the distance. They started to walk towards him, and with each step they took they started to come into clearer focus. Suddenly the light flashed bright again and Thomas saw his mother and his father.

As they smiled at him, Thomas noticed someone else was behind them. It was Pam and she was smiling ear to ear as she held a baby boy in her arms. Pam kissed Thomas on the cheek and then handed him his son. He had the bluest eyes Thomas had ever seen and he smiled when Thomas said, "Hey there." An overwhelming feeling of peace overcame him as his mother kissed his cheek and his father patted his shoulder. Gone was all of the sadness he had known, replaced now by a feeling of joy and comfort.

Marie looked at him and then at his son while smiling. "We've been waiting for you Thomas, we've missed you," she said. "Now come with us, we have to go."

"Go where?" Thomas asked as he kissed his baby on the head.

His mother smiled again and brushed her hand against his cheek, "To a wonderful place where you meet up again with the people you cared about who passed; a place where no one is sick or in pain. A place where no one is sad and everything is beautiful."

www.ingramcontent.com/pod-product-compliance
Lightning Source LLC
Chambersburg PA
CBHW062129170626
46813CB00002B/621

* 9 780615 812984 *